SONGS OF TRIUMPHANT LOVE

While the celebrated opera singer Terri Ivory is in hospital, facing what could be the end of her career, her daughter Julie discovers a long-buried secret. This forces her to question her past and her place in her mother's affection. Their empty house no longer seems a home. Mother and daughter try to keep their closeness to each other and to the men they love: damaged Teo, whose passion for Terri borders on the self-destructive, and Julie's first love, Alistair, who fails to predict the consequences of his decision to join the army. When calamity strikes, all four must make vital choices to find their way forward. Can love and music heal when medicine cannot? And are there some secrets that should never be shared?

Books by Jessica Duchen
Published by The House of Ulverscroft:

HUNGARIAN DANCES

JESSICA DUCHEN

SONGS OF TRIUMPHANT LOVE

Complete and Unabridged

CHARNWOOD
Leicester

First published in Great Britain in 2009 by
Hodder & Stoughton
London

First Charnwood Edition
published 2010
by arrangement with
Hodder & Stoughton
An Hachette UK company
London

The moral right of the author has been asserted

All characters in this publication are fictitious and
any resemblance to real persons, living or dead is
purely coincidental.

British Library CIP Data

Duchen, Jessica.
    Songs of triumphant love.
    1. Life change events- -Fiction. 2. Family secrets- -
Fiction. 3. Large type books.
    I. Title
    823.9'2–dc22

    ISBN 978–1–44480–153–8

Published by
F. A. Thorpe (Publishing)
Anstey, Leicestershire

Set by Words & Graphics Ltd.
Anstey, Leicestershire
Printed and bound in Great Britain by
T. J. International Ltd., Padstow, Cornwall

This book is printed on acid-free paper

For the several Marie-Thérèses who have
made this book possible . . .

Author's Note

I first became fascinated by the story of Pauline Viardot and Ivan Turgenev in 2004, when the violinist Philippe Graffin commissioned me to write a script for a narrated concert involving them and the composers they inspired. The programme culminated in Ernest Chausson's exquisite *Poème*, which is based on Turgenev's short story *The Song of Triumphant Love*, and we also featured works by Gabriel Fauré, whose biography I'd written several years earlier. The history of Viardot, the great singer who lost her voice, and Turgenev, the writer who loved her too much, haunts the background of this novel; its title is a tribute to the Russian author whose writing has always been very close to my heart.

Fauré was briefly engaged to Pauline's third daughter, Marianne, a shy girl who had a beautiful singing voice but hesitated to develop it. Fauré himself appears to have returned from the Franco-Prussian War suffering from what today might be termed post-traumatic stress disorder; its disturbing effects on his personality may have induced Marianne to break off their relationship. Two characters in Turgenev's story seemed to me to have been based partly on Marianne and Fauré. Perhaps Julie and Alistair have a little in common with them, 130 years later, while young men and women are killed every day in senseless wars, or return scarred for life.

If you'd like to hear some of the music of the book, Philippe Graffin's recordings of Chausson's *Poème* are on the Hyperion and Avie labels. Viardot's songs have been recorded several times, notably by Opera Rara in another scripted concert (regretfully, not ours!) live at Wigmore Hall in 2006: 'Pauline Viardot and Friends'. Several Viardot numbers feature in Cecilia Bartoli's 1996 CD *Chant d'amour* (Decca). The songs by Bach, Schumann and Schubert, and the Fauré Requiem, are widely available in innumerable recordings. And the raw, passionate albums of the Mostar Sevdah Reunion and the exciting young Bosnian singer Amira marvellously demonstrate the haunting and seductive sounds of *sevdah*.

Jessica Duchen, London, 2009
www.jessicaduchen.co.uk

1

When the laser makes contact with Terri Ivory's throat, she is dreaming of Teo. Or perhaps not Teo. Certainly she's with someone, transformed or idealised. Her spirit flies free, anaesthetically unbound. In the operating theatre, her body lies still while a gloved hand guides the beam to the mid third of the vocal fold where the polyp has formed. For the first time since her diagnosis, the sleeping singer is unaware that at any moment, with one false move, her career may be over.

★ ★ ★

She comes to, shivering. A silver blanket crackles round her shoulders. The cold is dense; she closes her eyes, wanting escape. Malaise blooms dull and wild in her mind, flickering through the drugs.

She registers the blue eyes of a friendly young nurse. 'How are you doing, Teresa? Waking up?' She sounds Australian.

Terri shakes her head. She isn't allowed to talk, not even a whisper. Nausea rings through her with the chemical odour in the ward, which she hopes is disinfectant.

'Do you feel sick?' The nurse reaches for a kidney-shaped container.

I'm not going to throw up, Terri decides. I

refuse. Escape; sleep. Blessed relief. Her blood pressure drops. The nurse calls a colleague and together they tip the bed so that her blood will run towards her head. She tries to resist. Just let me sleep.

'Teresa.' The tone is reassuring. 'You're going to be just fine. The surgeon's removed the polyp.'

Terri nods her thanks. If he hasn't, she reflects, I *personally* shall put his nose in a sling.

★ ★ ★

When she next looks out of herself she's been returned to her hospital room. A lamp casts a wing of brightness across the curtain, inter-rupted by a silhouette.

'Mum.' Julie's voice.

Terri smiles and lifts an arm towards her. Julie's fingers touch hers: soft, young, healing. Her lips brush Terri's forehead. So tender. Terri takes a notepad from her bedside table and writes: 'Hello, darling. How was school?'

'I've been sitting there all afternoon crossing my fingers for you.'

Terri scribbles: 'Are you OK in the house on your own?'

'Maybe I'll go to Alistair's tonight. We'll get some mates round.'

'Make sure you sleep. It's important, with the exams.'

'Mum, don't fuss, you've got to rest. Look, I brought you grapes and juice and bananas. Stuff that slips down easily. You'll be home soon and I'll look after you. Are you sure you don't want to come home now, or in the morning? They said you could.'

Terri has never been so afraid of anything in her life as of this operation; she's begged — and paid — the hospital to keep her in an extra day to make sure everything is all right. 'Prefer to be on safe side,' she writes. 'Tomorrow evening.'

'Is there anything you want? Books? Magazines? Some music?'

Terri lies back on her pillow and breathes deeply. Stay positive: throat temporarily buggered, but nobody's hand slipped. Cords will be fine, polyp gone, lungs unaffected. Time to start again. You can do it. And yes, music would help. 'My iPod's in my study. You know how to put new tracks on it?'

'Yes, Mum, I know how to use an iPod.' Julie seems annoyed, though trying not to be. She's no longer a baby, Terri reminds herself. She's eighteen. Finishing school, discovering sex with Alistair, thinking she'll be young for ever.

'What do you want?'

Terri writes. 'My own Mozart — *The Marriage of Figaro* — to keep me sane. And Varya Petrovna's new album — *Angel of the North*, to see what the bitch is up to . . .'

'Are you sure?' Julie's forehead crumples upwards under the wisps of dark hair, as it always does when she's puzzled. With a rush of tenderness, Terri understands that her daughter is concerned on her behalf: after all, she's asking to hear a CD of the woman who's become the biggest threat to her work and her sanity for donkey's years. It isn't Terri's fault that a nubile

3

Russian starlet has a similar type of voice to hers and is eyeing the same lyric-dramatic soprano repertoire.

She's still astonished to think that she's managed to create and raise a young woman who has the sensitivity to worry about such things. How did she ever deserve a daughter like Julie? Back in the Gorbals, she'd never dreamed she would one day be singing in the world's top opera houses and bringing up a beautiful, intelligent and gifted girl whose energy lights up her world even when she's six thousand miles away.

'Love you, my angel,' she writes. She'd looked like Julie once, with the same shaped eyes, as round as ripe grapes — though Julie's are warm brown, not turquoise. Terri's hair had been gold, not chocolate like Julie's, and, back then, naturally blonde; today it receives its colour for a large fee at a West End salon (Julie jokes that her mother goes there for 'resprays'). Because of Julie, Terri doesn't mind middle age. She'd been far happier in her forties than in her teens anyway. Then she turned fifty. The day after her birthday she found herself repeatedly trying to clear her throat. She'd blamed her party, thought nothing of it, then set off for the airport and Carnegie Hall.

'I'll bring your iPod along first thing in the morning,' Julie says.

'As long as you're not late for school.'

'I *won't* be late. I'll get up extra early.' Julie rolls her eyes heavenwards.

Christ, thinks Terri, can't I do anything right? Love or none, there's only one thing on the humanity planet thornier than fathers and sons, and that's mothers and daughters. At each other's throats.

'What's the joke, Mum?'

Terri smiles, then writes. 'A private pun that I couldn't have made up if I'd tried. Go home and get some rest.'

★　★　★

Julie makes her way down a staircase and through shiny corridors lined with arty photographs of trees. This hospital is devoted to patients with private health cover. On one hand she's convinced, along with Alistair and his mother Sue, that private health care is designed to close the NHS by stealth, running it down until nobody dare use it any longer and everyone will have to fork out huge sums for insurance instead. Yet she can't help being glad that her mother isn't incarcerated in the nearest NHS labyrinth, a place as gargantuan, impenetrable and forbidding as the Vatican, if less architecturally impressive.

Terri is rarely ill. Glaswegian childhood, she insists, toughens you up. The worst she's had before was a touch of exhaustion after her first run as Wagner's Isolde, and she'd stayed positive: it was a perfect excuse to take Julie on holiday for two weeks. There've been occasional ups and downs — Terri has explained to Julie that everything, but *everything*, affects the voice. Aeroplanes, pollen, dairy produce (which Terri won't eat), pregnancy, time of the month, the menopause, emotional traumas like divorce and bereavement, passive smoking, screaming matches with a difficult lover — the list is endless. A singer's voice is her musical instrument and she mustn't take risks with its efficiency. 'It's a wonder there are any female singers on this earth,' said Terri. But having clambered up a longer and steeper ladder than many of her colleagues, she never gives up and she never shirks a challenge. If there's an extra mile to go, you can bet your life that Terri Ivory will set off along it at once, flying the flag for Scotland.

Julie turns right at the main road. Ahead lies the Thames and its tree-lined embankment. On the bridge, strings of lights loop from Chelsea on the north side to Battersea on the south. The sun is sinking due west, painting gold leaf on the water. Julie crosses to the south. She senses men glancing at her, interest, approval. She's slim and looks good in skinny jeans — one benefit of living mainly on soup, fruit and the occasional toasted sandwich. Across the river she passes grey-brown terraces, the dilapidated shop fronts displaying cheap electrical goods or clothes sold for charity, alongside laundrettes, off-licences, and a greengrocer struggling in the shadow of the nearest supermarket. She turns under a railway bridge, finds the station and takes a train to Clapham Junction, where she changes to travel from south-west to south-east.

Crystal Palace, Gipsy Hill, Honor Oak Park, Forest Hill, Falcon Park. The hills and their poetic monikers are Julie's favourite aspect of south-east London. They undulate as if they mean business. A hill here boasts a real gradient and serious views — a perfect mix of breadth and depth. The houses — when there are houses, not the council blocks that have sprung up since the Second World War — are generously proportioned Victorian affairs, with bay windows to make the most of the light. On rare occasions when there's time, Julie and Terri love to stroll through the gardens of the Horniman Museum in Forest Hill, a weird extravaganza of artefacts collected from distant corners of the globe; from its panoramic perch, you can see all the way across London and beyond.

Their street, Livingston Road, is the steepest in Falcon Park. You have to go into first gear to climb it in winter or wet weather, according to a wide variety of taxi drivers. Terri, who has never learned to drive, points out that walking up that hill is what keeps them fit. 'Keeps *me* fit,' Julie returned. 'You're never home long enough to do any walking.'

The Blitz had hit Livingston Road, destroying the houses on either side of theirs; in their place makeshift blocks of flats had been erected, the concrete stained greyer by the year. Nobody takes care of them, Terri grumbles; it's always someone else's problem. South-east London is cheaper than the capital's other quarters, scruffier, as if patched together with string and sellotape; but, Terri insists, it's all the more charming because of this. Their house bears its own war scar: a crack down the length of the front wall. And the roof 'needs some attention' — as the estate agent had put it when a third

7

prospective buyer chickened out during Terri's one short-lived attempt to move.

Terri won this crazy, old-fashioned bohemian home in the divorce settlement, as Bernard was moving north; Julie has never lived anywhere else. Once it felt fuller, busier and a little warmer, holding two parents, an au pair and a tetchy Scottish grandmother who used to melt visibly whenever Julie twirled through her doorway. Julie still retains a faint impression of a large yet not especially comfortable lap, a housecoat, lilac hair rollers, fuzzy slippers. Poor but respectable, Terri told her. Churchgoing and 'decent', despite the absconding husband, or perhaps because of him. Forced me to be in the church choir, which I thought was desperately uncool until I realised I was good at it.

Terri's mother, Finnuala, died when Julie was eight; the divorce followed within a year. Julie doesn't like to dwell on that time; neither does Terri. Now, beyond the wooden central staircase, two bedrooms stand empty, ready for occasional but mainly hypothetical guests. One used to be Finn's, smelling of talc, wool and old lady; another had been assigned to whoever was the au pair of the moment and usually bore whiffs of sickly sweet perfume, hair spray and cigarettes, even though they weren't meant to smoke inside. Two more rooms have been transformed respectively into Terri's office and, where Bernard's study had been, a TV den. A drawing room with three tall, arched windows overlooks the garden, where Terri installed a compact swimming pool as soon as Julie had learned to

8

float. Underneath the kitchen is a wet room for the pool, and a cellar that holds, among other things, a rack of French wine that Terri orders annually from Berry Brothers & Rudd.

The rest of the basement is Terri's studio, the place she goes to sing, undisturbed, at an upright piano. Upstairs in her office, she's installed a desk, computer and shelves for her growing library of books and CDs.

The grand piano presides over the drawing room, where they throw parties when Terri is home long enough. Pink damask on the walls handily covers up the cracks; an ancient crimson carpet sprawls over the floor and the white sofas are arrayed with whiter cushions. Julie sometimes hovers there, remembering the party nights: her mother, splendid in her trademark ivory dresses or trouser suits, shimmering like a gold and rhinestone angel — assuming angels wear rhinestones. Pianists would take turns to accompany her as she sang — Strauss, Schubert, Brahms — and in between songs, the guests would drink the French wine and network in the corners. Once the chief conductor of Covent Garden turned up with Varya Petrovna on his arm. Another time, Teo lost it in the middle of some Schubert; Julie had to go with him to the kitchen and hold his hand while he calmed down over a whisky.

Now the room is silent and the piano needs dusting. Alone, Julie prefers to sit on the other side of the wall, in the kitchen, drinking instant soup made from powders.

'Why don't you move?' Alistair sometimes

9

asks. 'Your mum could cash in and get somewhere smaller.' Home is home, though; besides, as they've already discovered, nobody's going to buy this house with the roof in such a state, let alone the crack. For Julie, the house is an anchor — almost the only anchor she has, other than Alistair himself.

Until their *annus horribilis* of the death and the divorce, home was relatively calm, with routine maintained partly by her father, partly by her grandmother, but mainly by the au pair. Julie, boiling the kettle for a cup of mushroom soup, remembers Bernard upstairs in his study, helping her with maths homework that she couldn't understand. 'How can a daughter of mine be lousy at maths?' he'd tried to joke. Julie hadn't found it particularly funny.

Since landing a mathematics professorship in a university in the north, Bernard Mason has settled in a nauseatingly pretty Yorkshire dale with his second wife, Jane — a blonde GP who has green Wellington boots and no sense of humour. Julie loves her nine-year-old half-sister, Ellen, but towards Jane she turns all the nose-in-sling disdain she's learned from her candid mother. Terri has never hidden the truth from her: when Bernard took up his post, he'd attempted a weekly commute from London, but before they could blink, he met Jane, made her pregnant and moved out — then blamed Terri for everything. Julie sometimes thinks that life might feel easier if she didn't know this.

Now Julie is eighteen, the au pairs have gone and she often has the house to herself. Terri, who's relaxed and open and doesn't care what happens when she's away, lets her have parties whenever she likes, but Julie prefers not to. It's Terri who thinks it's fun to toast marshmallows over an open fire or to invent mysterious cocktail recipes that leave your guests unable to stand up. In summer they often hold gatherings around or in the pool, but Julie is terrified lest anyone should get drunk and drown. When she's alone, the house gapes. She prefers to stay down the road with Alistair in an environment that, if less bohemian and beautiful, feels a little more lived-in.

Slurping soup, Julie trails to her mother's study to hunt down the CDs. The image churns in her mind: her mother in bed, complexion ghostly, hair unleashed, unbrushed and unbleached. She was asleep when Julie arrived. Waiting for her to stir, Julie thought silently: 'My God, she's going to die.' She isn't, of course, not now, hopefully not for decades, and technically it was a tiny operation; but the idea had planted itself in Julie, along with the anxiety about drunk people in swimming pools, bicycles speeding on pavements and countless other worries that bug her irrationally, too often.

She closes the curtains against the dusk, switches on the lamp and bends it towards the CDs, which Terri keeps neatly in order on the shelves alongside her books. Terri has been reading constantly, far more than she used to: she's researching for a film she's wanted to make for years about the nineteenth-century diva Pauline Viardot. With the onset of the polyp, the hypothetical film has acquired a new significance.

11

'TV, Julie,' Terri announced with increasing frequency, between visits to the laryngologist. 'I've always wanted to be on TV and I've always fancied trying to have this film made, but I've never had the time before. Teo can help me with the writing. Besides, we have to eat.'

'Why her?' Julie protested. 'Why not Maria Callas?'

'For one thing, darling, Callas has been done,' Terri pointed out. 'Next, nobody can buy recordings of Viardot: no disc, no threat. Third, she wrote a lot of fantastic music, and I could sing it myself, all being well. And because the writer Ivan Turgenev might have been her lover, the whole thing is incredibly sexy. You need sex these days to get anybody interested, that's what everyone tells me.'

Perhaps what Terri's agent, Martin, has started to call 'filma-exmachina' is simply a form of escapism? The more Terri talks about the marvels of the mid-nineteenth century, Julie reflects, the less she had to think about the bank statements, accounts, VAT returns and health insurance documents that await her attention in the twenty-first.

Terri keeps her own recordings on a separate shelf. Julie quickly locates *Figaro*. The Varya Petrovna CD is sitting aside, as if contaminated. Terri probably thinks it is — Varya is the latest Russian babe to be signed up by a top record-label as much for her snowy bite as for her Bach. Terri's nickname for her is 'Taps'. Julie isn't sure whether it's a reference to her jutting

12

bosom or to a Broadway show, based on a Fred Astaire and Ginger Rogers movie, that Varya once tackled with mixed results.

Julie waits for the computer to boot up, spinning herself slowly round and round on Terri's swivel chair. The study exists in ordered chaos: papers, books and correspondence are piled systematically but statically. Terri is good at organising things that need doing, but less good at actually doing them. Julie spots a letter from the opera house in Vienna, dated two weeks ago, lying centre stage: 'Dear Terri, we were so sorry to hear about the back injury that kept you away from us . . . '

The screen brightens: the desktop shows the proscenium of the Royal Opera House, Covent Garden. Even in her study, Terri's virtual home is the theatre.

Julie pops the CD into the drive, then plugs her mother's iPod into a USB cable. While the sound of Varya Petrovna's singing fills her ears — younger and sexier than her mother, but a tad tarty in comparison — she browses Terri's books. There's a Viardot shelf: biographies of Pauline Viardot and of Turgenev; books by Turgenev; others by his friends Dostoyevsky and George Sand. A row up, there's other stuff: Anaïs Nin — an arty French writer, Julie thinks; a history of Italian film, autographed by its illustrious author ('To Teresa, with all my love and a thousand thanks for your glorious voice'); some worthy books involving human rights, politics and wars, including some tracts by Teo; and a rack of detective stories, which Terri likes to read on aeroplanes.

Julie peers closer. A small notebook bound in black leather, its spine unadorned, is tucked deep into the shelf between two crime novels — almost as if someone were trying to hide it. Julie hesitates. The cover gleams like lacquer. Read me, it begs. She resists. It's not right to look at your mother's private things.

She watches as her right hand, moving as if unguided, extracts the notebook. On the desk, it falls open. Her mother's handwriting parades across the pages like an army of ants streaming out of an inkwell.

A diary. A date: 30 June. Which year? She flicks through the pages. No clues. There's only one way to find out when her mother kept this diary, and that is to read it.

She knows she shouldn't. But, in deciphering the handwriting, she has already begun.

30 June
At Charles de Gaulle, waiting. Plane delayed — storms. Bloody mess. Packed painkillers in suitcase, now checked in, can't find chemist this side of security control. C d G is weird, run-down space-age concept, desperately dated. Next time perhaps the train will be ready.

So this is before Eurostar. Julie can't remember travelling to Paris on anything but a train. Before its genesis in the mid-1990s, she'd have been no more than six years old. Baby ballet class. Au pairs meeting her after

14

school. Nanna in the spare room. Terri would have been in her late thirties.

Still reeling from time with T. I've never been with any man who makes me feel so complete. In bed I'm so free with him. My soul goes out to him. I'm his. I can't put into words how much I want him. Just seeing the shape of his shoulders and his face, I want to drag him to bed and swallow him whole. And it's like that, it's ecstasy, we devour each other's bodies all night and in the morning I still want him, but I have to go away.

I can't be his, he can't be mine. Part of us holds back — me as much as him. Sometimes I think he can't let go enough, that he's just not all there — whatever his body is doing, his mind is somewhere else, and then I can't lose myself either. Perhaps it's because his traumas are beyond anything I can grasp and either they get in the way or I imagine that they must do. Am I making excuses for him?

OK, I had hard times as a kid, but to think what he has gone through: Bosnia; Mostar; his house; his family — he's lucky to be alive, let alone sane. Reasonably. My God. And now he's in Paris, looking lost, needing me, begging for me, but if I give myself to him, how can I keep my singing? He'd be like a great sponge, soaking up my energy. It's too much. It's too intense. But now I have to go back to bloody B. Why the

15

fuck did I ever marry him? TI wants me to divorce, but the truth is that I don't have the time to get divorced, let alone shift to Paris. T won't move to London, and I can hardly insist that he does, not even after all this time. Sometimes I feel as if we've been in this stalemate for half our lives.

It's not fair on J, poor little thing. Maybe I shouldn't have had her. It's selfish to have a child if one's not willing to put everything else aside to look after her.

But it's also selfish of other people to expect me to. If I don't sing, I'm not alive. It's almost impossible for anyone who hasn't experienced this to understand it — they just slag it off as artistic temperament, selfishness, pretentiousness — but it's actually true. Besides, without my singing I'd be back in the Gorbals being a school dinner lady. I can give J a much better future as things are.

I wouldn't be without J, but she's very demanding.

Sometimes it's more than I can take. The tantrums — she should have grown out of them years ago. It's as if she's deliberately turning herself back into a baby to manipulate me. Sometimes I think she's too young to know what she's doing, but other times I think no, she knows exactly: every tear and every shriek is calculated down to the last split second. And then I feel she is not a daughter but a millstone, dragging around my throat.

This, then, is why you're not supposed to read other people's diaries.

Perhaps the words don't mean what Julie thinks. But the more she rereads them, the more they refuse to change; their message reinforces itself, layer upon layer. That was written by her goddess-like diva of a mother? That was what Terri really thought about Julie, her own daughter, and had thought about her all along? Can it be that she really doesn't know her mother at all?

She bites her lip, feeling ice-cold, then wanders to the bathroom and dabs at her watering eyes with some loo roll. She sits down on the bathroom floor and stays there, musing, for what she later realises has been a good quarter of an hour. There's a new crack opening within her, as jagged as that on the house.

At last she collects herself enough to hunt for her phone and call Alistair. 'Can I come over?'

'You all right, Jul?'

'Not very.' Julie gazes at the shaft of light from the study, the inviting doorway of her bedroom. It's as if she's seeing the house's interior for the first time. 'I'll be along in a few minutes.'

First, she must be organised. She makes sure that the music has loaded on to the iPod, puts away the CDs and shuts down the computer. She replaces the diary precisely where she had found it, handling it by its edges as if it's radioactive. Then she splashes cold water on her face and shoves some clean underwear and a T-shirt into her bag. A few minutes later, the door slams behind her; she turns down the hill towards Scargill Tower, where Alistair and Sue live.

* * *

Julie jogs most of the dark five-minute walk and arrives in three. Then an extra two for taking the stairs to the seventh floor — she doesn't trust the lift, which is plastered with graffiti, reeks of piss and sometimes breaks down. Alistair is waiting for her in the doorway; a second later his stubble is sharp on her skin and she can smell peanut butter, beer, sweat and cats and the sense of people, of livingness, that always surrounds him — not much different now from her impressions on the first day she went home with him after school. Back then, they were only fourteen, and they'd noticed they were pulling identical faces of hatred and incomprehension in the maths class.

She'd cuddled the cats, eaten the biscuits Sue offered her, and wondered why this little flat in the most frightening estate in the borough somehow felt warmer than her own home. Sue, like Terri, was a single mum, but there didn't seem to be the acrimony around the ex that there was in Livingston Road — because there wasn't one. 'I never met my dad,' Alistair told her. She didn't like to ask if he knew his father's name. The two of them sat munching on opposite sides of the table, gazes occasionally colliding, cheeks a little flushed, still too shy to ask each other out.

They'd managed eventually; and now Alistair

is thirteen inches taller. He's just in from his shift at the supermarket and has been enjoying a well-earned lager.

'What's going on, Jul?' His bright eyes see straight into her.

'Is your mum in?'

'Nah, she went to work. Left supper for both of us, though. She guessed you'd be along.'

'Great. I'll tell you about today later.' She grabs his hand. In his bedroom, Alistair tips the tabby cat off the duvet and Julie peels off her jeans.

He comes up behind her and puts both arms round her waist. 'What's up, love?' he presses. 'You're not yourself. Tell Uncle Alistair.'

'Don't you uncle me!' Julie laughs. The warmth of his arms and his breath is as necessary as a fix to an addict. She grabs his belt and undoes it. He hesitates — torn between wanting to talk and wanting to shag — but the second option wins and he dips under the bed to find a condom. Julie pulls him down on top of her and as he plunges inside her the tears well up and won't be kept back. She doesn't want him to see. 'More,' she says into his ear. He holds her hips, hoists her legs against his shoulders. Julie squeezes her damp eyes shut. Lost in sensation, he hasn't noticed. Soon, she's lost too, as she wants to be. Nothing is real for a few minutes except her nerve endings — escape and freedom at last.

Alistair, getting his breath, licks her nose and grins. 'Lager?'

'Yes, please!' Her legs, satisfactorily, feel like

jelly when she pads to the bathroom while Alistair, in his underpants, fetches beer and crisps. The shower is furred with limescale and only lets out a trickle, but it's enough to soap away some of the dregs of this confusing day.

'How's your mum?' he asks, sitting back on the bed, opening the cans.

She takes a long draught, grateful, and tells him about the operation.

'Will she be able to sing?'

'It's going to take her a good few months to get better. I'll stay home to look after her. After the exams.'

'Jul, she's your mum, you're not hers, so don't let her hold you back. You'll get your place at uni and you're going to go.'

'I don't want to.'

'You get the chance, you go. Cos I can't.'

'You could, if you try,' Julie encourages. 'You're always telling yourself you're hopeless, but you're not!'

'Maybe they'll start an A level in sex,' he jokes.

Julie picks at the crisps. Normally she tries not to eat junk food, but they've just burned off a few calories and she'd skipped lunch, having had no appetite while she imagined her mother in hospital. She's on tricky Alistair territory. It's not as if they hadn't tried to persuade him to stay at school to take A levels; the art teacher had lectured him about not letting peer pressure stop you if you have an affinity for something that requires effortful development. But he hadn't listened, and now he's been stacking shelves for eighteen months.

He crunches. 'You'll swan off and be a posh student. I don't know what the fuck's going to happen to me.'

Julie knows him so well — or she thinks she does. Each day he's a little different. She looks at the pulse flickering near his Adam's Apple, the soft but defined hairs on his forearms, the way he bounces one leg repeatedly, a nervous habit. He's just nineteen. He's fit, good-looking — even after four years of being his girlfriend, watching him develop from spotty schoolboy to hunk, she's still amazed by the strength of her physical pull towards him. And he's always saying perceptive things, taking the trouble to give her a present or do something kind, always knowing when something is wrong, taking her part, making her laugh. They started having full sex two years ago, the moment she turned sixteen — well, just before — and the others at school and beyond no longer compete for their favours or make an issue of their different backgrounds. They simply belong to each other.

'Thing is,' Alistair says, 'your mum sings opera and mine cleans offices. Your dad's a university professor and I don't even know who my dad was. You talk BBC and I talk estuary.'

'What's that got to do with anything?' Julie protests. 'We grew up together. We do everything together. And everyone on the BBC is Scottish anyway. Al, all I want is to be with you.'

'Yeah, me too. You're great. You're clever, you sing like a bird, you get more gorgeous all the time.' He hugs her. 'You used to be a pretty girl, and now you're a beautiful woman. But you're going to go away and study and someday you won't want to know me any more.'

'I won't do that! I won't!'

Julie's university offers are buried in a drawer in her desk. Any of these eminent institutions will accept her as a music student even if she only gets three Bs in her exams. Dad's influence, she grumbles. Mostly the top universities insist on three As, seventeen pole-vaults and the ability to levitate. Julie has one gift that's a mixed blessing: she can achieve good grades without feeling particularly involved in her studies. Her mind may be academic, but her heart isn't. Still, neither parent will hear of her not going to university. Nor, annoyingly, will Alistair.

'I can't win,' she says. 'You won't let me not go, but you say I'll forget you. What do you want me to do?'

'I want you to have a chance.'

'But why are you so negative about yourself? Mum's always going on about positive thinking. She says she'd never have . . . '

'It's easy for her. She's famous.'

'Easy? For Mum? She started from nothing and she only got a break because she was working in a pub opposite the Usher Hall when . . . '

'Yeah, I know, I know. But your mum's special. She's got charisma, guts and a gift. I've got fuck-all.'

'But you can choose — '

'Me? *Choose?*'

Julie stops, resigned. She knows what's coming next.

Alistair begins to grumble: he's never seen much except the inside of Scargill Tower. His dyslexia means he can't spell — at school they'd twigged too late what was wrong — so he'd learned to believe he was stupid. He's got no money and only passed three GCSEs, so he's convinced he can't get a job except the one he has. If he's lucky, he might work his way up to the fresh meat counter.

Julie fights back with the words she's been repeating for months, indeed years. Dyslexia is a physical problem, not a mental one; you're bright, you simply haven't had the chance to do anything about it and our school didn't do enough to help. Inwardly, her mind's eye is still tracing its way over the scrawled loops of her mother's handwriting.

'Al,' she says eventually, 'can I tell you something? I found this diary that my mum kept when I was little . . . ' She trails off.

Alistair snaps out of his rant. 'Did she write about you?'

She nods, a lump in her throat larger than the polyp in her mother's.

'What?'

'Well . . . ' She can't find the words, let alone form them into sentences.

'I can't know what you're on about if you won't tell me.'

'I dunno what to say . . . but I just don't want to be on my own tonight.'

'All right,' Alistair grunts. 'Be like that.'

Sometimes Alistair takes her introversion as a personal affront and rolls up like a petulant porcupine. Unable to get past the prickles, Julie withdraws. She wanders away to his computer, which is her old one, to look at her email and Myspace page.

The browser is open. The picture on the screen shows a muscular, close-shaven young man clad in khaki. White lettering on a black background reads: ARMY JOBS.

'Al? What's this?'

'What does it look like?' says Alistair.

2

An electronic hum; the clunk of rubber and metal doors reuniting. The métro glides onwards. From the platform Teo Popović can glimpse the next station, some way down the open track. Lights in darkness, dots waiting to be joined up. He blinks. He's half climbed, half tumbled off the train. His limbs are stiff from sleeping wedged between seat and seat back — he's not sure for how long — and the fingers of his right hand are numb. He shakes it to get the blood flowing, then slumps onto a damp bench. The spring morning is fresh, scented with last night's rain. His shoes glare up at him; on the left foot, the sole has split at the side, letting in the puddles. Get some new ones. No excuse for hanging on to the old. Fear of losing the past, even if the past is better lost.

Teo watches another train approach. The rising sun glints, dazzling orange, off the windows. Each day is new, each day could bring a fresh start, if he let it. He shields his eyes, looking for a clock. Six a.m. He stares at the letters that make up the station name. The end of the line. How did he get here?

Such evenings are less frequent than they used to be, but they still happen. It was so civilised, at first. He went out for dinner at the bistro on the corner with his upstairs neighbours — Dominique the young lawyer and his wife Anna, the

25

grey-eyed schoolteacher. It's always the same: they encourage him, treat him with respect, laugh together; then something gets in the way.

The waiters knew them and greeted them, brisk and polite. Steak frites, green salad, cheese with chunks of fresh baguette, a couple of carafes of red wine. Some students from the Sorbonne recognised him; one came up and grasped his hand: 'I read your book, I don't know what to say.'

'Don't worry,' said Teo. 'Nobody ever does.'

Something must have set him off; he doesn't know what. Outside, inhaling warm breath from the mouth of the Luxembourg RER station, he waved his friends away and watched them vanish through the drizzle. Something about vanishing. He'll see them again, possibly tomorrow. But he couldn't make himself go home. He lives in a good area in a tiny flat, which he's rented for years from a government organisation that supports writers in exile from troubled states. It was waiting for him, empty, and after an evening enjoying good company, the idea of being alone with himself heralded pain. The keys in his pocket nipped his fingers. He couldn't pull them out and let himself into a space that is sometimes a home and at other times a prison. He felt incarcerated in the future, unable to access the past where the love lives. Or where it had lived until he first saw Terri Ivory and heard her sing.

He took the stairs down to the RER; at Saint-Michel he changed to the métro, the trains on which were slower and friendlier. There he sat alone, watching people. Normal people, chattering in Parisian dialect, or north African, or West Indian. Businessmen leaving work late; couples going home after a night out, a girl resting her cheek against a boy's shoulder; a group of men engaged in a discussion in a language he didn't understand, possibly Arabic, so intently that they nearly missed their stop. The métro has become his favourite refuge.

Sometimes he watches men trying to chat up women; the French don't make heavy weather about this, unlike the British, Terri told him. The girls smile or scowl, depending on the bloke, as they brush aside the advances. When he first came to Paris, he tried talking to girls once or twice himself; some were polite, others less so. Most had barely heard of Bosnia. It doesn't matter any more; he only wants Terri.

With the comfort of anonymous travellers around him, he nodded off, lolling against the window, and when he awoke the train was at the terminus and a guard was tapping him on the shoulder. It was too far to go home, so he managed to hide in the station while they locked up; he slept across the hard orange seats until the first train of morning rattled in, when he roused himself, climbed aboard, then curled up to finish his kip in the warmth.

After such nights he always feels ashamed, slightly sickened. He's endured everything that he's endured — and now, when he has a home in the most beautiful city in the world, he can't face going back to it? Self-hatred eats away at him.

He knows it's a vicious circle, but he can't stop it.

He once went to a doctor, who talked vaguely about post-traumatic stress disorders, then suggested psychotherapy. Teo visited a well-established Freudian off the boulevard Saint-Germain, and described in the simplest possible terms something of what had happened.

He was a teacher in Mostar; a writer in what time was left after work and family; a Bosnian who was ethnically a Serb and nominally an Orthodox Christian, but in practice believed in nothing except the essential goodness of the human spirit. Now he felt he'd been wrong to believe even in that.

In the decade following the death of Tito in 1980, Yugoslavia fell apart. By the early nineties, Belgrade and Zagreb, Teo told the Freudian, were fighting each other, but both fancied a land grab in Bosnia, while the West swallowed whole the Serbian propaganda about the 'flaring up of ancient ethnic tensions'. Boundaries were shredded, both in the land and inside people's heads. The Bosnian Serbs — supposedly his own people, yet individuals, he thought, from another planet — carved off a Republika Srpska from Bosnia and Herzegovina, intending it to be 'ethnically pure', which meant evicting or murdering its Muslims. Teo was one of some twenty-four thousand Bosnian Serbs who lived in Mostar before the war, but faced ethnic cleansing himself, since now Mostar, situated in Bosnia-Herzegovina, was designated half-Croat and half-Muslim. Neighbours who had lived amicably together for decades began to murder each other. Those of the 'wrong' religion were forced out of their homes, many into concentration camps. Teo was convinced that everything had been stirred up cynically for territorial and nationalistic ends. The Western politicians, he grumbled, were so hung up on reverence to race and religion that they completely missed the point. Or else they were just fucking idiots.

His house, the family home for generations, went up in flames. His children died with the house. His wife, Mila . . . he couldn't tell anyone what had happened to Mila. There, Teo's words dried up.

The therapist sat there like a lemon. Then she asked Teo to describe his relationship with his mother. He never went back.

It comes and goes. He writes, he teaches, he lectures about his experiences. He reads his work and people listen, dumbstruck, many in tears. Most assume that writing about it helps. If only it were so simple. He makes friends, meets women, flirts and jokes, finding that words build him footholds to scale the rocks from night to day. His foundations may be shattered, but he has to construct new walls on them because there's no alternative.

Normal life, the sight of ordinary people on the métro, is his balm; yet there are days when even this strikes him with revulsion. An image as simple as tourists photographing Notre-Dame, an orderly queue in Monoprix or a child riding a tricycle past the manicured flowerbeds in the Luxembourg Gardens can cast him into a rage that he suppresses violently until it turns inward. Sometimes he tries to quell it with drink; later he wakes up parched, his heart and head hammering, to find himself surrounded by broken glass, a smashed bookshelf or cupboards emptied and their contents scattered, and over-polite notes from the neighbours pushed under the door, asking too tactfully whether he is all right and whether there's anything they can do to help.

The lowest point came soon after he'd found his way to France. Black hole years, a time of flames and mourning. When the silence is so dense that you can touch it, and you know everything will continue regardless whether you're there or not, you wonder why you should stay. Teo bought four packs of painkillers and swallowed most of them before his body rebelled at facing such a pathetic death after having escaped the conflagrations of Mostar and the siege of Sarajevo. He vomited out the pills before they could work.

A week later, Teo, wandering the streets of Paris with his pipe, found himself outside the Opéra Bastille. He thought it looked like a Bastille: stainless steel, glass, functional clean-cut modernism. A poster announced *Der Rosenkavalier*, opera by Richard Strauss, starring Teresa Ivory as the Marschallin. The photograph showed the diva in her ivory dress, huge blue-green eyes upturned to the light with wonder illuminating her face. He'd seen posters of gorgeous actresses and singers many times and walked by unmoved. This time he stopped. On impulse, he went into the box office and bought the cheapest ticket available.

Teo wasn't a regular opera-goer and he had never heard *Der Rosenkavalier* before. The moment the orchestra began to play, energy blazed through him. Fireworks ran amok in this music, shimmering explosions and soon, a primal, utterly unmistakeable whooping from the horns. Teo couldn't believe his ears — music could convey an ejaculation? The lights went up on the set: sure enough, a couple in bed. Teresa Ivory lifted her head into the spotlight. Her costume was a scanty silk nightdress. She luxuriated, stretching out her bare arms and toes; she was the Marschallin, considering herself ageing at thirty-two, enjoying the illicit love of her seventeen-year-old page boy, Oktavian — who, to Teo's amusement, was played by a woman. As Teo watched, Oktavian kissed the Marschallin's toes one by one, and she tipped back her cascade of golden hair and laughed to the heavens, her face brighter than all the lights of the Paris Opéra put together. Transfixed, Teo somersaulted out of his world into hers.

The evening suspended him beyond time, while the music glimmered, laughed and waltzed, then found its catharsis when the Marschallin gave up Oktavian to a girl his own age. And while the three women sang their last trio, there settled upon the theatre a moment of ecstatic stillness, through which Teo felt the tears he normally couldn't shed sliding from his eyes, freed at last.

He went to the stage door to try to see her, but

the doorman wouldn't let him in — his name wasn't on the backstage list. He thought of lurking outside, waiting for her with the crowd of fans; but, knowing how crushed he'd feel if she walked by without a glance, he decided to write instead, sending flowers.

Later he kicked himself for leaving and for missing an opportunity, however tiny. He had no idea whether she'd received the bouquet, and the run had just one more performance. He called the Sorbonne to say he was sick and couldn't lecture that day, then began to telephone everybody he knew in Paris until, after three hours of fruitless chit-chat, he found someone — Daniel, a critic who'd praised his latest book — who knew an influential member of the theatre's administrative team. No problem, said Daniel. Free tickets and backstage pass coming right up.

By the time Daniel arrived to meet him in the foyer, Teo was dreading the evening. He hated the suits, handshakes, cheek-pecks and small talk involved in socialising with people who had cultural power but no talent. Besides, after last time, surely it would be impossible to re-experience the same sunburst.

They were in better seats, though, and he could see her closer to; and the rapture not only came back but transformed itself into the conviction — plainly ridiculous — that this woman was destined for him, and he for her.

He read her biography and asked nonchalant questions of Daniel and Benoît, his directorial friend. Where is she from? Poverty in Scotland, said Daniel. Where is she going? Straight to the top. She's thirty-eight — in her prime. What's she like to work with? Fearsome but phenomenal, said Benoît; generous but exacting, an inspiration to everyone. When Terri was there, the whole place caught fire. She pulled everyone up to a new level, made them achieve standards they'd never dreamed of. She gave so much that she made them believe they could as well.

Teo nodded: that made sense. That was who he'd thought she was.

'The Celts are good at singing,' remarked Daniel. 'Look at the Welsh.'

'Terri is Scottish,' Benoît pointed out.

'Ah, but look at those eyes. She'll have Irish roots. Skin like milk, eyes like the sea. I wonder if she could sing Isolde.' The Irish princess, Teo remembered, who travelled to Cornwall to wed the king but fell in love with his emissary, Tristan.

'Wagner?' mused the director. 'That's interesting. Terri Ivory as Isolde . . . '

Teo was barely listening. He'd fallen under every spell that could invade his mind while it was open enough to let them and Terri Ivory in. When she sang, her voice, as strong as quartz, as pure as distilled water and as essential, to him, as oxygen, sliced aside the pain and plummeted him into a consciousness in which nothing was real but now. All that existed was the present: a state of grace.

Benoît opened the pass door that led backstage. Teo followed his companions along the corridors, blinking in the fluorescent lights.

33

Steel, banisters, corners, people hurrying, laughing and arguing. And then the last door opened and it was hers.

She was tiny. The top of her head was level with his armpit and though her bust was full, her waist was as slender as a hornet's. From the auditorium, he'd thought her larger than life. Instead, he was towering over his dream woman.

'Terri, this is Teo Popović, the celebrated author,' said Benoît.

'I'm so glad you could come.' Terri Ivory looked him straight in the eye. Her hand, shaking his, made up for its smallness with strength and warmth. 'It's an honour to meet you. Please forgive me, my French is terrible, but I know your work, I read your novel. Someone gave me the English translation for my birthday. It moved me tremendously.'

Teo spoke English, retaining her hand for the contact with her physical reality. 'And you have moved me beyond all possible words,' he said. Her fingers pressed his in response. She looked not just into his eyes, but behind them. Perhaps he was imagining it, but he thought this was the look he'd sometimes received from women who knew they were going to sleep with him.

'Thank you for the beautiful flowers,' she said.

'Flowers are corny. I'd write a poem about you if I could, but I am a very bad poet.'

'I'm sure that isn't true.' She flashed a smile at him, then the others. 'Teo, Daniel, Benoît, won't you please join us for dinner? Let me get changed and I'll meet you over the road in fifteen minutes.'

Crossing the Place de la Bastille with the critic and the administrator to the bistro where Terri had booked a table, Teo wondered what 'us' meant. A husband, no doubt; American, probably, with the build of Arnold Schwarzenegger and the wealth of Bill Gates. But when she arrived — after thirty minutes rather than fifteen — her companions were a woman friend who worked in haute couture in New York, a French student who wanted to sing to her, and an extremely effete young man from her artists' management company in London. Teo had made sure a place remained empty beside him. Sit here, his eyes beamed towards her; and he watched as she turned, understood and complied, kissing him on the cheek as if she'd known him for ever. Her scent brushed his nostrils — floral yet ambery, rather like her voice.

'I want to hear all about your work,' she said to him, while Benoît ordered a St-Emilion wine and the others studied the after-theatre menu. 'Tell me about you. Tell me everything.'

'That's boring. *You* tell me everything. Tell me how you came to be where you are today.'

'That could take a while.'

He loved her accent: it tumbled and rolled like waves in the Hebrides. His fingers itched to light his pipe. He must resist, sitting next to an opera singer; she wouldn't like smoke. She sensed his edginess, he noted. A perceptive woman; one who wanted to be considerate, not one who knew only that she was a star. Two rings caught the light on her left hand — gold and a solitaire diamond. Of course, Teo remembered, the

British, besides driving on the wrong side of the road, wear their wedding rings on the wrong hand.

'Is your husband a singer too?' He tried to be polite.

'No, he's a mathematician. I think he's tone deaf.'

'You've been married a long time?'

'Too long. I'm home so little and Bernard isn't best pleased with me at the moment. Nor I with him . . .'

Benoît clapped his hands for silence; there ensued a speech in eloquent French about the wonders of Terri's performance, the glory of Strauss's music and the Bastille's privilege in presenting both. Under the table, Terri tapped Teo's knee.

'Guess what?' she whispered. 'I can't understand a *bloody word*.' Her breath tickled his ear; he closed his eyes, his hormones popping their corks.

'May I volunteer to teach you French?'

'Perhaps I should learn Bosnian instead. It might come in handy.' Something warm touched his ankle: the gentle pressure of a small foot in a high-heeled shoe.

Dinner whirled on. Teo was never sure how he managed to eat anything at all that evening.

'French lesson number one,' he said to her, much later, while the waiter was fetching their coats. 'Where are you staying? *A quel hôtel demeurez-vous, Madame Ivory?*'

'Oh, please,' she responded, 'call me Terri. And call me 'tu'. That much French I know.'

'*Bien, ma chère Terri, nous allons nous tutoyer.*' Teo liked speaking French. In a language that wasn't his own yet in which he was comfortable, he could turn himself into a different person, and a better one. '*A quel hôtel demeures-tu, Terri?*'

'A cute boutique place in the Marais,' she said in English. 'Very cosy. And they have a delightful little lounge bar. Would you like to stop for a nightcap on your way home?'

Teo's home was nowhere near the Marais, but he didn't care.

★ ★ ★

Her hair gleaming dusky gold against the bar's wooden panels, Terri insisted on ordering and paying for the drinks — Scotch whisky, naturally.

'I'd never have dreamed, when I was a little girl in the Gorbals, that I'd end up here,' she confided. 'Singing in the world's best theatres, staying in lovely hotels, dining with fascinating writers. I still can't quite believe it. Pinch me?'

Teo did.

'Ouch.' Her grin broadened. 'So, you are real, and so am I.'

Her voice enchanted him; speaking, it seemed much stronger in the quiet of the bar. 'What are the Gorbals?' he asked, sipping the whisky.

'I don't think you really want to know, darling. Let's just say that the truly incredible thing about singers — and I see this all over the world, talking to my colleagues — is that we come from anywhere and everywhere, and it never matters.

We're from the streets of Lima, the outskirts of Mexico City, the finest suburbs of old-world Europe or, in my case, what remained of a Scottish slum. We find our way to the opera houses even if we started out skinning kangaroos in the Australian outback or singing in churches in the Midwest Bible Belt. I never knew my father, at least not after I was two; he was a shipbuilder in Glasgow. I might never have known what an aria was if I hadn't been lucky enough that my music teacher at school took charge of me. And it's all because we open our mouths and out flies . . . this voice; then if we're lucky, someone notices it. We have just four things in common, we so-called divas, and our leading lads: we have a voice, we work hard, we take hold of life with both hands, and we are bloody lucky.'

Teo gorged on the sight of her in the lamplight, sitting with legs crossed on an armless pink leather chair, the raised knee pointing in his direction. Her sparkling necklace looked as soft as her skin, and her light eyes seemed oddly dark. An Ella Fitzgerald record pulsed along quietly in the background.

'Did it ever occur to you to do anything else?' he asked.

'Not really, though sometimes I think I'd have loved to make films. Documentaries. Directing or presenting or both. I can dream. Who knows, I might do it yet. A film about a great historical singer, perhaps.'

'I've got someone for you,' said Teo. 'Do you know about Pauline Viardot?'

'Tell me more.'

'She was — well, a great historical singer. One of the most important nineteenth-century divas. She inspired the greatest composers of her day, and everyone fell in love with her, especially Ivan Turgenev. I heard about her because rather a long time ago I did my dissertation on Turgenev.'

'Turgenev?' Terri echoed. '*Really?*'

That was Teo's first inkling that Terri wasn't so much a social climber as an intellectual one. She longed for the respectability she thought literature and learning might bring. Maybe that was why she'd married an academic whom now she evidently couldn't stand.

'Ah,' said Teo, 'I see the penny has fallen! She was the great love of Turgenev's life.'

Terri leaned her head to one side, laughing. 'The expression is 'the penny has dropped', darling, not 'the penny has fallen'.'

'I will try to remember that. But she would be a wonderful topic for you. There was so much potential between them. A singer and a writer, inspiring each other. And she's fascinating in her own right — a powerful woman, ahead of her time. Then she lost her voice. Some say she ruined it by singing too much. She had to retire from the stage when she was forty-two.'

Terri pulled her chair closer to him. 'I must confess, if I may, that I find that very frightening. Because what are we if we lose our voices? We're singers. We are our own musical instruments. The voice is something we're born with, it's part of us — and if our voice goes, the better part of ourselves goes with it, maybe our soul. That's what I dread, Teo, if I can tell you something intimate and if you won't find it ridiculous after losing all that you've lost. I dread losing my voice.'

'I know.' Teo covered her hand with his. 'Sometimes I dread losing mine too.'

Terri downed the last of her drink and said, 'Shall we go upstairs?'

In her room — the largest in the hotel, overlooking the place des Vosges — Terri kicked off her shoes and perched on the bed, no longer a diva but more like a little girl, swinging her legs, mischievous rather than guilty. She had dimples, Teo noted, the one in her left cheek deeper than the one in her right.

'Have a look in the minibar,' she said. 'There should be a half-bottle of champagne. Would you like to open it?'

He obeyed, pouring two glasses, filling them too full. This scenario was impossible, even in a life as bizarre as his, which he thought resembled a poker game where he drew either the worst hand in the pack or — as tonight — straight aces. She clinked her glass against his and the foam spilled over and mingled on their fingers.

'Let's talk.' Terri patted the bed beside her. 'We couldn't in the restaurant. Not the way that I'd like to.'

Teo, not certain that talking was uppermost in his mind, asked whether it would bother her if he smoked his pipe. She opened the window, but smiled as he pulled out his tobacco tin, filled the bowl and lit up.

'It smells nice,' she remarked. 'Spicy, fruity. A

bit like Christmas pudding. Have you ever eaten Christmas pudding?'

'It sounds full of pine needles.'

'It's a dense plum cake that's boiled rather than baked. We have it every Christmas in Britain.' She'd propped up three pillows and was leaning back against them, feet outstretched. Her toenails were painted very pale gold. Teo thought of Oktavian kissing them. 'Come and sit here. I want you to tell me about Bosnia.'

Teo inhaled fragrant smoke. 'Doesn't your husband mind you asking other men to tell you about Bosnia in your bedroom at one thirty in the morning?'

'My husband,' said Terri, 'doesn't bloody care. Anyway, in London it's only twelve thirty.'

He stretched out beside her, putting down his pipe in an ashtray under the lamp. She shifted across to lean her head against his chest as if she hadn't only met him that night; as if she knew him, trusted him, felt no urgency over what would happen later. He imagined she was a rare bird that had dropped out of the sky straight into his lap. When he closed one arm across her, the bolt of tenderness left him winded. 'Why?' he asked. 'Why do you want to know? Why do you want me to be here, now, like this? I don't understand.'

She smiled at him, simple, blinking. 'Darling, why *not*?'

'Why not, indeed.' He brushed a lock of hair back from her face, rested his palm against her cheek.

41

She closed her eyes, smiling. 'Warm, sweet hands.'

'Not really. Crusty old fingers, stained with tobacco and worse.' He held her shoulders with them. 'I never believed in angels. I don't know what to think now I've found one.'

She lifted her mouth to kiss him. 'But,' she mumbled into his lips, 'I do still want to know about your life. I want to know everything about you.'

'Later.' Teo was adrift. He needed to find out if her skin was as ivory-smooth as her name.

'*Now.*'

He lay down and took a breath. 'Where shall I start?'

'Mostar?'

Theo said nothing for a few minutes. He wasn't used to people asking him outright for his story; they usually assumed it would be too painful to discuss. Apart from the fact that they were right, his memories weren't ideal for this occasion. He would be selective.

'Until 1993,' he began, 'I lived in Mostar, in a house that had belonged to my family for generations, with my wife and two children. The river in Mostar, the Neretva, is green. Deep green, like malachite. There's power in the hills there, Terri, an extraordinary power. Above our house is a mountain called the Hum. There's an energy about it; it is somehow luminous. By night you can almost see it shining. Something to do with the limestone. But I'm no geologist. I taught French and English to high school students, and I always had this silly notion inside me that I needed to write. Then . . . '

The night drew on; the trees of the darkened square hissed in the October wind; the moon sank behind the baroque turrets. Terri listened as nobody had ever listened to him before. Now and then she nodded, or prompted him to go on, or held his hand, gripping hard, when he described what happened on the Hum. 'The best way to attack the town from the mountain was to fill tyres with explosives, set them alight and roll them down on to us.'

'And your house . . . '

'Destroyed. If it hadn't been that, it would have been something else. First the Serbs shelled us to hell, then the Croats decided they would too.'

'I never really understood what was going on in that war,' Terri admitted.

'It was like a triangle,' Teo suggested, 'with numerous smaller sub-section triangles within each triangle. Put it all together and it looks like a crazy geometry lesson — and none of the lines were straight. Does that help?'

'Not exactly.' Terri smiled. 'Go on. What happened to you?'

'I seemed to be on the wrong side of every triangle. Before the war I was just me. Just this dopey teacher, would-be writer and papa. Everybody got along, before this. I'm a Bosnian Serb, so what? Nobody cared about that crap. Suddenly, oh my God, a Bosnian Serb in Mostar! I happened to live in the wrong place. East Mostar is Muslim, West Mostar is Catholic, they even drink different beer, and they wanted to throw out the Serbs, who in turn were busy throwing them out of what would become the Republika Srpska. On the Hum, my mountain, where I used to walk as a boy, dreaming about writing and travelling, not only did they attack our town from here, but they shelled and destroyed the bridge.'

'What about your family?'

Theo paused. 'They were in the house.'

Terri kissed his forehead and cheek, pressing her hands against his shoulders. He thought he could feel energy fizzing through her palms and radiating into his blood. 'I wish I could do something to help,' she said.

'You do help. Most people don't want to know. They can't cope. You tell them a little, and then they say, 'oh dear me, how very nasty, would you like another cup of tea?''

'Well,' said Terri, 'I make the best cup of tea in south London.'

'And will you make me some, if I come to visit you?'

'Perhaps. If you're very, very good.' She threw herself flat on her back and held out her arms.

He surveyed this glorious white, gold and blue apparition, inviting him. 'Now you know, do you still want me?'

'More.'

'Aren't you tired? You sang that whole opera tonight.'

'I'll be much more tired if you don't come here and make love to me right now, instead of spending another half an hour saying 'are you sure?'.' Terri unfastened her blouse and bra. Teo threw his shirt across the room, then his trousers.

Terri's gaze lingered on the damaged patches of skin.

'Burns,' he said. 'Don't ask.'

'Do they hurt?'

'I don't think so.'

'Good. Make sure?' She put her lips against a scar on his left elbow, and pressed. And it didn't hurt, not at all.

At six, they passed out in each other's arms.

* * *

Teo drags himself up the station stairs and round the corner to the apartment block, where he presses the door code into the keypad, hoping not to bump into anyone inside. It's half past seven, though, and Dominique, the young lawyer upstairs, is setting out for his morning jog in the Luxembourg Gardens. 'Bonjour, Teo,' he says, bounding past.

Teo mutters a greeting. His throat is bone-dry. His clothes need washing; he must have breath like a donkey; and he hasn't shaved for over twenty-four hours. What must Dominique think — especially after their oh-so-civilised dinner? Then again, why should he care what anyone thinks?

Upstairs, his flat is ridiculously tidy. Jadwiga, the Polish cleaner, had made her weekly visit yesterday afternoon. Teo thinks there's something inhuman about tidiness. He likes a place to bear evidence of life. He doesn't let Jadwiga touch his desk.

A hot shower, a strong Bosnian coffee and he begins to feel more like his official daytime self; he kills an hour on administration and reading online newspapers, waiting for nine o'clock. At nine sharp, eight in London, he dials Terri's number. There's a female voice on the answering machine: not Terri, but Julie. No longer a little girl with a hairband, but a young woman, and one who could, if she wished to, sing like her mother.

Of course, Terri was in hospital for her operation and Julie would be staying with her boyfriend. Teo is horrified to realise he had temporarily forgotten about this.

He should be there; Terri would need him. He should have got his act together sooner — they'd known about the operation for several weeks — but he hadn't been organised enough. He finds it difficult to think ahead, even to book a train ticket to London to look after the love of his life.

He calls Julie's mobile. 'Julie, dear.'

'Hello, Teo!' She sounds bright, but a little down.

'How is everything?'

'The operation went fine. She'll be home tonight. Are you coming over?'

'I will try, as soon as she feels strong enough.' He's bluffing, and loathes himself for it. 'I don't want her to strain her voice by talking to me. And you? What have you been doing? Working for your exams?'

'Yes, but Al and I went out last night.' Julie stifles a yawn. 'We went clubbing with some friends. I was out too late, now I'm going to the hospital to see Mum, and then it's school.'

'Try to concentrate on your work, it's important. Are you still eating soup? Eat proper soup, homemade, with vegetables. In fact, chicken soup is the best nourishment. Not the powdered stuff.'

'Teo! It's bad enough Mum going on at me all the time without you starting too!' He can hear her smiling. It's a source of considerable pride that Julie is so fond of him that she treats him as genuine family.

'Teo . . . ?'

'What is it, my dear? Something is the matter.'

'I don't know how to put it, but I was wondering . . . because I never knew . . . when did you and Mum first get together?'

'So long ago that being not enough together has become a bad habit. Why do you ask?'

'Dunno, really. But . . . sometimes I think I don't know my mum at all.'

Teo tucks the phone under one ear while his hands reach for the tobacco tin. 'I imagine you would have preferred a mother who stayed home with you.'

'No way!' Julie insists. 'I'm dead proud of Mum. I wouldn't change her for anyone. I used to love it when my schoolfriends were, like, going on about their boring parents with boring jobs, watching boring TV every evening, and I was off to Covent Garden to see my mum sing! But — it's like she's one person onstage and another

47

at home with me and then there's another Mum, one that I don't know about, and that's her real self . . . I'm sorry, I'll shut up.'

'Julie? Are you all right?' There's an unfamiliar tone in her voice. She sounds shaken; destabilised. Teo attributes it to Terri's operation, for lack of anything else to blame.

'Fine. Yes, really, I'm fine. It's just, like . . . oh, never mind. Teo, come over soon? *Please?*'

'I will, dear. Take good care. And do remember, please, about the soup.'

Hearing Julie's voice is the next best thing to hearing Terri's, but talking to her always leaves Teo aware of the emptiness where his daughter, Gabrijela, should have been; this year, 2007, she'd have turned twenty-two. And though he longs for Julie to fill the gap, Terri doesn't encourage it.

In the time he's known her, Terri has grown from hot, youngish diva to senior opera star; from being adored yet bitched-about to being untouchably respected; from sex symbol to mother figure. Meanwhile he has morphed from struggling, traumatised refugee to slightly older, struggling, faintly calmer refugee, and from schoolteacher to — so he's told — literary giant, or similar rubbish. They can't even pretend that they're still young. He is fifty-two, but looks ten years older; Terri is fifty, though acts much younger. Yet the more he wants her, the more she manoeuvres herself to arms' length. All these years, Teo agonises, they could have been building a life together.

'Wouldn't you rather grow old together than

48

apart?' he'd asked her.

'We *are* together.'

'Not to me, we're not.'

'Then don't wait for me. You might do better elsewhere.'

'I don't want anybody but you.'

'Tough,' said Terri. 'I love you, but this is who I am. End of story. Put that in your pipe and smoke it.'

3

Terri, head thrumming and body feeling fragmented by the anaesthetic, climbs the stairs to her front door. She's liberated herself from the hospital a few hours earlier than intended, and Julie's still at school; the house is empty. She dumps her case in the hall, opening it only to remove her toiletries; then makes some tea and drags herself to bed where, curling up, she closes her eyes, wondering how on earth she got here.

'You must tell me exactly what's going on. No bullshit, no bedside manner, thank you,' she said to the laryngologist, waiting for his diagnosis. 'I can take it.'

He'd seemed more interested at first in talking about Glyndebourne and Covent Garden — angling, as people often do, for complimentary tickets. As if he needed them, the amount of cash he must rake in per annum. Terri stared him between the eyes and demanded, 'What exactly is the cause?'

'That,' he began, 'is a very good question. A number of different factors can contribute to the formation of polyps, Miss Ivory. Of course, the greatest part will be physical strain to the voice, and some of this is probably cumulative. But we have to look at why you should have developed this problem at this time.'

'Do you mean it's psychosomatic?'

'It's very difficult to separate the psychological and the physical. When the voice is the focus of your whole life, it becomes the focus, too, for a lot of tension. So, the important thing now is how we get rid of this little problem and ensure it doesn't return.'

It didn't feel like such a 'little' problem to Terri.

It all began with a common cold. Aeroplanes, Terri's convinced, are lethal weapons. The supply of oxygen is limited; you breathe in other people's germs, which hold all-night parties in your lungs. During the flight you make sure to get up and stretch regularly so that you don't develop thrombosis; therefore you don't sleep, so your resistance to those living bacteria is reduced through tiredness. Then you arrive in New York, you have to sing at Carnegie Hall and you have a bit of a cold. A tickle in the throat, like a grain or two of sand.

She swallowed a ton of Vitamin C, sucked lozenges, swallowed the only painkillers her New York friend Dora had to hand, and sang. Onstage, with the white and crimson auditorium filling her gaze, she sensed something was off kilter. In her middle register, on three or four adjacent notes, the sound wouldn't focus. That had never happened to her before. Fear doused her, the sweat erupting on her upper lip and the back of her neck. She dared not sing full out. Through her mind hurtled the worst images it could invent: bad reviews, lost voice, cancelled engagements, blank future. Note by note, she continued, praying that her technique could get her through to the end.

One critic later wrote that she wasn't at her best, but the audience didn't mind; the standing ovation went on for ten minutes. Two thousand, seven hundred and ninety-nine people couldn't be wrong. Perhaps it wasn't so bad after all. She decided to give it two weeks.

The voice wasn't itself after that, nor after two more weeks. She still felt that scratchy sensation in the larynx, compelling her to clear her throat again and again. Her voice began to sound hoarse. She took herself to a hassled-looking GP, who shone a light down her throat, then explained that there were lots of viruses around at this time of year. 'I know you're a musician,' he remarked, 'but do try not to worry so much. We have a cognitive therapist available in the practice twice a week if that might help.'

Terri tried not to panic. She'd thought she was the most honest, forthright, clear-headed opera singer on the circuit. That meant not fussing, not cancelling, not throwing fits that could have her dubbed a classic prima donna. By the time she understood she'd been in denial, and that her GP had been plain wrong, it was a little late.

She decided to find a way to sing around the problem; Anita could and would help her. She had a run of *Ariadne auf Naxos* at the Deutsche Oper, Berlin, but marked the part through the rehearsals, not singing out, and putting the high line *tessitura* down an octave. Then she was struck with the idea that everyone was bound to notice what she was doing and would twig that something was wrong. The moment any opera house knew that her voice was in trouble, they'd drop her and her work would dry up.

At night her heart thumped, her body overheated and sweated until she felt parched while her mind whirled into vortex after vortex; then she began to fear that the palpitations were hot flushes, the start of the menopause racking her voice with its muddle of clapped-out hormones. Sleep? Impossible. Exhaustion threw itself into the cauldron that her body had become, two slender white vocal cords boiling red at its centre.

Nobody back in the Gorbals would ever have let a sore throat stop them doing anything, she told Teo on the phone. That, he contended, was hardly the point. 'For heaven's sake, *rest*.'

She should have. She didn't. Some stupid, irrational, stubborn twit inside her head kept telling her that if she didn't admit the problem and see a specialist, perhaps it would just go away. What caused it? A screaming match, years ago, with Bernard? A long fight on the phone with Teo? Singing too hard on the wrong kind of painkiller, a type which she'd just learned expands the blood vessels and makes the cords more vulnerable? Singing Isolde — repertoire that was too heavy for her? Or just the black hole of anxiety that was swallowing her up? She might never know. She only knew that she hadn't believed it could happen to her.

★　★　★

'Terri Ivory, you're a chump,' she tells herself. 'It's your own fault, so take responsibility and be positive. Now, one must heal, each day a little more.'

She isn't allowed to talk for ten days. She'll have to see a voice therapist and exercise the larynx with supreme care. She isn't allowed to sing for a month. After that, she must start slowly, only a few minutes a day, building up from a hum. Every case, says her specialist, is different; she must pace herself and do what's right for her, not what may be right for someone else, if she happened to compare notes with friends. 'Don't worry,' said Terri, 'I'm not telling a living soul about this except my daughter, my partner and my agent.'

'It might help to talk to someone who's been through it and come out the other side,' the doctor suggested. 'It can be a comfort. These problems are much more common than you might expect.'

Terri forced a smile. 'I'll bear that in mind,' she lied.

Martin — no longer a minion but her manager, nicknamed Dry Martini throughout the music business — hadn't reacted with the sympathy she'd wanted when she called him to say she was going into hospital. 'Do you mean you have to cancel Munich?' he protested.

'On the opening night of Munich,' said Terri, 'I shall be at home, in bed.'

'It's very short notice.'

'Martini, darling. If you want me to sing Wagner when my throat's buggered, I'd possibly

54

be forgiven if the audience thought it was in a zoo, not an opera house. I have a problem. I'm sick.'

'But what shall I say?' She could hear the anxiety in his tone, suppressed for her benefit.

'Tell them that I've hurt my back. I've got a slipped disc.' It was partly true: the disc that had slipped was her next planned recording.

Why can't she fast-forward through this? Press a button and whizz to a few months hence? She'd tried to save, as her mother would have, for the proverbial rainy day, and she's made some canny investments over the years. But the temptation of designer concert gear (especially when facing competition from Varya Petrovna, who does a spot of modelling in her spare time), or a hotel or apartment that was slightly more comfortable for a little more money during a two-month opera run abroad, had — at the time — seemed like a good way to spend a healthy fee. Now her investments are mainly tied up in long-term stocks and bonds, and she's left contemplating one limited savings account for 'emergencies' and a cupboard full of expensive dresses that are out of fashion or don't fit.

Each dress has a tale to tell — some because she'd only worn them once. Most of them are white or cream-coloured; it had been Martini's idea to 'brand' her with an image that matched her name, so she wore ivory suits and dresses for every public engagement or photo shoot. It worked a treat. But she drew the line at ivory jewellery: no elephant would die because she happened to share a name with its tusks. She'd stick to rhinestones.

She runs a fingertip across a satin gown that she'd worn to sing a charity recital at Glyndebourne. A fond memory: just after she'd finished the performance, a thunderstorm knocked out the place's power supply while Bernard and Jane happened to be in the lift. Then there's the Chinese silk jacket in which, backstage at the Met, she'd walked innocently enough into an unoccupied dressing-room to use the loo, only to find her lead tenor in the shower-room in semi-upright flagrante with Varya Petrovna, who was holding on to the taps. Ever since, Terri has wondered what Varya's bathroom is like.

And she still has the St Laurent suit that Teo had helped her to shed the night she met him. It looks desperately dated and pongs of mothballs, but she can't bear to throw it out. She could auction the finest dresses on eBay for charity — or for a personal SOS fund (Save Our Soprano) — but they're all she has, along with a few posters, programmes and the odd CD, to prove that her 'glittering career' was ever real. What if this is *it*? What if she never sings onstage again?

Singing is evanescent. You sing — you have sung — and it's gone. No recording, broadcast or film can bring back the living energy of the song once it's over.

Terri hides her face in the pillow. She's had rough moments — the deaths of her brother and mother, the divorce, and certain other things that happened years ago in Scotland. But she can't remember ever feeling as bad as this before. With the polyp, the surgeon seems to have cut away part of her mind: the section that controls confidence and hope.

★ ★ ★

She used to be Terri the troublemaker, Terri the wild child who loved to go tearing along by the Clyde with her gang, feeling the wind hooting in her ears, loving the adrenalin, the thumping heartbeat, lifting sweets from tubs in Woolworth's and spiriting them out when nobody was looking, and getting away with it. They hung around on street corners, yelling at passers-by. At school, they set booby traps for the teachers — tricks involving mice, buckets, water and well-placed string — mild tricks by modern standards, but she ended up suspended once or twice. Her father left her mother high and dry when she was two — she can't remember his face. She has a faint recollection of a smell that she hadn't known was smoke and beer — sometimes when she walks into a pub, the air brings her an uncanny flashback to infanthood. Or it used to, before the smoking ban.

Her mother, Finn, never talked about him. She was eternally stressed out by her two difficult children, though she proudly refused to admit it. The stoical Finn had grown up in post-war austerity Scotland and still believed with touching faith in mend-and-make-do. Terri the teenager answered back, shovelled on make-up, slashed away her skirts — she'd never

57

let Julie walk around dressed like that — and respected nothing and nobody, except possibly her big brother Robbie, until Mary Hoolihan noticed she could sing.

When Finn died and Terri steeled herself to clear her room, she discovered a photograph concealed amid a pile of ancient legal documents in a shoebox: a black-and-white print much bent and faded. It was their wedding photo. Finn and Georgie outside the town hall, with a posy and a buttonhole. The grieving Terri stared at her mother — a vivid, dark young girl, barely nineteen and full of life — and at the father she couldn't remember. That moonless night she wept for hours. At dawn, she hauled herself out of bed, flushed her heap of tissues down the loo, then put the photograph back into its shoebox and the box into the depths of a disused cupboard. She hasn't seen it since. It can wait there for Julie to find it, after another fifty years.

★ ★ ★

A slam of the front door: Julie is home, with Alistair. 'Mum?' she shouts. Terri can't call back, so she whistles. That was one useful thing she'd learned in Glasgow. A second later the youngsters are in the doorway, where Julie hovers, gazing at her mother with a concern that Terri finds both touching and uncomfortable.

Alistair is too hefty to hover. He's been body-building at the sports centre, aiming for a six-pack. The mumbling schoolboy little Julie had brought home for tea, piping 'This is my boyfriend,' had transformed almost overnight from boy to bloke. At sixteen, he'd had a growth spurt; Terri thought his legs doubled in length, his shoulders trebled in width, and his alert eyes began to look at everything, not only Julie, in a new and noticing way. She suspected he was bored at school because he was too bright for it; she knows that look, because she'd felt exactly the same. Terri's friends sometimes think Alistair is unsuitable for her precious Julie, but she suspects he's more like her, Terri, than her own daughter is — closer to the forthright girl from the Gorbals who still stews away under the civilised mask she's put on for the sake of her career.

She reckons, too, that Alistair has a talent which nobody's bothered to encourage. His hands are extraordinary, with palms as thick as lamb chops giving way to remarkably long, straight fingers. The art teacher at school used to exhort him to stay behind and use the facilities to experiment with clay, papier mâché and stone carving. Sometimes he did. He refused to stay on to take art A level, though — he insisted he'd be killed for it the minute he left the gates.

So it was Terri who gave him the art materials for his birthday; later his mother arrived on the doorstep in Livingston Road and hugged her. Usually Sue Ross declined her invitations, feeling intimidated by Terri's fame. Alistair keeps the clay, pencils, pens and paper under his bed; Terri hopes he still uses them sometimes.

'You all right, Terri?' he asks politely.

Terri holds up a thumb and beams at him. She

always smiles when she sees Alistair. He has that glow of youth that lads develop around that age, just for a few years. By twenty-five, it will have gone. It must be hormonal; she can't help responding to it.

'She's not allowed to talk,' Julie explains.

'You look great.' Alistair's gaze is approving, given Terri's state of dishevelment; hair messy, no make-up or nail varnish and her cream silk dressing gown wrapped hastily over a matching nightie. At least they're designer jobs from Milan. She, like most of her fellow divas, wouldn't want to be seen dead in anything less.

Julie, though, seems to be suppressing a scowl. What does she expect the day her mum comes home from hospital? A photoshoot for *Hello* magazine?

'Anything we can do?' Alistair asks.

Terri holds up her empty mug. He flashes a grin and thunders down the stairs to the kitchen. Julie wanders up and hugs her. Bluish shadows lurk on either side of her nose. Worried? Terri takes a piece of paper out of the printer and writes 'OK?'

'Not really.'

'What's up?'

Julie sits down on the side of the bed. 'He's joining the army.'

Terri writes capitals. 'WHAT?! WHY???'

'He doesn't think he's good at anything non-physical, because of the dyslexia. I'm like, 'that's total crap, some massive proportion of the millionaires in Britain are dyslexic', but he won't listen. He's been planning it for ages, but he

60

never said so because he didn't want me to worry. They had someone from the recruitment department come to an open day at school before he left and Al talked to him for ages and took the stuff home. His uncle John's all for it, he used to be in the Territorial Army and apparently he's like, 'discipline and teamwork and training will do you good, and you'll be living away so you won't be a burden on Sue'. And Al's like, 'it's a real meritocracy so I could have a good career there.' John likes the Queen and Country thing too.'

'CRAP,' writes Terri. 'Queen not in charge of where British army goes. Is our government kow-towing to mad American neo-cons.'

'That's what I told him, I said, 'are you *crazy*?' But he's all, do I think my country is shit, then, and would I refuse to serve and defend it? He really thinks he'd be doing something worthwhile. And he's like, 'well, I could see something of the world.''

Terri chews the end of her pencil. Where exactly would 'the world' mean?

'He says he mightn't be sent to any of the wars,' Julie continues. 'They have soldiers in, like, eighty different countries, doing different stuff. Humanitarian aid work, rescue missions in floods, peacekeeping.'

Or killing innocent civilians, thinks Terri. Or falling in the line of 'friendly fire'. If only she could talk so that she could put him straight.

'Sounds like you're in favour,' she scribbles.

'I dunno . . . It might give him some kind of direction? I'm trying to be positive, because he's

61

going to do it anyway. He's starting infantry training at Catterick, like, the week after next.'

'YOU ARE JOKING.'

Alistair appears in the doorway with a tray of mugs. Julie glances at him; she doesn't need to speak for Terri to know she's scared witless.

Terri quickly scrunches up her scribbled paper and uses a fresh sheet. 'Thanks. Need to sleep now,' she writes.

★ ★ ★

Alistair wanders into the garden and begins to tidy up, pulling out some bindweed that's invading the clematis on the fence, then worrying at a dandelion, its taproot plunging deep beneath a rose bush. The one thing he'd always longed for was a garden — nothing could be further from Scargill Tower, so he used to go and help his uncle in Sidcup with his whenever he could. Julie follows him, hovering again, trying to imagine him in uniform, carrying a gun. Yet here he seems so calm, so at peace. Why couldn't he just become a gardener instead?

'Your mum's dead sexy when she's not trying too hard,' he remarks, tugging at the weed's base. The leaves come away in his hand; the root doesn't budge.

'You should tell her. It'd do her good. Look, I've got to go to my singing lesson. Will you hang on for me to get back? Mum'd like it if there's someone in the house.'

'Yeah, no problem. I'll get rid of the rest of that bindweed for you, maybe cut back some of this mess. Doesn't look like your mum'll be up to gardening for a bit.'

Julie wanders towards the swimming pool; its shield of plastic sheeting has accumulated a sprinkling of stray twigs and petals. 'Al,' she remarks, 'do you think it's possible to know too much about your own mother?'

He thinks for a moment, then says, 'Do you know anything about your mum at all?'

★   ★   ★

Julie stands poised by the piano in Anita's front room. She fills her lungs with air, deep in her abdomen. Anita strikes a chord; Julie pitches her voice and sings an arpeggio, up and down. The harmony sidesteps upward; she takes another breath, sings again. The high frequencies buzz through her head from one ear to the other.

'Good,' says Anita. 'Make sure you keep back enough air to get you through to the end. Try and crescendo to the top — phrase it like an arch in a cathedral.' For Anita, there's no such thing as an exercise: everything is music. She's an old friend of Terri's, half Spanish, who long ago gave up performing to teach. The front room of her flat, in a terraced house in Islington, is chock-a-block with pictures, posters and volumes of music. Outside, handily, is a bus stop. The traffic doesn't seem to bother her; she says there's music in its sound, too. In summer she opens all the windows; as Julie sings, she notices people peering in from the bus queue at the genial chaos and the baby grand piano

63

— curious, even astonished. She never understands why the sound of singing, which is so natural, should be surprising.

Julie had found it easier at first to sing in a middle-range mezzo-soprano voice, but when Anita took her on two years ago a period of experimentation, stretching and exploring revealed that her true voice came out a little higher. Now she's becoming a lyric soprano, though her timbre is much lighter than her mother's 'lyric-dramatic' *fach*, due to her age. She's passed her Grade VIII singing exam with flying colours, singing arias by Bach and Mozart; now she's learning more Bach and a Schumann song called 'Der Nussbaum', which describes a young girl listening to the whispers of the tree outside her room, telling her she will soon be married.

'Are you sure you don't want to apply for a choral scholarship?' Anita asks her. 'It's not too late — you can easily sing that Bach back in as an audition piece.'

'I think I've got enough to worry about already, with the exams,' Julie admits.

'You do look worried.' Anita's heavy-lidded brown eyes give her a shrewd look. Julie flushes; her teacher knows her extremely well. 'Is it your mum's operation?'

'Yes and no. Can we start with the Bach?'

Anita plays her in. The aria is called 'Bist du bei mir'; the story goes that Bach gave it to his bride, Anna Magdalena, on their wedding day. 'Be thou with me and I go with joy towards death and my peace.' Its simple harmonies take an unexpected turn that always kicks at the pit of Julie's stomach.

All her childhood she had felt so safe when her mother was around. Idolising her. Running down the hill brandishing flowers to meet her when she came home after weeks away. Listening to her voice soaring through the house, a sound that could have come straight from heaven. And all that time Terri had been feeling her daughter was a 'millstone'? As she tries to sing, her throat tightens and her eyes begin to water.

Anita stops playing. 'All right, Julie. Take a moment to breathe.'

Be thou with me and I go gladly towards my death. Now she imagines Alistair in uniform, boarding a plane. Her voice is packing in. If you lose emotional control, the voice is the first thing that goes.

'It's OK, love.' Anita soothes her, passing her a box of tissues. 'Let's have a cup of tea and you can tell me what's going on.'

'There's nothing to tell,' Julie insists.

'I've got a new book of songs for you to look at. Why don't you come and have a browse while I make the tea?'

Julie blows her nose, then obeys. Schubert. She opens the first song: 'Gretchen am Spinnrade'. Words by Goethe, from *Faust*. *'Meine Ruh' ist hin, mein Herz ist schwer, ich finde, ich finde sie nimmer, und nimmermehr.'* My peace has gone, my heart is heavy, I shall find it nevermore.

'Anita,' says Julie, 'I'm sorry, but would you mind if I went home? I don't feel great.'

Julie doesn't go home. Instead she takes a bus to the South Bank and wanders along the river, past the London Eye, the Royal Festival Hall and the National Theatre. The sun has come out and with it half of London; the parades of restaurants swarm with families at wooden tables chomping their way through Chinese dim sum, French salads, Japanese noodles and mountains of chips. Tourists slurp cappuccino out of paper mugs with slotted lids; a bearded violinist with lanky limbs busks, dancing while he plays like a stringless marionette. Julie stops to browse the second-hand books stall under Waterloo Bridge. Old paper, faded covers: lost worlds for sale at a pound apiece. She doesn't take in the titles. A fog seems to be drifting between her and them.

This is stupid. She must be like her mother, think positive, keep strong. On one hand she's trapped by her imagined picture of Alistair going to Catterick; on the other, by the words scrawled across the old diary in her mother's hand. Why should a handful of sentences scribbled out so long ago throw her so far off balance?

She moves on, remembering cherished images. Terri at the Vienna Opera — was it *Madama Butterfly?* Backstage in the dressing room, drinking herbal tea (Terri never drinks anything milky — she says it causes phlegm), greeting her agent and the opera house manager and Teo, who'd come from Paris; Terri could talk to everyone at the same time and make each feel he was the most important person in the world.

When she saw Julie, her face lit up like the sunrise. Julie jumped into her arms, smelled the stage make-up and felt the sweat that clogged her mother's silk kimono costume as she asked, 'Did you enjoy it, darling?'

'You were wonderful, Mummy.' Julie was shy in front of all the important men.

'That,' said Terri to the assembled acolytes, 'is all that matters. That my daughter should be proud of me.'

What an example: a mother who's radiant and fulfilled, loves her work and shows her the marvels that human beings can achieve if only they put their minds to it. A few stupid words, written more than half Julie's life ago, shouldn't make any difference, should they?

Julie leans on the railing, staring down at the water. A few seagulls ride the current, their yellow eyes fierce, their squawks hectoring her. She ought to go home; she has to revise for the exams. Yet her focus has shattered like a windscreen.

Perhaps the weekend would be a good time to go away. As Terri has insisted that she doesn't mind being left alone, and feels grumpy as well as being medically incommunicado, maybe she should visit her father. It's a long time since she last went to Yorkshire; perhaps she ought to give Bernard — and Jane, and Ellen — another chance. They're family too, the only family she has.

Julie takes out her mobile phone and dials her father's number.

Bernard, Jane and Ellen live in a caricature of a cottage near a village in the Dales, close to the dual carriageway on which Bernard drives to work. The cottage is dark stone, but painted white, its door centre front, between squat windows. In winter, woodsmoke pirouettes from the chimney. It's a house that a child, maybe Ellen herself, would draw, complete with a climbing rose curling round the porch. The garden sits, well primped, inside a dry stone wall; the cars live round the back, out of sight, to give visitors the impression that they're arriving in an idyllic English past, even if it's one that probably never existed. Jane cycles to her practice wearing a long skirt and a Barbour jacket. Ellen attends the village primary school, in which the children are taught to share and help each other and win gold stars for citizenship. It couldn't be more different from south-east London.

Julie waits an hour at York station for a connection, using the time for her revision. After the little train has meandered through a succession of fields and back gardens, she disembarks into a lukewarm evening under the chestnut blossom to find her father waiting for her in his car, listening to the cricket on the radio.

'Dad.' She gives him a kiss.

He pecks her cheek in return. 'What a nice surprise. It's been quite a while.' Bernard only comes to London if he has something to do there besides seeing Julie.

'I kind of had to get away,' she says, feeling awkward. 'Too much work, and Mum's in a filthy mood because of her throat. I was worried about leaving her on her own, but she said it was better because she knows she's being ratty and she can't talk in any case.'

'Your mother's ratty moods were never much fun.' Bernard accelerates along the road that runs between expanses of deep green grass towards the next village. 'Hope you don't mind, but dinner's going to be late because Jane's at the Women's Institute charity tea.' Jane never misses village events; she says she's expected to be there as an important member of the community.

'Whatever.' Julie watches the light and shade on the shiny hills and wonders how two hundred miles can feel like two thousand light years.

* * *

In the cottage, Julie dumps her backpack in the room that's officially hers, though she spends only a few days in it per year. She switches on the two-bar heater; the old stone house is never entirely warm, but Jane disapproves of central heating in May. The windows admit a copious draught, but the old diamond panes are so pretty that the Masons won't even think about replacing them; besides, the place is Grade II Listed. Julie texts Alistair to tell him she's arrived, then pads downstairs to try to chat to her father.

Drinking tea, Julie and Bernard sit together in

opposite armchairs, just like a real family. Julie describes her exam preparations, Alistair's impending army training and Terri's operation — though the latter not too much.

'The army?' reflects Bernard. 'He's a brave lad.'

'But what if he gets sent to Iraq or something?'

'I'm sure he'll have some say over where he's deployed,' Bernard opines. He has plenty of views about politics and the current conflicts, but Julie has no idea why he should know anything about army practices, even if Catterick is in the same county. 'Don't worry too much, Julie,' he goes on. 'You've got to think of your future. I reckon you'll sail into Cambridge. You know, you have to be ready for the possibility that life may take you and Alistair in different directions.'

Outside, the dog barks: Bradman the Labrador lives in a kennel beside the garage. Jane won't let him into the house: apparently it's not hygienic. Julie wants to run out and give him a cuddle.

'Alistair mustn't hold you back,' Bernard says.

'Back from what?'

'That's just what I mean. He's not had an easy life and I have the impression that he can be quite negative. I don't want you to pick up that attitude from him.'

Bernard's dark hair is inching back from a pink saucer of scalp. He has pin-thin lips and rather protuberant ears. His gaze is astute; Julie suspects that his favourite part of life takes place inside his own brain. She remembers him darting through maths equations that she couldn't begin to understand with the concentration of a ferret on the hunt. He's wearing the same thin blue jersey he's worn for the past six years. The cosiest thing about him is his unworldliness.

'What do you want to do eventually?' he's asking. 'If you could do anything at all, what would it be?'

'I'd like to be an astronaut and go to the moon,' Julie declares.

'Come off it. What you do with your life is a big decision.'

'Well, you did ask.'

There's a rush of cool evening as Jane strides in with Ellen in her wake. As soon as Ellen sees Julie her small face lights up; Julie runs to hugs her. Ellen is nine — shy and childish, far removed from the streetwise and foul-mouthed pre-teens who populate the junior section of Julie's school. Julie half expects her little half-sister still to suck her thumb. Poor thing, it's not her fault that Jane is her mother.

Julie's eyes meet Jane's over Ellen's soft hair.

'No, Ellen,' Jane directs, 'don't go another step without taking off your shoes, please. I don't want mud on the carpet.'

'Yes, Mum.' Ellen shuffles away from Julie. There's something robotic in the flat tone of her reply.

'Hello, Juliette. Nice that you wanted to come and visit for a change. I've made a cake.' Jane crosses the room without removing her own muddy shoes and Julie kisses her cheek, as obedient as Ellen in her stepmother's strait-jacketing presence.

'Are you really Julie or Juliette?' Ellen asks her. 'Cos everyone calls you Julie except Mummy.'

'My real name is Juliette, after a character in an opera,' Julie confides. 'But I prefer being called Julie for short.' She winks, and Ellen gives her a conspiratorial wink back.

Dinner, when it's ready, is a strained affair. After dishing out the pork chops, Jane rarely takes her gaze off her daughter. 'No, Ellen, hold your fork properly. Like this.' Ellen lifts resigned blue eyes towards her and copies the movements.

'Julie's thinking of putting in for a choral scholarship, but it's rather late in the day,' says Bernard. 'I reckon the best thing is just to get yourself in, then you can always go to the college's director of music and tell him you can sing.'

'No, Ellen, don't chew with your mouth open. How many times do I have to tell you?' says Jane. Ellen lowers her head.

'I'm not sure about the singing,' Julie admits.

'No, I imagine your mother has views on that.' Jane says. 'You're not planning to go the same way as her, I hope?'

'If I could, I would. But I'm not good enough.'

'You've got a lovely voice,' Bernard defends her.

'I don't see what use that is to anybody,' Jane opines. 'Life's a privilege, not a right, you know. You should do something that benefits other

72

people. Not waste time warbling away on a stage, thinking it makes you the greatest person on the planet.'

Julie thinks of Teo in tears over her mother's singing; the ovation in Vienna; the uplift at the end of the operas, when the audience releases its thanks in what Terri calls 'catharsis'. You emerge feeling cleansed, healed and enriched. You feel lucky to be alive. That's why we sing, Terri would say. To make that deep a connection with the people who listen to you.

'If you want to help people, study medicine,' says Jane.

'I can't. I'm doing the wrong A levels and I'm too squeamish.'

Jane shrugs. 'I fainted the first time I watched an operation. Most people do. You get used to it.'

'It takes all sorts to make a world . . . ' Bernard tries to ease the hostility.

'I don't see why,' says Jane. 'Ellen, stop kicking the table, *now*.'

'I think if you're a doctor it helps if you're very thick-skinned and insensitive,' Julie declares. 'If you can treat people like machines. If you think everybody's the same and can be cured of anything with a stitch here and a pill there.'

'You'd be only too happy to be given stitches for a bad cut or antibiotics for a throat infection.' Jane munches pork, unperturbed.

'But there's stuff in people that can't be cured that way . . . '

'What, like your mother's fancy-man from the Balkans? No, trust her to get together with a self-obsessed nutcase with nothing better to do than sit in Paris on someone else's money writing about how awful his life's been.'

Julie can't swallow the dried-out chop, which used to be part of a pig. Why had she forgotten what it's like here? 'You don't even *know* Teo.'

Ellen stares across her plate, periwinkle eyes glassy, lip wobbling. Julie reaches out a hand to squeeze hers. Ellen leans forward, fingers outstretched. Jane slaps her daughter's wrist lightly but firmly. 'Sit properly, Ellen.'

'I was thinking,' Julie mutters, 'I don't want to leave Mum on her own too long while she's not well. It's not fair, though she did tell me I should come up. She was just lying in bed staring at the ceiling this morning. She didn't even want tea.'

'Well, *I* spent this morning seeing patients non-stop from eight thirty till one,' Jane declares. 'And nobody's at my beck and call to make *me* a nice cup of tea.'

'Don't go, Julie,' Ellen pipes quietly.

'No, she'll go if she needs to,' Jane cuts in.

'I'll see,' says Julie. 'I have to revise.'

'Maybe you girls would like to walk the dog after dinner?' Bernard suggests — and Julie and Ellen brighten at once, happy at the prospect of twenty minutes alone together.

'Please can we get down now, Mum?' Ellen asks.

'All right, off you go.' It's the kindest phrase Julie has heard Jane speak all evening.

Outside, beside the garage, Ellen bends to fasten the leash to the Labrador's collar. 'Come along, Bradman!' The dog turns to lick her face.

Julie beams. 'Lead on, McDuff, you know the way.'

Ellen is small for her age; it's Bradman who bounds ahead, as quick as his namesake cricketer, pulling the little girl behind him. Ellen slips her leash-free hand into Julie's.

'Tell me about school,' Julie prompts. She listens as Ellen rambles on about her friends, her teacher, sports lessons and the pony club.

'I've never ridden a horse,' Julie admits. 'We don't really have them in south London.'

'How awful.' Ellen clearly can't imagine such a life. 'I love riding Blackbird. He was really mean the first time, though — he could tell I was a beginner and that I'd let him stop and eat whenever he wanted to.'

'I wish you'd come and stay with me in London. We could do all kinds of things together. We'd go shopping in the West End and we'd see a musical, and we'd eat sushi and go to the zoo. How'd you like that?'

'Fun!' Ellen grins and skips. 'What's sushi?' She looks liberated. Out here, wandering through dappled shade in a grove of beech trees, with the breeze drifting off the hills, she's like a different girl. 'Shall we sing a song?'

'Let's. Which one?'

Ellen chooses 'Early one morning'; the music teacher at her school is fond of folk songs. Julie joins in the choruses. Ellen doesn't really understand the words but knows how to repeat them, and she sings in tune. Their voices rise together: '*Oh, don't deceive me, oh, never leave me. How could you use a poor maiden so?*'

75

Ellen's is a clear, schoolchild voice, Julie's stronger, solidly pitched and musical.

'I *love* the way you sing,' says Ellen.

'I love the way you sing too.' Julie hugs her. If visiting Yorkshire was all about taking Ellen and Bradman for walks, she'd come up every weekend.

The stroll is too short. Back in the cottage, Jane is holding forth to Bernard, who looks exhausted, about the medical practice's office politics. Julie's used to her mother's lilting voice and sackfuls of charm. She wonders how her father, after living with Terri, can stand being in constant company with those hard, flat vowels and the strained voice in which Jane delivers them. Ironic, she thinks, that he'd exchanged the first for the second. He'd divorced her mother, accusing her of being overbearing and bossy, only to choose a second wife who, in Julie's opinion, far exceeds her in both these qualities. It would have been less hypocritical on his part, she reflects, if he'd left Terri accusing her of infidelity.

'Come along, Ellen. Homework, *now*,' Jane barks.

Ellen's face crumples. 'Julie's here.'

'You can play a game with Julie when you've finished your maths.'

Ellen's eyes glaze over. 'I don't know how to do it. Don't want to, either.'

'Ellen! Snap out of it and get on.'

The little girl turns, drooping.

'Never mind, El,' Bernard soothes. 'Come upstairs and I'll give you a hand when Mum's looking the other way.'

Julie's stomach turns over and she feels tears just like Ellen's threatening in sympathy. She hurries up to her room in order to hide them, and to make a start on some Shakespeare revision. Then, after fifteen minutes, she glimpses through Ellen's bedroom door Bernard and his younger daughter at the desk, heads bent together over the books.

Sometimes she thinks each of them exists in a separate world, differently designed. Her mother's globe is gem-studded, gleaming with stage lights and pulsating with music. Bernard and his planet form a ball that's neat, green and little, packaged tightly in clingwrap for Jane's approval. Ellen is proprietress of a slightly squashed pink circle. Teo — God alone knows what Teo's world comprises: blood, pipe smoke and baguettes, perhaps. What about her own, when she can't see further ahead than a few months? She feels permanently in transit, travelling from one person's home to another, journeys that are mainly out of her control.

Except now, she decides, she will take control. She'll leave at once and go straight back to Falcon Park, and nobody is going to stop her. She throws the few clothes she'd hung up back into her rucksack, pulls on her shoes and sneaks out of the house while no one's looking.

The walk is lengthy, along a dark, winding country road, but Julie doesn't care. She drinks in the freedom of the friendly night and the stars brightening over the distant moors; she sings to herself as she goes. The last train has left when she arrives an hour later, but the village has a small taxi company which ferries her to York just in time for the final Intercity back to London. She thanks heaven that her mother always furnishes her with enough cash to take taxis in an emergency. By the time her father realises she's no longer in his house and calls her mobile in a panic, Julie is half-asleep in the last carriage, sailing south through Doncaster.

4

Pauline Viardot, as every commentator insists on remarking, wasn't beautiful, writes Terri, working on her film pitch. *She had heavy features, a recessive chin and a mouth that could have been better shaped. As a child, she was constantly in the shadow of her much older sister, the famed soprano Maria Malibran. Yet this put-upon little girl grew up to be a diva who inspired the greatest composers of her day. With such a family, there was never any question that Pauline, too, would sing. Maria had taken the world by storm. Their brother Manuel became a teacher who determined the course of operatic singing throughout the twentieth century. He was also an expert on voice health and invented the laryngoscope, a diagnostic tool for problems in the vocal cords that's still used today.*

Terri puts a hand to her throat. How strange that Pauline's brother's invention should have been the means by which her own disaster had been identified. She tries to plough on. She needs to find a quality in this forgotten singer that will make directors in the world of film and TV sit up: notably the possibility — the probability — that Viardot, her husband and Teo's beloved Turgenev had

79

ended up living in a *ménage à trois*.

The phone rings. Terri stops writing and stares at it. Two weeks have passed and she's allowed to talk — briefly. For the first time since the operation, she reaches for the receiver, anxiety swamping her.

'Teresa Ivory,' she whispers.

'Terri, *darling*. You can talk?'

'Martini, darling, I'll try, but not for long. How are you? What's the news?'

'I'm having some positive reactions to your recital suggestion,' Martin tells her, officious yet precious — he reminds Terri of a pedigree dog in a show. 'But though the fish are jumping, they haven't bitten yet. And yourself? Up and about again?'

'I'm working on the pitch for my Viardot film. Don't you know some TV people we can approach?'

'Darling, nobody's ever heard of Pauline Viardot.'

'That's the *whole point*. It's time they did.'

'I know, I know, but the climate is *so* difficult at the moment . . . getting anything onto the television . . . '

'Please, Martini, won't you just give it a try?' Terri cajoles. 'You will, I know you will. Please, just for me? And I'll take you to lunch at The Ivy. What do you say, darling?'

'I know better than to argue with you, Terri Ivory. All right, I'll try — but I can't guarantee the response. And as you know, it's not really my field. We should maybe find you a film or literary agent . . . '

'Good, I knew you would help. I must go, Teo's coming over from Paris and I have to do something about the landfill site inside my house.'

'Look after yourself, Terri. Don't *talk*.'

Terri hangs up and makes herself the latest in an endless series of throat-soothing herbal teas with honey.

A mad mix of emotions fills her first thing every day. First, she can't do her rapidly hummed-then-sung note that's her normal wake-up routine — she's done this to test her voice each morning for more than a quarter of a century. Life without it feels altogether unbalanced. Next, she tries the counting of blessings. She's home, actually *home*. She can live like a normal woman, do the grocery shopping, read the newspaper, cook dinner, gently fend off — once she can talk properly — the bewildered blustering of her ex-husband who splutters down the phone about how Julie could have been so ill-mannered as to walk out in the middle of the night without a by-your-leave. She can see her friends and be a Lady Who Lunches. She can slob about in a T-shirt and no make-up. She can comfort her daughter, who's crying her heart out over Alistair's imminent departure for Catterick.

Then Terri starts wondering whether she's going to live like this for the rest of her life, if her voice decides not to return.

'For you, I think it'll be around nine months for a total, back-to-normal recovery,' said the laryngologist.

'Last time my body took nine months over anything, I had a baby to show for it at the end,' Terri quipped, trying to hide her panic.

Think positive: Teo, Julie, film. But beyond that, blankness. It's absolute terror. She's used to stage fright, but this is something new: *lack-of-stage* fright. How would she live? She could coach young singers, embark on high-profile masterclasses. She could try directing opera — that might be fun: she could set *Der Rosenkavalier* on a cruise ship, or *The Magic Flute* in an Indian ashram. And of course there's Viardot. But she's accustomed to the urgency of the next engagement, the imperatives of preparing, planning, rehearsing and performing, the unstoppable flow of adrenalin. This home-bound silence, broken only by cars changing gear as they drive up the hill, the chiming clock in the drawing room, or the soft twinkling of rain on the roof could be blissful, as long as it lasted for no more than two weeks. How can she survive without the stage? Maybe she's addicted to adrenalin. Without it she'd exist only in half measures. Terri has never been a woman to do anything by halves.

Sometimes — as now — she craves the presence of an understanding and supportive partner who, just occasionally, might bring her a cup of tea when she feels low.

★ ★ ★

The school doors fly open, letting in the summer air. Julie and her friends Patti and Lara take one look and break into a run. The exams are finished, and they're no longer schoolgirls. They hug each other, squealing with joy. It's the end of an era.

Julie thinks she's flunked the last French essay, but she doesn't care. She tries not to think about her father's expectations; now it's time to celebrate. A quick flurry of texts among their friends determines that they'll all go for a drink later, then head for a club in East Dulwich.

She trots the short distance from school to the supermarket where Alistair works. It's his last day before leaving for Catterick; he's free for the afternoon and had made sure to celebrate his departure with his workmates the night before. The aisles feel too noisy and busy, as well as bizarrely normal compared to the steamroller intensity of the exam. She picks her way between trolleys and pushchairs, hunting for Alistair in his shop uniform; soon she spots him by the fruit juice, loading orange and white cartons into tidy rows in the chiller cabinet.

'Al!'

He turns. A second later she's in the air, feet dangling. 'Go all right?' he grins, holding her aloft.

'I don't know!' she shrieks. 'I think so. But it's finished!'

'I've got something for you in the back.'

She follows him, the words of her last essay still jumping in front of her eyes; in the staffroom, he dives under a table and retrieves a bunch of bright tiger lilies.

'Oh, they're wonderful!'

'Let's get out of here.' He packs away his overall for the last time.

'Have you said goodbye to everyone?' Julie prompts; he seems remarkably unbothered about leaving.

'Only five hundred times,' he grins. 'Today's your day, love.'

'*Our* day.' She grasps his hand and out in the fresh air they walk homewards together.

At the bottom of Livingston Road, he stops. 'Race you up the hill.'

'That's not fair!' Alistair has been doing the army's fitness training programme — now she knows what the six-pack workouts are really about. He tears off ahead, noticeably stronger than he'd been a few months ago.

'We've got to get you fit too,' he teases as she pants along behind, carrying her lilies. He jogs on the spot outside the house, waiting for her while she gasps for breath.

'They make you run uphill?'

'I've got to get what they call 'army fit'.' Their friends have been looking at him with more respect recently; and since he's been saying the words 'Infantry', 'Catterick' and 'Royal Kent Regiment', even the local thugs have been giving him a wide berth. 'You ain't seen nothing yet,' he teases her.

They fall into the house, laughing and sweaty. Julie spots a suitcase in the hall — a battered old Bosnian one, plastered with ancient labels, that she knows well: Teo has arrived, at long last. Her mother's lover may teach at the Sorbonne, but he still hasn't got himself a decent bag.

'How was it?' comes Terri's voice, or what's left of it — quiet, husky and measured. Julie skips into the kitchen. '*Brava bravissima, Giulietta mia!*' Terri beams.

'She's a star,' Alistair grunts. 'She'll have done brilliant. Good evening, Mr Popović.'

'Ah, Mr Ross, how do you do? How very nice to see you again.' Teo, opposite Terri, is nursing a cup of black coffee; he adopts as fine an aristocratic English accent as possible, pumping Alistair's hand exaggeratedly. 'What a nice young man,' he says approvingly to Julie, pumping her hand too.

'But a very sweaty one.' She hugs him instead. 'We ran up the hill. Alistair's starting army training, so he's trying to . . .'

It's the slightest flinch, but a flinch nonetheless. Only Julie or Terri would have noticed it: a flicker of Teo's lashes, a momentary deepening of the hard-etched lines in his forehead. The army is not Teo's favourite organisation. Terri jumps up and creates a distraction, ceremoniously unveiling a cake she's made to celebrate the end of the exams.

Teo pulls out the other two chairs at the round table and fusses over the youngsters, giving them both napkins and forks. He takes Julie's orange lilies and arranges them in a blue vase. Only then does he ask Alistair: 'Why do you want to do this?'

'It's a chance for a career, Mr Popović. I think I might be good at it. I was never much good at anything at school, and my job's dead boring.'

'Please, call me Teo or I shall have to keep

calling you Mr Ross. Now, listen. Do you *know* what you are letting yourself in for?' His eyes are more serious than he usually allows them to be.

'The chances of being sent into action are quite small,' Alistair mumbles, looking a little intimidated despite his height. 'There's so much else — peacekeeping, development projects . . . '

'An army exists for one reason, and that is to wage war,' says Teo. 'War does lots of little things to one big end: bringing a country to its knees, subduing it by force to another's will. This usually means a great many people killing each other, and most of them will be innocent individuals who want nothing more than to live in peace. Are you willing to be part of that?'

'If it's better to do it than to have Hitler run England, then yes.'

'Hitler's been dead for more than sixty years.' Teo inhales from his pipe and blows the smoke out through the window. 'You don't need to worry about him. Look at the insurgents in Iraq, or the Taliban in Afghanistan. You'll have to decide whether it's worth risking your life over them; and whether you can live with yourself afterwards, knowing that you killed people, as you'll have to if they're not going to get you first. I hope someone told you this?'

'I know you know more about war than anybody else I've met, sir,' Alistair defers. 'But I don't want to do anything bad. I want to be helping people rather than killing them, and I'll want to make sure I come back, for Julie.'

'*What* a nice young man. Listen, Alistair. You'll have to follow orders, no matter what they are. And you must be aware: the chaps at the top sometimes get it wrong. Sometimes they get it incredibly wrong. I don't just mean Iraq and 'weapons of mass destruction'. Have you heard of Srebrenica?'

'Yes, sir,' Alistair mumbles. He'd been seven years old at the time. Julie reaches for his hand.

Teo leans forward. 'Is there anything I can say to persuade you to reconsider?'

'The truth is, I'm leaving tomorrow.'

Julie, fingers curled hard around Alistair's, watches his bright blue eyes and Teo's dark ones interlock their gazes. She thinks back to the first time they all sat together like this, just like a family. A family that isn't a family, and with Teo the survivor of one war while Alistair may soon face another.

'So, it's too late,' Teo says. 'Well, you'll learn a lot. Good luck to you.' He gives Alistair's back a pat. Julie notices Alistair stiffen; he's not used to a reassuring touch from another man.

'Julie, darling, why don't you cut your cake?' Terri encourages. 'And make a wish.'

Terri's cakes are Wagnerian cornucopias stuffed with fruit, chocolate and brandy, and this one is no exception; its aroma alone is a veritable banquet. Julie glances at her mother, Teo and Alistair. Her only wish is that this time next year, they will all be here, together and safe. She lifts the knife and plunges it in.

★ ★ ★

They wolf down as much cake as they can — Alistair augments his with toast and peanut butter; finally the youngsters bound away to the shower and emerge transformed, ready to go out. Alistair reappears first; in the hall, he turns to watch Julie cantering after him down the stairs; hulking, awkward and proud, he can't take his eyes off her, Terri notes. And she's beautiful, in a skimpy black top and loose, silky trousers; her arms are slender and muscular, her skin glows with the bloom of youth, exams or none. Alistair too has a gleam about him: his hair, close-cropped in army readiness, gives him a tidier appearance than usual and he's been taking the trouble to shave properly.

'My dear, you are flowering like a rose.' Teo embraces Julie. 'I am proud of my honorary step-daughter.'

Terri shifts in her chair. Teo has his place: and it's Paris, not Falcon Park. When she's with him, she gives as much as she can. When she isn't, her mind is full of other matters, tranquil in the knowledge that he's there, waiting for her a safe distance away. Family? No, thanks. She's had quite enough of that.

Besides, something in Teo's hunger for her love stops her feeding it to him in the quantities he desires. When they were first together, she'd thought he held back, that he couldn't give completely because so much of him was still missing in Bosnia. But now, a corner of her mind remains detached, observing him. To commit herself fully to such a damaged and needy man would be a risk too far. He has his place: lover and friend. Not husband.

'We're going down The Chocolate Drop,' Julie says. 'Back *late*, or we may stay at Al's. Don't wait up!'

★ ★ ★

When Julie and Alistair have vanished down the hill, Terri and Teo smile at each other, link hands and head for the bedroom, where Teo dumps his case in the corner.

'I've brought you a present,' he says.

'Ooh, show me? Can I open it now?'

'No. First, *love*.'

'No. First, present!' Terri's dimples deepen.

He strokes the dent in her right cheek with his middle finger. 'I missed you.'

'I missed you too. Give me a clue. Can I eat it?'

'You might, but I'm not sure it is advisable. It's a story. The draft of a story.'

'What? You wrote something for me?'

'I always write for you. You're my creative wellspring. All I need to do is dip my pen into that great pool . . . joking aside, my love, I can't work without you.'

'Shite!' Terri laughs, deep and tender. 'Your work is *yours*. It's nothing to do with me. You mustn't give away your power like that.'

'What would I want with power?' Teo says softly.

Terri draws the curtains; behind her, he runs an electric razor over his chin. She can feel his eyes following her. She turns, unbuttoning her blouse. 'What's the story called?'

'It's something I've wanted to write for a long time. At the moment the title is *Songs of Triumphant Love*.'

'It's your retake on the Turgenev?' He's mentioned, many times, his idea of rethinking a peculiar Turgenev short story, 'The Song of Triumphant Love', a romantic triangle set in Renaissance Italy that involves music, mysticism and the occult.

'It is. Now, hush.' He holds out his arms to her. 'Come here.'

A shaft of evening sun filters past the curtain, throwing a golden stripe across the bed. Teo, lying back, puts up a hand to shield his eyes. Terri kneels over him and moves her mouth on to his. He rolls her over and she melts, covering him with kisses, the roundness of his shoulders, the tendons in his neck growing rigid, the wide, slash-shaped cheek bones, the ripples of his ear, the burn scars close to the elbow on which he's propping himself up. She closes her legs round him and squeezes. She loves every inch of him and she adores sleeping with him — the sex, fantastic from the start, has only grown better. After so long together, it's difficult to imagine life without him.

What's the matter, then? Why can't she give him the final ten per cent of herself? She shoves the thought aside, for the moment.

Later, he lies with his head on her stomach and his feet dangling off the end of the bed, his heartbeat and breath calming. She feels his body damp with expended effort, and his ribcage shuddering with something extra; then the warmth of his tears on her midriff. He often cries after they make love. She never does. Terri can only remember crying once since the death of her mother — when she'd cried for nearly two months — and that was after she performed Isolde for the first time.

'I love you,' Teo mumbles into her navel. 'I love you so much that there's nothing left of me. Don't make me leave you again.'

'So don't.' Terri caresses his head — squarish, and large for his body. His dark hair is streaked with silver threads that grow dramatically in groups, as if for safety in numbers; it sweeps back from his forehead, like that of a nineteenth-century Parisian artist. The contrast of colours has intensified since she last saw him, only three months ago. 'You look like a badger,' she teases.

'I need you. I can't work without your image in my mind and the sound of your voice in my ears. I dread nothing more than losing you.'

'Darling, why ever should you lose me?' Terri doesn't want to lose him either; perhaps the difference is that she's confident she won't. In bed, he cries and she laughs. At least they balance one another out.

Teo's breathing slows towards sleep. She can't follow. Absorbed in the physicality of her love for him, she doesn't have to think. Now, though, the sensation comes back, repeating and repeating: what will she do if she's lost her voice?

Perhaps she's wrong to hold back from Teo.

Perhaps she needs him as much as he needs her, only she's too pig-headed to admit it? Why does she attract needy men? Bloody Bernard, prize wimp, had supposedly been a step in the aspirational direction of the intellectual elite, to which she didn't belong; she'd been too young to know better. At least Teo creates from the gut, much as she does. The voice is the mirror of the soul, she'd told him; he'd been overwhelmed by the concept until she explained that singers have been saying so since the beginning of time. Terri yawns. She'll read his story, praise it and give him the boost he needs — a little later.

★ ★ ★

Terri wakes to find that the shaft of sun has turned silver. Moonlight. It's ten thirty and she's alone on the bed. Teo's bag is open and the light is on downstairs. Pulling on her dressing gown, she pads after him.

She finds him in the drawing room, kneeling by the fireplace, a tumbler of whisky on the coffee table.

'Why do you want to light a fire? It's warm tonight,' she remarks, rubbing sleep out of her eyes.

Then she realises what he's doing.

'Teo, no!'

'Why not?' He doesn't look up from the tongue of flame that's teasing the typescript.

'My story, the one you wrote for me! I haven't even seen it!' She makes a dive for the unburned pages, but he tugs them away and in two swift motions rips them in half and tosses them after the others.

'Jesu Maria,' says Terri.

'It's no good. It's not worthy of you.'

'But, for God's sake, it's not about whether it's 'worthy of me'. Bugger that! It's about *you*, what you want to say . . .'

'Why should anyone care what I say? I'm a hopeless old badger, not a Turgenev. Who am I to name a story after one of his?'

'But so what?' Terri stamps with frustration. 'I'm not Maria Callas, but that doesn't stop me bloody singing! How dare you burn my story?'

Teo pushes the poker into the grate; the last of the manuscript combusts in a fountain of sparks. 'Because,' he says, 'it is my choice to destroy my useless work.'

'You'll still have it on the computer,' Terri points out.

'No, I deleted it before I left Paris. You can't tell quality on screen. The print-out is the test. That's all there is.'

A pang of fury shoots down Terri's arm into the palm of her hand. She clenches it. She'd been about to surrender, to give herself to him completely. Her instincts had held her back for a good reason.

It's not as if she doesn't know this. Year upon year, she teeters on the brink. Love is unconditional, she tells herself, love is entire, why not give it? Yet then there's the destruction, always Teo's drive to self-immolate, and she retreats, reeling, from the precipice. Usually she re-erects her invisible wall and absents herself for her next role, with relief.

'I'll see you in bed.' She turns her back. As she trails upstairs, she's wondering how to go abroad again as soon as possible, how to busy herself, away in that welcome space where he can't reach her.

5

The Gorbals weren't quite the Gorbals any more by the time Terri was growing up in them; or so the theory went. There'd been spates of cleaning up, sporadic repairs, the sending in of social workers, the efforts of the Salvation Army not far from the shipyards where many of the men worked — including, at one time, Terri's father. When she was two or three years old, just after he left, a shoal of shiny new tower blocks went up to rehouse thousands of locals from the tenements, though not Finn Ivory, who'd held out against a proposed move tooth and nail because she was afraid of heights. In the end she hadn't had to worry; many of the old buildings were demolished, but not theirs.

Terri often waxes lyrical to interviewers about the marvel of the Gorbals' melting pot, where immigrants flocked in the hope of a better life that they sometimes found and sometimes didn't: Jews escaping war-torn Europe, Italians seeking a path out of poverty and Mussolini's fascism, the Irish — like her grandparents — who'd arrived fleeing hunger and deprivation. Still, she'd add, it wasn't exactly a Glyndebourne picnic.

She lived with her mother and brother in a tiny flat on the first floor, which Finn used to scrub every day. The back window overlooked the dustbins ('the middens,' Terri would recount) and a constant whiff of damp and decay drifted through the whole block. The council kept promising better upkeep, which never happened; it was more worth their while, it seemed, to pull the whole lot down, as they kept wanting to but never quite did. To this day, Terri finds the smell of rotting rubbish vaguely comforting; damp less so, since she blamed her mother's arthritis on it.

Five minutes away, though, sat a popular pub, where the Irish community tended to congregate; it shone gold lamplight and rich dark colours out into the grey grimness of winter. Terri and Robbie weren't supposed to go in there — they were too young — but music came out of the pub, same as it came out of school and church and the radio. It was alive and it was warm. And it seemed, as Terri watched the singing start, that it was as natural as breathing, as natural that song should follow beer as that day should arrive at the end of night.

She was only ten when the wake took place. She didn't even know who'd died — some relative of a neighbour? She'd thought you were meant to cry over a death. Instead, everyone went down the pub and Finn took her and Robbie because it was going to be a long night and they shouldn't be alone in the flat. She never knew why they were let in.

It began with a tap. Someone tapping out a pulse on the side of a glass. The rain was battering down and she was surprised that anyone could hear the tapping — she was used to hearing things that other people couldn't. And the next man along from the tapper, who happened to be the postman, began to sing. Only it wasn't singing the way they sang at school. With his voice, he was imitating a violin; no words, just fiddly twiddles in a song for all seasons, and the propulsive rhythms caught at Terri's stomach as she pushed forward through the jungle of damp coats and beery fumes to be closer to the sound. And while the postman sang and his neighbour tapped, and people began to clap in time and the clapping spread through the gathering, their upstairs neighbour Donald spotted Finn and grabbed her round the waist to dance.

It was the first time Terri ever heard her mother cry out with joy. 'I can't, I've got bad ankles,' she protested, but Donald said, 'Rubbish, lass, just dance!' And Finn smiled, she actually smiled, with hands on her hips and feet lifting, like an ancient memory resurrected full of life and hope. Terri and Robbie caught each other's eyes, open-mouthed. Then Terri felt her throat vibrating, almost of its own accord, as her voice box told her she wanted to join in, not with the dancing but with the singing, the mouth music.

★   ★   ★

Terri and Robbie used to walk to school together past the Clyde and its long flat bridges, clutching their bags of sandwiches, their school uniforms too small for them because they grew faster than Finn could afford to buy them new ones. Robbie, two years older than Terri, was supposed

97

to keep an eye on her, but after school he didn't fancy spending his time watching over little girls; he preferred to join up with a local gang that used to take on another local gang behind the warehouses. Nearly forty years on, Terri can't remember what pretext they found for fighting — the usual, she supposes, territory, race or drugs. For Robbie, any excuse would have done.

Being a 'troublemaker' was a cool option, or at least passed the time when she couldn't be bothered with homework. The only subject she liked at school was Home Economics; there was music, of course, class singing, which didn't count because she was good at it. She happened to have the loudest voice in school and she could sing in tune. Troublemaking time was the first thing to lose out when the teachers appointed her to sing solos in the school concert, join the school choir and then the church choir, enter competitions, keep on singing just because she could. What she didn't understand was why other people couldn't. She'd have been happier out in the open with the gang, messing around on the riverside.

'Jesu Maria!' Finn protested when Terri bunked off choir and she caught her and the girls stuffing gobstoppers into their pockets between the shelves in Woolworths. 'You can *do* something, hen. They *want* you in the choir. So get out of here, Teresa Ivory, and *go and bloody sing.*'

Terri didn't know that you could sing for a living, unless you were Lulu or the Beatles. They were good examples, especially Lulu who came from the East End of Glasgow and won the Eurovision Song Contest. When Terri and her brother were smaller, their next-door neighbour, a lumbering woman named Maisie who reminded Terri of a big placid cow, used to invite them in for a glass of milk and some biscuits once a week. Maisie was a dinner lady in a school, and while Terri and her friends poked fun at the very idea of such a job, privately Terri wondered whether that was where she'd end up. She found peeling potatoes oddly calming, and couldn't help a slight but definite sense of wonder when she saw batter that had gone into the oven as brownish gloop come out again transformed into cake.

Both she and Robbie had enough heart to feel slightly sorry for the dour-faced Finn who tried so hard to make them a home; they had an unspoken pact to act like the respectable kids she wanted whenever they were inside, which wasn't often. As long as they went to Mass, Finn would be content.

At fifteen, Robbie left school and found a job in the docks. Two years later, Terri, preparing to follow suit, ran into trouble.

As the man of the family, Robbie had made a unilateral decision to stop going to church; Finn accepted this, though didn't hide her disappointment. He had been calling spades spades since he was four years old and their father didn't come home one day, nor the next, nor ever again.

Terri hoped that when she left school she need no longer bother with the Sunday rigmarole either, though for the moment she still sang in the choir at her mother's insistence and sat occasionally transfixed despite herself by the rolling waves of Monsignor's weekly rants against the iniquities of modern life. She saw little of that at home; while the seventies swung into action around them, Terri noted with early-teen fury, her mother still seemed to be living in the Second World War. She waited for Finn to dance again to mouth music in the pub. And waited some more.

A week before Terri's fifteenth birthday, a new music teacher appeared at school. A few days later, she turned up to rehearse the church choir too. They'd thought the choir would fold when the choirmaster left, since the church had no personnel except their beleagured priest and a rumoured resident rat in the vestry. But Mary Hoolihan, Monsignor announced, would save the day. She was young, pretty, dark and Irish, from County Clare, with a lilting voice in which she sang hymns as if every word were sincere. She sat at the piano, her dark hair hanging long and free down her back, leading the singing with a well-timed upward flourish of an arm off the keyboard.

The first time she heard Mary sing, Terri felt a small but definite shock. It was like an electric spark leaping between positive and negative, a bolt of colour shooting across the aural space towards her. The sound, the energy in it, lifted her soul for reasons she couldn't begin to explain.

Terri started to attend church choir practice

with a little more eagerness. She wanted to try copying Mary. The vibrations of her own singing struck a point in her solar plexus where her ribs seemed to resonate in response. This current was so strong and pleasurable that she sang louder to enhance it. Mary Hoolihan stared straight at her; a smile lit up her face. Terri found herself smiling back. Why should this astonishing young woman come to their corner of the Gorbals in any case, let alone give up her Tuesday evenings to coach a lousy church choir? She couldn't be that wonderful, Terri reflected, because she obviously didn't have much common sense.

After the practice was over, Mary caught Terri's eye and beckoned. Terri was about to run off to join her friends and chew bubble gum by the river, but she found herself hesitating. Talking to Mary was too tempting — her eyes possessed not just sweetness but something uncannily like understanding. Anyway, Terri thought, after next week she'd be out of school, out of the choir and away from all these silly expectations that people had of her and her loud voice. She trotted forward.

'You know, Teresa, you sing very beautifully,' Mary said. 'Do you *like* singing?'

Terri turned red. 'I don't know. It's just something I can do.'

'Come over here, now.' Mary ushered her towards the church piano, a scratched and sticky-keyed upright slouching against the wall near the vestry; it bore scars from the candlesticks it had carried in the early years of the twentieth century. Mary struck a chord, then played a sequence of rising notes. 'Can you sing what you hear, Teresa?'

Terri listened and sang. Of course she could. What a silly question.

'Try this one.' Mary played another chord and another arpeggio, this time both upwards and downwards. Terri sang. What was the point of this?

'Now will you sing me a tune?' Mary said. 'What's your favourite hymn?'

Terri didn't much like any of them, but earlier they'd sung 'Sweet Sacrament Divine', so she chose that one. Mary accompanied her on the piano, her fingers working automatically, her eyes never budging from Terri's face. Terri sang the familiar melody and words without thinking, but part of her, watching this peculiar day unfolding, was a little surprised at the power of her own voice, alone with the piano in the empty church. The stone-enclosed space amplified the sound; there was a purity to it, a cutting definition that struck Terri as a thing of startling and extremely unexpected beauty. And as she sang, she understood that she could control this beauty; it came from within her own body. It belonged to her, and she could make it louder or softer, more extreme or less, more meaningful or less, according to her will. As long as she didn't run out of puff.

When the hymn was finished, Mary nodded, then said, 'Let's do 'Soul of my Saviour' next.' Terri didn't see why not, so she sang, obedient to the lovely girl at the piano and the sounds that shimmered like falling stars through the air. She was vaguely conscious of people who hadn't been there earlier, milling at the back of the church, listening. Instead of shrinking and faltering as another child might have, she drew herself up and sang louder. Outside, the rain was relentless, a mean westerly wind was grumbling and nobody would think it was meant to be summer. But Terri felt hot and buzzing, warmed from within by the music and by a sensation when she looked at Mary that was surely love itself.

After another two hymns, Terri was beginning to feel tired. She turned. Sitting in a nearby pew, framed by one of the church's supercilious arches, was a hunched figure in a raincoat, her hair wrapped in a damp scarf, a handkerchief pressed to her nose. Her shoulders were moving up and down ever so slightly.

Terri stared. 'Mammy?'

'Your mother?' Mary caught her eye and mouthed the words. Terri nodded, chin wobbling.

Mary, brisk and soft in her long brown skirt and sensible shoes, paced over to Finn and sat down next to her. Terri hung back as the two women talked; her mother's eyes, though red from crying, were wide, apparently amazed. She couldn't hear what they were saying, only the soft purling of their accents, her mother's a deep, jigging Glaswegian, Mary's an Irish twinkle, the syllables twirling like swallows skimming over a lake. She wondered what they were cooking up. Perhaps she really could sing. Perhaps someone would spirit her away to London and let her join

103

a pop group. She'd grow her hair long, wear false eyelashes and the shortest skirts on earth and all the boys would fight over her and her picture would be all over the —

'Terri, come here a moment, *a chroi?*' said Mary. Terri, heart pounding, went forward, wondering what *a chroi* meant.

'How'd you like to go back to school next year?' her mother asked.

That was not, emphatically not, what Terri had been hoping for. That was the trouble she was in.

★ ★ ★

It only takes one astute person to change another's life. Terri has always told Julie this. But at King's Cross Station, staring up at the departure boards for the train to Darlington, with Alistair carrying a rucksack almost as big as he is, Julie wonders why, in his case, that person had had to be an army recruitment officer.

During a long conversation at the open day at school, Alistair had told her, the chap not only encouraged him but flattered him. 'You're just the kind of lad we want,' he said. 'You're strong, determined, positive. And you keep yourself in good shape. You've got the attitude.'

Positive? Alistair? That has to be a good thing. Somehow he's made it through the selection procedure; he's been to the assessments, talked to soldiers, had a medical, and managed to convince everyone that he's what they want him to be: a fit, go-ahead youngster who can't wait to learn to use a rifle. If he'd expressed any doubts, his uncle John would have turned them round with talk of subsidised housing and reliable pay — the army, he says, can't go bust — plus prospects for career development that are a tad more exciting than those at the supermarket. John didn't seem to notice that that development would be conditional upon his nephew not being seriously injured or killed first.

Julie has read through all the information, numb with misery. Six months from now, Alistair will be a combat infantryman. Next time she sees him, he'll be in uniform. He'll probably be carrying a gun. His mind will be full of quick reaction, fast thinking, regimental loyalty, first aid, weapon handling, health and safety. She's also been trying to grasp, so far without success, the differences between a unit, a regiment, a battalion, a platoon and a company.

'Don't cry, Jul,' Alistair mutters. Other lads are heading for the same train for the same purpose, Julie realises; he's embarrassed that they might see him for the first time in company with a snivelling girlfriend. She hangs on to his neck, hiding her face on his chest.

'I'm going to miss you so much.'

'You won't have time to. You'll be going out with the girls and your mum'll take you on holiday.'

'But what will I do without you?'

'Go to uni. Like I said.'

'I flunked the exams, I know I did. I'm not like my dad, I'm not academic.'

'Don't be daft.' Alistair kisses the top of her head. 'I've got to go. We'll talk, yeah? Visit my mum sometimes, will you? She'll be lonely.'

'Al . . . ' Julie trots along the platform after him. He turns and his blue eyes sparkle down at her as they always do. What if he's sent to Iraq or Afghanistan? What if he's hurt? Killed? How could she bear it? She wants to say that she can't live without him, but that's no way to encourage him on his first day. 'Be careful,' she falters instead.

'Christ, Jul, stop fussing. I'll call you soon as I can.'

A number on the station clock flips forward. A guard blows a whistle; with a last wave, Alistair jumps into the nearest carriage. The doors close; she waves back and keeps waving while the train pulls away, heading north. When there's nothing to see but empty tracks, she sits on a metal bench and watches, numbly, a few disoriented pigeons fluttering above the signals towards the open air.

★　★　★

When the disconsolate Julie lets herself into the house around three o'clock, all the windows are open and a draught is whirling up the stairs from the garden door. There's no trace of tobacco smoke. Teo's linen jacket has vanished from the coat-stand. Terri is talking on the study phone in her filthiest mood, barking — as far as she can — at Martini about 'Taps', whom she declares shallow, money-grubbing and contemptible. There's a click as she hangs up. A moment later, she's taking out her fury on her shredder, the

106

whir of its blades chopping up the past into diamond-shaped confetti.

Julie follows the sound. 'Where's Teo?'

'Paris.'

Julie had stayed the night with Alistair in Scargill Tower. She hadn't thought to wonder what was happening at home. Teo wasn't supposed to leave for ages. He'd only just got there.

Life seems to be full of people jumping on trains sooner than they were meant to. Julie knows why she'd decided to escape Yorkshire and how furious she'd felt there; nothing less would have made her go. She can scarcely imagine what must have induced Teo to leave after just one day. 'Did you have a row?'

'No, we were in the garden making daisy chains,' Terri glowers. 'What did you expect? Wedding bells?'

'No, but . . . '

'Sorry, darling.' Terri slumps at her desk, her forehead on her fists. 'I don't mean to yell. I can't yell, anyway. Listen, angel, I was thinking. You can't make your plans until your results come and I can do fuck-all until I'm better. Why don't we plan a holiday? Wouldn't you like that?'

'Where'd we go?'

'Somewhere peaceful and healing. Somewhere interesting and beautiful. I was thinking of Baden-Baden.'

'Where's that?'

'Southern Germany. Not far from the Black Forest and the French border. It's a famous spa town, very beautiful and unspoiled. Pauline

Viardot and Turgenev lived there once.'

'Oh.' Julie tried not to sound crestfallen. She'd enjoyed a brief vision of beaches, barbecues and serious heat.

'There's a wonderful hotel where I always stay. It's like stepping back into the nineteenth century, but with twenty-first-century mod-cons. I know the manager very well — he can give us a good deal if we go in August. It's a little way off, but it would give us something to look forward to. And you have to try the baths.'

'Baths?' Julie's been to day spas with Terri before. You sit about in a dressing gown drinking herbal tea, swim in overheated pools and have an overpriced massage. Then you feel so tired that you can't do anything except go to sleep.

'*Roman* baths.' Terri explains. 'Like nothing you've experienced before. It takes about three hours and there are around twenty different . . . well, you'll see. It'd be a girlie pampering trip, just the two of us. Terri-and-Julie time.'

Julie looks at her mother's dimples and smiles, despite herself.

★ ★ ★

Teo makes Bosnian coffee in a *džezva* from Sarajevo: a brass jug patterned with garlands and faces, tapering inwards before broadening at the spout. A long handle gives it the look of an upright rodent with extended tail. He grinds the coffee as finely as possible, then mixes it with boiling water in the *džezva* and reboils the lot. Plenty of sugar, then let the grounds sink to the

108

bottom, and name according to time of day. First thing in the morning, it's *razgalica*, wake-up coffee.

Not that he needs to wake up. He's been sleepless for hours, watching the charcoal night and listening to Paris clanking by — voices bidding farewell, the putter of a motorscooter, a rumble of métro deep beneath the house — each noise a comfort that reminds him where he is and why. Nothing new there. Nor is the fight with Terri anything new; there've been enough over the years.

The coffee bittersweet on his tongue, he watches his computer screen brighten. He types the germ of an idea:

Two damaged people trying to help one another.

Then he scrubs the words. Stupid concept: it can only lead to tragedy. Teo doesn't write tragedy; there's too much of it already. He likes to give his fiction hope and humour, or at least a positive twist — though to him it always feels contrived, no matter how many people tell him how marvellous they find his optimism in the face of Bosnia's living hell.

Even the rebuilding of Mostar's bridge, the Stari Most, going up block by block at the end of his latest book — named, appropriately enough, *A Bridge at Mostar* — was contrived. To him, there is nothing heroic or hopeful about the real thing. However much trouble the reconstruction team took, and it was immense, the sixteenth-century stone bridge can never return.

His cousin Sonja and her Swedish husband Stefan, the last members of his family left alive in Sarajevo, have written to tell him about it. The new bridge that's replaced the ruin, they say, is the right shape — a pointed arch, high above the deep-cut valley — and is made of almost the right stuff; but one crucial component is missing. The river used to sing beneath it. The Stari Most, dreamed up by a Turkish architect named Mimar Hajrudin, used to resonate with the waters of the Neretva: overtones echoed around the stone as the powerful current flowed underneath. But the secret of that acoustic seems to have eluded everyone. The river can't sing against its bright new bridge, any more than Terri could with the polyp in her throat. It's the right shape, but it's only for show.

★ ★ ★

He should have seen the trouble ahead from the start, but he was too dazzled by Terri to recognise that the magic was magic, and not real. Under it hid a frightened little girl. A child who never stopped weeping inwardly for her mother and brother and who, having grown up without a father, had little predisposition towards closeness to any man. Sex, yes; intimacy, no. At least, that was his theory. The angel's wings were slippery and the feathers would slide out of his hands — and anybody else's — when they tried to take hold.

But she'd have done the same. She'd have burned that manuscript. If it had been a

110

recording, she wouldn't have approved its release. She's a perfectionist, like him. There, they're the same. Teo smiles at his own silly reflection in the dawn-lit window: that's why he and Terri are soul mates. Each, in the other's place, would have behaved in exactly the same way.

He spotted a sliver of that on her first visit to him in Paris. She was married, and she'd made excuses at home about a concert or a rehearsal, he didn't know what and he didn't care, as long as she turned up. For two months he'd sat alone in the flat feeling his sanity would tumble clean off the roof if he didn't see her soon. And one day, there she was on the doorstep, twinkling up at him with her dimples and saying, 'So did you miss me, then?' and suddenly he couldn't remember how it felt not to be with her. They'd raced up the stairs to the bedroom, giggling like schoolkids; and life seemed idiotically simple after all.

They closed the curtains, locked the doors, then fell into bed. Neither of them wanted to go out again into the space where they had to pull the clothing of their outer selves back on. He tickled her until she screamed, traced her flanks with the tip of a biro, drew smiley faces on her buttocks, threatened to leave a love bite on her breast so that the Hopeless Husband would know exactly what she'd been up to.

'You haven't a good word to say about him,' he pointed out on the third evening, while they were eating pasta and salad by candlelight in the kitchen. 'Why did you marry him?'

'Well,' Terri sighed. 'It seemed like a good idea at the time.' Bernard was everything Terri hadn't been. Privileged, academic, a brilliant intellect. 'He has a good brain,' she remarked. 'Shame about the heart.'

'Leave him. Move here, with me.'

Terri stirred the penne around in the sauce with her fork. She couldn't meet his eye, and it struck Teo that she was afraid. Of what? Making a mistake? Backing a loser and ending up alone? Was that how she saw him — a bad bet? If so, she was right. For his part, how could he think her a good bet? If a woman behaved this way with one man, she could do so with another. But Teo was infatuated; he wanted to convince himself that if he loved her enough, she'd stay with him, be faithful and be happy. The age-old mantra was as mythical as full-moon charms against warts, but the temptation was more than he could bear.

She raised her eyes at last and he saw the pain in them.

'Did you ever love Bernard?' he asked.

'I thought I did. At the time.'

'And now?'

She lifted his palm to her cheek, as she had done that first night after the opera. 'Warm, sweet hands,' she said. 'You see, love, real love, is frightening. I guess I didn't want to be frightened.'

'I'm in love with you, Terri. I want you here with me.'

'But still, it's frightening.'

Later, Teo held her while she slept, snoring

softly against his chest. He'd survived the destruction of his home, house and family; falling in love again was the last thing he'd intended to do. When you know what it is to lose someone, how dare you hand over so much of yourself to anyone else? Pragmatically, it's like investing in a business that you know is bound to fail. But in bed with Terri, pragmatism wasn't an issue.

He turned the sleeping woman on to her back and kissed her slightly open lips, which tasted of remembered pesto sauce and a strange herbal toothpaste she liked that could only be bought in Germany.

'Asleep . . . ' she muttered.

Teo kept kissing her. A mouth isn't really there; it's empty space. His lips explored the springy softness of hers, but it was the space he was kissing: the mouthful of universe that was Terri's but, now, also his. She turned, opened all her spaces to him and later he couldn't sleep so he got up and wrote down everything that had passed through his mind in those hours when she gave him all of herself except the one thing he wanted, which was her essence, her blue kernel of love out of that inner cosmos. The last ten per cent, but the only part that matters. And she was right — it was frightening.

There's a familiar, enervating nature to the latest quarrel, his early return to Paris and the strain vibrating through him like a sharp note in a chord. All because he'd ripped up some work that wasn't good enough. How dare she decide that his work is good enough when she hasn't even read it?

Teo takes a sip of brain-blasting coffee. It's nine o'clock at last. He knows never to call Terri before eight, British time. He picks up the phone.

'Darling. Are you all right?' says Terri, as if everything is back to normal.

★   ★   ★

'It's good,' Alistair says. Julie tucks her phone under her chin while she folds T-shirts for the trip. In the background, around Alistair, she can hear the clank of plates and the boom of male voices.

'Is it still so tough?' she asks. The first weeks, he'd often texted to say he was so knackered he could hardly stand. Several guys were too unfit and had dropped or been pushed out. A few of the officers grumbled that youngsters these days eat and drink too much rubbish and don't exercise enough.

'Yeah, it's bloody tough. That's why it's good.'

Julie listens to him describe the pressure, the rain, the weight of the loads, the guns. They'd been on an exercise in the moors which simulated an ambush. Alistair had had a role, of sorts, in which he'd saved the 'lives' of three fellow trainees from balaclavaed 'terrorists'. And he'd done it well. Plaudits all round, but afterwards he'd wanted to sleep for a year. At least the barracks are new. 'The old ones are shit,' he remarks. 'Broken pipes and stuff, and

114

mildew. Nothing worked. Us lot've been lucky.'

'But . . . aren't you scared?'

'What for? It's the only adventure I'm ever going to have, innit?'

'Isn't Sue worried about you?'

'She's dead proud. Like Uncle John. I can't remember any time he's been proud of me like this.'

'When can I come and see you?'

'You have a good holiday with your mum, yeah? Maybe you can come up when you're back, I'll get free weekends by then. Have fun. Not too much fun with the Krauts, mind!'

'No chance. I'll be with Mum.'

'And is she going to be with you?'

Last time Julie and her mother went on holiday together, to Italy, they'd met another English family with teenage kids and Julie had joined them to go sightseeing. Terri saw her local agent, visited the managers of the Verona Arena and La Fenice in Venice and was wined and dined on what she called the Diva Drag. Julie had had plenty of fun — just not with Terri.

'I don't care,' she says. 'If she goes off diva-ing, I can look after myself.'

'Miss you.'

'Miss you too.' Julie kisses the phone, then puts it down.

6

Julie stands on the balcony, breathing deeply. The chestnut trees and weeping elms beside the fast-flowing water are heavy with late summer leaves. The river is a glorified stream; but then, she's used to London and the wide grey Thames. Here in Baden-Baden, everything is a little smaller, a little slower and a lot more beautiful.

'Wasn't this a good idea?' Terri beams from her bed, where she's lying flat, shoes off, a damp cloth on her forehead. The journey had begun with a hot and aggravating trundle through Heathrow, where they queued at the 'fast bag drop' for forty-five minutes, then security for nearly half an hour. Stuttgart airport, where they landed, had been clean, efficient and quick.

Julie feels guilty at finding the journey frustrating: for Alistair and Sue, such a trip was out of the question. She's glad to have been at a school where her friends were local and where she wasn't cosseted away from the boggling melange of south-east London. Her classmates' parents came from Sudan, Pakistan, India, Nigeria, Poland, Croatia, Wales, Somalia, France and Lebanon and many of the children in the primary section's reception class spoke next to no English. Terri had wanted to send her to a private school, keen to guarantee her the fine education she herself had never experienced; it was Bernard who insisted, 'She can go to a

116

normal school like everyone else. That's what they're for.' Julie was happy there and had always done well in her exams. But squaring term-time with the holidays had never been easy; however much she enjoys the luxury of travelling with Terri, she can never quite relax. Eating in upmarket restaurants from Italy to New York, she'd think of her evenings with Alistair and Sue at MacDonalds, which she enjoys almost as much. Not that she'd admit that to Terri. Whichever way she turns, she feels guilty.

'Lighten up, sweetheart,' Terri says. 'You're allowed to enjoy yourself. Let's go and have coffee and cakes in the garden.'

Terri has changed into white linen slacks, a white top with a deep V-neck and some gold jewellery. Julie, following her down a wide staircase to the foyer, wonders how her mother manages to look expensive even when she's wearing cheap high-street stuff. Something to do with being onstage, switching on the headlamps. Passing guests and staff glance her way, fascinated by her full-beam charisma. Trailblazing through a besofaed lounge where a pianist is playing 'Smoke Gets in Your Eyes', Terri glows like a film star. No wonder she had felt that her child was a millstone. Julie feels the familiar cloud of doubt and depression settling on her neck.

They march through an airy conservatory into the garden by the river, where tables are set with white linen cloths, silver cutlery and white china. Groups of guests relax at the other tables, though most, Julie thinks, are dressed as if

117

they're going to an office, a wedding or a funeral. There's only one family with small children. The little ones don't run about on the grass but are regimented to their places by a young woman who, by process of elimination, is probably a nanny.

Julie smiles when people greet her; she says 'ja', 'nein' and 'danke schön' when necessary. A waiter offers Terri an umbrella to provide shade, but she waves him away, smiling. 'We need sun,' she declares. Opposite Julie, she explores the menu. 'Now, what would you like? Look at all these different teas.'

'Madame Ivory!' A besuited young man is striding towards them across the gravel. Julie wonders why he calls Terri 'Madame' — she's Scottish, not French, and he's German. He lifts her hand, kisses her knuckles. 'What a pleasure to see you again!'

'Joachim, darling.' Terri is entering Diva Drag mode. 'Lovely to see you too. It's wonderful to be back, a real treat. This is my daughter, Juliette. Julie, sweetheart, this is Joachim, who always looks after us when we stay here to sing.' Julie knows that 'we' indicates 'we singers', not Terri regarding herself as royalty, though she wouldn't much blame her if she did.

Joachim kisses Julie's hand too: 'As lovely as your mother. And do you sing too?'

'A little,' says Julie, as she usually does.

Joachim turns back to Terri. 'Madame Ivory, I appreciate that you're on holiday, but if at any point during your stay you would like to try out any new repertoire, we could easily arrange a small recital . . . '

Terri's smile becomes fixed; the twinkle drains from the back of her eyes. 'That's kind, Joachim, but I'm definitely and entirely on holiday. Julie and I are having quality time before she flies the nest to university. I wouldn't *dream* of singing.'

'Of course, I understand perfectly.' He gives a small bow, clicking his heels. 'Now, what shall I ask them to bring you?'

Julie picks Darjeeling, with carrot cake. Terri asks for a special green tea blend that is unique to the hotel, and a slice of *pflaumtorte*. She winks at Julie. 'If only the boys could see us now.'

Julie thinks of her father and his prominent ears in his cottage, marking maths papers, wearing his blue jersey. She feels abruptly sorry for him.

'By the way, darling . . . ' Terri leans towards her. 'Not a word to *anyone* about the operation. Not a syllable. If anybody asks why I'm not singing, I've had a back injury and I'm taking a break to learn some new roles. Please don't forget.'

'Don't worry, Mum, there's no way I'd forget. Promise.'

Terri clinks her cup against Julie's. 'Thanks, darling. You're what they used to call 'a real brick'. And of course the wonderful thing about you being grown-up now is that we can be friends, not only mum and daughter.'

★　★　★

119

The next morning, after a palatial breakfast, they set off for a stroll. Julie takes in the undulating garland of tree-lined landscape encircling the town, larger than hills, smaller than mountains. The pedestrian centre of Baden-Baden makes her imagine some uninvented Disneyland Germany. Pointy roofs like gingerbread houses, geraniums cascading from self-conscious window-boxes, onion-domed churches bashing out chimes on the hour. The aroma of sausages and mustard drifts from a street stall; under the chestnut trees that line the road, shop windows boast designer watches, art deco antique lamps and dark green Loden coats. 'Do you think that'd suit me?' Terri jokes. 'Or maybe I should get one for Teo.'

'Would it suit me?'

'Heavens, no. Much too old for you.' Terri puts an arm round Julie. 'I still think of you as about eleven, you know.'

'I bet.' Julie looks at the ground. Millstone. 'Is Teo talking to you, after the other week?'

'Of course. I've spoken to him nearly every day.' Terri takes off her sunglasses and polishes them. 'It's never been straightforward, it never will be. He's a very complicated man.'

Julie hesitates. Should she tell her mother that she found the diary? Perhaps she should come clean; it may clear the air. Still, so many of her childhood memories involve confrontations grating the atmosphere between her parents before they split up that she'd do anything rather than create another.

'What would you like to do later?' Terri changes the subject. 'The baths?'

'The idea is for you to rest and get better, isn't it? We should do what you want to do.'

'But what do *you* want to do?'

'But you're the priority.'

'No, you're *my* priority.'

Julie, given the choice, would just want to be with Alistair. This pretty, affluent town heaving with sausages and cake is all very well, but it would have been nicer if he was there — not that he could have been.

'Let's walk over to the Festspielhaus,' Terri suggests. 'I'll show you where I sang Isolde for the first time.'

★ ★ ★

The theatre stands back from the street, a sprawling building with great arched windows, dazzling Julie with an expanse of mosaic floor in the entrance. It used to be the station, Terri tells her. This was where Pauline Viardot, her husband Louis and Ivan Turgenev would have arrived, catching their first glimpse of the turrets and tree-lined hills from the shallow steps at the front. Brahms would have passed this way, too, and Clara Schumann after the death of her composer husband. Dostoyevsky would have walked the route they're walking now; a plaque and statue commemorate the house that was his. In those days everyone came to Baden-Baden.

'*Why?*' Julie sounds a tad scathing.

'This is a tremendous cultural centre. It's only

little — a hundred thousand people — but this theatre's one of the biggest in Europe and every international star performs here. I can tell you, singing Isolde for the first time in this city was no small order.' She glances with irritation at a poster bearing the huge eyes and pouting lips of Varya Petrovna.

★ ★ ★

Memories surge back across the empty foyer, all glass, wood and grey carpet. Three years ago, Terri stood onstage here, wearing a red wig, a dark dress and a silver shawl, listening to the orchestra playing the prelude to *Tristan und Isolde* and knowing that in a few moments she would begin the longest and most daunting task she had tackled since giving birth. She was so nervous that she'd been sick that morning — though she'd told no one, terrified that the incident would have a noxious effect on her vocal cords.

It took her two and a half years to learn the role, and that was after she'd spent a further year trying to convince herself, and Martini, that she could do it. She'd never sung a note of Wagner before and she'd had to twist Martini's arm, hard, to find her short runs first as Verdi's Aida and then some less taxing Wagner — Elisabeth in *Tannhäuser* — to ease her towards music that was much heavier than her usual roles. She was known for Beethoven, Richard Strauss, lyric Verdi or Puccini and the occasional Mozart; pure lines, direct emotion, nothing requiring truly excessive meat — until she found herself in Vienna, sitting over a candlelit dinner at the Hotel Sacher with a Hungarian conductor named Ferenc, who, while busily taking away any breath that she didn't need for singing, rubbed her knee and remarked: 'You should sing Isolde.'

'Don't be silly,' Terri laughed.

'I tell you, it's true. I don't just say this for fun.'

Ferenc had small, blue eyes that burned like torches; he was a compact figure, only a few inches taller than she was, but the palpable crackles of electricity that surrounded him when he took the podium brought a commensurate fizz from singers, orchestra and audience. Besides, she adored his accent.

'You are made for this role,' he said later, in bed. 'It's not histrionic. It needs lyricism like yours — with inner strength, and mystery in the soul. Isolde is the inheritor of magical arts and her purity is a force that is immense. It shouldn't be done, you know, *bel canto can belto*.'

'I never even thought about it.' Terri rubbed his chest, which wasn't as hairy as Teo's. She liked a good amount of fuzz under her hands. 'They suggested it in Paris once, but I laughed them out of town.'

'Don't laugh. You should try. You go home and start to learn the role. Take your time, nice and slow; explore each word and every phrase. When you are happy, you call me, then we schedule, no?'

'Well, why not, indeed?' She kissed the tip of the maestro's nose. It was easy to say yes, basking in his energy. Teo left her exhausted, sometimes enervated; of course the emotion was all there, but sometimes in those long months alone on the road she craved the solace of another body, and one who would replenish her spirit rather than drain it. Those other bodies, also belonging to itinerant musicians, usually had the same idea. This encounter was especially creative: Ferenc's heat fed hers and vice-versa, with delectable results both private and public: in the theatre the following night, they received a fifteen-minute ovation.

Back in Falcon Park, she foisted off loneliness by ordering the score of *Tristan und Isolde*. It was too fat for the letter box; she had to fetch it from the sorting office. At her piano, she turned to the 'Liebestod' and began to sing quietly. '*Mild und leise, wie er lächelt . . .* '

Every soprano knows the theme, so iconic that it's hard to imagine any human being could have thought it up and written it down. Terri, following the notes on the page, heard the harmonies that changed the world. She wasn't much of a pianist, having not learned until she was at college, when she absorbed some basics by sheer willpower. '*Wie das Auge hold er öffnet.*' She knew the sound by heart, because the power of it could set the greatest musicians cowering in awe.

She picked her way through, very softly. She couldn't do this. To sustain that line — and at the end of an opera that involves nearly four hours' singing — was a crazy idea for her vocal *fach*. She was a lyric-dramatic soprano, not a full-blast, Valkyrie-winged Wagnerian, end of story. She phoned Ferenc to explain.

'No, no, no, this is nonsense!' he protested. 'You impose, or Germany imposes, this silly *fach* system. This does not concern you and your individuality! Who are they to say there are only a handful of voice types and you cannot venture beyond one set of roles? The bloody Germans! One day, I tell you what Germany does to Hungary in war. So ignore them, Teresa! Sing what you like, what suits *you*. Tell them to go jump in Lake Balaton! And by the way, you know what opera houses will *pay* for sopranos singing Wagner?'

'No?' said Terri.

Ferenc told her. Then, while she was still getting her breath from the shock, he added — for he was a clever fellow: 'But maybe you are right, Terri, maybe it is too much for you to take on. Perhaps you shouldn't.'

Terri was not one to chicken out of a challenge. She remembered assessing a wall by the docks in Glasgow — it was five feet up — and Robbie, who always knew what she'd do before she did it, yelling, 'Terri, *no*!' At once, she'd sought toeholds in the bricks. Telling Terri not to do something had always been the best way to ensure she'd go and do it at once. Eventually Robbie had to help her instead, standing by to catch her while she hoisted herself on to the top of the wall. She never imagined what might happen if she fell. She fixed her gaze on her goal, set her focus, placed her feet securely and at the end Robbie lifted her down while she screamed with laughter and triumph.

Isolde, a five-foot wall? Bugger that, thought Terri. It was the bloody Matterhorn. She remembered Ferenc. She took it slowly, gave herself time between runs of Mozart, Verdi and Strauss, letting the phrases sink into her subconscious.

The scale of it was unlike anything she'd tried before. When you think a phrase can only last a certain length of time, Wagner doubles it. When you think the intensity can go no further, he blasts open the horizon and propels you into a sphere where everyday emotion pales to nothingness. Then there's the volume, the power. The action takes place more in the orchestra than on the stage; she must make her voice soar over the top. Wagner's theatre in Bayreuth has a sunken orchestra pit, partially covered; the sound is distanced enough for the singers to perform without straining their voices. This, though, is the only opera house of its kind. Mostly you have to let rip.

'I'm learning Isolde,' she told Martini.

'Are you *serious*?' He clearly didn't know how to respond to the idea that she had started tackling the longest soprano role, as far as either of them knew, that a single opera had ever presented, one that required a stamina and a volume that exceeded anything she'd attempted before.

She invited him to a party, and sang the 'Liebestod', *Tristan's* closing scene, in her own home with her piano accompanist; by the end the gathering was speechless. It was a treat, she discovered: not remotely difficult when sung in isolation with a piano, but still guaranteed to send everyone into ecstasies. That, of course, has nothing to do with performing the whole opera. The next day Martini phoned with the news that Baden-Baden would book her. Ferenc wasn't free to conduct, but she didn't care any more.

'You didn't think I could do it, did you?' she teased.

'One thing I've learned,' said Martini, 'is never to underestimate Terri Ivory.'

As for the character — that wasn't difficult either. Terri knew Isolde as if she were etched inside her DNA. Strong, yes, but not harsh; her strength was in her giving. She healed Tristan not with medicines, but with the life-force that she channelled. She made him love her by harnessing that same universal energy. Love potion? What crap. Drinking the stuff is only an excuse for the pair to face their feelings for the first time. Terri's Isolde wasn't Amazonian; she was vulnerable, transcending her vulnerability — open to the possibility of miracles even when she suffered the most. Terri's Isolde was, in two words, Mary Hoolihan.

Two years later she was in Baden-Baden, throwing up. Since that day she's never been able to walk through the park along the Lichtentaler-allee without thinking of the way the seconds had dragged her on, lurching towards four o'clock — *Tristan* started at four and ended only after ten. She'd stopped by the statue of Turgenev and left a flower for him, silently cursing Ferenc, Martini and her own stupid, pig-headed ambition.

Four o'clock came. Terri sang. She had no idea how it was going across. The music carried her; she abandoned all sense of self, because there was no other way to keep the line other than to cease to exist and let it inhabit her. All she knew was that the opera was passing, while the music resonated through the open landscape of her mind and body. After the final curtain, she stepped out in front of it. The roar that greeted her nearly knocked her flat.

'You looked like a rabbit in the headlights, Mum,' Julie told her later, pink with pride, when they were bundling up the bouquets in the dressing room.

'I *felt* like a rabbit,' said Terri. 'A squashed one.' She thought she'd sung OK, but to her horror, the audience was going bananas. They were on their feet, the whole theatre load of them, yelling. She'd stood there, bedazzled, wondering whether all this fuss could really be for her.

★ ★ ★

What Terri has never known, and may never know, is whether singing Isolde started the polyp. She searches the angled staircases, the deserted champagne bar and the vaulted roof as if they hold the answer she needs. She'd never had any trouble before it, that much was certain. This doesn't mean, though, that it wouldn't have been brewing, imperceptibly. If in doubt, blame Wagner. Anything rather than blame herself.

'What's the matter, Mum?' asks Julie.

'Nothing, angel. Shall we go and find Turgenev's house?'

★ ★ ★

A little while later, Terri and Julie come to a halt on a wide road that curves up a hill towards the woods. The dove-grey mansion is symmetrically proportioned, its façade lavish with windows and curlicued carving; the whole could almost have been designed by Alphonse Mucha. It looks as if light would fly through the particles of its walls at one snap of the occupant's fingers. The gate is padlocked. Beside it, a plaque reads:

VILLA TURGENEV
KEIN ZUTRITT

'The house that Ivan built,' Terri muses. 'That means that Pauline lived *there*.' She points at a modern block of flats next door, functional brown and beige. 'Jesu Maria. They pull down Pauline's house and her theatre, and they build *that*.'

'Good place for property developing,' Julie remarks. 'It looks like St John's Wood.'

'I imagine Pauline must have found this place a bit . . . '

'Sleepy?'

'I guess, if you're a singer and you're stopping singing, this is quite a good place to come and *not* sing.'

'Mum,' Julie ventures, 'why do you have such

a thing about Pauline Viardot? I've never really got what it's about.'

Terri smiles, wry. 'I'm not sure I get it myself, darling. Something about me and Teo, Pauline and Turgenev — I only got interested because Teo adored Turgenev, then decided to be a writer falling madly for an opera singer. It's almost as if the whole story is trying to tell me something. But I'm not too sure what it is.'

'If you find out, will you tell me?'

Terri gives a brisk smile. 'You bet. At least we found the house. And it's private. This great Russian author built it, lived in it, loved in it and wrote in it, but, oh dearie me, you can't go in. It's *private*.'

Just like a diary, Julie reflects, staying silent.

'Hungry, sweetheart?'

'Not remotely,' says Julie. At the thought of the diary, her appetite has vanished. Perhaps she'd just eaten too much breakfast.

★ ★ ★

There's nothing private about the Friedrichsbad: instead, everyone's privates are on display. It's a world of steam and flesh, of muzzy moisture on the skin and floppiness through the muscles after the soap-laden pummelling by a masseuse with hands like elephants' feet. Terri tastes the water — bitter, sulphurous, but apparently good for you.

She stretches out on a lounger alongside Julie. They're both naked. So is the entire spa. Julie had been horrified for a few minutes when they

130

went in, but Terri assured her that in a few minutes it would feel like the most natural thing in the world — which, technically, it is. Post-massage, pre-final dip, it's time to relax. Terri can't help admiring her daughter's body. To think that these slender, tender limbs had grown from that bundle of mucus and blood that was her newborn baby.

'What?' asks Julie, seeing her smile.

'I'm so proud of you.' Terri doesn't waste her time wondering how Julie sees her. Orange-peel flesh on the bum. Long-lingering stretch-marks. Breasts with a half-century's incipient sag. Batwings where there should be triceps. Sod it, Terri tells herself, I am not going to be jealous of my daughter. Had she been happy at nineteen? Had she, hell. She'd been working in a pub beside the Usher Hall in Edinburgh, dating an ice-cream salesman and living in a bedsit where the heating only worked when you shovelled sixpences into a meter.

Some sections of the baths are mixed. Few male bodies, Terri reflects, are good enough to make their nakedness a pleasant sight. Drooping tums, breasts where there shouldn't be any, turkey necks bouncing about. Everyone respects the bath culture; notices request silence, and Terri has the distinct sensation that anyone who tries 'inappropriate behaviour' will be carted out on the spot, or forced underwater and held there. One becomes necessarily sexless. It's not escaped her notice, though, that when men do walk past, it's towards Julie that their gazes flicker, with one or two exceptions. She tries not to talent-spot on her own account. Here she's neither opera star nor elegant older woman; she's an invisible mum, with cellulite. Julie ignores the lot of them. It's impossible, when you are young and beautiful, to know just how exquisite those qualities are to anyone who no longer possesses them. Everybody is beautiful in youth; few realise its value until it's gone. Terri forces a smile. This is a moment to count one's blessings, not mourn the past. She is indeed a lot happier now than she was thirty years ago — or she will be when her voice returns.

★   ★   ★

Dressed and ready to leave, Julie waits for Terri to finish putting on her make-up, responding with monosyllables to her mother's through-the-lipstick-pout questions.

'What are you thinking about?' Terri asks while they wander out through the foyer to a leafy square where early evening suggests it could be time for a glass of wine.

'Alistair,' Julie sighs. 'Wondering how he'd have liked this.'

'He'd love it.'

'Yeah. It's a bit different from where he is right now.'

'I know, darling. Now, what shall we . . . '

'Miss Ivory? Please pardon me?'

Terri and Julie stare up at the accoster, a tall man with more hair than would be natural to most European males of the same age. His accent has a strong Californian twang.

'Please forgive the intrusion, but I'm a great fan of yours.' He extends a hand. Terri realises she'd spotted him inside the baths; he'd been one of the more presentable males, one of the few who'd been worth noticing. She beams up, all too aware that he'd have first seen her stark naked while she was imagining herself anonymous.

'I don't know when else I'd have gotten a chance to say hi,' he goes on. 'Things being as they were, I couldn't really talk to you in there.'

Terri laughs. 'I'm amazed you recognised me with my clothes on. Are you from the States?'

'Yes, I'm here filming. We're making a biopic about Dostoyevsky.'

'You *are?*' Terri's smile widens. 'How amazing. I didn't think Hollywood was interested in nineteenth-century Russians. I once told an American journalist that I wanted to make a film about Turgenev's lover and later she said, 'This Eye-Van Toogayinev guy, he sounds kinda neat, do you have his email?''

The American laughs; his teeth are ridiculously white.

'So, which side of the camera are you on?' Terri asks. 'You look familiar.'

'You found me out — I'm an actor. My name's Tom Cruise — no, just kidding, I'm Brett Herman. Doomed for ever to be 'best supporting actor'.'

Terri's eyebrows aim for the sky. 'Heavens,' she says. 'I know your name so well — it's a pleasure to meet you.' Her dimple deepens. 'What a very interesting situation this would have been a bit earlier! Did you know that the bikini was invented by a French designer in the 1950s, and was very, very tiny? The problem was, it didn't take off!'

Brett Herman laughs, too loudly. 'What a marvel this is,' he enthuses. 'If you have the time, may I treat you to a cup of English tea? And if you're interested, I'd be very happy to show you round the set.'

'That would be lovely. Brett, this is my daughter, Juliette, Julie for short.'

Julie, copying her mother, holds out a hand to the Hollywood semi-star.

'Charmed,' says Brett, taking it. 'And do you sing too?'

'A little,' says Julie.

★ ★ ★

Brett's suggested tea morphs into a stronger drink in a bar at the top of the old town, near the Schloss. They order local white wine, which to Julie tastes as sulphurous as the water. She's torn between wanting to ask Brett for an autograph and wondering whether he'll spirit Terri away, as men sometimes do. Brett, his teeth twinkling, invites them both to dinner with the director, a staggeringly famous Italian-American, at a French restaurant nearby. Julie's limbs feel plush and boneless after the spa; besides, the image that fills her mind of Alistair in combat gear makes it hard to concentrate on the conversation. All she wants to do is go home and sleep.

'Julie, what do you think?' Terri says.

'Wouldn't you like to meet Vincent Pollani?'

'Whatever.' Julie is too tired not to yawn visibly.

'If you'd rather not go, that's fine.' Terri brushes the actor's arm. 'Maybe tomorrow, Brett.' Julie watches his face melt down to goo, as men's tend to when her mother touches them.

'Mum, you go. I'll stay in. I've got reading to do.'

'She's applying to university,' Terri explains. 'We'll be hearing from Cambridge any day.'

'Cambridge? How amazing.' Brett looks impressed. 'I remember being there as a tourist one time. I couldn't imagine anything more magnificent than studying in a place like that.'

Julie catches her mother's eye. 'You go. Really.'

'I don't want to leave you on your own.'

'I'll be fine.'

'But darling, it's not fair.'

'Mum, don't *fuss*. I'll get room service.'

'She misses her boyfriend,' Terri tells Brett.

'Oh, Mum, just *go*, don't mind me.' The wine has given Julie heartburn.

'I wouldn't want to take you away from your lovely daughter, but . . . ' He hesitates. 'If you're sure . . . '

Julie knows that Terri will go. 'I'm sure,' she says. And indeed, a few minutes later, Julie is wandering alone back to the hotel, while Terri, her face betraying guilt to her daughter if nobody else, vanishes towards the Dostoyevsky House with her new friend.

★ ★ ★

135

Julie settles on the balcony of her room, a book open on her lap. She reads a few sentences, then closes her eyes. She drifts in and out of daydreams about Alistair, most of them involving love, sex and anxiety. Over the park, the sky turns violet as dusk approaches. Julie calls room service and orders a toasted sandwich, soup and some tea, which arrive on a tray borne by a waiter in white gloves. The soup is not out of a packet; the tea stews in a silver pot. Minutes tick by.

At ten, Julie, goes to bed and falls instantly asleep. She wakes up once to go to the loo: the moon is high over the hills, the sky an odd shade of dark pewter. She wonders whether Terri has returned — there's been no sound next door. Then she goes back to sleep and stays there. The first she knows of her mother's presence is when she peers out of her room at eight thirty and sees a new sign on the handle of Terri's door: *BITTE NICHT STÖREN*.

★   ★   ★

Terri appears in the hotel dining room while Julie is finishing her cereal. Shadows haunt the sides of her nose, but her eyes are smiling, ever so slightly triumphant.

'There's coffee,' Julie grunts.

'Darling, you're an angel.'

Julie stares at the laden platters on the breakfast buffet. Faced with a spread involving every kind of cold meat, smoked fish, cheese, eggs, yoghurt, patisserie, waffles and fresh fruit in Germany, all she wants is bran flakes.

'Everything all right?' Terri prods.

'Yes.'

'That means no.'

'When did you get back?'

'Seven a.m.'

Julie is silent.

Terri gives an exasperated sigh. 'Darling, what can I do to make you feel better?'

Julie swallows coffee. Her mother's entitled to a sex life. It's not meant to make her feel useless and millstone-like. Terri has always let her and Alistair sleep together at home if and when they wanted to, as long as they used condoms; other mothers might have collapsed at the notion, since most seemed incapable of even saying 'condom', let alone buying some and leaving them strategically placed on a bedside table complete with a diagram of how to put them on. In return, Julie has inferred, she's expected not to object to anything that takes place in her mother's bedroom.

'You're a snob,' she accuses Terri. 'Just because he's in a film about Dostoyevsky.'

Terri laughs. 'Darling, he was telling me last night how he grew up in the roughest part of the Bronx. And I told him a thing or two about the Gorbals.'

'But he wears a toupée! Or didn't you notice?'

'Sweetheart, I'm going to make a film in which . . .'

'*You're* going to make a *film*? No, you're not!' Julie cries. 'You just want to get yourself on TV! Who's going to accept a thing like Pauline

Viardot? Out in the big wide world, nobody gives a fig about her any more than about you!'

'Juliette, I may be a stupid, uneducated singer, but what have I done to deserve this?' Terri asks quietly. 'You know what the Diva Drag's like . . . '

'This isn't the Diva Drag. This is you pushing off with the first man who chats you up after seeing you sitting in a public bathhouse stark naked.' Julie realises, to her horror, that she's about to cry.

'So?' Terri says. 'It's nothing that most girls your age wouldn't do. Am I undignified, wanting sex at fifty?'

Julie blows her nose on the white linen napkin. 'What about Teo?'

'Well?' says her mother. 'What about Teo?'

Julie gets up and marches out of the breakfast room without looking back.

★ ★ ★

Upstairs she calls room service for more coffee — they'll be getting used to her soon — and ponders her options. She can't stand her father's house. To her mother, she's a millstone. Alistair is away training and may then be sent to war. She, too, will have to go away. The exam results will determine where and whether she can go.

Alistair had been determined to go into the army, and wouldn't let her hold him back. So, if she's at the bottom of everyone else's priority lists, then she must force them to the bottom of hers, however unnatural it feels. It's time she got away from them all. University, then. If she gets the grades, she will go. Even if she doesn't think she's academic, maybe it doesn't matter. She will have a space of her own at last.

7

Terri stands dead centre in Anita's front room, amid the clutter of books and sheet music. Anita is at the piano, her brown eyes filled with sympathy. Those eyes sometimes remind Terri of Mary's and at other times of Pauline Viardot herself; perhaps that's why Anita has always been her favourite teacher, the one Terri trusts not only with her career but also with her daughter. Outside, a double-decker disgorges a crowd of office workers heading for home. It's unseasonably warm — there's been an Indian summer and the leaves seem to be hanging on to their branches as long as they possibly can. All the same, Terri feels cold: a draught garlands her neck from the gaps around the sash windows.

'Ready?' Anita encourages.

'Almost, but please could I borrow a jersey?'

'Of course.' Anita heads for her basement bedroom to find one. Terri suspects that her old friend is tactfully avoiding to comment on her evasion tactics.

Terri's innards feel as if she's swallowed a live pigeon. She hasn't dared do more than hum until now; even that fills her with terror. Supposing the doctor was wrong and it's still too soon? Yet he insists that she could have started again weeks ago, if she'd wanted to. She's lost her courage as a side effect of the operation; she hadn't realised how much else had vanished with the polyp until she returned from her check-up, sat at her piano, played a note and opened her mouth, only to find she couldn't persuade herself to make a sound.

At last she'd forced herself to call Anita and ask for a session. 'I thought you'd never ask,' Anita said. 'Come and have a sing any time you like.' Anita, bless her, has more than an astute ear and a total understanding of vocal technique: she has enough Spanish warmth to carry Terri through this ordeal.

Anita returns with a cardigan, and Terri pulls it on. It probably wasn't the draught that had made her feel cold.

'OK,' says Anita. 'Let's begin. Very quietly.' She plays an arpeggio in the middle range. 'Try starting with the hum. Then on the last note, very gently, try to open the sound.' She demonstrates. 'Don't be afraid. You've got to do it sometime.'

'I know.' Terri fastens the last button. Her fingers are like ice-lollies.

'One arpeggio won't hurt. Honest. Just one. Then we'll stop, if you want to.'

Terri takes a breath. The bottom note is in her ears. Her tongue lifts, her throat vibrates. She keeps still, feeling, assessing. The note is where it should be. There's no sensation of sand.

'Good. Now, keep the level steady, as long as it's comfortable. Next note.'

Terri's hum rises by a major third. It's still comfortable. She is halfway through the exercise. One more note; she follows.

'Good,' says Anita again. 'We're just trying to

141

bring the vocal cords together, very gently. And on . . . '

Terri reaches the top. It's still her voice, recognised like an old friend who's been away on a long journey, plodding homewards with a backpack of unlikely experience.

'Now open. Very slowly, very quietly.'

Terri obeys; the sound echoing around her head brightens, as if emerging from behind a gauze of cirrus. But then there's a raspiness, a grating —

'Oh no.' Terri stops. She's never made an ugly noise before. She wants to curl up and die.

'It's OK. The cord they operated on is slack, that's all. We need to get it back in shape, tauten it up. It's going to sound crap for a little while, Terri, but that's all right. Just accept it and remember that if you build it up, it will be fine again very soon. Yes?'

Terri nods.

'One more.' They move to the next key, a semitone up. Terri repeats the process, opening gradually. The sound is horrible.

'I can't stand it.'

'We'll get there. We'll have regular sessions to exercise that lazy old cord. Come on, Terri, you know you can do it. Nothing ever fazes you.'

'First time for everything.' Terri tries to laugh. 'Annie, do you think it's going to be all right? Am I going to go around sounding like this for ever?'

'You're going to be absolutely perfect.' She surveys Terri, her dark eyes perceptive. 'Believe me, Terri, I know voices and I know *you*. If

142

anyone can be all right, it's Terri Ivory.'

Terri sits down and hides her face on her arms. 'Maybe I'm just a lousy singer. Maybe I've been a lousy singer all along: bad technique, no brain . . .'

Anita hugs her. Terri fights herself; she never cries. If she cries, it means that something has upset her as much as Finn's death.

'You're nothing of the kind, and you know it,' Anita says firmly. 'You wouldn't believe how many people this happens to — and it's something that just *happens*. It can happen to anyone, to people who've never sung a note in their lives. And if it were only bad singers — well, I can't tell you the number of terrible singers with no technique whatsoever who sail through life without ever having a minute of vocal trouble. You're a good singer. The best. You've just been hellishly unlucky.'

'Thanks, Annie.' Terri, mortified, wipes her eyes on her sleeve.

'More?'

'Not sure.' Terri admits.

Anita closes the piano. 'That's enough, then. You've done it, Terri — you've made the leap. I think you've earned yourself a nice cup of green tea.'

★   ★   ★

Terri had never realised how intensely she depended on her work. Without concerts and operas to prepare, she doesn't feel liberated; she feels lost. An academy for young singers in

Australia has contacted her via Martini to beg her to give masterclasses. Terri could have used both the sun and the money, but decided against it. If she were to give too many masterclasses, everyone would think her career was over.

There's enough gossip on the Internet about her already. Googling her own name, she discovers comments she wishes she'd never seen. 'Ivory faces extinction,' declares one forum. 'Terrified Terri blames withdrawal on back injury . . . '

'Ignore them,' Teo urged her from Paris. 'They are — what are they in English, those very little fish that swim in streams?'

'Minnows.'

'Yes, minnows. How was the holiday?'

'Good escapism.'

Terri half dreads that Julie will tell Teo too much about Baden-Baden. Not that he has anything to worry about — the actor had looked better than he'd felt, though she'd enjoyed the excitement and the romance, if you could call it that. Baden-Baden is a romantic place, after all. Julie had seemed oblivious to this quality, perhaps because she'd been catching up on her reading list, or perhaps because she was bored; it's so bloody difficult to tell with sulky teenagers. She's sure, though, that Julie's been viewing her with an odd new detachment. Is it just that Julie's grown up more than she'd imagined — or is there something more to her cynicism?

Julie's detachment in Germany had been her loss, of course. Some of the young actors had attended the dinner at the French restaurant, as had a chocolate-eyed assistant producer from Brazil. 'I wish my daughter had come along,' Terri told him. 'You'd like her, she's nineteen and very lovely.'

He begged her to call Julie and persuade her. 'Does she sing too?'

'Beautifully.' Terri took out her phone. But Julie wouldn't be persuaded. She was in the hotel, swotting over a *Life of Bach*. What can you do, Terri reflected, swigging Rhineland wine at the director's table, with a daughter who prefers to sit in her room and drink soup on her own, rather than exchange a word with a young man who wasn't her boyfriend?

The day after they got home, Julie's A level results plopped onto the doormat. Even Bernard couldn't have found anything to criticise. 'Everything but a damehood!' Terri declared, as she embraced the laughing and shrieking Julie.

So now Julie is preparing to go to Cambridge. And Terri prays that there she may find ways to spend her time that don't involve turning herself into a nun.

★ ★ ★

'No,' says Jane, 'he's at the office. You could try him there, or I can give him a message.'

'Just that I'm going up on the first weekend of October and I wondered if he'd maybe come with me?' Julie tries not to falter.

Jane's hesitation suggests that neither she nor

145

Bernard has thought of this. 'I'll pass that on,' she says.

'How's Ellen? Can I speak to her?'

'She's having her maths coaching now.'

'Could you ask her to call me when she's finished? I just want to say hello.'

'No, not until she's finished all her homework.'

'After that?' Julie wonders whether Jane also begins every sentence to her patients with the word 'no'.

'We'll see. Oh, congratulations, by the way.'

'Thanks.' Julie hangs up, with relief. She imagines Ellen skipping along under the trees, singing — then going home to the tourniquet of Jane.

Letters arrive from Alistair — sometimes emails, sometimes physical letters by post, handwritten and misspelled. Better than phoning when all the lads can hear you and there's no time to talk properly, he says. Julie writes back, telling him about her camping trip to Devon over Bank Holiday weekend with Patti and Lara — they'd returned early, drenched and suffering raging colds; but everything she says feels desperately trivial compared to what Alistair's undergoing, running cross-country carrying almost his entire bodyweight in his backpack. She tries to accustom herself to the jargon: 'tour' for going abroad, 'theatre' for battlefield, 'engagement' for battle itself. The words remind her so much of her mother's operatic terms that she's almost surprised he doesn't call his commanding officer 'maestro'.

He uses these expressions infrequently, though.

Instead, his missives feature everyday life: his new friends, who have names and nicknames like Han, Ben and Gerry and call him Rosso; a power failure in which he couldn't find his boots; an exercise when he'd been distracted, dangerously so, by a passing badger. He's not looking ahead, at least not when he writes to her. Julie, working through her reading list, tries not to look too far ahead either.

'You'll have such a wonderful time,' Ellen says, phoning her back. 'Can I come and see you?'

'Yes, please! Whenever you like.'

'Everyone says it's really cool, and you go punting, and you do acting and singing and go to balls and have masses of boyfriends . . . '

'Oh, really?'

'You don't sound very *interested*,' Ellen protests.

'I'm not.'

'Why not?'

'I'm just not. How are the riding lessons?'

'Great. I have to go, Mummy says it's time for bed.'

★ ★ ★

Out in the twilit garden, Terri has decided it's still warm enough to swim, and has switched on the lamps in the bushes and at the edge of the pool. The water, taupe flecked with indigo in the gathering evening, ripples under the white-gold light as she cruises back and forth. Julie pulls on her flip-flops and wanders down the mossy steps towards her.

Terri surfaces with a splash. 'Coming in, sweetheart? It's good. Bracing.'

Julie shakes her head. She's happy to watch. The garden, near the top of the steep hill, offers a broad horizon; far away, pinpricks of brilliance glimmer from the edge of London. Overhead, the purple-brown sky is trying to summon the stars. A patter of TV reaches them from the block of flats next door, which is shielded from view by dense fir trees. Somewhere a neighbour has mown a lawn and the air is filled with the scent of cut grass. Terri in her white swimsuit turns on to her back and propels herself along in slow motion, rivulets sliding from her broad forehead into her hair.

Julie looks at the white plastic loungers, folded against the shed wall. Only two are habitually open on the terrace. A third could have held Bernard or Teo. A fourth could have held Ellen, not that Ellen ever visits. Watching Terri swimming, graceful and self-contained, Julie nevertheless senses completeness: Terri and Julie, together, inhabit a sanctuary removed from real life. It's Terri's creation, entirely deliberate. 'You may think you don't need a sanctuary,' Terri would say, 'but I do.'

Julie perches cross-legged on a lounger. 'How did it go with Anita?'

'Good, thanks. I'm glad you're learning with her. She's sensitive and sensible, which is a good combination.'

'But how did it feel?'

'Scary,' Terri admits. 'There's still a voice, somewhere. I just have to exercise the blasted

148

cord. What's she given you to learn recently?'

'Bits and pieces. More Bach and a Schumann thing.'

'Tomorrow, why don't you sing them through to me and we'll have a session?'

Terri doesn't often try to help Julie with her singing, unwilling to interfere with her regular lessons. Besides, in front of her Julie turns tense and embarrassed — everything that's least helpful to voice production. Terri reverses direction in the water, pushing herself away from the wall and comforting herself and, she hopes, Julie with her broadest smile.

'Tell me about how you started singing, Mum,' Julie asks.

'You've heard it a hundred times!'

'But I'd like to hear it again.'

★   ★   ★

Aged fifteen, caught between Finn and Mary, Terri amazed her friends by obeying them and going back to school. The rest of the gang disappeared. One girl went to work in Boots, another in Woolworths. The prettiest of them vanished altogether until Robbie told Terri, months later, that he'd seen her in a club at the other end of Glasgow, wearing sequins but not much else, writhing through some interesting moves involving a pole and a top hat. Another girl, Kirsty, was five months pregnant. Terri had found her crying in the school loos; her mother had told her she'd have to give the baby up for adoption and, when she protested, insisted she'd have no choice. Kirsty didn't know whether that was true or not.

'Who's the father?' Terri asked.

'Don't know,' said Kirsty. 'I don't care. I just want to keep it.'

Terri hugged her and said, 'There's got to be a way.' But after Kirsty left school, Terri never learned what had become of her.

She felt lonely without the gang, but not as much as she'd expected. Twice a week, she took a bus to the sloping street of terraced stone apartment houses where Mary lived. Here, Mary would give her a singing lesson, herbal tea and toasted crumpets; while they ate, she'd play Terri record after record after record. Terri snuggled up in the armchair near Mary's fire with the big grey cat on her lap and the heat on her face, drinking in every note.

She'd never known there could be so many different ways to sing. American gospel choirs, to which she clapped along and stamped her feet (the cat didn't like that). Billie Holiday or Ella Fitzgerald jamming, irresistible — if only she could join in! And someone called Maria Callas, singing in Italian, which Terri couldn't understand but was nevertheless a familiar sound, like some unexplored realm within herself. She was accustomed to hearing it around Glasgow, especially at church where a third of the congregation were foreign, mainly from Italy, Poland and Lithuania. Italian was a lot easier to grasp than the other two languages — and something about the way Callas sang twisted her heart clean out of her.

'Can we hear that one again, please?' she asked.

'Do you know what this is, Terri?' Mary smiled. Terri shook her head, drinking in the warmth from Mary's kind eyes. 'It's 'Casta Diva' by Bellini. It's from an opera about a woman called Norma. It's a prayer. Norma is a priestess in a temple; she's in trouble and pleading to her goddess for help.'

They listened in silence. Terri was startled and rather embarrassed to find a tear slithering down her cheek. 'It must be very bad trouble,' she remarked afterwards.

'It is,' said Mary. 'She's a priestess and she's supposed to be a virgin. But she's in love with an enemy Roman and she's had two babies with him! If anyone finds out, she'll be burned at the stake. Some operas have wonderful music, but the stories can be hard to believe — why, Terri, what is it? What's the matter?'

A jolt had gone through Terri: Kirsty. 'It's not hard to believe at all,' she said. What was stranger was that music, sung in a foreign language by an opera star who knew nothing about suffering because she was rich and famous, could express all that better than Kirsty ever would, howling in the loos while her baby grew inside her.

It was only much later that Terri would learn just how much Maria Callas had suffered; and that being famous was no guard against pain. For now, all she knew was that she wanted to sing like that. She wanted it so badly that it sucked the breath out of her. She'd never wanted anything so much except her first taste of

151

chocolate and her first kiss.

'Are you feeling all right, Terri?' Mary asked.

'A little odd. Sort of stirred up.'

'I'll make some tea,' said Mary. 'Listen to this one while I do it.' She cleaned another LP with a felt cloth sprayed with anti-static fluid; Terri watched the needle settle on the revolving grooves, wondering what would come out this time.

She knew the voice at once: Katharina Strashilova. Mary had played her a recording of Strashilova before; her tone was like clear, golden syrup. But this music was new to Terri, and it was so beautiful that she thought her heart might stop beating so as not to disrupt it. As she listened, two more women's voices joined in, one higher, the other lower.

'This is the last trio from *Der Rosenkavalier* by Richard Strauss,' Mary called from the kitchen. Terri couldn't move: her limbs, heavy as the shipyard cranes, seemed welded to her chair while the music shot cannonballs of incredulity, want and need through her middle. She had never imagined that anything so miraculous could exist anywhere, let alone in Glasgow.

In the kitchenette Mary was spooning dry herbs into a teapot. They rustled, as if conspiring, when the hot water tumbled over them. Terri wiped her tears away with her sleeve before Mary could turn round from whatever she was concocting this time.

Mary kept a row of jars above the kettle, twelve or fifteen of them, each containing a different variety of funny-smelling, dried-out leaves and twigs. She had a remedy for everything. Period pains? Drink this, said Mary. Terri drank: the knots in her stomach smoothed, the bleeding slowed, her head cleared. Sore throat? Here you go: just add a little honey. Terri imagined a force-field fizzing out of Mary's palms, into her tea and thence on to the offending tonsil, which was duly zapped out of its grumbles.

'Is it magic?' she asked.

'I suppose in the Middle Ages they'd have burned me for a witch at the stake,' Mary said, with a laugh, 'but it's not magic. It's just common sense. Nature's there to help us when we know how to use it. There's nothing supernatural. Nature is strong enough already.'

Terri had one dread: that someone; a man presumably, might take Mary away from her.

'Miss Hoolihan,' she said one winter afternoon — she called her 'Mary' only in her thoughts — 'you're not going to get married, are you?'

'You know, Terri, I was engaged once.' Mary knelt on the hearth, stirring the logs with a poker. Sparks danced up the chimney. 'There was a boy I loved who wanted to marry me, at home.'

'Why didn't you?'

'He died.' She seemed calm as she spoke, firelight glinting on her hair. 'You'd never believe it, but he died because he lost his spectacles. Handsome, clever, but blind as a bat without his glasses. One day he couldn't find them and he was late for something and went out without them. A motorbike hit him. It was very quick

— he'd never have known what happened, and I'm glad of that. But, yes, that was my young man. I came here to get away.'

'That's why you came to teach in Glasgow?'

'There are only two comforts as great as God in my life now, angel. One is music and the other is helping the children and watching them learn, feeling I've had a hand in guiding them. I don't mind that they're not mine. They're all mine, because they're all God's, and in His eyes, I believe, we all belong to one another.'

'I like that,' Terri mused, watching the flames. 'But — poor you.'

'Poor in fate, but rich in spirit.' Mary smiled. 'I'll play you another song, shall I?'

Terri watched Mary's every move as she drew an LP out of its cardboard sleeve and cleaned it with the felt cloth. Mary herself reminded Terri of felt; her shape seemed malleable, her angles curved rather than pointed, her face and eyes as round as if a child had cut them out and stuck them on. The sound crackled from the speakers and Terri heard another voice, a duskier sound than Callas or Strashilova, singing something which was also in Italian but had a streamlined, unadorned tune that was easy to remember.

'It's this one.' Mary pointed at a line on the record sleeve. 'Mozart. 'Voi che sapete', from *The Marriage of Figaro*.'

'Could I sing it?'

'Sure you could,' said Mary. 'You, *a chroi*, can

sing anything you like. And don't you forget it. Now, somewhere I have the music . . . '

* * *

It took Terri a long time to learn to spell the composer's name without writing 'Motzart'. Learning the song was easier.

She practised it at home. 'Why can't you sing in the King's English?' Finn demanded.

'It's in *Italian*.' Terri was scathing.

'Oh aye,' Robbie jeered. 'Could have fooled me.' Terri's Italian had a distinctly Glaswegian tang. 'You should go and see Joe, he's a real Eye-Tie, or his parents are. He'd put you straight.'

Terri itched to sing the song properly, her determination fuelled by the fierceness that had awoken in her when Mary played her the Strauss. The sensation, hungry as a tiger cub, wouldn't leave her alone. Nothing had ever felt so important. If that was what it took to make it sound good, then that was what she'd do.

And so, that weekend Terri found herself eating her way through an outsize bowl of strawberry goo in the back room of the Moretti family's ice-cream bar in the cinema, with Joe Moretti's black eyes glittering at her while she tried to pronounce the words of the aria through melting pink mouthfuls. His real name was Giovanni.

'They make that stuff with whale blubber and cochineal,' he told her. 'And flavouring. You don't find strawberries in these parts.'

155

'Whale blubber?' Terri put down her spoon. He grabbed her free hand, laughing — at her or with her, she wasn't certain.

'*Allora*, Teresa! What'll you give me if I show you properly?'

'You're not Italian at all,' she protested. 'You're Scottish just like us.'

'Mamma,' Joe called, in response, '*vieni qui?*' A second later Mrs Moretti's rotund form was filling half the little office, and the air was full of enchanting and vigorous sounds that Terri felt she ought to understand — the vowels stretching wide, the consonants enjoying their own flamboyance, just like Joe. Again the sensation swept over her of having known them before, perhaps in a previous life.

Eventually Mrs Moretti left them to their own devices. 'Aye, lass,' Joe said, 'Italian enough?'

'Where does your family come from?'

'Sorrento. On the coast. Beautiful, beaooooti-ful.'

'D'you go back a lot?'

'Me? Never been there in my life. But that's what they tell me, and I'll go one day.'

Terri didn't know what she was looking for in his face. Some clue to his real self, hidden behind the denim and leather. Who was he? Who was she, for that matter? What was she doing in the Odeon ice-cream bar, asking some pal of Robbie's she'd never met before how to pronounce Italian? What was happening to her?

He sized her up in a way she hadn't meant him to. 'So, sing me the song, we'll get the words right and then we'll choose my fee.'

Terri couldn't see a way round it. Alarming though the prospect seemed, it might just be a good way to learn more Italian than she'd expected. 'Well,' she said with a grin, 'here we go.' She began to sing.

* * *

Glasgow is full of Italians, Joe confirmed later, ensconced in the back row of the cinema with her, eating yet more ice-cream and watching a James Bond movie. Just like it's full of Irish, Poles and the rest of it. They'd come by sea, up the west coast and into the docks, looking for a land paved with gold, which they'd thought was New York. His grandparents had run away from Italy to escape Mussolini, bringing his parents as young teenagers. When their ship pulled in to Glasgow, they'd been told they were in 'Ame-e-e-rica'. They disembarked, noticing that the place was chillier than they'd expected. By the time they discovered they'd been cheated, the boat had gone. And here everyone called them Tallies, or Eye-Ties.

'I see,' said Terri. 'I never really thought about that.'

'So, you want to learn my language?'

'Yes, please.'

His hand went up the back of her neck and pulled her head towards him. Their ice-cream tubs rolled under the seats in front; it wasn't long before he wanted to roll after them. They slunk out of the cinema the back way; stumbling

157

and giggling in the dark, they found their way to the Moretti family car and rolled inside that instead.

'Your father didn't believe me when I told him I lost my virginity to Don Giovanni in a cinema car park,' Terri tells Julie.

'How old were you?'

'Sixteen. Just.'

'*Did* you learn Italian?'

'A bit.'

Terri went to Mary's class a few days later with the song memorised; even Mrs Moretti approved of her pronunciation. But she'd never be able to hear it again without remembering the stabbing pain under her jeans, or the way she'd scrubbed at the blood stain on her pants in cold water for an hour to hide the truth from Finn.

She'd been horrified by the size of what he wanted to fit inside her; but after a moment of acute pain, she'd experienced a seeping, expanding sense of marvel in parts of her body she'd not known she had. She liked Joe; she knew she didn't love him, because she loved Mary Hoolihan and real love felt different, gold rather than copper. But the closeness of his body against hers was comforting nonetheless; perhaps copper was all right. She wasn't used to feeling close to people; it was a surprise to discover that after the initial terror, she liked it. A strange sensation like urgent thirst told her that she wanted more.

'You sure you haven't done this before?' he'd said to her, looking down.

Terri touched herself and lifted her finger to

show him the blood.

'Am I hurting you?'

'A little.'

'It won't hurt next time. You'll see.'

It was only after their second or third date — when, indeed, it didn't hurt — that she began to panic. She'd forgotten about Kirsty.

She didn't know what to do. As far as she knew, there wasn't much she *could* do. She wouldn't show Joe how scared she was; she didn't want to tell Robbie, because he'd tell Finn and she'd unleash hellfires on Terri that would burn her spirit to charcoal. She wondered whether she could believe in God hard enough for Him to hear her; she certainly couldn't tell anyone real.

Unless perhaps Mary Hoolihan would listen.

After a long night when her heart thudded too hard in her throat to let her sleep, she walked into choir practice with her hopes fastened on to Mary like safety-pins — only to see a strange woman marching to the piano and making an announcement: 'Miss Hoolihan's not well today. My name is Mrs McFarlane and I'll be taking the practice this week.'

Mary was never ill. Why would this happen now? Could betrayal, even unknown betrayal, make a loved one fall ill? Was this *her* doing? Terri staged a coughing fit to justify escape, then fled the church. Her breathing had gone haywire and wouldn't let her sing in any case; if she was missed, she didn't care. Twisting her fingers together, she scanned the horizon for a bus, but as there was no sign of one, she began to run instead, the pavement jarring her feet and sending impacts up her legs. Even running, it was a good twenty minutes to Mary's flat.

She rang the bell. No reply. She pressed harder, again and again. After a long and horrible silence she detected, at last, the shuffle of slippers; and Mary, hair dishevelled, spectacles perched on the end of her nose, peered round the door. She was wearing an old towelling dressing gown. 'Goodness me, Terri! What are you doing here?'

'Miss Hoolihan, are you sick? Can I help?' Terri blurted out.

'Come in out of the cold, *a chroi*. But stay back, I don't want you getting my germs.'

'What's wrong?'

'It's only the flu. I've got a fever and lungs full of phlegm. Not very pleasant.'

'Miss . . .'

'Terri, please, just call me Mary. I'm too sick to think of myself as Miss HoolySchoolmarm. Come along, I'll make you a cup of . . . why, Terri, what is it, now?'

Terri didn't have a hanky so she wiped her nose on her sleeve. 'I missed you so.'

Everything she'd wanted to ask had gone clean out of her head. She still felt as if the world had tipped over and spilled like a dustbin, but now she blamed herself; she didn't want Mary to know how stupid she felt. She kept quiet, snuffling. Mary gave her first a handkerchief, then a cup of herbal tea — anti-bacterial, she said — and finally, a smile. 'So, Terri, will you sing me the Mozart?'

Terri obliged. Mary's fever-dimmed eyes widened as Terri twisted her tongue around the Italian inclinations — 'sa-peh-teh', not 'sa-pay-tay', Joe instructed, and roll the r of 'amor' — that's easy, very Glaswegian.

'D'ye know what it means?' he'd asked.

'No.' She was flat out underneath him at the time

'It means: 'tell me, fair ladies, what is love? What is this burning, yearning, seething desire?''

Terri's body was full of that. But while his hairy arms gathered her up, she found herself imagining, completely by accident, what it would be like to be clasped close and bare-skinned against Mary instead. Joe would go on believing that all her responsiveness was really for him.

Sin, Monsignor thundered in his sermons. When unnatural passions seize you, tear them out by the roots and repent. Terri couldn't. Why should it be unnatural to love someone? She sang to Mary, meaning every word.

Mary's eyes filled. 'Sorry, *a chroi*. You sing so beautifully, and I just don't know how it happens.'

'How what happens?' Terri was confused — did Mary mean Terri's voice or her feelings? Or maybe, even, her own response to them?

'It's a mystery. You were born with such a beautiful voice, and you use it so well, so naturally, and I don't know how it can be.'

'I don't know either,' Terri admitted, disappointed. 'Mary, what does *a chroi* mean?'

161

'It's Gaelic for 'my heart'.' Mary smiled through her fever.

Terri had meant to explain the Italian lessons, the anxiety, the way that it wasn't really Joe that she loved, but she didn't know how to begin; and Mary was so pale and ill that now all she wanted to do was tuck her under a blanket and make her feel better. 'Why don't you lie down and keep warm, and I'll sing something to cheer you up?'

'That's sweet.' Mary looked so surprised that Terri began to wonder how long it was since anyone had done anything to help her, as opposed to vice-versa.

'Not really.' Terri dared to touch her arm for a split second. 'I'll make you some more of your special tea.'

Mary let Terri lead her through the narrow passage towards the bedroom, where the curtains were drawn and a much-ruffled pack of soluble aspirin sat on a battered bedside table. The room smelt of sweat and cough mixture, but it was too cold to open the window. Mary slid under the sheets; Terri drew the blankets up to her chin. She wanted to beg Mary to tell her which herbs she needed to do the job that might need doing; the words wouldn't come out. Besides, Mary was distressed enough already; she couldn't add to that.

Instead, she perched on the side of the bed, wondering what to sing. She didn't know the other arias Mary had played her well enough, and hymns didn't feel right. But there were the folk songs that Finn used to hum at home, years

162

ago, in the days when she still wanted to. Terri began, her heart hurting.

> *Vair me oro van o*
> *Vair me oro van ee*
> *Vair me oru o ho*
> *Sad am I without thee.*
> *Thou'rt the music of my heart,*
> *Harp of joy, oh cruit mo chridh,*
> *Moon of guidance by night,*
> *Strength and light thou'rt to me.*

Mary must have felt the sadness in the 'Eriskay Love Lilt'; she of all people was sad without her love. But she smiled as Terri sang; perhaps because sharing her loneliness helped to dispel it. She joined in, very softly, her voice low and sweet.

> *When I'm lonely, dear white heart,*
> *Black the night or wild the sea,*
> *By love's light my foot finds*
> *The old pathway to thee.*

Terri kept singing, softer and softer, until Mary fell asleep.

★   ★   ★

Two months later, Terri made her first visit to a hospital. She'd had to tell Robbie, now that it was all real; she'd thrown herself on his mercy and, thank heaven, he agreed to cover up for her, telling Finn that she was going

163

with him to visit a friend in Edinburgh for a few days. 'Stupid girl,' he accused Terri. 'You should have been more careful. Why didn't you take the Pill, for Christ's sake?'

Terri, too upset to cry, couldn't explain that she hadn't the guts to go to the doctor and say that she wanted to go onto a contraceptive pill, against which Monsignor constantly ranted in his sermons while she sat in the choir waiting to sing, listening by default.

She wondered how you were supposed to square all this. On one hand, Joe was a lot bigger than her, and insistent; she enjoyed having sex with him, but even if she didn't, it would still be almost impossible to say no. On the other hand, you weren't supposed to do anything to stop yourself getting pregnant, according to Monsignor. And on the third — if you could have a third hand — having an abortion meant murdering your baby. What in heaven's name were you supposed to do?

'Church?' Robbie half shouted. 'Nobody believes that crap any more except our mother. You have to look after yourself, Terri, because nobody else will. You want God? God helps those who help themselves.'

* * *

'Is that why you only had me?' Julie asks. 'Did the abortion damage something — did it make it, like, difficult to have kids when you wanted them?'

'Well, I *do* have you.' Terri opens one eye in a

sly wink. 'And thank goodness for that. By the way, I wasn't really lesbian or bisexual, I was just sort of in love with my music teacher. It took me a while to work out that there was a difference.'

'I see.' Julie isn't sure she does.

'We should go in. You mustn't catch cold. Come inside and sing me something.'

Julie, obedient, pulls on her blue cardigan, though it's Terri, in the cooling water, who's more likely to need the warmth. 'Dad says I should be thinking about getting into choirs and stuff when I go to Cambridge.'

Terri hauls herself out of the pool in one smooth motion. 'Well,' she says, 'we'll make sure you knock the buggers flat.'

*   *   *

Terri is hungry and thirsty after her swim, so they indulge in extra tea and cake before going to the piano in the drawing room.

'Let's have the Schumann,' suggests Terri. Julie's trying to perfect 'Der Nussbaum'. Her voice is precise, pure and cool.

Terri stops her after the first stanza. 'Try and mean it,' she says. 'It comes across, you see. There's nowhere to hide when you sing. You have to become your character, even in a song that's just a few minutes long.'

It's difficult to mean every word of a song that's so far removed from your own experience. The girl in the poem is innocent. She won't know that there's more to marriage than the baking of bread and the holding of hands; she probably thinks you find babies gurgling under gooseberry bushes. This little nineteenth-century maiden will never dare undress in front of her husband, no matter what the tree tells her.

Terri agrees, when Julie explains her problem. 'You need to reach into yourself, find something you identify with that you can give to this girl, and, through her, to the audience. It's all about giving.'

'I don't really want an audience. I just want to sing it right, for its own sake.'

'And then? Will you want an audience?' Her mother's blue-green eyes are astute. 'Julie,' she says, 'do you think you might want to be a singer?'

'Like you?'

'Not like me. Like yourself.'

'I'm not good enough.'

'You could be. You've got a super voice. It's a question of what you want to do with it. A question of finding it, and its direction.'

'I don't *know*, Mum.'

'Can you imagine life without singing?'

'I don't have to decide yet, do I?' Julie stalls, squirming.

'Of course not, angel.' Terri seems to relax a little. 'You're young — you've got bags of time. Let's have a bite of supper.' For Terri, Julie's noticed, every meal at home is an event to cherish.

In thirty-two years' time, Julie muses, chopping onions, she'll be the age her mother is now. Maybe she does have a voice; maybe it's good enough to develop professionally. But would that mean never being at home, never seeing your partner or husband, never spending enough time with your child or children? Julie doesn't want to replicate that situation in her hypothetical family-to-be with Alistair. What price the Diva Drag if it takes you away from the people you love?

Fortunately, she doesn't have to make up her mind. Not yet.

8

'Do you think it's possible to know your mother too well?'

It's mid-October and Julie is in the Buttery near the music faculty, drinking coffee with her Russian next-door neighbour from college, Irina Ovchinikova.

'How do you mean?' Irina has lived in the UK just long enough to speak fluent English without losing her excessively charming accent. She has huge blue eyes, which she elongates with ultramarine liner on the upper lids. Beside her, Julie feels like a duck paddling desperately in the wake of a swan. Still, two weeks into term, Irina has decided that they are inseparable, and they finish every evening with a cup of tea together.

'Well . . . does your mother . . . ' Julie stops. Not many mothers are as open-minded as hers, let alone as promiscuous. 'Does she treat you as if you're her friend, rather than bossing you about?'

'It's my dad who bosses,' Irina laughs. 'Anyway, you know, they are divorced five years and I live with my dad — my mum is in Russia. He's very protective. If I bring a boy home, he must leave by eleven thirty and never be in my room.'

'Home', it emerges, is plump in the middle of a Highgate enclave not far from Kenwood House. Sergei Ovchinikov has something to do with diamonds. Julie hasn't worked out what, but it involves plentiful journeys by private jet.

The more Julie talks to her fellow students, the more confused she feels. Her schoolfriends had been used to Terri, the relaxed, chaotic house, the long absences, the laid-back attitude that let Julie sleep over with Alistair, or vice-versa, whenever they liked. Everyone accepted their different circumstances; it wasn't a problem unless you made it into one.

Here it's different. In the college bar, Julie explains her absentee boyfriend. 'Is he at Sandhurst?' is the most common response. 'Does he know Prince Harry?' Julie mumbles evasive words about the training, the forthcoming passing-out parade ('Because you faint when you see him?' quipped smart-alec Raff) and her anxiety about boots, bullying, helicopters and rations.

'What's his rank?' asked Chris the organ scholar, when Julie went into the chapel to audition for the college choir.

'Private.'

'Oh. And where's he going to go?'

'I don't know yet.'

'Does he have any say in it?'

'No,' said Julie, who now knows this is true, contrary to her father's platitudes. 'He'll have to go wherever they send him.'

'I see . . . Well . . . come over to the piano and we'll start. What have you brought?'

'Bach.' Julie gave him the music. The sun caught in the stained-glass window and splashed coloured light across the page. In the top right-hand corner, splodged with passing violet, the name 'Teresa Ivory' was inscribed. 'My mum,' Julie explained, watching astonishment cross his specs. It's hard to be taken on her own terms when her mother's name is scrawled on everything.

'Cool,' said Chris. 'So, you sing too . . . '

Julie sang. The next day Chris left her a note saying 'Congrats, old girl, you're in.' She wonders whether she might still have been 'in' even if she'd sung badly; the expectation of what Terri Ivory's daughter should be able to do often outweighs the reality of plain Julie Mason.

'I would like to hear you sing.' Irina sips her cappuccino. 'You sing solo?'

'I have lessons. I go to my mum's friend who teaches her.'

'Your mum has a teacher?' Irina looks amazed.

'Most singers do. It helps keep them in shape. Mum usually goes for a sing at Anita's whenever she's home, and there's also a coach she likes who helps her learn new roles. Trouble is, now Mum's taking a sabbatical, she wants to hear what I'm doing.' Terri had left Julie at college on the first day with strict instructions to keep stumm about her operation, on pain of nose in sling.

'This is *trouble*?'

'Well, pressure. Hardly trouble, compared to yours.' Irina was kidnapped in Russia when she was eleven. 'I don't know how you stand walking down the street after what happened to you.'

'Some things upset me,' Irina admits. She can't bear confined spaces — Tube trains, windowless rooms, anything dark or locked. She sleeps with a lamp on. Even theatres are problematic. She'd been grabbed from behind on her way home from school in the finest part of St Petersburg and bundled into a van with a blanket over her head; her hands and feet were tied, her mouth was taped and she spent two terrified hours trussed up like a turkey, being driven to a hide-out in the distant suburbs. There they held her for three days in a lightless basement before her father paid the ransom.

'Who were they? Were they caught?'

'Crooks.' Irina shakes her head. 'They are dead.'

Julie hesitates, imagining: a ransom paid, a daughter returned, a hitman hired, shots. If that's true, if Irina's father had organised the murder of her kidnappers, she's not sure she wants to know. A Lithuanian bodyguard named Vaslav, who's six foot four and considerably more than 'army fit', escorts Irina between college and faculty and is constantly on hand in case Irina should need him, and often when she doesn't. Desperate for freedom, she'd refused to live in the flat that her father wanted to buy her, which would have accommodated Vaslav as well. She preferred to be in college with everyone else. Tolerantly — or for money, Julie isn't sure which — Vaslav has been awarded a college room too. Irina likes to know he's there at the touch of a button on a high-tech device that she calls her 'talkie-walkie'.

'What did they . . . ' Julie stews with questions. Were the kidnappers kind or violent? Was she raped? She doesn't know how to ask.

'They gave me food and let me watch TV.' Irina reads her mind. 'It wasn't so exciting. Sorry to disappoint you!'

Julie pats her new friend's arm and Irina's wide smile blossoms behind her cup. For all the luxury that haunts her every step, Irina strikes Julie as slightly sad and lonely.

★ ★ ★

The girls cycle back to college along the Backs. Leaves spiral down from the lime trees over the towpath and there's a wintry nip to the air. Julie's bag of books, files and notes weighs down her bike basket. She relishes the sight of the ornate college buildings beyond the river. She's here because her father expects it, but with such history underpinning the view, she can't help feeling sneakily proud. Isaac Newton once walked this route; Samuel Taylor Coleridge; Rupert Brooke. Scientists, poets, philosophers and some of her mother's least favourite conductors have all passed this way, thinking the same simple thoughts: 'God, it's beautiful.'

'And the spies,' Irina reminds her.

'The boys who defected to Russia. What do you think of that?'

'They were crazy. They support that system! Jeeeez.'

'You didn't grow up under communism, did you?' Julie pedals hard; Irina's bike possesses more gears than her own.

'I was born in year the Berlin Wall came down.

172

An interesting time to enter the world. So, no, things changed and I do not experience the old Russia. But I think maybe new Russia is more dangerous . . . My father cannot go back, you know.'

'Would he be arrested?'

'More probably murdered.'

'But what did he *do*?'

'Nothing. He is a good man. But he made money, and some people don't like this.'

'So you've never been back to your own country?'

'I don't think it is my country now.' Irina is studying Russian, with a focus on nineteenth-century literature. 'It was a great culture,' she explains. 'It really was. Just not today, because of the greed, and because if someone is good at something, they leave.'

Round a few corners, they reach their college, St Barnabas — less grand and famous than King's and Trinity, but no less beautiful, in an overshadowed kind of way. A team of gardeners takes pride in making the grounds the best kempt in the university. On the pond a colony of ornamental ducks live and breed, much to the delight and frustration of the college cat.

Irina and Julie's rooms are twin bedsits in a modern block at the back of college, constructed well out of sight of the tourist-trapping courts. They share a shower room and kitchenette with two other girls. Irina has adorned her pad with sophisticated pale throws and cushions; a brand-new iMac with an integrated sound system has pride of place on the desk. Julie hasn't brought much except a kettle, some volumes of songs and a supply of soup sachets. 'Like we don't have shops here.' Irina teases.

They prefer talking to working; and now it's afternoon dip, the worst time to try to achieve anything academic. They decide on a last cup of tea in Julie's room before parting company. On Julie's desk sits Teo's new book, which had arrived from Paris that morning. Irina picks it up and opens it at the title page, where Teo has written:

> '*For my dearest Julie, with all the*
> *love of a crazy writer. Teo*'

Irina, with her startling background, is not particularly easy to impress, but she seems genuinely surprised. 'You know *Teo Popović?*'

Julie fills the kettle at her basin. 'He's . . . a friend of my mum's. They're kind of involved.'

'They say that that book could win every literary prize in the world.' Irina strokes the cover reverentially with one finger. The blurb describes the novel as 'the story of four ordinary families whose lives are torn apart by the Bosnian war'. 'What's he writing next?'

'Actually, he was trying to write something for my mum, but he tore it up without showing it to her. She was livid. She's the most incredible intellectual snob! She only has to hear the word 'writer' or 'artist' or 'Turgenev' and she starts slavering at the chops.'

Irina looks even more impressed. 'My father has friends in the opera world and he knows this very successful girl, Varya Petrovna, you know she is all over everything, modelling and so on. She models for my father's firm.'

'Really? Taps?'

'What?' Irina is bemused.

'Mum calls her Taps. I think it's something to do with her shoes.'

'They're friends?'

'Heavens, no. Mum can't stand her. She doesn't think she's, like, a 'serious artist'.'

'Your mum is right! She's sort of thirty-five going on sixteen. She loves bling, glamour, money and, OK, she sings well, but I don't think she ever read a book except for trash.'

'My mum grew up in Glasgow. She never had much chance at school, and she's always, like, 'you have to get a good education because I never had one'.'

'So why didn't she send you to a private school?'

'My dad doesn't believe in private education.'

'What does he do?'

'He's a maths professor. I know, it doesn't make any sense.'

'No, it makes perfect sense when you understand. My dad has rather Russian perspective. He says the English middle classes hate the English middle classes, so they will do anything not to look middle class, but they get everything they really want through the back entrance, while pretending the opposite.'

Trying to work this out, Julie hands Irina a mug of tea — Russian style, black, not too strong, with sugar; looking at her new friend's catlike eyes, she wonders how it can be that Irina seems infinitely older and wiser than she is, even if she is indeed sad and lonely.

Then the cat-eyes catch light like the wick of a candle. 'Julie, I have idea! You want to go shopping Saturday?'

'That'd be fun. I've not had much chance to look round the shops.'

'Not here. We go to Paris!'

'*What?*'

'We take the train to King's Cross, then train to Gare du Nord, we shop, we have lunch, we shop more, we come back. Easy! I pay, no problem. We'll go business class.'

'But I can't — '

'Yes, you can. Leave it to me.'

★ ★ ★

When Irina's gone, Julie shakes herself back in the general direction of earth. She arranges her lecture notes on the left of her desk; three reference books centre back; and a packet of chocolate fingers on the right. In the middle is her blank pad of paper. She has to write two thousand words about English sixteenth-century madrigals.

Her mind doesn't want to focus on the aural depiction of poetry in these settings. Isn't it obvious that if a stanza says night is falling, its music will descend and become quieter? This is noteworthy? She doodles on her pad, then scribbles, 'Word-painting: wow.'

Alistair's latest missive from Yorkshire lies

under her pillow. With a company of other newly trained combat infantrymen, including his closest friends from Catterick, he will be leaving a few weeks before Christmas for a very distant destination, the name of which made Julie howl aloud. He's worried about Sue, who's smoking and drinking too much in his absence; he's afraid that she could be forced out of her job because she's not young any more — the cleaning industry is full of East-European girls in their twenties who do crazy hours and work faster. 'Please call her sometimes,' he requests. He worries a lot more about her than about himself.

Julie chews the end of her pen, which is already riddled with tooth marks. How can she live in this rarified, wide-skied student community, writing essays on Orlando Gibbons and singing in historic chapels while Alistair will be flying east to fight fanatical insurgents? She pictures him asleep in the barracks. She'd barely recognised him last time she'd visited: he seemed stronger, cooler, more distant, strictured into conformity with the other lads from haircut to bootlaces. He's learning discipline, and he likes it. If he's proud of himself, then she must try to be proud of him. She munches a biscuit, staring across the courtyard, pen motionless.

The anti-war march earlier in the term had become difficult when the others she didn't already know in their college group learned where her boyfriend was. Their attitude first surprised her, then shocked her. She'd tried hard to explain, through the shouts and chanting and clapping of hands and waving of banners, that where he was to be deployed wasn't his choice and that this particular war had started when he was only twelve. She had to argue, yelling through the din, that because Alistair was in the army, she was the most anti-war of them all because she was the most worried; that just because he had to serve in it, it didn't mean he thought that joining it had been a good decision on the government's part; that even if he did think so, which he didn't, the fact that she was his girlfriend didn't mean that she'd automatically agree; and the bottom line was that he could be killed. Yet they seemed determined to equate having a boyfriend in the army with approving of participation in the war, no matter how stupid that conclusion sounded.

Julie left early. 'I thought students here were meant to be intelligent,' she told Terri by phone.

'Darling, put their noses in a sling! Defend yourself!'

'I did try.' The incident had done nothing for Julie's confidence.

Essay unfinished, Julie lets Irina drag her to a party in a room at the top of the college's oldest court, given by a third-year called Charlie who'd gone to Elthingbourne, is studying Russian and chases Irina with flowers, opera tickets and, of all things, golf. Irina doesn't fancy him, but dresses up anyway in a black silk dress with plunging crossover neckline and sparkling jewellery. Julie goes in jeans and her blue cardigan.

'*Solnushka!*' Charlie hugs Irina, shouting the Russian pet name through the thumping music. 'You look scrumptious!'

178

'Thank you! You know Julie, my next-door neighbour.'

'Great to see you, Jul.' Charlie looks her approvingly up and down.

'Julie's mum is Teresa Ivory, the opera singer,' Irina tells him, leaning forward to display cleavage and necklace.

'Oh, yeah? Do you sing too, then?'

'A little,' says Julie.

'Great necklace,' someone compliments Irina. 'Topshop?'

'This was my present from my father for eighteenth birthday.' Not everyone knows, yet, what that means.

'They're real?' Julie asks.

'Of course.'

'But you wear them here? To a party?'

'Why not? I have beautiful things, I should show them off. Besides, Vaslav is outside with talkie-walkie. *Da, Carlyusha — champagnski, spassiba*!'

After two rapidly-downed glasses of champagne, Julie slips out onto the stairs, away from the heat, crush and noise. Safely on the landing, she presses Alistair's speed-dial number on her mobile. As usual, his phone is off. It's ten thirty; he's probably asleep after a tough day's training. The wooden banisters smell of waxy polish and a hint of dust; smoke from cigarettes, and something sweeter, drifts out under Charlie's door. Julie sits on the top step and curls her head down to her knees. She knows thousands of kids would give their eye teeth to be in her shoes — as Bernard reminds her constantly — but she still can't work out what the hell she's doing here.

There's no point disturbing Irina, who's networking for all she's worth, which is lots, among the other Russian students and former public school boys who've concertinaed themselves into Charlie's room. Irina would say Julie should be in there too, making the most of herself instead of the least — preferably wearing something other than the blue cardy she's had since she was fourteen, which contains at least two moth-holes. She should be joining in, fielding questions about whether she wanted to become a singer like her mum. And she should be saying that she did. Never mind if it wasn't true.

Here, masks reign supreme. You must show nobody your true self. If you let anyone know how vulnerable you feel, how out of your depth, how chilly, miserable and intimidated, it's not a plea for friendship, but an invitation for them to trample on you. Terms are short and sharp; you race against the calendar to earn your grades, make your contacts, meet rich boys, bump up your CV with extracurricular activities and show your strength by drinking your companions under the table. And this is what her father has been pushing her towards for the past eighteen years? Julie already suspects that if she learns anything here, it probably won't be thanks to her studies. She picks herself up and starts off down the stairs.

A clatter at the top and Charlie calls after her, 'Julie, you're not leaving us?'

'I'm knackered.' Julie forces a smile. 'I need an early night.'

'It's great to see you. Come for a drink with me and Rini and the others soon?'

'Cool.' Julie takes another step down.

'You know, I've seen your mother sing loads of times.' Charlie's trying to slow her exit. 'It's so cool that you sing too.'

'Only sort of.'

'Funny, you don't look a bit like her. D'you take after your father?'

'Not really,' says Julie, without thinking about it. 'See you soon.'

Irina appears beside Charlie and leans on the banisters. 'See you in morning, darling!'

'See you in morning,' Julie echoes, something warm brushing the inside of her ribs.

★　★　★

Back in her room, she can't sleep. With the whirl of brain-chatter amplified by the champagne, it takes her a while to work out what's wrong. Charlie's words keep coming back to her.

He's right. She doesn't look much like her mother. And nothing like her father, not even in the days when he had more hair.

She rolls off her bed and peers at her face in the mirror. It's not her best moment — half past midnight, eyes red and shadowed, frown-lines picking at her forehead. Her face is the same shape as her mother's, with round eyes and similarly tilted nose. It's her colouring that's different. Both her parents have light eyes. How

come her irises are a deep chocolate brown,
verging on black?

★ ★ ★

Back in the days of the siege when everyone else
was trying to get out of Sarajevo, Teo was trying
to get in. He'd never imagined he had such an
instinct for survival. Part of him marvelled at it
as the days went by. Amid the ear-blasting shots
and shells, the ground shivering as the great
Habsburg mansions plunged to earth, he had
one cousin left alive and all he could do was
follow the sensation in his skull that carried him
towards that cousin, even when it meant hiding
in the woods for three days, finding berries and
mushrooms to eat, throwing himself flat on the
ground whenever he heard a shot or even a
footstep, until Mostar was far behind and he saw
ahead of him the grim humps that were Sarajevo
under bombardment.

Unharmed, miraculously so given the sniper
fire all around, he found his cousin Sonja and
her Swedish husband Stefan haggard, skeletal
and confined to the flat. They hesitated to come
to the door, but finally embraced him for long
and silent minutes. Teo's solitary presence told
them all they needed to know. He could see the
compassion in Sonja's sunken eyes, as well as the
silent, unmentionable relief that someone had
had it worse than she had.

They were living on false coffee made from
ground wheat; a handful of potatoes; and the
occasional tin of fish. Teo wasn't sure where

these came from, but the Western names on the labels suggested an humanitarian air drop — a sporadic event and one that the besiegers were doing their best to obstruct, blockading outside help by shelling the airport. Sarajevo's inhabitants risked their lives occasionally to reach the relief office for food supplies or to fetch drinking water, standing in queues at which snipers loved to take pot-shots from the hills.

There was no electricity and the winter temperatures were plummeting. A stench of something rotting and animal saturated the air. Teo thanked heaven that it was cold, because summer heat would make the decay worse. At night they wrapped themselves in blankets and rationed their light. Stefan improvised a candle by pouring car oil into an empty fish tin and adding a string wick. They found ways to pass the time. Stefan, who had been the manager of an upmarket restaurant that was now a bombed-out wreck, tried to tell stories about Sweden; Sonja occasionally tried to keep their spirits up by trimming the men's hair and fast-growing beards.

Teo felt like a sleepwalker, existing in a state of half-life, as if someone had stabbed him but he'd not been able to die of the wound. The siege resembled an externalisation of his inner self. The air resisted him like water: each step took innumerable kilojoules of energy, each moment of waking meant longing for sleep. Hunger left him debilitated, but he grew accustomed to it; after Mostar, the inside of his mind was a worse place than that of his stomach, or the flat, or the city itself.

Some quiet nights he couldn't sleep. He'd lie watching the moon, hearing his cousins' soft breathing — perhaps they too were only pretending to sleep — and listening to the scuffling of rats, the few creatures who benefited from the siege. Yet oddly he often slept through the bombardments, as did Stefan and Sonja. With the noise of shelling as loud as a deathly orchestra in the room, it was as if their bodies decided to take time out and transported their consciousness somewhere a little pleasanter, requesting to be woken, please, when it was all over.

Once he surfaced to find the walls of the room drizzled with holes that hadn't been there before and the ground thick with debris, yet he hadn't stirred a muscle from his dreams. On the floor lay a lump, a spiked oval that for one dopey second he identified as a model of a hedgehog. It was only when he'd rubbed the sleep out of his eyes that he realised it was an unexploded hand grenade.

'Fuck!' Stefan and Sonja stood beside him, staring. 'If it didn't explode on the way in, it's not likely to now,' Stefan pointed out. 'Let's throw it.'

'You can't do that!' Sonja protested. 'Supposing it goes off?'

'Well, it can't stay here.' Stefan advanced, scooped up the grenade in his bare hand and marched towards the front door with it.

'*Stefan!*' Sonja shrieked. She covered her eyes and Teo hugged her until they heard Stefan's

184

footsteps on the stairs as he returned, his Swedish equanimity intact, without the grenade. They waited for an explosion in the distance. For once, there was silence. If the blasted thing had worked, they'd all be dead. Teo imagined someone in a factory telling a joke to a colleague and maybe taking his or her eye off the work for a moment, just long enough to let through a faulty grenade or two. He hoped there were more where it came from.

Someone had decreed Sarajevo the fourteenth worst place on earth. Teo amused himself by imagining the thirteenth, never mind the twelfth. Besides, nobody had told the rats. They thought it was Christmas. As indeed it was.

★　★　★

Landing in Sarajevo for the first time since the end of it all, Teo is in an aisle seat beside a young British couple who've spent the flight perusing the *Rough Guide to the Balkans* over each other's shoulders. While the plane sails down, they exclaim in wonder over the view. Green hills, little pointy-roofed chalets, a dusting of early snow on the pines.

'It looks like Switzerland,' cries the girl.

'With a little Soviet architecture.' Her long-haired boyfriend points at the brown glass and concrete supermarket nearby. Teo, his innards twisting into knots that he fears might confine him to the airport loos for hours, wonders whether he's mad to come back. He stands aside to let the young couple leave the plane first. He waits until everyone else is off as well before he pulls his case down from the overhead locker and walks out into the chilly, clear air of his homeland.

Life continues in Sarajevo. The tourists are coming back. Part of the place has been rebuilt; part hasn't. Just like him. And perhaps it still possesses the charm and charisma that had made Stefan stay after he initially arrived by mistake. He'd been interrailing with friends and got extremely drunk on a train, which then stopped for several hours in the middle of the most beautiful field he'd ever seen. Needing a pee and desperate for some air, Stefan got off. When he turned round again, buttoning his flies, the train had gone. Since all his worldly goods were swanning away towards Dubrovnik, he'd had little choice but to hitchhike to the nearest town, which happened to be Sarajevo, and present himself at the first restaurant he found to plead for an overnight stay in return for washing up. He loved it so much that he never left.

Stefan and Sonja are standing beyond customs control, waving; a second later Teo is enfolding them by turns in his best bear-hug. Sonja has succumbed happily to middle-aged spread, and Stefan sports a shirt with a green crocodile logo. They've made a success at life. Their sons are both working in IT in Stockholm; Stefan has opened another restaurant; Sonja has resumed work as a hairdresser and has her own salon. Bosnia, with a little money trickling its way and the infrastructure slowly being recreated, has been forgotten while the world focuses on new concerns, further east.

'But nothing works,' Stefan remarks, leading the way to the car. The two parts of the country, Bosnia-Herzegovina and the Republika Srpska, he tells Teo, won't even share a police force; without a unified administration, progress is utterly impossible, even while Serbia and Croatia, the countries that destroyed Bosnia between them, are heading for EU membership. The landmines, too, are still there and occasionally, Sonja says, they take their toll on children who don't heed their parents' warning not to play in the velvety green fields.

The apartment has been repaired inside. There's fresh paint. A sheet of glass has replaced the gaping hole that had let the faulty grenade in. Water pours from the taps when you turn the handles. Evening brings lamplight, television, central heating, then silence while the inhabitants sleep, vermin-free, as peacefully as they can. In the Austrian part of town, a Christmas market, Stefan says, is in preparation.

On the first morning, Teo slips out of the flat at sunrise to head for the town centre. Stefan and Sonja's row of concrete apartment blocks bears heavy scars from the shelling. He hasn't seen it since the siege; he still feels compelled to glance back over his shoulder while walking down this street.

Wandering into Sarajevo, Teo gazes at the bullet holes in the walls, brick or marble or concrete. Here and there, the bare bones of mansions stand in ruins. He eats spinach burek in the Turkish area, then a Danish pastry with

Julius Meindl coffee on the other side. This chameleon of a city changes its identity across just one road.

'People are different, though,' Sonja had remarked, on the way home from the airport. 'The trust has gone. Now the siege is inside us.'

In the days when Teo had his first teaching job in Mostar, he'd once held forth to a cluster of friends in a café about how to teach fourteen-year-olds *Romeo and Juliet* without the whole class dissolving into hormonal meltdown. In their group, some were Catholic, others Orthodox and more Muslim; some were married to each other. Nobody had given it a second thought. If you want something universal, Teo thinks, try hormones.

He follows the curve of rickety pavements that he knows as well as his own feet. The stones are slimy with melted snow and the wind snaps at his ears round the street corners. There is no metallic smell of blood, no encroachment of earth and death in the nostrils — yet without it, the place, for all its prettiness, feels oddly sterile. Everything has been wiped away, superficially normalised, sent, Teo thinks, into denial. He walks through the Old Town amid the mosques, constantly aware of the hills rising beyond the street ends, the steep slopes thick with white and terracotta houses. The hills hold an intensity that makes them mythic; the same intensity that drew Stefan to them all those years ago and wouldn't let him leave.

Teo sees his goal ahead: the plain grey stone and red roof of the Stara Pravoslavna Crkva Old

Orthodox Church. Inside its complex, he goes up to the heavy door and through it. He makes chilly progress under the rounded arches towards an array of candles. Familiar icons — golden, brown and blue, non-feeling images — plaster the screen under the dangling incense burners. There's calm here, an unpretentious simplicity he's always loved more than the grandeur of the Orthodox Cathedral; yet this place too has been sanitised. The bell tower is as shot to pieces as the rest of town; the Serbs, attacking Sarajevo, had nearly blasted apart their own church.

Teo takes a taper and begins to light candles. One each. His wife; his son; his daughter. His mother and father. His in-laws, their children and grandchildren. His sister. The candles cast golden haze around him, across the stone and the icons, intensifying with each new flame.

Afterwards he kneels down on the flagstones in the centre of the empty space. He stays there for a long time.

9

On Saturday, Irina taps on Julie's door at half past six. 'It's time, darling! Are you ready?'

The girls cycle to the station and chain their bicycles to a railing while the dawn is still pink in the east. They've brought backpacks with ample space for prospective purchases. Julie gazes out of the train window at the brightening day: an unwarranted patina of glamour surrounds the journey to London until she nods off, head against the glass.

From King's Cross they make their way through subterranean tunnels to St Pancras International, where the station's Gothic arches, crowning a shining gallery of new shops, pose above the girls as if designed solely for their benefit. They wake themselves up with extra-strong coffee; then Irina, waving a blue ticket folder, strides in her high-heeled boots past the queues of tourists towards Business Premier check-in.

'Shall we look up Teo?' Julie suggests.

Irina nods, hard. 'I'd love to meet him. Call him once we're on the train?'

Perhaps it's Irina's leggy confidence, something about the blue eyeliner or the wide-slanting cheekbones, but people jump to her aid the moment she even thinks of asking a question. On the platform, she pauses, examining their tickets for the carriage number. Instantly two officials materialise at her elbow, ready to assist; moments later, Irina and Julie are being personally escorted to their seats in the pink-lamped Business section. 'Would you like some champagne with your breakfast, ladies?' the steward asks with a bow.

Soon, as the Eurostar accelerates through the tunnel under East London that will take them to the coast in forty minutes flat, the girls are giggling over champagne, coffee and pots of yogurt with muesli. Unused to alcohol in the morning, Julie quickly feels woozy; she's about to succumb to it and fall asleep when she sees that Irina is bending forward, head in her hands.

'What's wrong?'

'Channel Tunnel. I'm no good in tunnels.'

'So why on earth do you want to go to Paris through one?'

'End justifies means.' Irina muffles her voice in her knees.

Julie reaches out a hand, which Irina — no longer the self-assured Russian princess — clasps hard for twenty minutes until daylight floods in once more and they glimpse a booze hyper-market designed for British daytrippers.

'*Harasho*. That's better.' Irina relaxes. 'So, you want to phone Teo?'

Julie hesitates. She hasn't told Irina her new suspicion. Irina had been scathing enough about her other anxieties — the tale of the party at which Julie had watched over the pool for hours in case someone fell in had caused humiliating hilarity. Having someone laugh first at her, then with her, had done Julie some good. But this is

191

too personal to laugh about.

Julie presses in Teo's number, trying to hide her nervousness.

'Darling,' says his distant voice, 'I am in Sarajevo.'

'*Sarajevo?*'

'I have to come back to my home country sometime. So, my book is released here and I come back now. I tell you about it soon, no?'

'Er, yes.'

'But you are in Paris for one day? So come again. Come for longer. We'll go have fun.'

A lump rises to Julie's throat as Teo rings off. Was that the voice of her real father?

★ ★ ★

Arriving in Paris, Julie and Terri would normally take the RER to the Luxembourg station for Teo's flat in the Left Bank. Instead, Irina ferrets through the station crowds towards the entrance, rounds several corners and brings them to a taxi rank.

'Isn't the métro faster?' Julie suggests.

'Vaslav tells me always not to use public transport. We leave him and talkie-walkie at home, so we must be careful!' Climbing into a taxi while an extremely willing driver holds the door open for her, Irina crosses one silky leg over the other and asks in perfect French to go to the rue de Rivoli; she dumps her bag beside her as if to hasten its demise. 'What you want to buy, Julie? I want new bag, winter coat, dress for my father's Christmas party.'

'Dunno.' Julie stares at the traffic; she half expects the little terrier-like cars to start clambering over one another's backs. 'Maybe a bag.'

'Listen, you must come to our party. My father will adore you. And your mother too.' Irina slips an arm through Julie's and squeezes. 'My father would love to meet her. Perhaps she'd sing? I don't know whether is right thing, to ask her to sing at party. Varya loves to sing at parties.'

'If it was a question of outdoing Taps, Mum'd be at it like a shot! But . . . ' Julie isn't sure how her mother's vocal state is progressing, other than that she's been going for various therapies on a regular basis. 'It depends on how her back is,' she stalls.

On the rue de Rivoli, the taxi pulls up and with November chill on their cheeks the girls pile out into the throng, lapping up the sight of the Tuileries over the road and the distant Eiffel Tower rising into clouds that obscure its tip.

'Phallic,' remarks Irina.

'Yeah?' To Julie, this is obvious.

'You know, Julie,' Irina confides, tucking Julie's arm through hers, 'I am virgin!'

'Really?'

'You're surprised?'

'You seem so — I mean, I've been with Alistair for ages but . . . you seem so much more *worldly* than I am.'

'But my father doesn't let me go near boys. Now I'm at college, he can't stop me. So I must find right boy to show me what to do.'

'I'm sure Charlie or Raff would love to help you out.'

'No, I find special one first, someone I will love. Then I learn better. Anyway, I think Raff is really gay.'

'Why?' That hadn't occurred to Julie.

'Look at his socks. Straight boys don't wear socks like that.' Irina pulls up short outside a designer store and casts an expert eye over some suede heels in electric blue. 'Is Alistair home for Christmas?'

'No way.' Julie, worried about pickpockets, clutches her bag closer. 'He's only going next week. I think it'll be six months before he has any leave.'

'Come on, let's try those on . . . But you wait for him?'

'Of course I'll wait for him!'

Inside, Julie, nursing distress over the thought of Alistair's destination, watches Irina don the blue shoes and twirl before a mirror, pale coat and golden hair swinging as she spins.

'*Oui, je les prends.*' She pulls out a platinum credit card that's linked to her father's account and the shop assistant, glancing at the name, looks startled, then rattles off something about how nice it is to have Irina in the shop.

'Nothing for you, Julie?' Irina asks.

Julie shakes her head. She'd seen the price on the till. This is the kind of shop that doesn't put prices in the window. If you have to look at them, you needn't bother going in.

'I buy for you. Is no problem.'

'No, Rini! It's not right.'

'Why not? It makes no difference to my father whether is for me or my friend. I invite you to our party, so you must have lovely clothes, and it gives me pleasure to make you feel good. Julie, you can make so much more of yourself, you know?'

Julie doesn't tell Irina that many of her evenings out, until now, have been at McDonald's or the pub with Sue and Alistair or her schoolfriends, and she doesn't need blue high heels there or anywhere else. 'Rini, what *is* your father's business?'

'I show you.' Irina slings her carrier bag over her shoulder. 'We go round this corner . . . and now look . . . Voilà!'

Beneath five storeys of carved stone and wrought-iron balconies crawling with Art Nouveau tentacles, the store gleams from a portico of greenish marble; its windows reveal gems so large and brilliant that Julie can't believe they're not fakes. OVCHINIKOV, says the logo.

Naïvely, Julie had never associated Irina's surname, Ovchinikova, with the diamond brand that advertises in opera programmes via the Petrovna pout. She's briefly speechless.

'I show you what happens when we go in.' Irina swings open the door. Julie falters, aware that her boots are scuffed, her hair's turning frizzy in the damp air and her coat comes from a charity shop in Crystal Palace.

Strolling up to the desk, Irina utters her name with perfect smile and outstretched hand. The shop is promptly struck by lightning. A manager bounds to attention, chairs are brought, coffee or sparkling wine offered and a box of chocolates virtually jumps on to the desk.

'*Je voudrais voir quelque chose pour mon amie*,' Irina announces.

'No!' Julie protests. 'Rini, I can't! You can't!'

'Silly, of course I can. Come on, take off your coat. You are wearing something under that jumper?'

Julie is — a once-white vest with a lace trim. Embarrassed, feeling scrawny and plain, she hauls her jersey over her head. Irina and the manager, who introduces herself as Madame Pilonger, assess her skin tone and the colour of her eyes and hair.

'Sapphires,' suggests Madame Pilonger.

'Amethysts?' Julie squeaks.

'We don't really do semi-precious stones,' Madame Pilonger explains.

'Diamonds.' Irina is adamant.

Madame Pilonger smiles assent. 'May I suggest, Mademoiselle, for your first diamonds, something simple and classic?'

Julie watches, horrified, as the besuited manager takes a locked velvet box from a deep drawer and applies a tiny golden key before lifting out its inhabitant. Something cold and hard settles on her collar bones; Irina's fingertips brush her skin as she fastens the clasp. Half afraid to look, Julie turns to the mirror.

Her breath briefly deserts her: this single string of stones has transformed her in a split second from scruffy student to glamour puss. How these look different from her mother's rhinestones is anyone's guess. But, ineffably and undoubtedly, they do.

'Perfect!' Irina declares. 'We take this one.'

'Rini, I can't! I'd never dare wear it. And we can't carry it through Paris all day.'

'We don't need to. Madame Pilonger, would it be possible to have this sent to us in Cambridge? By courier, please?' Irina hands over her credit card. Julie stares at the carpet, flushing carmine with embarrassment. Yet Madame Pilonger, to her surprise, seems touched by her diffidence; when they get up to go, she gives Julie a kiss and remarks: 'Your first diamonds, *chérie*, but certainly not your last.'

Irina leads the way out. 'One day we go together to St Petersburg and I show you the Hermitage.' Behind them, the necklace is being wrapped in bubble-plastic, ready for dispatch. 'Some of the pillars are malachite, the paintings are the finest by Matisse and Gauguin . . . if you think we live well, you should see how the Tsars lived.'

'But they were royalty.'

'Today there is no royalty, except your British ones which I don't count. Money is royalty now. Therefore, by logic: we have diamonds, we are royalty! Easy.'

'Why don't you count the Queen?'

'Because her family are cousins of our Romanovs, but when the Revolution comes, 1917, and the Romanovs are threatened, the British king does nothing. He could have given them refuge in England. But no. They let their cousins die, because they were scared. They thought there'd be a revolution in Britain too.

They were cowards.'

'The last revolution in Britain was Oliver Cromwell.' Julie pulls on some threadbare gloves and fastens her coat's top button.

'Yes, the British never had the balls to join in in 1848. Now they're too drunk. Can you imagine a proletariat revolution in Britain? All the beer guts and slobby slags trying to shoot straight!'

'Where we live, boys knife each other quite a lot.' Julie is well aware that many of the recent teen murders in London have happened in its south-east corner.

'But those are just gangs — it's not political. They can't even organise themselves, never mind anyone else. Nobody shoots bankers or politicians or Royals, not since the IRA, unless al-Qaeda . . . '

'Can we change the subject, *please*?' Julie interrupts. 'Alistair might have to shoot people, and I just can't bear it. The idea of him with a gun makes me feel sick, because I think of Teo and everything that happened to him . . . '

'Ach, darling, let's forget it for today.' Irina puts an arm round her. 'Why don't we go to Le Printemps — do you know it? A beautiful department store. They have many fine labels, we find you perfect party dress to match necklace! And there is a nice restaurant, we can have lunch.'

Half an hour later, Julie is gazing at her own mirrored image wearing a long, draping creation in dove-grey silk. She looks like an off-duty Greek priestess heading for a night on the tiles.

Scratching the middle of her back is a designer label she's never dared look at before.

'Wonderful!' Irina applauds her. 'Alistair would be proud.'

'But what will he say when he sees this?' Julie points between her shoulderblades at the tag.

'He will be thrilled. It's about what you make of yourself. You mustn't always hold yourself back thinking it's for him. You have to be *you*. He'll love you more for that.'

'For a virgin, you know a lot about love,' Julie teases.

'Real love is not just sex,' declares Irina. 'Let me take your photo.' She whips out a shiny pink phone and snaps an image of Julie in the grey dress; then, putting away the handset, she takes out the now familiar credit card instead.

On the next floor, Irina chooses a winter coat in a matter of minutes — she knows what she likes and cream-coloured cashmere suits her to perfection. Julie points out that the coat will soon turn grey with grime, but dry-cleaning bills evidently don't alarm her friend. Next, under Le Printemps' stained-glass dome, a riot of Art Nouveau flowers and leaves in peacock blue, grass green and rose, they settle into the top-floor restaurant and order salads, mineral water and white wine. Eating, Julie notices that her heart, which had started to race in Ovchinikov's, is still doing nineteen to the dozen. And it's not only nerves and fright, but excitement.

In the beauty section they talk their way into a makeover, which leaves Julie with huge, smoky eyes and polished complexion and Irina looking less like a swan and more like a bird of paradise.

'Let's pretend I am your fairy godmother.' Irina leads Julie by the arm out of the store and across the road to the neighbouring Galeries Lafayette. 'I am an only child and it's boring! I am spoiled, I know, I'm spoiled all the time. It's more fun to spoil someone else.'

Soon Julie, kitted out with a white cashmere sweater, designer jeans and a pair of spiky-heeled boots, has to admit that she feels like Cinderella, and she's loving it.

They finish with a trip to the food hall where they buy two bottles of Côtes du Rhône, a jar of foie gras, some brioche, several cheeses that emit pungent gases, a tub of apricots from Provence and a ripe melon the like of which would be tricky to source in East Anglia.

'Tomorrow we ask Charlie and Raff round to eat everything,' Irina suggests, tucking her packages into the train's overhead luggage rack. 'How do you feel?'

'Amazing! I'm glowing all over.' Julie is as light-headed as she'd felt over the champagne that morning.

'Good. This is how I want you to feel.'

'But why?'

'Darling, why not? We're friends, we're having fun. You don't have enough fun. Anyway, I know how worried you are about Alistair.'

Julie opens her mouth. All along she'd wondered whether Irina had an ulterior motive, such as free tickets to hear Terri sing at Covent Garden. Of course, the Ovchinikovs don't need freebies. It had never occurred to her that an ordinary if wealthy friend, knowing that her boyfriend was soon off to a war zone, could simply have the generosity to want to cheer her up.

Irina pulls off her boots and sits back while the train doors slide shut. 'You probably think I always feel like you do now,' she begins, 'but I don't. I am poor little rich girl. You have to have someone to share it. I never had that before.'

'Not even at school?'

'No, because the girls were all like me. Spoiled, pretentious. Wearing masks all the time. And now there's always bloody Vaslav watching me. It is such a relief to get away from him.'

'You're not pretentious at all. And Vaslav's nice, I really like him. I think he studies harder than the rest of us put together.' The bodyguard applies himself with a passion to improving his English, listening to podcasts from BBC Radio 4 over and over again.

'You don't wear a mask, you let people take you as they find you,' Irina remarks. 'I like that. It's genuine. You know who you are, more than anyone else at college.'

'But I can hardly take a step without people asking about my mum — '

'How do you think I feel about my dad? We are two of kind, you see.'

This much is true. 'But do you know what you want to do? After college?'

'*Bog znaet*. No clue. I don't need to work, you see. Maybe I do translation, or maybe I do tourism, taking people to Russia. Maybe I get married. But I have no *vocation*. And you? You are going to sing? Because you have a vocation, I think.'

'Everyone always says that, but I don't know. I like singing, it's just . . . I don't know. I look at my mum and I'm like, heck, do I want to live like that? And then I look at Alistair and his mother and how they live and I feel guilty that I do have some sort of gift for singing but maybe don't want to do it. I feel guilty all the time, no matter what I do.'

'But Julie, now you feel good? You have dress, you know you look beautiful, doesn't this help?'

'Of course, but . . . ' It's true, she does feel more confident; she knows she could stand up on a stage and look and sound good. But she can't relax. She can't stop thinking of what Sue and Alistair could have done with the money that has been spent on her today.

'Stop beating yourself up!' Irina commands. 'You don't need to. Let yourself *enjoy* things. Then you'll start to fly. Oh God, here's the tunnel . . . '

And for twenty minutes from France to England, Julie holds the frightened Irina's hand and chatters away to distract her from the tons of cold seawater pressing down on them beyond the tunnel walls.

10

Terri spends a morning bolstering her doors and windows with draught excluder against the deepening chill. Only after she has been round the entire house with it does she slink down to her basement to begin some tentative vocalising. She's taking things slowly, as Anita advised, but this has entailed enduring the ghastly grate of her slack cord as she tries to limber it back into shape. It's better than before; Anita's tactics are working. Underneath the crap, the voice is there, waiting for her: the sound that's the essence of her true self.

She's about to utter a prayer of thanks, when something goes wrong. She can't find the note. With a pang of fear, her throat and chest tighten. The sound falters, then breaks.

'Jesu Maria.' She slams the piano lid; the instrument jangles in protest. She's not ready, that's obvious. And however hard she stamps, however intensely she wills her recovery, nothing can hurry it. If she rushes, she'll do herself more damage. 'Be patient, darling,' Anita exhorted. 'But you never did know what patience was, did you? Time to learn.'

The panic swirls from mind to body and back again. Is her voice breaking down because it hasn't recovered, because something else is wrong with it, or just because she *thinks* there's a problem, so her body conspires to create one?

How much of this is caused by her own imagination?

She stomps away to the study. The phone glares at her. Anita's teaching. Julie will be in a lecture. She could call Teo, Martini or Dora. But if she calls Teo, he'll demand to see her; Martini would want to know how the voice is; and Dora would natter for hours, which is the last thing Terri should do. Talking, said her laryngologist, can be more damaging than singing: at least if you're singing you're using your voice sensibly, supporting it in the diaphragm, whereas if you're just yakking . . .

The Viardot shelf beckons. Perfect escapism: the past. The history of a woman she'd never met. A woman who was born to sing. Pauline was world famous by nineteen — at which age Terri had been slogging in a pub kitchen, doing industrial quantities of washing-up, making heaps of mashed potato from packets of instant mix and fending off the predatory brass sections of visiting orchestras fresh from the concert hall; they always seemed to come back for second helpings when she was on duty. Terri stares at the familiar picture of Pauline, recessive-chinned, heavy-eyed. Sometimes, when she looks at Anita at the piano during her lessons, she imagines she's seeing Pauline instead.

Aged twenty-two, Pauline Garcia had married the intelligent, middle-aged and distinctly dry impresario Louis Viardot. Pauline was trying to better herself, just as Terri was when she met Bernard. Both of them had been over-impressed by the wrong things, Pauline by security,

204

connections and career management, Terri by intellect and respectability.

⋆ ⋆ ⋆

Terri can remember vividly the first moment she'd set eyes on most of her lovers and friends — but oddly, not Bernard. It was a dinner party in someone's house, she can't remember whose; she must have blanked it out. She'd been placed next to him and he'd asked sensible questions, not the usual rubbish like what you think about while you sing. He'd wanted to know whether she related one composer to another — Strauss to Mozart, Wagner to Beethoven — or whether each existed purely in his own right. Did she think Debussy was a reaction against Wagner or towards him? Did she like contemporary music? Terri had had a little too much wine, so had he; and the evening progressed . . .

She can remember apricot walls, a Persian rug, a street in north London, getting into Bernard's car, and little else. Who on earth had hosted that dinner party? Whoever it was, she doesn't see them any more.

Bernard offered her safety. And at thirty, Terri needed safety. Glasgow had brought her two abortions, Edinburgh an assault and her first years in London more slimy City gits than she'd thought could squeeze into one opera house. They didn't like it when she saw through them. 'I don't want presents,' she'd told one, whom she'd liked. 'I want affection, not *stuff.*' After that, she didn't see him for dust.

Bernard wasn't rich or smooth; nor was he cruel, demanding or kinky. Terri decided that he was safe, dull and decent, with his sticky-out ears and his mathematical brain. Music and maths, he told her, go together. He'd keep her earthed, she considered. They'd be good for each other.

By that time she'd tried almost everything else. Jealous Joe from Glasgow. Abominable Alexander from the merchant bank. Creepy Conductors — one of them bought her a mink, which had mildly compensated for the night she'd endured beneath him until she realised that every other soprano she met in every opera house where he'd conducted was wearing exactly the same coat. She wondered whether he had a deal for buying in bulk.

Admirable Academics, though, were from another world. They valued knowledge ahead of money; they aimed to create a better world through education and enlightenment. Or so she'd thought. Bernard admitted on their first wedding anniversary that he'd only become an academic because he hadn't had a clue what else to do with his life. Terri, thirty-one and fresh from a visit to a gynaecologist who'd tut-tutted over the state of her uterus, which proved scarred by an infection after her second abortion, tried not to show her disillusionment while they celebrated.

The stupid thing, she reflects now, is that probably to a woman leading a 'normal' life, Boring Bernard wouldn't be boring at all. She herself had responded to him because he asked her interesting questions at that dinner party.

But his sedentary, staid routine, faculty infighting and a life lived more in the brain than the body could scarcely have been more different from hers. The fact that she was bored silly by him was as much her responsibility as his. Her nature was rooted in her own physicality and the perfecting of its voice, but Bernard had made the extremely common mistake of thinking that opera singers should be as intellectual as opera-goers. She admires intellectualism — Julie's not wrong — but while she could read as much Turgenev as anyone else, her brain simply couldn't latch on to the abstract concepts of advanced pure mathematics. That proved, as if it were necessary, that she and Bernard were wrong for each other. She'd grown up without a father; she certainly hadn't intended her daughter to do likewise. But when you feel so claustrophobic, so lifeless in your partner's company that you celebrate — preferably with another man — whenever you go away, the price of staying becomes too high. Besides, would Julie have benefited from growing up in a perpetually warring household?

The phone rings, jolting Terri back to earth.

'Mum?'

'Darling!'

'Can I come home today? I need a lesson with Anita. They've asked me to sing a solo in the college choir. It's the Fauré Requiem, the 'Pie Jesu', and I've never even looked at it before.'

Her daughter is nervous, excited, flattered, but to Terri's dismay, the current that charges through her at these words is as bitter yellow as jealousy.

207

'We can work on it together, love,' she suggests, fighting it.

'Thanks, Mum, but I've booked myself in with Anita. I wouldn't want to make you work. See you later. Love you.'

'Love you too.'

Terri abandons the study for the kitchen, where a homemade cake needs finishing. Once it's gone, she sets about baking a new one.

★ ★ ★

Julie has done something strange to her eyes. When Terri asks her what the warpaint's for, she mumbles something about makeovers in Paris.

'Are you sleeping enough?' Terri demands. 'Are you eating properly?'

'Yeah.'

'Are they working you very hard? Are you enjoying it?'

'Yes, then no.' Julie stifles a yawn.

'You look distracted.'

'Is there any cake?'

Terri's latest effort is still warm. She cuts Julie a chunk, packed with almonds and glace cherries.

'Alistair wrote.' The words make her look tired; it's not just the effect of 'smoky eyes'. 'He's arrived. He says he's all right. Actually he didn't say much, other than there's a lot of dust, it's freezing and the food's awful. Too many beans.'

'It sounds like a funny place to send someone who's only just finished training,' Terri comments.

'I guess that's where they need people. He says it feels a bit like being in one of those Westerns where the cowboys are holed up in a fort. I can't get my head around it — him being *there*.'

'Isn't he afraid?'

'If he was, he wouldn't tell me.'

'Come on, sweetheart. Why don't you sing to me? Show me what you went through with Anita.'

Julie is to perform the solo soprano movement from Fauré's Requiem: '*Pie Jesu domine, dona eis requiem*'. The breath control is extremely tricky, which is why, according to Chris, the organ scholar, Fauré liked a mature female soprano to sing it, rather than the usual choirboy at the Madeleine, his Parisian church.

'It seems that Fauré preferred a mature female to a juvenile male in most situations,' Terri remarks, carrying cups of tea to the studio. She's interested to see that Julie has stopped taking milk in her hot drinks. 'You know, he nearly married Pauline Viardot's daughter.'

'I didn't know. Does it help?' Julie plays a defiant chord on the piano.

'Let me play for you.' Terri pushes her off the piano stool. Obedient, Julie stands to one side.

Terri has never sung the 'Pie Jesu' — it doesn't suit her voice. It has to sound almost impossibly pure. Paradoxically, that's what makes it sexy. She reads the piano part in a basic form, just enough to give Julie the harmonies.

Julie's tone, she thinks, has a new focus, a certain bolstered quality around the diaphragm.

Perhaps it's developing through singing regularly in the larger space of a college chapel; perhaps she's maturing physically; or maybe Anita has shown her some new tricks. Certainly the effect is more defined and bell-like; there's a character coming through that is a step forward from Julie's timid schoolgirl efforts only a few months earlier. That's not to say her performance is perfect. Terri wishes Julie could relax, stop thinking so much about the notes and get the words and their message across.

Halfway through, Terri stops her and suggests refreshing the breath at a different point.

'I'm doing what Anita said.'

'But darling, it might work. Just try it once and see how it feels.'

Julie tries.

'That's it. Beautiful.'

'Are you sure?' Julie's brow creases upwards.

'Yes! Now think about the words. Do you know what they mean?'

'It's just 'please, Jesus, grant them rest'.'

'Yes, but that means quite a lot. Think about it. The Requiem is a prayer for the dead. You need to convey compassion, not just piety. If there's real compassion, it's from the heart and everyone can hear it.'

Julie tries again. The music sounds utterly wooden.

'You're worrying about it. Just let it flow out. Use the text, enunciate the consonants a little more strongly. The phrasing will come naturally.'

Julie puts down her music. 'You don't like the way I sing, do you?'

'Of course I do, I'm just trying to help. Come on, don't let one criticism knock you. You're doing wonderfully, but you can make even more of it. It's not such a big deal.'

'It's a big deal in that I have to perform it in a week's time. And why's everyone on at me about making more of things?'

'Like what?'

'Like the song. Like myself. Like *life*.'

'Are you premenstrual?' Terri demands.

'No!' Julie shouts, then bursts into tears.

Terri rolls her eyes heavenwards and lets Julie go. She listens to her footsteps pounding up the stairs to her room. Back in her study, she stares blankly at the computer screen, wondering how to deal with her daughter when her daughter couldn't deal with her. Absently she clicks the computer mouse on the BBC news site.

She reads:

FOUR MORE BRITISH SOLDIERS KILLED.

So that was it. Terri hurries to Julie's room. Inside, the girl is flat on her bed, face in her pillow. No wonder she can't sing a solo about compassion for the dead. It's a wonder she can sing anything at all.

Terri sits next to her and strokes her hair. 'Darling,' she whispers, 'it's OK. I just saw the headline.'

'It's not him,' Julie points out between sobs. 'But it could have been, so easily. I knew it was going to be awful when he went, I just didn't

211

know it would feel like this.'

Terri hugs her and says nothing. Her own heart feels ready to break. She suspects that the families left behind at home feel worse than the young soldiers do themselves — the lads out in the 'theatre of war' will be too occupied with the task in hand, the business of survival, to think about the whys and ifs of what's happening to them.

'I don't know how I can do the Fauré.' Julie flails around for a box of tissues.

Terri passes it to her. 'OK. We need a different tactic,' she decides. 'I'll tell you about another a trick. While you're singing, try to forget that you feel anything.'

'But just now you said . . . ?'

'Yes. You have to start there. But once you've felt it, you know how it feels and you have to convey it, cool and detached: try to evoke those emotions in your audience without getting involved yourself. Do you see?'

'So to feel it — ?'

'Yes, *beforehand*. Remember it and put it across using your technique.'

The light brightens in Julie's reddened eyes as she grasps the concept. Terri hadn't been sure she'd understand — but as so often, Julie surprises her. It's as if she already knew, but simply needed to be reminded. Terri feels a pang of yesterday's jealousy, but this time it's over the wonder of discovery: the moment of revelation when — in Teo-English — a penny falls.

★ ★ ★

In the stairwell of Scargill Tower, the teenage boys bellow at each other across several levels. Hearing their yells echoing round the concrete spiral, Julie shrinks back in the entrance. She's brought flowers for Sue and has to go up to the seventh floor. She can scarcely understand their words; this gang has its own dialect. Not that she wants to join in. Out on the high street the first Christmas lights are up, with strings of bulbs looped round the lamp-posts; Terri joked earlier that it looks like an airport runway. But inside, the block resembles a multistorey car-park: a lingering whiff of blocked drains, traces of vomit that haven't been properly cleaned up, a dank, airless trap that some fifty families call home.

The gang members scream expletives; Julie has the impression that someone has shopped someone else to the police. She peers round the corner, hoping against hope that she's still out of sight. Three of them are in hoods; some of the others wear fleece hats. She finds the hats, weirdly, scarier than the hoods; and the baggy trousers could conceal anything: guns, knives, broken bottles, pouches of drugs. She'd be one thin, timid girl trying to get past seven or eight zoning boys fired up by boiling testosterone. When one of them glances in her direction she catches a glimpse of the anger in his eyes: a flash of pure hatred. Perhaps he and his mates have never known anything except cruelty and violence, but she's no social worker to stay here and work her way past it. She turns and runs. As she bolts through the door, something thuds into her shoulder. For one terrified second she thinks it's a shot, but there'd been no sound of gunfire. She keeps going, breathing so hard that she's afraid she might faint.

A safe distance away, outside a well-lit middle-class café, she stops to examine her coat. Something raw and liquid is slithering down it; pieces of shell cling to the ends of her hair. The yolk drips faster than the viscous white. The gang, despite its infighting, had still found time to egg her. She rings Sue from her mobile.

'Hello, love,' comes Sue's comforting voice. 'You all right? Where are you? You didn't meet them rude boys?'

'I'm sorry, Sue, I chickened out. I so want to see you, but I'm scared. I couldn't get past them. I feel so pathetic.'

'You did well to keep away from them lot, love. I got the same problem, only I'm inside, and I got to get to work later. Everyone here's too scared to step out of their doors when those crackheads are around. That's all they are, see, and they're cowards, the lot of them, but they get away with it cos people let them.'

'Can't the police do something?'

'They're shit-scared too. These boys have knives an' all.'

'But what are you going to do about work?'

'I'll go when I have to, but I can tell you, love, I say a prayer every time. I've applied for a housing transfer, but the waiting list is thousands and they can't tell me when they might let me have a turn. Nobody knows nothing. You ring up

214

and there's some kid at the end of the phone picking his nose. Listen, love, go home where it's good and safe and we'll get together when you're back for Christmas, all right?'

'I miss you, Sue.'

'I miss you too. I had a message from him today, he misses you like the blazes.'

'Is he OK?' Julie tries not to be upset that she didn't get the same message.

'Yeah, just preparing for winter in a cold, horrible place. He says people are good, mostly, though there's some as aren't. And them Americans, there's hundreds of them, really tough and with all this great new kit.'

'Isn't his kit OK?' Julie reads obsessively all the newspaper reports which suggest that the British troops aren't well enough equipped.

'What he says is that the stuff's good — body armour, guns, boots and that. It's just there isn't enough of it. They rely on the helicopters and the armoured vehicles so much where they are, and it's like, there are too few and they're stretched. The Land Rovers were designed for Northern Ireland, not the bloody . . . well, he says we're not to worry because he's prepared and he loves us. Now listen, you look after yourself. Enjoy your college. I wish he was there with you.'

'So do I, Sue. Take care, and I'll call you next week.'

Julie turns homewards up the hill, her legs still unsteady with lingering fright.

★　★　★

'Your Russian friend phoned,' Terri tells her when she comes in. 'They've invited us to a Christmas party in Highgate. I wonder what to wear. Teo phoned too, he sends his love.'

'Is he coming over? Is he still in Sarajevo?'

'How did you know he was in Sarajevo?' Terri asks.

Julie hadn't told Terri about her attempt to call Teo in Paris. 'I tried to phone him and that's where he was.' Then she explains her evening.

Terri glowers, assessing the damage to Julie's coat. 'It'll wash out, but someone needs to put their noses in a sling,' she growls. 'I don't know what's happened to this city. And under a Labour government. I voted for these people! It wasn't always like this, so extreme. One minute you can't get past those morons and their knives because some miserable patch of street is 'theirs'. The next, a diamond mogul asks you to his bloody mansion that cost twelve million. I don't know what's going on. I just don't know where we fit in any longer.'

'*Do* we fit in?' Julie sighs. 'Because I don't.' She's hungry, depressed and not much inclined to listen to one of Terri's rants.

'Artists are like albatrosses,' Terri muses. 'We're further from it all, so we have a wider perspective. I sometimes think that at birth, the angels deal out your cards, your advantages and disadvantages and how you play them is up to you . . . '

Julie yawns. 'D'you fancy beans on toast?'

'You go ahead, angel. I'm not hungry.'

Terri waves her daughter down to the kitchen and closes the study door gently before ringing Teo.

* * *

To her surprise — though she doesn't know why she should be surprised by anything he says — he sounds angry when she tells him she's been trying to work with Julie.

'She's got a teacher and a life of her own,' he barks. He's in a restaurant somewhere in Bosnia; she can hear a guitar in the background, and the sound of singing.

'I was only trying to help.'

'Giving her advice that conflicts with her teacher's? I thought her teacher was your teacher, anyway.'

'Yes, but — '

'The girl's nineteen, she's not a baby. If she's going to sing, it's her business. Why push her? Just because you, currently, are not allowed to sing, you mustn't start trying to control her.'

'It's not about 'controlling her'. She's doing one small but difficult solo, and she wanted my help. And why should I justify myself to you? You haven't been in these parts much recently, unless I've managed not to spot a large, dark man smoking a pipe in my house.'

'I haven't felt precisely welcome. That's why I'm here, trying to do something positive for a change.'

'Oh, Mr Sanctimonious! You've been back so often, haven't you? Garnering brownie points with the Almighty?'

'I don't have to listen to this.' Teo slams down the phone.

Terri, waiting, begins her ritual count to a hundred. The phone rings four seconds early.

'So what would you prefer to listen to?' she asks.

Teo doesn't apologise; neither does she. After a brief silence, he starts over. 'I need to tell you something. You know, this book is making a sort of a splash. Today Xenia, my agent, called to say I am shortlisted for the Mandela Peace Award.'

'Good God.' Terri is dumbstruck. 'Not that you deserve anything less,' she adds hastily.

'I think this is very funny. Here we go again — burn down my home, kill my family, then give me a prize for telling what happened. Anyway, there will be a prize, I probably won't get it, but we're invited to the presentation dinner in February.'

' "We"?'

'I am invited with a guest and I want you to be that guest. Will you come, Terri?'

'Where is it?'

'This time they hold it in Bruges. It's a different city every two years.'

It's still a shock to remember that her diary for February 2008 consists of twenty-nine blank pages. 'Thank you, darling,' she says. 'I'd love to.'

'Good. I tell them.'

There's a pause. Terri can hear clapping, rhythmic and vaguely ecstatic; voices raised in song, a melody that strikes her even from this

218

distance as mournful and longing. 'Where are you?'

'In a bar, with my cousins and their friends. Everyone's singing *sevdah*.'

Teo has often played Terri recordings of *sevdah*, the melting pot of folk music that's the one common element throughout the quarrelling Balkan states. It's a light year away from *Der Rosenkavalier* and *Tristan*, but something about its off-centre rhythms and the unsuppressed sorrow in the arching melodies never fails to tighten a string around her heart. Teo has told her many times that '*sevdah*' means 'love' or 'soul'. She wishes, for one weak second, that she were there with him.

'Perhaps we bring you soon.' Teo's voice is softer now, warmer. 'You could have been here now.'

'You never told me you were going,' Terri points out. She's still trying to figure out why Teo has broken his exile for the first time. 'Has it changed?' The question feels dumb. Any question would.

'A little. Terri, I see you soon. Goodnight, my angel.'

Sensible man, ringing off before the sparring could start again. Terri opens her diary and writes BRUGES in large letters: a solitary blue word on a sea of white.

11

'If it's true,' Julie says to Irina, 'then they've been lying to me my whole life.'

'How long have they been together?'

'I don't know. I was really small the first time I met him. Or the first time I remember meeting him. That doesn't necessarily mean anything.'

'When I was a kid,' Irina reminisces, 'I had fantasy that I was adopted. It was only when I heard how much money my father had paid to that kidnapper gang that I realised I must be truly his.'

'It's not like that. I can't get my head around it — that there's this man I've been thinking is my father all my life and maybe he isn't?'

'Darling, hush. Don't add two and two and make ninety-nine.'

Julie can't rid herself of the idea. Why wouldn't they tell her? Why would they think it more important to preserve the respectable front that is Bernard than to let her know the truth? She hunts for a benign motivation, to keep herself reasonably sane. Perhaps it was to protect Teo, whose family was still alive when she was conceived? He wouldn't yet have been living in Paris — but there was no reason to suppose that he wasn't free to travel there, or anywhere else, before the war. He might have met Terri before he left Bosnia for good, not after. As her mother is not renowned for fidelity, there's no reason to suppose she ever had been. Did Bernard know? Is that why he's so reluctant to spend time with her? As the ideas wash through her, Julie feels as if her anchor has come loose from the seabed and she's adrift on a current that's stronger than she is, with nothing to pull her to shore — except, perhaps, Alistair.

Terri has never hidden from Julie the fact that she has an active and varied sex life; yet oddly, experiencing first the illicit diary, then her mother's adventure in Baden-Baden and now this has made Julie more squeamish about her own relationships, not less — as if to overcompensate. It's easier to wait for Alistair's sporadic communications than to respond to anyone else. Besides, when she thinks where Alistair is now, there is nothing else she can possibly do: it would be a hideous betrayal.

'Silly,' says Irina, who flirts with every boy in college but still hasn't picked one to divest her of her virginity.

'I love Alistair.'

'But never even to go out on a date, not even for a drink? Or if you do go, you wear your blue cardy!'

'You go, then. I don't go because I don't want to.'

'What do you do?' Irina presses. 'When I go out and you stay in? I worry about you.'

It's December and as the end of term approaches, Julie has plenty to do. She writes 'e-blueys' to Alistair on the army's site for the purpose; emails to Patti and Lara at their redbrick universities; floral cards to Sue and

221

quirky text messages to Terri. And she surfs the Internet for information about army life, Eurostar timetables and paternity tests, not necessarily in that order.

'It's not right,' Irina says. 'You make sure you come to our Christmas party and you must wear Paris dress and bling necklace. Bling looks good on you.'

'Mum would call it Wagner's Bling Cycle,' Julie jokes.

Less amusingly, Julie's tutor has left a message in her pigeonhole at the porter's lodge requesting that she should come to see him at once.

She sits on a cracked leather armchair in his book-lined study and twists her hands together while he talks. Some of her supervisors, he explains gently, are not pleased with her progress. One suggests she lacks motivation. Another wonders whether the lectures are going in one ear and out the other. Is something worrying her? Can he help?

'I'm fine.'

'I know,' he ventures, 'that this place can be difficult. I know you have some good friends and I've noticed your Russian neighbour taking you under her rather ample wing. But I'm concerned that you're spending a lot of time on your own. I understand your boyfriend is in the armed forces?'

Julie tells him where Alistair is and sees — or imagines — that he winces.

'I imagine that not everybody is going to react sympathetically to that.'

She nods; a second later she's battling tears. He extends a box of Kleenex towards her at arm's length.

'No wonder you're distracted,' he remarks while she mops up. 'I do understand. But you need to pay attention to your work, Juliette, because otherwise you could be in deep water when the exams roll round. Time goes quickly here — you'd be surprised how much you have to absorb in a matter of months. If you can't do it for yourself, then do it for him. He'll want you to.'

'Yes,' says Julie. 'Yes, he does. I'm sorry. I'm a bit of a mess right now.'

After the meeting, Julie wraps her scarf against the icy east wind and wanders out to the supermarket. There the last straw appears.

Approaching the shelf, she finds a gaping, dusty space where the mushroom soup should have been. A notice declares it 'temporarily out of stock'.

'Excuse me.' She accosts a shelf-stacker. 'Any idea when you'll have the mushroom soup again?'

'Could be Monday,' says the jaunty teenager. He gives her a wink. 'Cheer up, love. Might never 'appen.'

And Julie looks at the boy and sees Alistair, only half a year ago, meeting her in the aisle by the orange juice, giving her tiger lilies and racing her up the hill. At the same moment, she understands that that Alistair has gone for ever. Something inside her wobbles, then snaps.

She abandons her shopping, meanders back to

college and puts herself to bed, closing out the world with earplugs. At 6 a.m. she wakes, dresses warmly and packs a bag with more than overnight clothes, plus her passport. Minutes later she's on her bike, heading for the station.

The train whizzes to King's Cross; in less than an hour she's queuing with her credit card to buy a ticket to Paris. She half expects the ticket seller to refuse to serve her, but he simply presses some buttons and prints a boarding card.

'And the return?' he says.

'Open, please.' It costs more, much more, but she copies Irina and doesn't look at the number, although she knows her mother's attitude to this is going to be significantly different from Sergei Ovchinikov's. Moments later she's through the barrier, through security and boarding the train.

★ ★ ★

Julie reaches Teo's cul-de-sac, chilly from the winter air but sweaty from the crowded Saturday métro; at the apartment block's entrance she presses the code into the keypad. It lets her through into first the passageway, then the central courtyard. She crosses the sleek paving and walks up the wooden stairs to Teo's flat on the second floor, where she rings the bell.

Nothing happens. He's not home.

Wrong-footed, Julie sits down on the stairs beside her rucksack, pondering. She'd been so busy thinking how easy this was that she'd forgotten to consider the one crucial factor of whether Teo would actually be there. She tries his mobile; it's off. She doesn't leave a message; she's too embarrassed. Perhaps a note on the door while she waits in a café? She rummages in her pack, but, like the idiot she is, she's brought neither pen nor paper. What if he's not even in France? That'll teach her to pitch up unannounced in another country and expect a responsible adult to rescue her.

Footsteps pound down the stairs above her and a gangly, youngish man in a track suit and trainers arrives on the landing.

'*Bonjour, Mademoiselle.*' He glances her up and down the way that men tend to in France.

'Er, *bonjour,*' says the forlorn Julie.

'*Puis-je vous aider?*'

'Um, *peut-être.*' Julie is supposed to speak reasonable French, but real-life situations are far removed from her meagre classroom experience.

'It's OK, I can speak English.' The neighbour smiles. 'My name is Dominique, my wife and I live upstairs. You are looking for Monsieur Popović?'

'He's not away, is he?'

'I'm sure not, I saw him, maybe two days ago. Normally he tells me if he will go away. Are you from England?'

'Yes, from London. I came all the way to see him.'

'And how you know Mr Popović? I'm sorry, it's not my business, it's just that . . . '

Julie sees doubt on his face. 'He's my mum's boyfriend. Is something wrong?'

'I wonder, do you have time for a coffee? Because you look as if maybe you need one.'

She wonders if he's trying to chat her up, but his tone of voice tells her something else is afoot.

★ ★ ★

'Monsieur Popović,' says Dominique, sipping a *grand crème* in the café on the corner, 'is a very great puzzlement to all of us.'

'Why?'

'You see, I'm a lawyer. Would you like a croissant?'

'No, thanks. Please go on. You're a lawyer?'

'Yes, so I go to work early most mornings, and often I make jogging around the Luxembourg Gardens first. And sometimes I see him coming in.'

'Coming *in*?'

'Six thirty, seven. And he looks — you know — crevé. Not shaved, not brushed, sometimes there is dirt on his coat or his face . . . I pretend I don't notice, of course. And often if Anna and I go out to dinner, we invite him and we have a great time. He's good company, great fun.'

'He is, isn't he!'

'But I don't know what he does afterwards. I thought maybe — forgive me, I know he is with your mother, but I think that he goes out on the métro and he doesn't come back. He sleeps on the trains or on benches at stations. A colleague of mine who commutes very early in the morning saw him once at the end of a line on the other side of Paris, fast asleep, looking almost like, you know, *un clochard*.'

Julie's mouth freezes open.

'I don't want to distress you. It is not my business and anyway, maybe it's not so serious. Just that he's this celebrated writer, but sometimes he chooses not to come home. That's all I know. I wondered if you can tell me anything more.'

'Mum's never said anything.'

'Maybe I shouldn't have told you. You see, I like him and I am worried about him. He must have experienced hell.'

'Yes. Mostar. And other stuff.'

Dominique drains his coffee cup. Julie stares at some scratches on the formica table.

'The thing is,' he says, 'it is difficult to talk to him about what happened and how he feels. He doesn't like to discuss it. Still, I would love him to know that Anna and I are there for him, if he needs us. We would like to help if we can.'

'That's very kind. I'll try to tell him. Assuming he's here.'

'What will you do now? Would you like to wait at our place?'

'Thanks,' says Julie, 'but I think I'll go for a walk.'

★ ★ ★

Teo, relieved and distressed in equal measures to be back in France, has spent several days in meetings designed to further the fortunes of his abruptly famous book. Now that he's been to Bosnia, everyone wants to ask him why. He'd requested that all the interviews should take place on the same day in the same café, to get them over and done with; and on a Saturday, to deter as many journalists as possible. He sat at a table in the Café de Flore on the boulevard Saint-Germain facing the stream of questions. Why didn't he go back before? Why did he go back now? What did he want to achieve? Was there anything he could achieve? Had he waited until everything was back to normal before he retraced his steps?

'It is not back to normal,' said Teo. 'It never has been. I want to help.'

Why did he want to help, when apparently he never had before? Teo, lighting his pipe, attempted explanation. 'Some things can be healed, and some can't,' he told the reporter from *Le Monde*. 'Wounds in ourselves, wounds in others, wounds in our countries. Some can be cleansed and sewn up with medical intervention. Others can be accessed in the spirit by art, music or writing, whether active or passive. And still others cannot be fixed at all, except possibly by time on a scale beyond the span of our short lives. I want to do what I can to restore a little hope to my homeland.'

But why now?

'Why not?'

The fact that he can face Sarajevo, when he couldn't before, is something he understands little enough already; and it's none of *Le Monde*'s business that Terri's persistent semi-detachment has made him determined not to leave a void in his life where he wants her to be. 'There comes a moment when you're ready,' he ventured, 'and you must trust your instinct.

There's nothing more rational than instinct.'

There's been much to discuss with his agent. Money issues — whether to donate part or all of the prize, should he win it, to charities in Bosnia, and if so, which ones? Those that rebuild infrastructure, or those intended to help rebuild human beings? Invitations arrive, begging him to speak in universities, bookshops, schools and orphanages. He wants to go to Serbia and Croatia, but they hesitate to invite him because of the depiction of their forces in his book. 'I told nothing but the truth,' Teo explains, 'but that is in the past and to heal the future, we must include everybody in the present.'

Then came the culture minister, pleading for music: 'Isn't your friend the opera singer Teresa Ivory? Wouldn't she come here and sing?' Teo thought about this for several days before calling the minister back and telling her that he would explore the best way to make this happen.

★ ★ ★

When the last fellow has packed up his voice recorder and the waiters have opened every window to dispel the plum-pudding aroma of smoke, Teo stretches his arms, has a good yawn and begins to head homewards past the Odéon and the tall iron railings bordering the Luxembourg Gardens. After the smoking ban comes in, he decides, he'll have to do all his interviews in the Gardens; he'd never get through them without his pipe.

The prospect of the empty flat fills him with

the usual dismay as he crosses the place Edmond Rostand; perhaps dinner in the bistro and a ride on the métro will clear his head, or at least by-pass the mess that the journalists have left in it. He stops to buy milk, bread, cheese, coffee and some shoe polish, then rounds a corner into the cul-de-sac and makes his way up the stairs.

Outside his flat, sitting on a rucksack turned on its side, is a slender girl with long dark hair and an outsize stripy scarf.

Teo dashes forward and pulls her to her feet. 'Julie! What are you doing here?'

Julie, her cheeks like ice — the stairwell is draughty — hugs him hard. 'I tried to ring, but your phone was off. I've been walking in the gardens.'

'Poor thing! Come inside and get warm.'

She follows him, silent. In the flat, he shunts a mound of papers off the kitchen table and another off a chair so that she can sit down, then puts on a pot of coffee. A candle or two adds to the hominess as dusk falls. Julie's face, lit by the flames, is pale and anxious.

'Now, my dear.' Teo stirs sugar into the boiling coffee. 'What is this? I'm not used to you appearing by magic. Tell me everything.'

Julie begins. It's a long tale, existentialist in nature, Teo thinks. To many, it would sound like the usual student grumbles. Doubts about her future. Students with whom she doesn't fit in, a course that doesn't interest her.

'Darling,' he says, 'we all feel this way. You'll find that, behind those masks you talk about, every person would think this description applies

230

perfectly to him or her.'

'And they don't understand about Alistair,' Julie adds.

'No, I imagine they wouldn't.'

Julie, opposite him, sits with legs crossed and arms wrapped round her middle. 'The thing is, that place — it just isn't me. I feel so out of tune with it. I don't know how I can stand it for three years.'

'But running away to Paris? Suppose I hadn't been here? I'm only just back from Bosnia. And how long are you planning on remaining in the City of Light before you go home to face the music? People will worry.'

'I just wanted to get away.'

Teo takes her hand and squeezes. 'I know. But why here?'

Julie searches his face as if it's a faraway land — and her eyes turn moist. 'Teo, can I ask you something?'

'Of course. Anything.' He hopes desperately that she's not going to cry, because he'll blame himself if she does.

Julie opens her mouth, then closes it again. 'Maybe not.'

'Go on. I'm curious!'

She's struggling; he wonders what with. 'Can I just — could I stay with you for a couple of days? Please, Teo? I won't get in your hair, I promise, I'll just wander around Paris and . . . it would be such a relief . . . '

'Well. You stay tonight, at least. The sofa becomes a bed. But you call your mother and tell her, OK?'

'Oh Teo, thank you so much!' Her face breaks into a smile at last.

'I don't like to see you miserable. It's not my Julie as I know her.' The question hovers, unspoken; her tears linger, unshed. He waits; nothing. 'Why don't you relax, take a shower and watch the news, while I sort myself out,' he suggests. 'Tonight we go and have fun!'

'Thanks, Teo,' Julie beams. 'That would be *wonderful.*'

★ ★ ★

Teo potters about, making a mild effort to tidy up — not that his unexpected house-guest would notice. She spends a while in the bathroom, showering, washing her hair, then comes out smelling of shampoo, wearing grey jeans, her favourite blue cardigan and a towel over her shoulders. He makes more coffee, which she drinks sitting on the couch in front of the little TV, watching the news with her legs drawn up to her chest and shoes discarded nearby. When the latest report from the war begins, she tenses, scanning each uniformed or bandaged figure for signs of familiarity.

'Come along,' Teo prompts. 'Phone home. Make that call. Later I will show you my Paris.'

★ ★ ★

Christmas lights deck the city streets: on the boulevard Saint-Germain the trees are aglitter with tiny blue bulbs. Teo, fastening his furry hat's earflaps against the wind, picks a café by the Seine with a view of Notre-Dame, floodlit gold on the other side. They order two glasses of spicy *vin chaud* which brings a flush to Julie's face and starts to restore her sparkle.

'You see,' he says, 'each sip of this is like a little present. You can sit glooming the time away — or you can learn how to enjoy life. It's very simple.'

'It's so beautiful.' Julie gazes at the cathedral's great rose window, black and bronze. 'I love this city. I can see why you want to live here.'

'When does your young man come home on leave?'

'He only just got there.' She sips her wine, elbows on the table. 'The trouble is, everyone keeps telling me I shouldn't wait for him because we're too young and we're going to grow apart, or something stupid like that. And I miss him so much! It's horrible. People think I'm weird because I don't want to start seeing anyone else.'

'It's not their problem,' Teo promises her gently. 'I only worry for you because you're unhappy and I don't want you to waste your chance to get a good degree.'

'I don't see what the big deal is with that.'

'Come along, drink up. Good girl. Let's forget 'that' for now. We're in Paris and the night is young. Do you like shellfish?'

Julie's head is spinning after the *vin chaud* as they make for the métro to Montparnasse; the white-tiled tunnels slope and orbit as she hurries to keep up with Teo on the *escalier roulant*, then up one flight of stairs and down two more. She'd woken very early that morning; time seems distorted. So does her perspective on Teo — because now he's like a different man. His shoulders are back, his head raised, his steps faster: tonight he belongs to himself. She's more accustomed to seeing him trail in her mother's wake like a slightly disoriented dog. Perhaps it's the prize nomination, or the return to Bosnia, or just that Terri isn't there to damage his confidence?

She longs to tell Teo about the diary, but that is the last thing she must do; not only would he presumably tell Terri right away, but, worse, he'd want to know what Terri, in those long-ago words, had said about *him*. The situation, already messy, would become incrementally worse in seconds. Is it possible ever to know another person entirely, however close you think you are? And if she finds the courage to ask Teo her question, and he says what she thinks he'll say — where will that leave her?

★   ★   ★

That morning, holding forth about work, war and peace, trying to sound wise when he felt stupid, Teo had never imagined that later he'd be sitting in a leather-lined banquette in La Coupole, watching Julie sampling oysters for the first time. Their platter of shellfish is set over a dome of ice; it looks like a Turner Prize installation. He shows her how to dress an oyster. 'Try a little white wine mixed in this time . . . Nice?'

'It tastes like pearls!' Julie's eyes are round and delighted, as if she'd opened the shell to discover a whole necklace inside.

Teo, absorbing her joy, remembers that the best things in life are not only free but also frequently unplanned. 'Good girl. Next, a few chopped shallots, and a splash of vinaigrette . . . '

Julie tips her head back and pours the oyster into her mouth; her eyes close in ecstasy. She's never tried them before because Terri doesn't trust them. You place twenty-four hours of your life under threat every time you swallow an oyster, Terri insists. Tonight Julie has decided to ignore this.

'So now, what do we do with this fellow?' Teo lifts a great crab from the centre of the platter, where it's the crowning glory Julie has never tackled one of these either. She watches Teo crack the shell of an outsize claw with the stainless-steel contraption provided for the purpose, then tries to do the same.

'It's the remnant of the hunter-gatherer in us.' He squeezes lemon over the extracted crabmeat. 'You'd think the restaurant would do the dirty work, but it's more satisfying, in terms of instinct, to make a little effort for your food.'

Relaxed by the wine, thrilled by the shellfish and entranced by the glamour of the bistro's polished wooden pillars and chrome railings, Julie begins to talk more eagerly. She tells him about Irina's attempts to evade her bodyguard, and Teo throws back his badger's head and laughs like a lion.

What a marvel, he thinks, to see Julie transforming as if in a fairy-tale from stressed-out child to blossoming, enchanting woman. She has the same inner glow that he loves in Terri; the charm of naturalness at its most giving. His daughter Gabrijela would have been just three years older than Julie is now. He battles the stab of pain. This should be enough. A moment this beautiful should be sufficient in itself. He shouldn't wreck it by wanting the impossible.

★ ★ ★

Replete, happy and no longer remotely tired, they leave the restaurant, pausing on the pavement beside a tall advertising column so that Teo can light his pipe. Julie, looking up at the stars through the curling smoke, catches a glimpse of a film poster wrapped round the upper half of the pillar: Brett's face glowers down, incongruous, from one corner. It strikes her for the first time that maybe her mother isn't hugely good at managing her own life. Like the piles of paper in the study waiting to be sorted. It looks organised, but it doesn't progress.

'What is it? You sighed.'

'No, no, I'm having too much fun! I haven't had this much fun all term, not even with Irina.'

'Tell me more about Irina?'

Julie talks as they stroll. It's not too far from La Coupole back to the Luxembourg — just a good walk to shake down the shellfish. Teo laughs at her description of their shopping day in Paris, but shakes his head when she mentions the

Christmas party and the diamonds.

'Be careful. Now and then people ask price that you don't expect, and sometimes it is too high — but because of all this, you can't say no. Enjoy your nice new friend, but keep your eyes open. Now, the night is young! Are you tired? Shall we go somewhere else?'

'Where?' Julie's eyes brighten.

'I know a place you might enjoy, but it's very, very silly. Do you like Japanese beer?'

★ ★ ★

From the doorway, the nightclub's interior looks transplanted from another planet — or at least from Japan. The club serves sushi (which they're too full to eat), Japanese drinks and bean paste sweets. A montage of suitable photographs — skyscrapers, temples, bullet trains — covers every inch of the walls; the clientele too are mainly Japanese, but for a smattering of adventurous locals. On a dais beneath a mirror ball perches the star attraction: a state-of-the-art karaoke machine, over which a Japanese compère in heavy-rimmed spectacles and a brightly patterned shirt is wielding control, shouting in enthusiastic, accented French.

'I don't believe it!' Julie shrieks with laughter. 'You're not going to make me sing?'

'Ah, the penny has fallen . . . ' Teo pats her shoulder. 'I thought that, being a connaisseuse of singing, you might find this place rather amusing.'

They settle at a table near the back, order beer

and watch three young Japanese women, dressed in identical short skirts, take the microphones and launch into an Andrews Sisters number in close harmony. Julie's impressed despite herself. 'That's quite tricky,' she tells Teo.

'They'll have been practising for weeks,' he says. 'This is the high point of their month!'

'I'd find this more scary than singing the 'Pie Jesu' in the college chapel. At least the chapel's so resonant that it hides all your faults!'

'Did you enjoy it? The Fauré performance?'

Julie hesitates. 'I felt terrible beforehand, but it was lovely at the end when everyone clapped and they gave me flowers. And — knowing it sounded all right and that people were responding. That felt good.'

'Let's do a duet,' he suggests. 'We could sing a Serge Gainsbourg number.'

'Who's Serge Gainsbourg?'

'Oh, *mon dieu*, this girl is educated, this girl has French A level and she doesn't know Serge Gainsbourg! I fix this soon. Do you know Charles Trenet?'

'Who?'

'I show you. I go it alone. Be the angel that you are and order me another beer while I put in the request?'

Teo has barely downed the drink when a booming announcement calls him forward to the dais as the machine's next victim. If anyone recognises him, they don't say so. Perhaps nobody expects a Mandela Prize nominee to stand up in a karaoke bar, rather the worse for *vin chaud*, half a bottle of wine and two Japanese beers, and start to sing 'Quand notre coeur fait boum'.

Teo's features glisten under the lights, their plasticity expressing every word, conjuring up ridiculous, laughable pain and utter naïve delight within split seconds of each other. His eyebrows see-saw, his lips twist, snarl and smile, and his voice is its usual warm baritone except that it happens to be singing instead of speaking. He knows the song so well that he barely glances at the words on the screen. Julie tries to reconcile this image — Teo sparkling, laughing, entertaining a clubful of people he doesn't know — with the picture that his neighbour had painted of that devastated character who sometimes chooses to sleep rough rather than go home, for reasons that only he would ever understand.

At the end, the whole room cheers. A pink-faced waitress brings Teo a prize of a free beer to succeed the one on the table that he's just finished.

He takes a long draught, then turns to Julie: 'Now you.'

She flushes, giggling. 'But Teo . . . '

'You're English. Sing us a Beatles song.'

'Oh, I *couldn't*!'

'Yes, you could, because under the circumstances, I don't recommend the 'Pie Jesu'. Come along, *ma belle Juliette*. How do you feel? Are you a happier girl now?'

'You know what's funny? Last night I was so unhappy I never wanted to come out of my room ever again. And now I'm having the *best* time.'

'So sing for joy. Go on, choose something.' Teo

shows her the list of songs in stock that sits on each of the tables.

'They're all too gloomy.' Julie, who feels silly and free, rejects 'Yesterday' and 'Hey Jude'.

'Come on. We do one together. When they've finished.' Teo points at a familiar title, then tucks Julie's arm through his while a Japanese couple warble 'Endless Love' off key.

'No!' Julie protests, but Teo is a step ahead.

'I put in two requests just now,' he tells her. 'So this is going to be your big moment. *Our* big moment.'

As the other pair leave the platform, Teo jumps to his feet, pulling Julie after him; the compère declaims, 'Please welcome back Teo Popović, with Juliette Mason from England, to sing a song we all know!'

Cigarette smoke hovers round them while Teo watches Julie take a microphone, her smile under the spotlight casting brilliance across the room. Just like her mother. It's instinct; natural. What's most remarkable is that she doesn't even know that it happens. The fanfare which ought to open the Marseillaise rings out and there's a sprinkling of applause as it slides into 'All you need is love'.

'Alternate the lines,' he whispers to Julie. 'Then together at 'Easy' and the chorus.' She gives a conspiratorial nod.

And it's as he thought. She can sing for joy. She can. It's not difficult to sing here, whatever she'd thought; nothing like the chilly chapel concert that had her so worried. Reflections twang above them from the twirling mirror ball, the receptive faces fan the warmth inside him and after only a few nervous moments the girl opens out her sternum and sings for all the world like a nightingale taking the sky.

Maybe all you need, as Lennon and McCartney said, really is love.

★　★　★

Much later, they stagger home through the last streets; the shop windows are dark behind their decorations and only one or two lamps in apartment windows offer signs of life high above. Inside, the flat is warm and Teo fills the kettle to brew some tisane. His ears are buzzing uncomfortably from the volume in the club.

After kicking off her trainers, Julie sets about folding out the couch into a bed. She flops down and pulls out her mobile phone.

'Any news?' he asks.

'Mum's rung twice and Irina three times.' Yawning, she switches it off. 'I think they can wait a few hours, it's half past one.'

'In Britain it's only twelve thirty,' Teo remarks, a flicker of nostalgia crossing his mind.

'Teo,' she says, eyes half closed, taking the mug he hands her, 'can I ask you the thing I didn't want to ask earlier?'

'Anything, my child.' The room is whirling around him — he's due a massive hangover — and the light is too bright for his pile-driving head; still, he can't remember when he last felt so happy. He lights a candle and two lamps instead of the crass central fitting in the ceiling.

He's always hated it. Maybe it's time, finally, to make some changes to the way he lives.

'Teo, it's just . . . well . . . I don't look much like either my mum or my dad. And I don't really know when you and Mum got together, and I was wondering if . . . I don't know how to put it except to ask straight out.' She hesitates, fidgeting with her hair.

'Go ahead. Ask straight out.'

'Oh God.'

'You can't leave me waiting and wondering. Come along, dear, out with it.'

Julie says, very quickly: 'Teo, are you my real dad?'

Teo sits down in the armchair, sobering up fast. It's too cheering, being drunk; there's always a crash afterward. Julie won't meet his gaze.

He reaches out to her; she goes closer, perching awkwardly on the arm of his chair. 'I see,' he says. 'That is what all of this is about . . . Oh Julie, Julie. How you start to think so?'

'I dunno. I guess . . . I prefer you to my dad.'

This is the most touching thing anybody has said to Teo in over a decade — and she doesn't even realise how much it means to him.

'You were six years old when I first met your mother.' He takes both her hands. 'Julie, listen. The truth is this: I'm not your father, but I wish I was. Is that good enough?'

Julie, visibly crestfallen, is assimilating this information. 'It's nice.'

'I had a daughter once. I've never stopped missing her, not for one second. Sometimes I like to think you're my payback from stupid old fate.'

Julie stands and shuffles back to the couch that will be her bed. The moment she sits down, her eyes begin to close. Teo wishes she hadn't moved; the mood went with her. The answer's given, the hope has gone.

She flops to the side, head on the cushion. 'I honestly do prefer you to my real dad,' she remarks, sleepy.

'That,' he whispers, 'is probably because I'm not very real. Sleep tight, darling.'

'Goodnight,' mumbles the girl.

A moment later she's fast asleep, flat out in her jeans and cardigan. Teo smooths back a strand of her hair that's tipped over her eye, then plants a gentle kiss on the top of her head. He won't kid himself: Julie, though she probably doesn't realise it, has been swayed to this view not through any virtue of his, but more by Bernard's fatherly failings. Switching off the lights, he retreats to his bedroom where he lies awake, pain flickering like a candle flame in his chest where the ghosts of his family whisper for his attention to them, and them alone.

12

Terri stands transfixed in her entrance hall. The young woman in grey silk gliding down the wooden staircase looks like an advert fresh out of a programme from La Scala, Milan. Julie has pinned up her hair in a perfect chignon; and the Parisian dress clings and drapes in precisely the right spots. Against her throat, the diamonds that she should never have let Irina give her bare themselves like teeth.

'You look fantastic,' Terri says. 'I'd better change.'

'The taxi's here. Anyway, you look cool.'

Terri is in a cream-coloured trouser suit. 'Give me five minutes.' She bounds up to her bedroom without further ado.

Teo wanders out of the drawing room, pipe in hand. The house is marinating in the scent of his tobacco, though Terri has, as usual, opened the windows against it. 'Surprise for you on the Christmas tree,' he tells Julie.

He had brought some new decorations from Paris and now the tree, which stands to attention beside the drawing-room piano, is draped with copper-coloured tinsel. Julie hasn't grown out of a childhood love for all things sparkly; from the doorway she delights in the way the fronds trap the firelight. On the top balances an angel in a white robe with a golden halo. 'You see the angel?' Teo says. 'Now come out here.' He points upwards.

Terri has reappeared at the top of the stairs in one of her best evening dresses — ivory like her name, off-the-shoulder and heavily beaded. She bows with a flourish before sailing down towards them.

'I can hardly believe I am going out with two such glorious ladies,' Teo declares, offering an arm each to mother and daughter. And to Julie, quietly: 'You see the angel?'

Julie would call her mother many things; an angel might have been one of them until recently. She pulls her coat closed, trying to hide the diamonds as the three of them step out into the street.

★ ★ ★

The taxi trundles through Dulwich, Camberwell and Elephant and Castle; it crosses Waterloo Bridge — a minute of London glory, the dome of St Paul's sharp against the sepia clouds. There's a crawl north past Euston and Camden Town, then a steady climb to Hampstead Village and the flagpole that marks the highest point of London. Beyond it, the streets widen; everything expands by a size until finally they pull up outside a gated house that, to Julie, looks as megalithic as college itself.

'How many million again?' Terri whispers. Julie tells her. Terri pulls a face. She pays the driver and climbs out under the gaze of two

245

heavy-set guards who stand on either side of the door.

'*Privyet*, Vaslav,' says Julie to one of them. He gives her a brisk nod.

'You know him?' Teo asks.

'He's up at uni, making sure Rini's OK.'

'Jesu Maria,' Terri mumbles.

At the door a maid spirits away their coats and they find they're facing a baronial wooden stairway carpeted in white, with a Gothic stone arch at the top — though the rest of the house is as modern as can be. Jazz fills the air — a live band, somewhere inside. The air is rich with the scent of cinnamon candles. They pause, taking stock of these outlandish surroundings. Terri spots a painting that can only be a Miró.

A shriek of joy and Irina appears under the arch, radiant in black and gold. She dances down to embrace Julie and shake Terri and Teo's hands long and hard. 'It's so amazing you are here! Please, come and meet my father.'

'It's more amazing,' Teo whispers to Julie, 'that they let me in at all.' He's insisted on wearing his old corduroy jacket with the patched elbows. When Terri questioned his choice, he explained that it's because the pocket is big enough to hold his tobacco tin.

'You're not going to sleep on the métro tonight,' she'd growled at him, 'even if you're dressed for it.' She'd smarted for days after Julie's report of her chat with Dominique. Taunting Teo doesn't seem fair, but she hopes, beneath the apparent harshness, that it might

246

help him to gain a little perspective and snap out of it.

'I shall do what I like,' he returned, 'whether it's taking a cat-nap or refusing to show respect for the Russian mafia.'

Irina, arm tucked through Julie's, leads them along a corridor whiter than a hospital; a moment later a ballroom sprawls ahead, its giant windows bordering the fairy-lit garden where lanterns hang among the branches and the lawn's edges gleam magically with low-set lamps. A few couples are dancing to the jazz band. Julie senses, through the wailing saxophone, a buzz of languages: the gurgle of Russian, the light patter of French, a blast of operatic Italian and some East European spin-offs that she can't begin to identify.

'This is my father, Sergei Ivanovich Ovchinikov.' Irina holds out an arm to a middle-aged man of medium height, dressed in a plain dark suit. Julie is almost surprised by how ordinary he looks. Somehow she'd expected him to seem different — taller or broader, wearing outlandish clothes and/or a bullet-proof vest. Yet it's only his mercurial eyes that set him apart.

'*Ochin priatna*, Sergei Ivanovich,' Terri purrs. Irina's father raises her hand to his lips, his gaze taped to her face. 'This is my friend Teo Popović, and my daughter Juliette.'

'Julie is best friend I ever had,' Irina declares, arm around Julie's waist.

'And she is very lovely,' says Sergei. 'Dear friends, welcome to my home. What would you like to drink?' With a click of his fingers he

247

summons a waiter bearing a tray of glasses. Julie feels his eyes linger on the necklace from his shop.

'Is there a Mrs Ovchinikov?' Teo hisses to Julie.

'Divorced.' Julie watches the two men seeing through one another: Teo's expressive face as he looks past Ovchinikov's polished exterior to the smallness of spirit beyond, and the Russian's inscrutability as he sizes up the self-destructive Bosnian who wouldn't dress up for the smartest party in Hampstead.

'So what brought you to London, Sergei Ivanovich?' Terri asks, while he personally tops up her champagne.

'Teresa, I wish I could say that it was lure of greatest city in Europe.' Sergei's tone is confidential. 'I wish I could say it was wealth of culture, beauty of Hampstead Heath, convenient access to all parts of world. But you know what? It was tax laws!'

He roars with laughter and Terri joins in. Julie beams her a silent message: don't even think about it.

'Why do I suddenly feel like a spare part?' Teo growls, aside.

'Would you like to see house?' Sergei asks Terri. 'I show you house. I introduce you to my friend from management of Mariinsky Theatre in St Petersburg. And there is so much to ask about your wonderful singing.'

'I knew he'd love her.' Irina beams after them while they glide away.

The band begins 'Jingle Bells', jazzed up. Teo

248

— abandoned — smiles at Julie: 'We've sung together before. Now shall we dance?'

They haven't told anyone but Terri about their evening in Paris. There'd been nuclear fallout in Falcon Park, of course, but less than Julie had secretly hoped, mainly because Teo insisted on sending her straight back. In the morning, after croissants and coffee, he looked up the train times and bundled his sleepy guest off to the Gare du Nord. 'It's been great,' he said, kissing her goodbye at the check-in, 'but I must work and so must you. We can't have happy holidays all the time.' And Julie had little choice but to accept it.

In the end, he'd been the sadder of the two. Unable to stand the empty flat, he'd gone out late in the evening, consumed several cognacs in the nearest bar, then got on to the métro and stayed there. As far as Julie was concerned, all was well; with one night's absence, college hadn't been alerted, and when Teo called Terri, she promptly invited him over for a week — during which he could come to this blasted party.

To one side, their rainbow of colours reflecting in the white marble floor, food-laden tables offer cold poached salmon, mounds of wild rice, blinis with sour cream and caviar, green salad, hot chicken and potatoes, sliced tomatoes with red onion, piles of broccoli and cauliflower — enough, Julie thinks, to feed Alistair's regiment.

'Come and eat something,' Irina encourages after Teo has whirled Julie to the end of the dance. She pulls them towards the buffet, past a corner of the room where the wall bears a peculiar collection of switches, plus a red knob protected by a glass cover with keyhole. 'You see that button in corner, beside light switches? If we unlock it and press, floor slides open and underneath there is swimming pool! It's very funny to do this at the wrong moment, but I resist such temptation.' Irina catches Teo's eye and gives him a flirty wink, which he returns. 'My father keeps the keys in his study, so there's no danger — if we behave! Julie, when we've eaten, come upstairs, I show you my room.'

Sergei and Terri have long since diffused into the party ether. Teo, leaving the girls together, wanders outside to the terrace beyond the dancing and puffs on his pipe.

★ ★ ★

Julie has never seen so many toy animals in her life. Fifty? A hundred? They're piled all over the bed. Cats, dogs, lions, tigers, bunny rabbits, teddies, tortoises, fish, each fuzzier than the last. Everything else in Irina's room is white, unless it's fronted with mirrors: floor-to-ceiling wardrobes take up an entire wall. A white desk stands in one window with a white chair; the white carpet is spotless; the bedspread, underneath the furry toys, is snowy raw silk. Pale Viennese blinds loop themselves down the length of the casements.

'Is beautiful, no?' says Irina.

'Er, yes,' says Julie, more confused than ever.

'You are lucky, having your mother around.'

Irina curls up like a long-limbed cat in her armchair. Julie perches between animals on the bed. 'She is amazing. So beautiful.'

'She's hardly ever here,' Julie points out. 'This is kind of a one-off.'

'But my mother *never* is. I go to see her in Russia maybe twice a year. I miss her so much.'

'We're as bad as each other, really. Competing for whose parents are least there.'

'You know, it's not your fault, don't you? I know, is not my fault.' Irina stretches her slender arms into a balletic arc. 'It is *world events*. All we think is in our little lives is really because of world events.'

'I'm not with you.' Julie pulls three toy animals into her arms.

'Political Russia means my father cannot go back and thinks I am in danger if I go. And if mother comes over here, problems too when she returns. It's not my fault. This is world, Putin's world, you see? And world events determine why your mother must travel all the time. In the old days when they had only steam ships, artists would make a long tour, but not as often, and they would take whole family too. Now because of planes, it is expected musicians travel constantly, so they must even if they don't like to. It's not her fault. Is world events.'

'I'm afraid that my father moving out had very little to do with world events,' Julie remarks, picking up a fourth animal.

'Well, we make most of life for ourselves,' declares Irina. 'That is the secret. Champagne? No, don't get up!' She reaches out of her window and pulls in, from the sill outside, a bottle of Dom Perignon that has been chilling privately in the winter wind. 'All ours!'

Holding out her glass, laughing, Julie tries to banish a crawling suspicion that something in this house is very skewed indeed, and about to grow worse.

★ ★ ★

'I have seen you many times,' Sergei tells Terri. 'I see you sing in Covent Garden, Salzburg, Vienna, La Scala, the Met . . . '

'Oh, quite the groupie,' she teases.

'But you are Scottish? You have a very beautiful accent.'

'Funny, everyone says that,' Terri growls. 'Everyone loves the Glasgow accent except us Glaswegians!'

'Tell me how you became a singer. I want to know all about you.'

'Then let's sit down a minute.'

They're in a relatively cosy sitting room off the white corridor, where an array of cushions and a giant flat-screen TV suggest that Sergei and Irina retreat here to relax, when possible. Terri coils herself into a round chair lined with a shaggy white rug.

'It's a funny thing about singing,' she begins. 'You see, you don't have a voice, it has you. And it doesn't matter where you come from or what your background is. In my case it was the Gorbals. I was always singing as a child, and there was music everywhere, in church and

252

school and the pub, and free music lessons for everyone who wanted them — those were the days! But it was thanks to the woman who took class singing at school that I learned I had something a little different.'

'A clever lady,' Sergei comments. 'And then?'

'Well, I had this mad Italian — Scottish boyfriend who decided I could busk at the Edinburgh Festival and earn our keep by singing, so that we could go and see everything there. So we moved to Edinburgh with a backpack each, and it was fun at first. The place seemed a lot nicer than where we both lived — but I didn't make much money, so we had to look for jobs. He sold ice-cream, and I went to work at the pub across the road from the Usher Hall, in the kitchen. That way, you see, I could be close to the music and the musicians.'

'You knew even then that you belonged there?'

'More and more, music was an addiction. Perhaps an escape too, but certainly an addiction. I came from nowhere, Sergei Ivanovich. My mother was living on benefits in one of those old tenement blocks, and we had no hot water when I was a kid. Free music lessons yes; hot water, no.'

'Was it only you and your mother?'

'And my brother. He went to work in the shipyards — later he was very badly injured and then I needed to support him.'

'Injured? How injured?'

'An industrial accident. His leg had to be amputated.'

Sergei swears in Russian. Terri nods gently.

'It's a long time ago,' she says. 'Back to my story. One day I was working at the pub when Katharina Strashilova wandered in — the Bulgarian soprano who was very big-time in the early 1970s — she was my absolute idol, apart from Callas. She'd defected from Sofia, then married serious money, an American diplomat from a Texan oil background. I'd seen her once, when she came to sing *Norma* at the Theatre Royal. Believe it or not, I used to go quite a bit — there was a big drive to pull in primary schools when I was a wee thing, so we'd all go trooping in; and the tickets didn't cost too much, so later Mary, my teacher, took me with her several times. We saw Kiri te Kanawa, Janet Baker — loads of great singers visited Glasgow in those days.

'Anyway, I saw her looking at the menu on the blackboard — there was no catering in the hall so everyone used to come to our pub. And I dropped a tray and the food went all over the place. I thought I'd lose my job. But when I told my boss why I got such a fright, I was lucky — she loved music herself, so she understood. Then the 'artists' liaison officer', an officious little prick, came bustling in and said could we send some supper over to the hall for Miss Strashilova? She had all these special requirements: nothing dairy, no meat, herbal tea and so on. My boss delegated this to me. I nearly died — I had to take a special meal to my heroine in person!

'My hands were shaking as I dished out the spinach. I still remember that plate — overcooked white fish without the sauce, gloopy green stuff on one side, starchy white rice to the other, and I jollied it up with some tomatoes and a cup of peppermint tea. I had to walk up and down the corridor three times before I found the courage to knock on her door, and only then because otherwise her food would be cold and everyone would blame me.'

'I'd never realised how much make-up singers wore onstage. There were her great dark eyes staring at me, outlined with all this black stuff, and sparkly blue over her eyelids. I'd never seen anything like it! I smiled sweetly and she was so pleased that I'd got all her requests right that she started chatting to me — just about the weather, then was I from Edinburgh and did I like it there? I don't know what came over me, but I heard myself asking if I could sing to her and if she could advise me what to do. I'd never have imagined I'd have the nerve and I never thought she'd say yes. But she must have seen in my face how much it mattered to me, and she agreed . . .'

'This is remarkable,' Sergei comments. 'A beautiful story. So much was resting on chance and good fortune.'

'Indeed.' Terri sips her champagne; its bubbles fizz together with the distant jazz in her ears. She wonders what's loosened her tongue — perhaps the fact that she hasn't been to a party for months? Or has Sergei doctored her champagne? She keeps talking. She tells the Russian all about how she sang Mozart to Katharina the next morning before the singer left for London, the advice she provided, the references she wrote

255

that let Terri be admitted to the Royal College of Music and helped her gain access to the necessary grants and scholarships. 'It was like a fairy tale,' she remarks.

'But you dared to do this,' Sergei points out. 'You could so easily take the great singer her supper and never say a word.'

'I was lucky. She was a kind person, unusually kind. And maybe a little insecure — she loved being adored, and I think she still does. Obviously I adored her, so she liked that! She didn't have to listen to me, she didn't have to help the way that she did. Perhaps it was a whim; perhaps she was bored and lonely — it can be awful when you're on the road alone. And you know, singers don't often do this for new young talent — we're all paranoid as hell! I do think I was more lucky than daring.'

'Perhaps you, Teresa, are a lucky person. There are some whose natural disposition is so honest and true that they cannot help but be lucky. I believe you are one such.' Sergei kisses her hand again, then seems reluctant to relinquish it.

Terri senses it's time to get out. What *did* Sergei put in her drink? 'I left Teo on his own,' she explains.

'He is a big boy,' says her new admirer. 'He can look after himself. We are among friends. Tell me one more thing — which was the Mozart you sang to your heroine all those years ago?'

'Cherubino's aria, 'Voi, che sapete'. Funny, I never sang it onstage. It's completely wrong for my voice.'

'How it goes?'

Terri hums. Sergei nods, his eyes twinkling.

'Teresa,' he begins. 'I don't know how to ask you. But we have fine pianist here, in band, he can sight-read anything. I have little music library upstairs. May I beg you, on my bended knees, to sing Cherubino's aria for us here tonight?'

Terri's breath catches in her fragile throat. 'Oh, I couldn't. It wouldn't be fair to inflict a concert on all your guests! They're having fun dancing.'

'They should be so lucky as to hear today's greatest diva perform for them,' Sergei encourages.

'But I never sing this aria at all.' Terri glues on her grin. 'It isn't in my repertoire.'

'Then maybe you would sing something that is?'

Terri thinks fast. It's her own fault for not letting anybody know why she'd been off, so she shouldn't complain. At one time, she'd have been only too happy to comply.

A possibility beckons to her so unexpectedly, through so much champagne — spiked or otherwise — that she's swept away. Her laryngologist, a model of patience when faced with her anxiety, has remarked that most singers undergoing the same treatment would have been back at work months earlier. She's been careful, exceptionally so; the problem is her confidence, and the more cautious she is, the more cautious she becomes. Yet — heavens, how she misses it. If she doesn't try, how will she know whether she *can* perform?

One aria. Just one. Something easy; something in which she need not strain her throat; after all, the room is no opera house. A flash-flood of desire goes through her: physical longing, visceral in her nerves. The wanting cuts like a dagger, sending a shooting sensation down her arm and curling her hand into a fist. Some women feel this way over babies they don't have, others over neighbours' better houses. She feels it only for singing.

'Please, Teresa,' Sergei wheedles. 'It would be a moment that nobody present could ever forget.'

There's a swirl of grey, black and gold by the door and the two girls appear, breathless, laughing.

'Ah, there you are!' Julie cries. 'You have to see the tropical fish, they're incredible!'

Terri glances at Sergei. His gaze has drifted to Julie's neck.

'It suits her so well, this choker,' he remarks quietly. 'A very good choice. I would be so sorry if she felt for any reason that she had to return it.'

Gates clang shut around Terri as she understands. How on earth had she failed to see this coming?

She takes a breath. 'Just one, then.'

'Good. I show you library,' says Sergei.

'Mum?' says Julie. 'What are you doing?'

* * *

Julie plunges through the party, past the waiters and their trays, the businessmen shovelling food

258

high on to their plates at the buffet, the Russian models and escorts who have accompanied some of the men, out to the terrace where Teo lurks in the rockery with his pipe, his breath rising with the smoke through the bitter air.

'Come quick.' Julie grabs his arm. 'He wants Mum to sing.'

'No! She said yes?'

'Teo, it's like — ' She puts her hand to her throat, where the diamonds feel much too tight. 'I feel like it's my fault.'

'Bloody monster. I kill him. I get friends from the Bosnian army to come and kill him. Why doesn't she explain? Why does your mother have the head of a pig?'

'Sergei's got some friend here who runs the Mariinsky — but it's not just that, Teo, I think she *wants* to sing.'

'That, my dear, is the real problem. Come along, we must stop her.'

Julie senses a rustle of excitement behind them, the brush of figures rearranging themselves and finding the best places to stand while Sergei declaims a request for everybody to gather in the ballroom for a musical surprise. Teo and Julie slink to the side of the room.

The pianist of the jazz band looks pink-eared and reverential as he props a piece of music on the stand. Guests drift in, admiring the view from the giant windows.

'Which was the button?' Teo hisses to Julie.

'You wouldn't!'

'Try me!'

'In the corner, by the light switches. But you

259

need a key. Irina says they're somewhere in Sergei's study.'

'OK, I find the study and steal the key.' Teo slopes away before Julie can say another word.

Sergei claps for attention. 'Ladies and gentlemen, friends, comrades!' There's a chuckle from the older Russian guests. 'Tonight we are privileged to have amongst us one of the greatest stars in the operatic firmament, Teresa Ivory, who has agreed to honour us with Tchaikovsky's famous art song, 'None but the lonely heart'.'

★　★　★

Terri, waiting, feels sweat on her upper lip. She has to do this sometime. She'd rather have chosen the moment herself, without blackmail, but on balance it's as good as any. A test-drive in second gear through a backwater to check that the vehicle can actually move. It's a slow, intimate song; she won't need to belt it, and if she sings quietly, everyone will think it's a musical decision to draw a tear or two.

To the crackle of friendly applause she sweeps forward in her evening gown, its cream-coloured beads rattling against the marble floor, and takes her place beside the piano. In the far doorway, she spots the squarish silhouette of Teo's head — he's apparently in altercation with the Lithuanian bodyguard. Turning to the pianist, she smiles and gives a nod; silence falls as he begins the introduction.

Terri sings in Russian as best she can. She remembers the sound of the syllables more than their meaning — but at least she does remember them. The song is low-set, which is comfortable; and one of her special abilities is that, rather than projecting everything out to the audience, she prefers to draw them in towards her, forcing them to listen. One line into the song she senses the familiar velvet hush settling over the room. Her voice is doing everything she wants. So far so good.

Teo has finished his fight with the bouncer and is leaning against the doorframe, a misfit in this roomful of slick, moneyed Russians: a badger among the weasels, an albatross amid the gulls. She feels a rush of tenderness towards him, for his strength and loyalty; she curses her own imagination that's too easily led astray by fascinating newness. She fixes her gaze on his face and sings the love song past the crowd, entirely for him. As she watches, a glistening tear meanders down his cheek.

Her song is faultless, the applause fervent. Sergei embraces her and Julie virtually jumps for joy. There's a shout: 'Encore!' Left and right, voices echo the call. Terri bows, charisma ablaze. What now? She's a victim of her own success. One song, fine, but push it too far and anything might go wrong . . . yet she can see the director of the Mariinsky Theatre holding forth to Sergei in ecstatic Russian, and there's a future to form.

'Do you have 'Dove sono' from *Figaro*?' she asks Sergei; smiling from ear to ear, he gives one of his assistants a set of barked Russian instructions regarding the music library.

'A brief break, then more singing!' he announces.

Teo fights his way forward, eyes grim.

'Darling, cheer up.' She hugs him, keeping her voice low and speaking into his ear. 'I *can* do it, you see. I *haven't* lost my voice.'

'Be sensible,' he whispers.

'I can sing 'Dove sono' standing on my head underwater,' she insists. 'You wait and see if I can't.'

'But — '

The aide returns, brandishing the score of *The Marriage of Figaro* with Cyrillic writing on the front. Terri leafs in two flicks straight to the aria. She wonders why Sergei has so many volumes of sheet music.

'Once upon a time,' he explains, 'I wanted to be a pianist. I used to accompany local opera company's rehearsals. But I've hardly touched piano since things changed in Russia. There was winning to do, and to play piano when I was no virtuoso would not make me win.'

'Well, I'll sing you some Mozart and then you'll be sorry!' She flashes a dimple.

The pianist, his hands shaking slightly, begins to play. Terri earths herself and shapes the familiar Italian. She's flying high now, confident in her happiest skin, her stage persona. And what a relief: it's still there, it's still hers. No longer is she singing for Teo, but for the world around her, a world that needs art like hers in order to hold up its head proud and call itself civilised.

Afterwards, of course, everyone wants her to carry on. She'd anticipated this, but shakes her

262

head, smiling all the while — no, I'm at a party, I've had a little too much champagne and I've sung enough. But the seconds drag by and they won't let her go. Someone gives her a white rose, which she tucks behind one ear. Someone else brings her more champagne. Sergei walks forward with a small box bearing the Ovchinikov logo; something rattles inside. Terri kisses him, backing away from the piano as gracefully as possible. Another moment and she'll be free.

'Wait.' Sergei picks up a volume that had mysteriously appeared along with the Mozart. She can't read the title, which is in Cyrillic. It's the piano score of a huge opera.

'Most wonderful thing I ever heard,' he declares, 'was you singing Wagner's Isolde in Baden-Baden. It was your debut in role. It was most profoundly moving experience of my life, before or since. Please, Teresa, may I *beg* you to sing Isolde's 'Liebestod' for us tonight?'

'Oh, no!' Terri bats her eyelashes. 'Sergei Ivanovich, I haven't sung the 'Liebestod' for such a long time. I haven't practised it. It will sound terrible!'

'Impossible. Nothing you sing could sound terrible.'

'And it wouldn't be fair on my poor pianist, he's never seen the music before.'

'I can do it if you want me to, Miss Ivory,' the pianist interrupts, thinking innocently enough that he's helping.

'Mum, *no*,' Julie mouths.

'Really, I've inflicted enough opera on your long-suffering guests. It's Christmas. They're here to enjoy themselves!' Terri makes a last frantic attempt to escape.

'Ah, but it's my party. So, what I say goes.' He kisses her hand and at the same moment Terri knows that those words are directed not only at the guests, but at her.

She's well and truly trapped, so she'll have to be positive. The voice has worked, she feels fine, everyone has been paying her compliments. She doesn't have to sing full out. Sustained, yes; loud, no. Anyway, the 'Liebestod' isn't that difficult if you don't have to sing the other four hours of the opera first.

With an exaggerated curtsey, she hands her pianist the Russian edition of *Tristan und Isolde*, and issues quiet instructions: 'Not too slow, darling. And please don't bang.'

★ ★ ★

Julie dives across to Teo, who's heading out of the room. 'What are we going to do?'

'I couldn't get the key because of the thugs, but I'll find a way. Leave it to me.' He blows her a kiss, then vanishes round a corner.

Julie watches in horror as Terri takes up her position beside the piano for the third time. She's crazy. How can she risk everything for the sake of keeping up the appearance of perfection? Would she rather set herself back than admit that there's recovery in progress? She only need tell Sergei that she's had an operation on her throat and isn't fully better. But she can't — or she won't. The familiar harmonies, rhetorical and

264

sombre, rise from the piano. Terri closes her eyes and begins the 'Liebestod' almost in a whisper. '*Mild und leise . . .* '

And the rapture, Julie understands, is not only the listeners', but Terri's own. Julie's instinct was right: Terri is singing not just because she's been coerced, but because she wants to; and not only because she wants to, but because she must. If she'd declined to sing the 'Liebestod' tonight, she might never sing it again.

Terri is lost in sound. Arms outstretched, head slightly back, she's turning herself into a channel: Isolde's music passes through her and straight out to the audience, concentrating a century and a half of melody with a focus as intense as precision radar. Somewhere beyond the room, there's a commotion — shouts, slams and a thump — but Terri is oblivious, a white and gold vision reflected fifty times above, across and below in glass and marble, transformed by her stage magic and surfing the crest of the music as it surges higher and higher.

The transition from ecstasy to chaos takes place with a suspended shock like the aftermath of a bomb. Sound collides with silence, and Terri, coughing, hands pressed to her mouth, swings away, hiding her face, then flashes towards the door in a blur of golden light. All that remains is the startled young man at the piano, his hands frozen on the keys.

'Mum!' Diving after her, Julie's just in time to see a glint of beading as Terri plunges into the cloakroom off the white corridor. She shakes the door handle, shouting, but Terri's locked herself in and won't answer.

Reeling, she runs back to Irina. 'Where's Teo?'

'Vaslav and Vacek threw him out.'

'*What?*'

Sure enough, Teo is sitting on the garden wall not far from where the chauffeurs wait for their clients, his pipe giving out a bronzy glow in the dark. There's a streak of gravel, white and grey, on his corduroy jacket. 'They said he was trying to grab the key that opens the pool,' Irina whispers.

'Oh God,' Julie says, fighting tears. 'If only he had.'

★　★　★

In the bathroom, Terri, leaning on the basin with her fists clenched, has been trying to call back to Julie through the locked door. But her voice has turned so hoarse that there's not enough left to make a sound.

13

'I don't know what you expected,' says Teo. 'I don't know what you thought you were trying to do.'

'I was trying, in case you didn't notice, to sing,' Terri croaks over herbal tea with honey. It's past 11 a.m., but she's in her dressing gown and has switched on the answerphone.

'Why didn't you just say no? Isn't that what they used to tell kids to stop them taking drugs? *Just say no*?'

'And it really worked for the druggies,' Terri grumbles, sarcastic. 'Jesu bloody Maria. What am I going to *do*?'

She looks so frightened that Teo, though furious, hugs her, wishing that the will to heal could do the job on its own. 'Go and see your doctor, right away.'

'I can't! What's he going to say?'

'He'll say, my darling, that you're an idiot.'

'But if I hadn't sung . . . '

' . . . you wouldn't be in this state now.'

'But Julie — the necklace — and Sergei was saying that . . . '

'Are you sure that's really what he was saying? Weren't you reading too much into it?'

'I know a deep dark hint when I hear one, my dear. I wasn't born yesterday.'

'In that case, you shouldn't behave like a silly schoolgirl. Terri, what will it *take* to make you look after yourself?'

A huge bouquet of white flowers has arrived with a card, including a mobile phone number, from Sergei Ovchinikov. The night before, when Terri finally peered round the cloakroom door and explained her vanished voice in mime, Julie succumbed to hysterics and told Irina everything. The contrition was immense; the face of the Mariinsky director was never to be forgotten; there was even an apology to Teo from Vaslav, who nevertheless pointed out that opening the swimming pool beneath the ballroom would have risked lives, not to mention a massive bill for piano repair, and might not have been the best course of action given the circumstances. Sergei packed the three of them off home in his Lexus with his chauffeur, and Irina, hugging Julie, had insisted they meet today to make certain everything and everyone was all right.

A bit late, thinks Terri, stirring her tea. There's a prickling ache in the depths of her throat; she keeps wanting to gag.

'If you don't call the doctor right now,' says Teo, 'I will.'

'All right. You do it. I can't make myself heard on the phone anyway.'

'Give me the number.'

Terri does.

★　★　★

Three hours later, she's in Harley Street, mouth wide open.

'Singing for your supper,' remarks her

laryngologist. 'Just what you needed most, wasn't it?'

Terri can't respond in her current pose.

'How bad is it?' she whispers a few minutes later, upright again. 'Is it a haemorrhage?' Images flash through her mind — another operation, a disaster, the possibility that the problem will never clear up . . .

'The good news,' he says, 'is that it's not a haemorrhage. In fact it's more likely to be acid reflux.'

'Acid reflux?' Terri echoes. She knows of nothing else that sounds so undignified. 'But I shouldn't get that — I keep my bed tilted specially!'

'It can be down to a lot of different things. Adrenalin, hormones, the age that you happen to be, or simply that maybe you half expected something to go wrong. It's hard to pinpoint the cause, Terri, but I'd take it as a warning signal. You need to rest properly and for longer. R-E-S-T. Enjoy it while you can. Stop driving yourself so hard — do *nothing* for a while. You owe it to yourself.'

'I've never been much good at doing nothing,' Terri admits, 'and I've been doing nothing for half this year. It's been the longest of my life.'

'But if you want your voice to be its old self, you have to listen to its needs. Terri, I know it's difficult, but *you mustn't sing*. Promise?'

Terri, teeth clenched, promises.

★　★　★

Alistair, lying on his bunk at the end of a long day on patrol, is mainly aware of his feet. All his consciousness has swum down into them. It's as if they're blowing up to dwarf the rest of him; soon they'll only be two monstrous plates of red meat, with corns the size of Mount Snowdon against the bones, and he'll have to trail on them through the rocky terrain, dragging his head along behind.

He's incrementally fitter than he was when he left home — more muscle, less fat. He wonders whether his mother and Julie will recognise him when he returns, which won't be for a while. A war doesn't take time out for Christmas. Sue will spend the holiday with her brother, Julie with Terri. Teo, Julie writes, might go to Bosnia for New Year with his cousins. Since he's been here, Alistair has gained not only extra respect for Teo, but also a modicum of understanding about why he occasionally acts weird.

Inside the camp walls, constructed by fellow infantrymen a couple of years ago, they're to have Christmas dinner, with supplies flown in by helicopter. Some of the lads are preparing a few songs. His friend Darren Hanley wants to do a number in drag — homosexuality isn't smiled on here, but its aping is — and they've been trawling mothers, wives and girlfriends in the hope that someone can post them, in time, a pair of size twelve shoes with six-inch heels. 'Don't talk to me about feet,' Alistair said. Acknowledging that though at home he's surrounded by songbirds he can't string two notes together himself, he's volunteered to turn some cardboard boxes into rudimentary props.

E-blueys arrive regularly from Julie and his mum, when the computers are working. Family back home type messages into a centralised website and they come through, from worlds away, in the form of little blue printouts like airmail. Normally he writes back, but the computers have been down for four days so he's scribbled a letter instead. He can't bring himself to finish it — and not only because it will take at least a week, if not two, to reach her.

The first week, he missed Julie intensely — her warm, slender body, her wonderful eyes and her voice, which is as nice when she's speaking as, he supposes, when she sings. Not that he'd seen much of her while he was in Yorkshire, but now the psychological distance adds bizarre effects to simple non-presence. From Yorkshire you could phone and text, knowing that if you jumped on the bus and the train, you'd be together again in a matter of hours. Here twenty minutes a week is free by phone — you can pay for more time if you like — but that is it; and when, the day after Alistair and the others arrived, a truck was ambushed by a suicide bomber and two lads were killed, the first thing to go was the telephone. Nobody could ring home until the family had been officially informed, lest the news should reach them first on the grapevine.

He'd never realised before that missing someone can be a physical sensation. He felt it in his head, stomach, fingers, even his toes. Sometimes, staring towards the point where earth meets sky and the two blend ochre into grey, with the sand that swirls in the air stinging the side of his face, the pulsing sensation of *no Julie* nearly took away his breath. The first package she sent him — magazines, newspaper clippings, chocolate, peanut butter and Marmite — was a help, if a small one. He used to scoff at the much-repeated notion that Marmite tastes of home more than anything else; he's appalled to find that it's true.

Her e-blueys always remind him of her lack of confidence — it was a quality he used to think was appealing, maybe because he'd shared it. There's always been something *apart* about Julie; shyness rather than snobbiness — as the child of an opera star, she's always been hypersensitive if anyone thinks she's a snob. Now, though, he wonders if Julie's not so much shy as slightly lost. Alistair no longer feels lost. From this distance, he can recognise in her his own old way of being — those messages that either grumble about things she dislikes at uni or worry about her mother and always seem disappointed in her father, without ever exploring many solutions.

For the first time, here in this desolate place beside which Scargill Tower looks like the palace of the gods, he feels he's a cog in a wheel that has significance, even if he's not always sure what that significance is — the politics go way over his head. He knows it's something to do with West versus East, Christianity versus Islam, freedom against fundamentalism, even if it all sounds a bit far-fetched. But also he knows he's never been so fit, so stretched or so focused before, and he's never had so many friends. Extraordinary that if you've spent days on end firing guns side by side, avoiding what comes back, trying to get 'them' before 'they' get you, protecting and saving each other, you soon grow closer to those guys than you ever would to someone you've known all your life.

Perhaps the oddest thing of all is that he's enjoying it. The food's full of beans, the dust is everywhere, the nights are fucking freezing and his feet hurt, but the excitement and the adrenalin never stop. It beats the hell out of stacking shelves.

'Trouble is, Rosso,' Darren Hanley remarked when the two of them had a chance to talk away from the others, 'we shouldn't be here.'

Han had arrived in Catterick on the same day as Alistair. He'd been the brightest of their batch of recruits, eager to learn, raring to go, watching in dismay when those who weren't fit enough were weeded out lest he should be one of them next time. Alistair doesn't know when his doubts had begun. Before they flew out for the tour, people asked questions, lots of them; when they got there, everything was new and they'd been too busy adjusting to discuss such things; and soon they were occupied at every moment with the small matter of staying alive. Han couldn't wait to get started, or so he made out. These days, he's anxious and fidgety and smokes too much.

Alistair argued that since they were there, they had to do it properly.

'Do what properly?' Han retorted. 'These

273

bastards are trying to kill us all, every fucking day, and there's no way we can win. Everyone says that. Nobody's ever won a bloody war in this country. And you know something? What we're really doing here is propping up the dope trade. We stop them growing poppies, so they grow weed instead. It's fucking insane.'

Alistair had no answer for that. There was no point telling Han that he's the one who shouldn't be there if that's how he feels. Three days earlier, their section had passed the site of a roadside bomb minutes before it went off. A boy from the platoon's last section was killed; he was only eighteen. He'd had his head out of the vehicle, on lookout. He hadn't spotted the bomb before it seemed to spot him. And of course the phones went down again at once.

Alistair wondered how he'd ever be able to explain to Julie, Terri and his mum why he didn't feel afraid. The first week, he'd been petrified, every moment of every day. But soon he found it was easier to forget it and just live in the moment, because there was no time to do anything else. You can't stop a war in order to blub.

Han, though, was badly shaken by that incident; Alistair worries that he's lost his nerve. He tries to strike a balance between reassuring his friend and wondering whether he can speak to a senior officer about bringing forward Han's leave without giving the impression that he's seriously worried about him.

Beside Han, Alistair feels almost guilty at being upbeat. His abilities are assets here: he's

274

good with his hands and quick with his reflexes and he's discovered that he can make sensible decisions fast. These qualities seem to go down well. It doesn't matter if he can't spell 'tomorrow', or remember the date of the Battle of Waterloo. What counts is purpose, discipline, the pushing of self and others, and the camaraderie which isn't just with the guys but also, to his surprise, with the officers. Though he sometimes wakes up longing never to see this landscape again and wanting only to sleep, preferably with Julie, he knows that south-east London will seem odd when he finally returns.

And so he can't finish his letter. Talking to Julie in their old way feels wrong; it would be a sham. If he sends her his real thoughts, she won't recognise him; she will think that what's changed is his feeling for her, though that isn't the case. It is more that, like the fear, missing her has dissipated because there's no time for it. He could never tell her that.

When the skies are thick with starlight and the silence of the empty hills betrays the earth's longevity against the news of a comrade killed or seriously wounded, it's then that the most unsettling thoughts come crawling along. What would be the odds if he bet on not going home alive? What would Julie's first words to him be when he went back, given how little she'd understand about this life? What if Han was right — that, later, someone might prove that they shouldn't have been there at all? Fortunately he's too knackered to lie awake thinking such things for more than thirty seconds at a stretch.

Alistair tears up the letter to Julie. He takes a page from his notebook and writes: 'MISS U. X.' Some stray sand blows on to the paper. He should send her those little grains: they would tell her more than any words.

★ ★ ★

'We miss you,' says Stefan to Teo, clasping his hand. 'We need you here.'

Teo drops his hand and embraces him instead, then hugs Sonja too. They're at the airport, which has been shinily reconstructed; a plane taking off roars overhead, the vibrations rumbling through the floor and up his legs. Being in Sarajevo with his cousins for New Year's Eve has been like stepping through a time warp. Toying with words for his own amusement, Teo finds it appropriate that what carries you from one plane of existence to another is, well, a plane.

'I don't know what I can do,' he says, 'other than hugs. I do good hugs.'

'The best.' Sonja presses his arm. 'Teo, you're doing more than anyone else. You are helping to keep it in people's minds. Otherwise everyone will forget us.'

'They have to move on,' Teo points out. 'And so do we. I know that now. I'm glad I've started to come back, Sonja.'

'But we need you back, and back again,' she insists. 'You belong here. You're part of us in a way you'll never be part of anywhere else.'

Teo stands firm. 'I have to go home.'

'It's still Terri? I don't think you're only going back for your students.'

'Yes. Of course it's still Terri.'

'For God's sake, Teo, you have to forget her. She's no good for you,' Stefan urges. 'She picks you up and puts you down. You should find someone who can give you a home and a family.'

'I have to go.' Teo's flight is boarding. 'I'll be back. Promise.' He holds out his arms; the three stand locked together for a few seconds.

'Bring her here, then.' Sonja releases him. 'Bring her to us.'

★ ★ ★

The old Sarajevo airport, in the days of Yugoslavia, didn't do such a good line in duty-free electronics and alcohol. Teo stocks up on whisky for himself and Terri — fancy buying a Glaswegian woman Scottish single malt in Bosnia! — then wanders to the electronics outlet to explore the newest gadgets. Digital dictation machines, portable hard-drives with many gigabytes of memory, plus something he hasn't seen before that is called a terabyte, maybe a dinosaur with eight-inch teeth. It's all beyond him. His favourite numbers are those in a rumoured Indonesian system he'd heard of during a surreal conference in Bali: one, two, three, lots.

He flies to London, not Paris, to see Terri and Julie before the beginning of term. The levels of his life shuffle under him like cards, switching from spades to hearts. The endless corridors of Gatwick, its new bridge and towering escalators. Continual announcements. Do not leave your cases unattended or they could cause a security alert and may be destroyed. Do not allow your children to play on the trolleys or the luggage carousels. Do not take trolleys on to the escalators. Don't forget that we fly to hundreds of exciting destinations every day. Don't forget to visit our wonderful shopping mall and high-street restaurants in the departure lounge. The transit monorail is approaching its final stop, please take care while leaving the train. This carriage is protected by CCTV.

Teo wants to block his ears and scream. Are people in Britain so dim and desensitised that they have to be instructed by disembodied voices about what not to do at every juncture? Don't they know that there are places on earth where no loudspeakers exist to say DO NOT WALK HERE, THERE ARE LANDMINES? When he had small children, he wouldn't have needed anyone to tell him not to let them play on a luggage carousel. It's obvious that it's dangerous, and if you're a parent you don't want your children to be hurt, so you stop them, fast. Or are the loudspeakers intended to suppress instinct, because if people can't hear themselves think in the ambient din, they'll never be capable of questioning the systems around them?

He takes the train from Gatwick to Clapham Junction and changes via the underpass for

Falcon Park. People have fled town for the holiday season, and he has few companions except for a gaggle of teenage girls who've been out partying. They're so drunk that they seem to swim as they board the train, eyes unfocused, legs like jellyfish. They scream stories at each other about how drunk they've been and how funny it was. 'And she made me take off my clothes and it was like just in time cos I threw up into the dishwasher, it was like *gross*!'

Teo moves to the end of the carriage where he can't hear them squealing or smell their breath. He's glad when the train pulls into Falcon Park station and he sets off, suitcase in hand, for the familiar slopes of Livingston Road.

The street hasn't changed much in twelve years, though there are fewer cars because of the residents' permit scheme. Terri's house looks run-down: tall and grey with worn stone steps leading from street to door, the same old crack the length of the wall, a patch of undergrowth passing for a front garden, and a roof that had needed replacing a decade ago and still does. Inside, though, a lamp glows in the hall window; she's expecting him. Bring her to Bosnia? Pigs are getting very good at flying in south-east London.

* * *

It's Julie who opens the door, jumping into his arms with a flurry of long hair and delight. Teo

279

sniffs: an unusual pall of cigarette smoke lingers in the air.

'Sue's here,' Julie explains, taking his arm. 'She's just back from her brother's place, but she misses Alistair terribly. We've had her round a lot.'

Teo wanders to the kitchen, where Terri's turquoise gaze, cool, clear and pleased, meets his across the other woman's head before she gets up to hug him. Sue's opposite, her back broad in a much-mended pink jersey, her ginger hair laced with grey, and a column of smoke rising from her cigarette towards the ceiling.

'Sue, you haven't met Teo, at least not for years,' says Terri.

'Long time ago.' Sue pumps Teo's hand. 'Nice to see you.'

One empty and one almost empty wine bottle stand at the side of the table; the three women have been happily ensconced here all evening. Julie is nineteen, Sue forty and Terri ten years older, but clearly these differences don't matter. He's never seen them together like this. He vaguely remembers that last time he met Sue, the children were young teenagers 'going out'; she'd been hovering on the doorstep waiting for Alistair, too shy to accept Terri's repeated invitation to come in for a cup of tea.

'She's a dead good cook,' Sue confides now. 'I never dreamed. I thought opera singers would just go to posh restaurants all the time.'

'Teo, darling,' says Terri, kissing him. 'I'll get you a glass. Sue, once a journalist asked me what career I'd have had if I wasn't a singer and I said

I'd have been a school dinner lady. He thought I was joking, but it's true.'

'Lucky school.' Sue gives a contented hiccup. 'Don't know what they missed, do they?'

'There's still time,' says Terri.

Teo accepts the glass. 'Sue, it's good to see you. How is Alistair?'

'As well as can be expected. He rings once a week and when he writes he doesn't write much.'

Teo follows Julie's gaze: a lined piece of paper on the sideboard is scrawled with no more than 'MISS U. X.' 'I'm sure it's just because he's busy.'

'Or he doesn't want to say too much about what he's doing because he doesn't want us to worry,' Terri points out. 'Mostly he just grumbles about the food.'

'I'm glad you all got together,' Teo remarks.

'What's 'Cheers' in Bosnian?' asks Sue.

'*Živjeli*.' He raises his glass and there's a triplicate echo of the word — from his other plane — as three female voices, different ages, different timbres, drink the health of the same boy three thousand miles away in a language they don't know.

'Sounds like Drivelly.' Sue laughs.

'We drivel a lot after a few glasses. The wine in Bosnia is extremely good.'

'So how was Sarajevo?' Julie asks.

'Fine.' He knows that behind her cheerful exterior, Julie's worried sick. Talking about his trip seems ridiculous. His war is alive inside him, but to everyone else it's long past. Perhaps Stefan and Sonja were right — most people have

281

forgotten Bosnia, perhaps because they have to in the face of the new-generation wars. 'I'll go again soon,' he says. 'My cousins want me there. They feel that Bosnia has somehow lost its voice in today's world, if you'll pardon the analogy.'

'Haven't we all.' Sue puffs smoke, and Teo automatically reaches out to push the window — Terri hasn't opened it nearly as far as she would have to protest at *his* smoke.

'How's college?' he asks Julie.

'I don't want to stay there, but Mum won't let me leave.' Julie's face darkens somewhat.

'She's right. Mothers sometimes are.'

'Oh, Teo! Not you too.'

'Yes, Julie, because you'll never get another shot at a degree from this beautiful university. You have to grab your chances. They don't come back.'

'I feel all wrong there. I'd rather get a job, or study somewhere else.'

'Maybe you could study singing as well as your course,' he suggests. 'That would liven things up.'

'She's not ready,' Terri interrupts. 'Lessons yes, conservatory no. She needs to be a bit older first.'

'Oh, God.' Julie rubs her forehead with her fist. 'I can't get anyone to listen to me. It's like whatever I do, they think it reflects on *them*. It's nothing to do with who I am.'

'You know, I liked what Sue said just now,' says Teo.

'What? What did I say?'

'I mentioned that my cousin thinks Bosnia has

lost its voice and you said 'haven't we all'.'

'I was only thinking of her.' Sue indicates Terri, who's giving Teo an under-the-lashes 'bed soon' look.

'Well,' says Teo, 'do *you* have a voice?'

'Me? Try and stop me! Been rabitting on for hours, haven't I, girls?'

'But do you have a way to say the things you need to say, and make sure they're heard?'

'Christ, I try. I vote when we're supposed to. Loads in the tower don't, though, cos there's no difference between them politician crooks any longer. Something's the matter with our drains, too, and the bloody council won't come and look. The place stinks to high heaven.'

'You see?' says Teo. 'That's what I mean. People don't have *a voice*. Not against media self-interest, government or local government incompetence, illegal wars and so on.'

'Or bad smells,' remarks Sue. 'Same thing, I guess.'

'You can write anything on the Internet any time you like,' Julie points out.

'But someone will always hammer you if you speak or write the truth.' Teo fumbles for his pipe. 'It's only the *illusion* of a voice. People write all kinds of comments on news sites and blogs, but it's only a voice if someone listens. Mostly if you write on those things you're dismissed as a nutcase. I certainly am!'

'You do write the truth.' Terri's leg rubs against his under the table.

'Only because it's fiction.' He rubs back.

'I'm lost!' Sue laughs.

'Don't worry, Sue, he's trying to dazzle us.' Julie's face glows with affection as she watches Teo picking tobacco strands from his tin to fill his pipe. 'You love having three women to yourself, don't you, Teo?'

Teo, puffing, blows her a kiss. Terri's other leg moves around his ankle. Sue dissolves into giggles. 'This is the best evening I've had in weeks,' she declares. 'I was always so scared of you, Terri. I thought, me, I'm a washed-up old single mum scraping by for my boy, and here's this — angelic person. Talented, famous. She'd never want to know me, even if our kids have been seeing each other all this time.'

'So guess what? Now *I'm* a washed-up single mum and I'm a lot older than you!' Terri tells her. Through her ankle, Teo senses a wobble under the laughter. He glances from Terri to Julie, a silent question.

'You haven't seen yesterday's *Telegraph*, have you?' Julie asks him.

'Show me?'

She fetches it. A headline in the Arts section reads: OPERA STAR MAY NEVER SING AGAIN.

Teo throws the paper across the kitchen.

'Rubbish,' says Sue. 'Load of crap. Course you'll sing again, Terri.'

'Where did they get this shit?' Teo demands. 'You didn't talk to them?'

'I refused to. That's their revenge. Someone who was at that party spilled the beans.'

'Like I said, love, don't let them get to you,' Sue exhorts.

Terri drums her fingers, avoiding everyone's

gaze. 'I'll show them, just you wait. If I ever meet this journalist on a dark night, I shall do something to his nose that he'll never forget.'

'Hey-ho.' Sue glances at the clock. 'Time for me to roll down the hill.' She lumbers to her feet and Julie dashes to embrace her.

'I'm so glad you came,' she says. 'If he calls . . .'

'Don't worry, love, I'll phone and tell you everything. You know he misses you.'

Julie hangs on to Sue as if trying to hold on to Alistair himself. Teo watches; he feels excluded from this atmosphere. After a little consideration, he deduces that it's probably because he's a man. Neither Sue nor Terri had known their fathers. Julie knows hers, but doesn't rate him much — rather the opposite, since she'd come running to Paris hoping to discover that he wasn't her father at all. Alistair, too, is fatherless; maybe what he and Julie, as well as their mothers, have in common is the lack of paternal back-up. Teo, as a would-be resident male in this house, knows he's at a considerable disadvantage. The Mandela Prize jury praised his psychological acuity, but that doesn't make the insights it brings him any less painful.

'Are you sure you'll be OK?' Terri fetches Sue's coat. 'I'll treat you to a taxi.'

'No, no, love, it's only five minutes. Anyway, those sodding kids won't be there now. They go off somewhere else this time of night, God knows where.'

'Their parents let them?' Teo says.

285

'What parents? They don't have any, or if they do it'll be a mum on her own and off her head on drink or drugs because she can't cope. Me, at least I'm proud of Alistair — that's how I cope.'

'Come again soon? Next weekend?' Julie kisses her.

'You'll be back at college,' Terri points out.

'I'm not going back.'

'Yes, you are.'

'Goodnight, girls,' Sue interrupts. 'See you, thanks again.'

They see her out before turning on one another, faces alight with annoyance.

'Cool it, ladies,' Teo interrupts. 'Terri Ivory, you haven't said hello to me properly. Come here.' Embracing her, tracing her spine with his fingertips, he can tell just from the tension in her arms and the rapidity of her heartbeat that all is far from well.

★ ★ ★

The house darkens while Terri strolls from room to room, switching off lamps and blowing out candles. Finally she takes Teo's hand and they head for bed. Their silhouettes dusky in the silvered light from the streetlamps and what's visible of the moon, they lie wrapped together for a long time, in silence.

Terri luxuriates in the familiar touch and scent of him, musky and tobaccoey, his hands rough-skinned because he doesn't look after them, yet their caresses as gentle as a baby's. Whatever the hassles with Julie, the anxiety over Alistair, the irritation of Martini pressing her with questions that she can't answer about roles and dates, there's one refuge and this is it.

'What is it, my love?' Teo pleads. 'You're worried.'

She places her mouth over his to silence him.

Much later, they slide towards sleep. 'Better?' Teo mumbles.

Terri's arm drapes across his waist. 'Scared.'

'What of?'

'If I can't sing . . . '

'You will. In time, you will. Have faith.'

'I did, but now I don't. It's everything I am, everything I've always been. I was so nearly better, and then — wham. I don't know what I'll do if I can't sing any more.'

'You're going to be fine. Try not to worry so much. The more you worry, the worse you feel. It's a vicious circle.'

'I know. It doesn't help.'

'Your Russian friend sent you flowers. Did he ask you out?'

'Well, he had the grace to be embarrassed about what happened, so he took me to the Savoy Grill and I ordered the most expensive fish on the menu.'

'Then?'

Terri smiles in the dark. Ovchinikov took her home, expecting to be invited in, but she'd said a brisk goodnight and virtually slammed the Lexus door in his face. It was a long time since anyone could have called her a pricktease, but he deserved it. 'I told him I had to get an early night, for the sake of my voice.'

'You didn't . . . '

'Of course I bloody didn't. Come on, darling, sleep time.' She rolls away.

'Terri?'

'*What?*'

'Are you glad I'm here?'

'Yes! Goodnight.' She flips on to her other side and is out like a light.

Teo loves the way that Terri never loses sleep, no matter what. The night before her Isolde debut she'd slept like a happy cat for seven hours — then got up, tested her voice briefly, and vanished into the bathroom to be sick. Tonight he wants to stay awake, to appreciate her while he can. Her shoulder is warm against his cheek; he kisses her neck and buries his fingers in the furriness between her thighs. 'I love you so much,' he mumbles into her vertebrae. 'I can't get enough of you.'

'You've had plenty already.' She yawns, pushing him back to his side of the bed. 'Bad boy! *Sleep.*'

★   ★   ★

For Teo, sleep is easier said than gone to. His head full of his journey, Sarajevo, Terri, Julie, Alistair and more, he can't settle despite the aftermath of sex. He goes downstairs so that he won't disturb Terri. On the way, he notices that she's forgotten to turn off the light in her study. A few minutes later, cradling a whisky tumbler, he goes in and looks for the switch.

A printout of the latest draft of Terri's film pitch lies on the desk under the lamp. The words catch his eye. He reads several lines. Then he sits down to read some more.

Pauline's relationship with Turgenev, Terri wrote, was out of balance. She spoke often of the willpower she had applied to prevent her passions from getting the better of her — and she was nothing if not a passionate woman. Turgenev, though, gave himself up to his love. The more he pursued her, however, the more Pauline resisted. It was as if his extreme passion fed her with doubts she might not have entertained had he put less of himself in her power.

Being excessively adored can make the beloved rebound against the lover. In most relationships one person does more of the loving; though ideally giving and receiving should be equal, we all know that that's rarely the case. Here, the see-saw stood no chance of balance. Turgenev sat like a dead weight, propelling Pauline upwards into the sky of song — and away.

Just how deeply does Terri identify with this woman? Disturbed, Teo turns back to the beginning. Tucked inside the front page he spots an unfinished letter in Terri's handwriting addressed to Martini, who it seems has provisionally agreed to 'test-drive' the pitch on some film-makers and a BBC bigwig. Beside it, the quote on the title page leaps out at him:

'LOVE KILLS WHEN IT IS NOT ALLOWED TO BURST INTO FLAME'
Pauline Viardot

Teo downs the last of his whisky. Pauline was wrong. Love *doesn't* kill. That, to him, is its real tragedy.

14

Alistair perches with five other lads in the back of a Snatch Land Rover, rattling along the stony track that passes for a road through the hills. His eyes and ears are full of sand and every bump reverberates through the metal below him and up through his feet, legs and abdomen. Exhaust fumes waft through his lungs as the vehicle hops and plunges. It's freezing, but the guys are in good spirits. Since they left camp, summoned to help another group that had got into difficulties with some insurgents — they don't yet know exactly what difficulties — they haven't stopped baiting Han about his song in drag.

'I can get you a job in this strip club in Hamburg, drop of a hat,' says Gerry. He'd started out in the Territorial Army, which he'd originally joined so that he could have a free trip to Germany every year.

'Julie will be jealous.' Alistair pokes his best mate in the ribs.

'Lay off,' Han groans. He's had an upset stomach for two days and has also been grumbling that his feet still hurt from the high heels he'd worn for five whole minutes on Christmas Day. 'I've got gut-rot. I'm going to chuck up sometime soon.'

'Best thing to do with rat-packs,' quips Lee. 'I've had Menu D three days on the fucking trot.' Their commanding officer had put them on to ration packs when three boys were shot and one was killed trying to bring in supplies of fresh food.

'Get some air, Hanley,' their lance corporal suggests from the front of the vehicle.

Han hauls himself upright and puts his head through the hatch to take over as the lookout. Ben starts to sing a striptease tune and Gerry joins in — since discovering that together their names added up to fancy ice-cream, Ben and Gerry have been inseparable. Alistair screws up his eyes and tries to watch the land passing around them through the back of the Snatch, but the wheels on the makeshift road spin so much muck into the atmosphere that he can see nothing but a cloud of dust.

The boom comes out of nowhere. Alistair knows, or numbly thinks he does in the time it takes to blink, that because of relative speeds of light and sound, you're supposed to see things before you hear them, but the noise throws him before he can take in the flash and the smoke, the vehicle whirling into shattered components, the figures and their guns flying like angels, limbs outstretched, dancing, cascading upward against gravity over red flame and black smoke. Something metallic strikes him on the back of the neck, maybe his own weapon, and, falling forward, he finds his mouth is full of sand and viscous liquid. There's a roaring in his ears and a stench of burning rubber and he thinks, as his awareness fades, that he can hear an animal whimpering nearby.

Fighting back against the faintness, he forces

his mind towards home base. Stay awake. Someone needs help. Remember, there were only men, not dogs, in the van. He feels for his legs; they're still there; so are his arms; his hands too are intact. Applying sense, talking himself through it motion by motion as a training officer might have, he begins to haul himself along the earth towards the sound. One of his legs doesn't want to move, so he drags it too.

Red hair glimmers in front of him, under a paste of earth and blood. Han had been the most vulnerable — his head was exposed when the bomb went off. Alistair wipes the muck out of his eyes and tries to stand, to move faster despite whatever's happened to his left leg, but a crackle of gunfire throws him prostrate once more, shielding his head with his arms. He's shaking and can't stop. To his horror, his trousers are wet.

'Han. Hanley. Can you hear me?'

An indeterminate sound comes back.

'Hang on, mate.' Alistair slithers on his stomach, inching forward, trying to move from side to side the way a snake might — it seems to work. His tongue brushes something rough and raw on the lower right side of his mouth — he's lost a tooth, maybe more than one. His head feels as if the whole truck had landed on it. His left knee is swelling up like a football. The pain in his head is so strong that it masks the pain in the joint. He'd barely registered that his leg had been injured, only that it wouldn't move. He can hear someone, maybe Gerry, echoing his call to hang on, but can't locate him in the chaos.

Han is on his back, coughing and retching in the smoke. Alistair, breathing hard, tries to take hold of his shoulders to drag him further away from the furnace that used to be their truck, but the lad howls with a tone Alistair has never heard at such close quarters before. Now his spirit, which he'd thought steady despite his physical reactions, begins to quake as much as his body.

'Hold on, mate,' he says. 'All right, now. You're going to be OK.'

As he speaks, he knows that Han won't be. His clothes are soaking up his blood. Trying to keep his hands deft, Alistair fumbles for the medical pack in which they all carry morphine. If they can get Han out quickly, within the hour, to some treatment, then he might stand a chance. But that needs a helicopter, bloody fast. 'Someone help!' he shouts, but it emerges as barely a whisper. His head is threatening to overwhelm him. What's happened to the others? They can't all be dead? Though they could — the Snatch was made for Northern Ireland, not this little lot. Where the fuck is Gerry? 'Come on, mate,' he whispers, 'we'll get you out of here.'

A noise wells up, something between a howl, a choke and a gargle as Han's body jerks twice, three times, four. Redness bubbles under his lips, then he coughs and a spurt of blood comes out of his mouth and strikes Alistair in the face. Han falls back and is still. The last thing Alistair knows is the smell of blood trapped under him in the sand.

When Julie unlocks the door of her college bedsit, the room feels chilly and draughty. The wind, it's rumoured, comes straight from Siberia and her windows face east. She dumps her rucksack on the bed, turns the two-bar heater up high and begins to unpack. She has an instinct, when she lets herself listen to it, a voice that perches above the inner ear and gives an occasional tap: 'You are in the wrong place.' Her stomach churns; her feet itch to take her back to her bicycle and thence the station. She's done it a few times now; it's hard not to do it again.

Irina comes bounding in without waiting to be asked and envelops her in a Russian bear-hug. '*Solnushka*, unpack later! Let's go to bar to celebrate new term.'

Julie complies, pleased to see her friend despite everything; she hopes nobody will notice how not-there she is. It's as if her awareness has been airlifted out of the country. What's happening to her? Why does she feel like this? Something's wrong. She knows it, even if she'll be laughed out of town if she says so.

In the college bar, they run into Charlie and Raff; several beers later, they're all in Irina's room, stretched out on the floor smoking, munching crisps and handing round a spliff. Irina has brought some of her stuffed animals, which adorn the bed, pride of place going to a huge white bear she's named Knut. Raff, shunting himself along the ground to the desk, kneels up to explore the Mac's music content.

Julie, taking her turn on the spliff, glances at his famous socks — bright blue and apparently made of silk. She feels the stress sliding away, non-caringness starting its slow invasion. Nobody really chooses their life anyway. She beams at Irina, who's lying flat out with her head in Charlie's lap.

'Do you think we choose our own lives?' she asks, sitting back against a cushion.

'I guess,' sighs Irina. 'Don't you think?'

'No, I don't. I think we're stuck where we're born, first, and then things just happen to us that we've no control over.'

'Sure we can choose,' Charlie suggests. 'It's just that most people are too lazy.'

'The less you have to start with, the less choice you have,' Raff suggests. 'Because if you're born into poverty, chances are you won't get a good education and that's the only thing that can give you the tools to get yourself out.'

'I think less you have, more your chances to move,' Irina reflects. 'If you have nothing, you have nothing to lose. Expectations are less pressuring, so you make your own motivation. There is more freedom.'

'Only if you're not ground down by trying to survive and feed a family.' Raff points out.

'Hey, Raff.' Charlie passes him the joint. 'Sounds like you need more of this. Zat your phone, Jul?'

Julie, her brain numbed as if by three velvet blankets, takes a moment to recognise the purring in her pocket. The drug wraps invisible mittens around her hands. When she finally retrieves the handset, the screen shows it's her mother.

'Hey, Mum. I'll call you tomorrow, OK?'

'No, Julie, it's not OK.' Through the fug, her mother sounds strained. 'Go somewhere private where you can talk, and listen very carefully. And sit down.'

★ ★ ★

That instinct had been telling her the truth. After a sleepless night, the distraught Julie repacks her rucksack and sets out for the station, with Irina and Vaslav cycling alongside to make sure she is all right.

In the station entrance they pause. 'I knew,' Julie confesses. She can hardly see; her eyes, wept out, seem to hurt for the whole of her. 'Something in me knew.'

'If we can help in any way, me or my father,' Irina says, 'you ring *at once*, OK? Any time, day or night.'

'There's my train, I'd better run.'

'Call me later.' Irina blows her a kiss as she hurries away.

★ ★ ★

The day is grey and damp; on the train to Birmingham, alternating between trying to comfort Sue and being comforted by her, Julie imagines what a relief it will be for Alistair to see English skies again, free of sand and the Asian winter wind.

Except that he can't see anything yet: in the Selly Oak hospital, he's still unconscious after emergency surgery. Curtains encircle his bed, sheltering him from the other wounded servicemen on the ward. Julie, speechless with pain, bends to kiss his forehead. She doesn't want to cry here; she's determined not to upset Sue even further. She breathes a scant whiff of his familiar smell and feels the warmth of his breath.

'It's all right, love,' Sue keeps whispering, rubbing Alistair's good arm, stroking what's visible of his hair beneath the bandage, too quickly because her hand is shaking so much. 'You're home now. We'll have you right.'

The doctor on his ward-round talks them through what's happened. Alistair's physical injuries include two broken ribs, a shattered kneecap and fractured ankle, severe concussion, burns, and the loss of two teeth. They have yet to determine whether his eardrums are affected. As for the injury to his mind . . . 'He's a lucky lad. We've seen worse things come home from these Improvised Explosive Device blasts. There's nothing that can't be mended, but it will take time.'

'I'm here for him.' Sue lifts her chin, set in determination. Julie feels the older woman's fingers tighten around her own. Some of the lads caught by that IED hadn't made it.

'So am I,' she adds.

'And me,' says Terri quietly.

'We'll do everything for him we possibly can,' the doctor assures them. 'Then it'll be over to you — in some ways your healing powers will be greater than ours. When he comes home, you'll need to treat him gently. You may have to tolerate things that you'd otherwise find problematic. It's always hard for the lads coming back, even if they haven't been injured.'

The doctor isn't into music and doesn't recognise Terri. To him, Julie realises, her mum is nothing more than her mum. Terri, staring at the floor, seems miles away. Julie notices, for the first time, that her mother has gained weight. Strange how such everyday, disembodied ideas can invade her when she only wants to think about Alistair and stay with him, not leave him to bear his private chamber of horrors alone.

★ ★ ★

Terri remains dry-eyed, though she longs for release in the tears that she finds too hard to shed. She busies herself with practicalities: the buying of sandwiches for the train journey home, then the booking of a minicab from Euston to Falcon Park. Emotionally wrung out, the three of them sit in the cab together in silence, watching the grey-brown city hassling by.

'It reminds me so much of what happened to my brother,' Terri remarks eventually.

'I didn't know you've a brother,' says Sue.

'I used to.' Terri fidgets with the strap of her bag. 'He died years ago.'

Robbie — tough, no-nonsense Robbie, her chief ally and the only person other than Mary to whom Terri ever listened — was always telling her to calm down. Don't walk on walls, don't run across main roads just expecting lorries to stop, and for God's sake go on the Pill. Robbie was the last person who should have suffered a workplace injury. He cared everything for her safety, and other people's — but, apparently, not enough for his own. He'd become the union representative because he was so outspoken over working conditions, the use of equipment that was outdated or faulty, and the dangerous cutting of corners to save costs. Why he should have been so close to the crane was something Terri had battled with for months, indeed years, afterwards. It might have been his fault for lack of awareness, someone else's for not warning him or the crane operator's for not seeing him. He ended up with an amputated leg, internal injuries and a crushed spirit. The company was forced to pay 'compensation', but the sum was barely a gesture, and for Robbie it was ill-named. Nothing could compensate for what he'd lost.

'He was in a nursing home for several years,' Terri tells Sue. 'He couldn't look after himself in the flat and his girlfriend walked out. If I ever see her again, I shall murder her.'

'How old was he?'

'Thirty-six. Perhaps it was a merciful release.'

Terri, who has a gift for being economical with the truth, doesn't explain that Robbie had taken his own life with sleeping pills and a bottle of whisky. He shouldn't have had access to either; she'd never known where he got them. 'There hasn't been a day since when I don't miss him,' she admits. She sees the shock on Julie's face; this isn't something Terri talks about at home.

'Alistair's injuries aren't as serious, physically, and he's younger and stronger,' she adds. 'He'll be fine.'

'Can I stay and look after him once he's home?' Julie pleads.

'Not on your nelly,' Sue interrupts. 'You're going straight back to college. He'll want you to.'

'But — ' If those words had come from her mother or father, Julie would have rolled her eyes heavenwards and ignored them.

'When he comes to, how do you think he'll feel if he sees you sitting there making sheep's eyes and saying 'I gave up college to look after you'? You want to make him feel guilty and all, on top of this? I know my son — he doesn't need that. You go back, love. Make him proud of you.'

'But how can I concentrate on anything while he's in there?'

'Find a way. Make yourself do it. I feel the same, love, but I've got to work, or we won't eat. If I can, then you can too.'

Julie, struck dumb, gazes at the hills which show they're nearly home. Closing her eyes, she can still see bandages, monitors and drips. The more she tries to imagine how Alistair had come to this, the moment of the blast and the pain, the less she seems able to feel anything at all.

★ ★ ★

Irina refuses to let Julie succumb to her slough of misery. She drags her to lectures herself — and when she can't, because she has her own classes to attend, she assigns Vaslav to escort her instead. He hasn't much to do, she points out, while Julie takes in the sight of his hulking frame in her doorway. Soon Julie finds herself cycling to the faculty with this unlikely companion trailing her, his legs too long for his sit-up-and-beg bike. More often than not, he's waiting after lectures to guide her to supervisions, choir practice and even the college cafeteria ('Miss Irina says you must eat more than soup').

She likes his broad, open face and direct gaze, and she finds him entertaining. Besides, his diligence makes her feel guilty. He's working hard at his English and has wangled a permit to use the university language lab so that he can learn French as well. He regales her with stories of growing up in Vilnius, and the lawlessness that followed the fall of the Iron Curtain before the EU became the latest outside force involved in running the Baltic States, which had known little other than occupation. 'But this time is good,' he says. 'At least for now. My country is still polarised politically between the pro-West politicians and the pro-Russian.'

'I guess you're pro-Russian, working for Ovchinikov?' Julie munches her caff dinner of chicken and mashed potato.

'No, I am pro-West. Mr Ovchinikov can't go back, you know. If he goes back, probably someone kills him. That's why he employs people like me. Is good life, Miss Julie, I tell my family I study here in Cambridge and they think is something astonishing! Even if what I study is not only language but human nature, for which there are no exams.'

Julie, warming to the twinkle behind Vaslav's toughness, has begun, slowly, to trust him.

'Now what we do?' He waits while Julie downs the last of her chicken. 'Is Tuesday. So, is Chamber Choir.'

Julie hasn't slept properly since Alistair's injury; singing is the last thing on her mind. Especially Chamber Choir. It's the university's most select and demanding vocal ensemble; it involves concert tours in the holidays, sometimes recordings too, and in the summer a highlight of the post-exam festivities is always Singing on the River, when they perform *a capella* poised on a fleet of rafts lit by paper lanterns, for an audience assembled on the grassy banks near Trinity College. Chris, the organ scholar, persuaded Julie to audition — convinced she didn't stand a chance, she'd sung the 'Pie Jesu' and was accepted at once.

'I don't want to go,' Julie tells Vaslav. 'I need to phone Sue and see how Alistair is.'

'Miss Julie, *no*. You go sing,' Vaslav orders. 'You have phoned home five times today.'

'How do you know?'

'I notice everything. It's my job.' He grins at her. 'Honest, it does you good to sing. I read in newspaper on Internet today, singing is very good for health. It makes oxygen circulate. Let's go, I take you there.'

Vaslav pedals beside her to the rehearsal in a college chapel five minutes away. The town's Gothic rooftops and turrets are floodlit and the shops are bright-fronted. Their bicycles jangle softly over the cobblestones.

'Shouldn't you be with Irina?' Julie asks.

'She likes a little freedom. Anyway, she doesn't sing, and I like to listen to singing. Is very beautiful. You don't mind?'

'It's up to Dr North who conducts us, but he's cool, I think it'll be fine.' Julie dismounts and parks her bike. Vaslav's slouching figure sometimes reminds her of Alistair; he comforts her in a similar way, simply by being there. Pain twists in her; Alistair's image lingers like a stone lodged in her brain.

Vaslav lurks at the back of the chapel while Dr North puts the choir through its warm-up paces and the first chorus of the Haydn 'Nelson' Mass, which they're learning. Julie concentrates on following his directions. Her mind wanders while she writes essays, but not while she sings, endeavouring to produce the sound and observe herself producing it at the same time.

'Guys, guys, where's the enthusiasm? I know it's cold and you'd rather be down the pub, but let's give it some welly!' Dr North exhorts the group. '*Kyrie eleison*! Haydn's not saying 'Lord have mercy on us', he's saying 'Isn't it great to be alive?' Come on! Feel it in your gut, let the sound form in the tummy until you just can't keep it back another moment! Again. Off we go . . .'

Julie's voice rises with the others. Sound generates itself inside until it demands expression and as the music wraps her in its bright cloak she senses her knot of anger and sorrow becoming a ball of pure energy that swells, presses up and escapes, blending with twenty-nine other voices under the chapel ceiling. Into it goes her longing for Alistair, her terror for him, and all the useless questioning and frustration. The great messy jumble inside her latches on to Haydn's notes and soars up, out and away.

'Good!' shouts Dr North from the piano. 'Sopranos, excellent!' He's looking straight at her.

She feels knackered yet oddly calm afterwards, packing away her music and chatting with some of the others, who are understandably curious about Vaslav. 'A friend from Lithuania,' Julie explains.

'Was good?' he asks while they cycle home by moonlight.

'Yes. Very good.'

'They say music is, how you say, cath-something?'

'Cathartic?'

'Yes, that is right. Cathartic. That to sing can help to heal.'

'Maybe.' Julie holds an arm out to indicate she's turning right.

'You think is true?'

'I don't know. But it's possible. I do feel sort of — well, better.'

Tonight, she almost believes it for the first time; and later on, for once, she sleeps for eight solid hours, the soundwaves from the chapel still vibrating inside her.

15

'I brought you a cake,' says Terri.

It's Alistair's first weekend home from hospital. Terri, cup of tea in hand, perches on the end of his bed. Questions fill her; asking them is impossible.

His room is much as he'd left it, though the clothes, which would once have been heaped on the chairs, have been put neatly away. The art clobber lies neglected in its plastic box, covered by a tea-towel. The room is stuffy and smells of male sweat and socks; the tabby cat has settled down beside Terri on the duvet and is washing its paws. She strokes the animal, since she can't stroke Alistair. 'Cherry, almond and vanilla,' she adds. 'One of my best.'

Alistair nods his thanks. He's been up and about, but neither for long; all his energy, Sue remarks, has to go into healing his wounds. Most of the time he's in bed or, at most, hobbling to his computer, surfing for information about what's happening in the war and writing laborious e-blueys to his mates, plus emails to the ones who'd been with him in the explosion and have been sent home, likewise, to recover. Ben and Gerry are both in the Newcastle area; two of the others are respectively in Carlisle and Penzance. Darren Hanley is dead. His coffin has come home, draped in a Union Jack. Alistair is desperate to be well enough to attend the funeral.

'Julie sends lots of love. She'll be down to see you very soon.' Terri reaches out. She wants to take his hand; she'd like to pat his stubbly cheek and ruffle his fast-growing hair. 'Let me cut you a slice?'

Alistair gives a faint smile and the slightest of nods. He's still in some pain — the ribs have to heal of their own accord and it won't happen overnight.

'Sent him home too soon,' is what Sue thinks. He needs physiotherapy, but getting him to and from the hospital for it is problematic without a car. The dodgy lift does nothing to make the prospect easier, as Alistair can't possibly walk up and down seven flights of stairs. Sue spends half her time calling her brother John for help, and the other half trying to organise lift repair and hospital transport, never mind the smell from the basement; getting anyone at the local council to answer the phone is a challenge in itself. Terri finds her in the kitchen, puffing a cigarette and grazing at a packet of crisps. Terri dips in. They munch together, seeking comfort in salt and company.

'I'm getting fat,' Terri grumbles.

'So stop eating crisps!' Sue laughs, grabbing another handful. 'Get away with you!' They push at each other, competing for space in the packet and giggling like schoolgirls letting off steam.

It's true; since Terri's been 'off', she's had no incentive to keep fit. Normally she'd be in hotel gyms abroad, or an opera director might be instructing a hefty physical workout onstage.

307

Instead, she's home and underoccupied; and though the cakes she bakes are ostensibly for Julie, she ends up eating most of them herself. Calls from Martini asking about her progress or her likely availability for a performance three years hence send her scurrying to fridge, cupboard and kettle for reassurance.

★ ★ ★

There's nothing like cake for inducing instant contentment — except, perhaps, a fresh outsize chocolate brownie.

Preparing for a lunch meeting with Martini in which staying positive was paramount, Terri had put on her favourite ivory winter trouser suit, only to discover that the button at her waist wouldn't meet the hole. A last tug made it fall off, straight into a crack between the floorboards. She replaced it hurriedly with a safety pin.

'Glass of wine?' Martini offered in The Ivy.

'Yes, please,' said Terri.

★ ★ ★

'It's kind of you to come round.' Sue refills their mugs. 'A few times this week I've thought I'm going to go gaga sitting here with him, but it's worse having to leave him on his own when I go to work evenings.'

'Listen, darling,' Terri begins, 'I'm stuck, I've nothing much to do, and I can't get used to the empty nest, let alone the empty diary. So if I can help, if I can make myself useful, it's really a pleasure. I hate to see you suffering.'

'We just got to get him better.' Sue shrugs away Terri's sentimentality. 'There's no point whingeing — this is how it is and we have to deal with it. Cos there isn't another way. I spoke to Darren Hanley's mother. She's a wreck. I'm lucky, my son's alive. Then you start wondering what it was all for, why they were sent into this, without the right gear . . . '

'I'm here, Sue. You won't have to handle this alone, I promise.'

'Thanks, Terri.' Sue's eyes are lowered. 'I don't want to impose, but it's kind. *You're* kind. Just come over, anytime.'

Terri remembers how it felt to watch Robbie slowly losing his willpower day by day in those rooms that stank of urine, with adjustable metal-rack beds and railings everywhere to help mobility, and how she'd tried to keep him smiling and alive; then later, how she'd tried to keep the grieving Finn smiling and alive. 'Yes,' she says. 'I will.'

She kisses Alistair goodbye, a peck on his forehead above a scar from a piece of shrapnel; he grunts a response. His skin is so smooth, so ridiculously young. Terri seethes with fury. If there's an emotion she loathes, it's helplessness. She's always helped — others or herself. She has to find a way to help him.

★　★　★

'Shall I come to London?' Teo asks. Terri, at her computer, adjusts some uncomfortable headphones. She's installed Skype, and now she and Teo are trying to communicate through it. The conversation is riven with minor cut-outs, hopefully just teething problems. They're navigating a peculiar tranche of the early twenty-first-century: a ridge of an era between old communications and new, between CDs and digital downloads, war and peace, love and independence, hurt and healing. Terri has just remarked that amid all this it's easy to feel slightly lost.

'Come if you have time,' she says.

'If you need me, I'm coming.'

'I don't need you enough to disrupt your work, but I'll see you in Bruges next week,' Terri points out. Teo has been talking to her at less length on the phone recently; he's busy. As a Mandela Prize nominee, he's submerged under a heap of requests and demands that he's dubbed 'a terminal case of piles'.

'You don't want me there?'

'Of course I do. But . . . '

'*But*. I see. Well, then, I shall leave you to your empty house.'

These days, there's a new tone in his voice. Since his first return to Bosnia, something in him has begun to sew itself together. Or perhaps the nomination has gone to his head. Certainly one breakthrough seems to have given him energy for the other. She wonders whether he'll drop her, now that his world status is changing — as hers may be, only in the opposite direction.

Terri lies awake, overheated and sweating. Teo thinks that she never does this; she hasn't the heart to tell him that she's a good actress and can feign sleep as easily as operatic death by suffocation, suicide or consumption. In the morning, she braves the bathroom scales. She doesn't believe the electronic numbers, so she picks up the machine, shakes it, puts it back down on a different spot, then tries again. The same figures flash by her toes. 'Jesu Maria,' Terri mumbles, heading down for a breakfast of croissants with plenty of honey.

At the kitchen table, she stirs sugar into black coffee. She's fifty-one and her periods are as confusing and chaotic as a government initiative. She knows that her disturbed night was not only psychological but physical too — the dreaded hot flush. No doubt the hormonal mayhem impinges on her weight, moods and general appearance. She must make a trip to the hairdresser for a respray before Bruges, and she desperately needs a dress she can fasten. Everything in her cupboard seems to belong to a different woman — the one she used to be until only a year ago.

Muzzy with tiredness, she can't focus on Pauline Viardot, and she feels stumped by her lengthy list of TV People to Call — the BBC, Channel 4, Channel 5, Arte. Martini has reneged on his promise to pitch her idea, pleading excessive work for other artists. His job is selling musicians, not film scripts. But if he won't pick up the phone, how can she? Does he know something she doesn't? After a few minutes' thought, she abandons the idea for now and instead pulls on a coat and scarf to head for Scargill Tower.

On the seventh floor, she's amazed to hear music even before Sue opens the door. Mozart. In Alistair's room.

Sue hugs her. 'Julie's here.'

'What?'

'Didn't she tell you?'

'That girl would run away from college every day, given half a chance.'

'You should see them. But keep quiet.' Sue leads the way round the corner towards Alistair's door.

The curtains are drawn; in the half-light Alistair is a dark mound under the duvet. Julie is stretched out on top of it, beside him. They're motionless together, listening to Mozart's *Ave Verum Corpus*, which the Chamber Choir had sung alongside the Haydn 'Nelson' Mass a couple of nights earlier. Julie, eyes closed, looks peaceful, maybe asleep; Alistair is stroking her hair with one hand. Terri, a massive lump in her throat, hovers outside so as not to disturb them.

Julie has got through to him. Of course she has. She's been his girlfriend for five years. There's no reason Terri should be able to compete with that, and no reason she should want to. Yet the bitterness gripping her is definitely jealousy. Of what? Youth, strength, the blank life-canvas of unlimited possibility?

The music comes to a soft conclusion; there's a rattle of applause on the recording. 'Hey, Mum,' Julie says without moving.

312

Terri lifts a hand and gives a little wave.

'Hello, Terri,' says Alistair. He holds out an arm and lets her kiss him on the cheekbone.

'You look as if you're on the mend,' she remarks.

'Julie singing,' he says. The words are an effort.

'This is the concert we did the other night and I wanted Al to hear it,' Julie explains, sitting up, 'so they gave me a CDR of the recording they made. He loved it so much.'

'Does it hurt less when you speak?' Terri asks Alistair. Like her, he had virtually been forced to lose his voice.

He glances at Julie. 'His ribs hurt, his leg's bad and the teeth are a nuisance,' she supplies.

'I didn't know you were coming down, sweetheart.'

'I'm going to see Anita later and then I was going to call, you and come home, if that's OK.'

'Terri?' Sue is at the door, looking on. 'Can I show you something?'

Terri suspects she wants to leave the youngsters alone together — which is fair enough.

In the kitchen Sue offers biscuits and tea. 'Julie arrived with this CD,' she explains, 'and then he just sort of flopped, and when it finished he began to talk to her like he hasn't since they carried him off the frigging plane. I couldn't believe it. Oh, you should have seen her face — she was so thrilled! And he looked so . . . I dunno . . . relieved . . . '

Terri passes a box of Kleenex across the table and gives her hand a squeeze. 'Did he say

313

anything about what happened?'

'Not much. Except, he said at first he didn't know where he was — because the last thing he remembered was Darren Hanley dying in front of him somewhere in those godforsaken hills. Next thing he knows, he wakes up in Birmingham. He said there was something obscene about it. He was just glad it was a military ward, because some of them are mixed, you see, and he didn't know what he'd have done if he'd found some old biddy in the next bed saying 'so what you here for, then, love?' As it is, some of his old mates from the supermarket called by, and it was good that they wanted to say hello, but it ended with one of them saying, like, if he thought he ought to be doing it at all when the place is chaos and we shouldn't be there anyway.'

Terri helps herself to a third biscuit. 'What did he say?'

'Not a lot. Christ, I get so angry.' Sue slumps back in her chair. 'I mean, in the Second World War they knew they were doing the right thing. The Falklands too. And Kosovo and that, I don't know about Bosnia. But how can they carry on if they don't believe in it? And if they do, what can they say when they come back and find nobody else does?'

Terri thinks of Teo. 'There's never any sense. It's innocent people who are killed, and often the real criminals get away.'

'I get so *angry*.' The release in Alistair seems to have set off a release in Sue; the more she dabs away her tears, the faster they flow. 'He was

314

watching this cartoon on TV last night — *Tom and Jerry*. And you see, in real life, the cat always wins. Look at him.' She points at her black-and-white cat, lounging near a radiator, grooming its tail. 'He gets the mice sometimes — we're not supposed to have mice here and the council says we don't so they won't have to do nothing about it. But there *are* mice, he catches them, he plays with them for ages and then he kills them. And it's always the same. The cartoons are lying. The cat always wins.'

'Isn't that why we like the cartoons?' Terri suggests.

'I don't care.' Sue blows her nose. 'What I mind is lies.'

Julie wanders in, bag over her shoulder, and remarks, 'I have to go to my lesson. Mum, see you later?'

Terri jumps up and hugs her daughter as if she mightn't see her again for years.

★ ★ ★

Towards Brussels, the land flattens out. Sipping coffee and enjoying the last of a very buttery, chocolate-filled pastry from St Pancras, Terri leafs through her newspaper. Teo's prize book is in her bag. She hasn't dared to tell him that she's finding it almost impossible to read. Every word hurts. It's another life, his previous life — and it's a howl of mourning for another woman, and the children he'd had with her.

It reminds her that her body is busy closing down its egg factory and will, if left to its own devices, push her through the menopause within the year. Teo, if he wanted to, could at any time choose a woman twenty or thirty years younger than she is and have a new family, just because he's a man. When they met, he was too damaged to consider a home and children, while she was too busy. Now, for her, it's too late.

Not that she'd ever seriously considered having another child, with Teo or anyone else. Presumably the only reason she's regretting it is that it's safely impossible.

'*Prochain arrêt: Bruxelles,*' comes the announcement. These days it's quicker to get to Belgium than Bradford. Terri wheels out her case and prepares to change trains.

★ ★ ★

The hotel room shows that Teo has been in, left shoes and clothes everywhere, and gone. A pink cardboard box decorated with olde-worlde script lies on her pillow, beside a note in his writing: '*Darling, there are more chocolate shops per square metre in this city than anywhere else on earth. Don't eat them all at once.*'

Terri pops a rum truffle into her mouth and savours ripples of delight. Then she has another. She must stop this. Maybe just one more.

Teo is no doubt busy with meetings, interviews and the rest of it. Everything that Terri is more accustomed to doing herself. She, though, is as free as the proverbial air until the dinner tonight; it's only 2 p.m. Still, if she were champagne, her bubbles would have flattened hours ago. She hangs up her evening dress and places her bag of toiletries on a bathroom shelf beside Teo's razor. Today she's a trophy partner: the supporting act. Spoiled girl, she tells herself: not good. She should be so lucky as to be here, meeting Nelson Mandela. It's time to distract herself by exploring Bruges. If there really are so many chocolate shops, she wants to see them for herself.

She wanders out of the hotel and along the cobbles towards the centre of town, where the canals lap grey and quiet under the medieval terraces. There'd been no great fire to sweep away the old, no bombs to flatten the town's beauties or bulldozers to clear the way for skyscrapers: Bruges has always known that its strength is in its age. And its chocolate. With puffy clouds overhead and a hint of spring sap filtering through the aroma of cocoa that hangs about the doorways of chocolatier after chocolatier, Bruges is watercolour rather than oils, eau de toilette rather than eau de parfum. Low-slung bridges curve over the passing barges, bicycles hiss by unhurried, and as the hour approaches the bells peal out of churches near and far in a symphony of overtones that silvers the air.

Terri is a brisk walker but soon finds herself trapped behind trundling tourist parties who linger too long at each shop and pause at every corner to photograph anything that looks old — as most of the place does. To avoid them, she alters her route towards a path that leads her across a muddy park and over a bridge on the Minnewasser. A stone portal beckons: she

317

discovers she's entering the grounds of the Begijnhof, a sizeable convent enclave protected by distance from the tourist drag.

In the gateway she hesitates. To her left is the church; enclosing it, a courtyard of ancient buildings which house the nuns. Trees weave a delicate lattice of branches above the central lawn, where daffodils are sprouting, ready to bloom. Another couple of weeks and the place will be carpeted with gold.

Tranquillity creeps through Terri: she breathes deeply, relishing it. She's encountered no atmosphere of peace like this in years. Calm is all around in the Begijnhof, smoothing her ruffled mind. Perhaps she should have been a nun. Imagine going through life in a state of spiritual ease, ego negated, anxieties about money and career non-existent, at one with yourself, your sisters and God.

One problem: no sex. Perhaps she'd be permitted chocolate as a substitute? Still, she could sing. The nuns sing every day: the most natural and least costly form of beauty, art and worship rolled together. Mary might have been a good nun. Thinking of her, time-travelling across thirty-four years, Terri wanders up to the church and pushes open the door.

The smell of cool stone and polished wood reminds her of her old church in the Gorbals — without the tough neighbourhood festering beyond the gates. She wanders to a pew and sits there, breathing in and out, eyes closed. Familiar but lapsed words whisper in her memory: Holy Mary, Mother of God. Perhaps such patterns latch themselves on to your brain during childhood more deeply than you realise. Guidance, she prays silently. Please, if you're there — anybody — couldn't you help me with some guidance?

★ ★ ★

In 1975, Mary Hoolihan began to teach Terri how to use her voice properly.

Terri and Joe were planning their trip to Edinburgh for the festival. They'd stay in a youth hostel first and busk — well, Terri would busk while Joe persuaded passers-by to cough up — and when they'd raised enough money, they'd move to a bed and breakfast so that they could sleep together. Terri embroidered her jeans with images of angels. Joe had acquired some flares so broad that they made her hoot with laughter when he paraded them in his bedsit, aping Mick Jagger.

Finn pursed her lips and told Terri that no good would come of it. 'The Gorbals is good enough for me,' she declared, 'and it's good enough for your brother. But not for the likes of you. Why don't you get yourself a sensible job?'

Apart from her mother's daily disapproval and the troubling, unexpected legacy of her abortions — frequent nightmares, plus an unuttered howl of pain on glimpsing small children around the shops — Terri was reasonably happy that summer. She'd discovered that it was more fun to sing songs by the Beatles, the Rolling Stones and Joni. Mitchell than hymns — but she'd also learned, oddly, that Mozart sounded better on her voice than did the ballads of Paul McCartney. This voice had a mind of its own. It didn't always do what she wanted. Instead, it wanted to rule her.

'Come on, Terri,' Joe encouraged. 'Everyone loves 'O sole mio'.'

'It sounds silly when I sing it. You'll have me punting a bloody gondola on the Clyde next!'

'Right, then, what about 'Goldfinger'?'

'That's even sillier. Especially without the trumpets.'

'You don't need trumpets. Just do it like Shirley Bassey. You can sing. It can't be that difficult to sound like Shirley Bassey.'

'Joe, you don't get it — it's not difficult, it's impossible. My voice is my voice. I can't make it into something it's not.'

'Bollocks.'

'*You* sing like Shirley Bassey, then. That'd bring the crowds running, so it would.' Terri put her nose in the air.

'I thought you said everyone can sing if they try,' he glowered.

'Sure they can,' Terri explained. 'It's just that they all sound a bit different, and you don't always want to listen to them.'

'You see,' said Joe, backing off for once, 'I could listen to you all day and all night. And I don't know why. Your voice isn't *that* great.'

Terri told Mary what was happening. 'Well, then, it's time I gave you some real coaching,' was her pragmatic response.

At first, her techniques didn't involve much

singing. Terri stood still while Mary adjusted her posture. She had to centre her weight. 'You've a tendency to lean to the left,' Mary pointed out. 'One shoulder's higher than the other.' She guided Terri's shoulderblades into a position of 'maximum ease' with her fingertips. Terri closed her eyes and savoured the touch, light, strong and sure while it lasted, moving along her vertebrae one by one.

Soon she was copying Mary's exercises to release her muscles: shoulder rolls, spine rolls, head rolls — anything, it seemed, that would roll. Then she stood in front of the mirror, while Mary taught her how to yawn to open her throat. First upwards, lifting the soft palate, keeping the tip of the tongue against the lower front teeth. Then sideways, stretching the cheek muscles; finally, with the mouth closed, feeling the space behind her molars and above her tonsils. Next, she had to stick her tongue far out, so that the tip licked her chin.

'Did you know that the tongue is attached to the larynx?' said Mary.

'What's the larynx?' asked Terri.

She could hardly bear to watch herself in the mirror, but Mary encouraged her: 'Don't think about how you look, just notice how you feel. Don't try to do it 'right'. It's about letting out the tension.'

After that she lay on the floor, patting her tummy. Earth yourself in the ground, Mary instructed. 'The voice doesn't come from your voice box. It comes from the central force in the abdomen, just below your belly button, and you can picture it rising up to there out of the core of the earth. Now, imagine all your tension draining out and away . . . '

By now Terri had a slightly difficult relationship with her lower abdomen. She lay fighting the upset, feeling tension and hurt boiling there together.

'Let it all go,' Mary said, kneeling beside her. 'It's in the past. It's gone; you don't need it. Put your awareness into your feet and let the tension sink out of them . . . '

After another minute, Terri felt as floppy as a dishcloth, so relaxed that she feared she might nod off. Suspended between waking and sleeping, she had to force herself to remember that she was meant to be following Mary's instructions, not just listening, and certainly not taking a nap.

Gradually, Mary brought in sound. First, a faint whistle, a flurry of exhalation between the upper lip and the teeth. Then a vocal noise, let out with a physical release. Build up the tension, then let it go and feel the voice rising as you do so. Sense the energy sucking up from the earth to the pit of your stomach, then let it slide through your body and finally emerge from your mouth and fly towards the ceiling. A strange sound, not a polite one. Something animal, something natural.

'The kind of sound you'd not normally want to make in public,' Mary suggested. 'The kind of sound you might make in an intimate situation. You see, the voice is a primal force. If we earth ourselves and let go of the tension, the voice can come out as it's meant to be, unimpeded.'

'How do you know all this?' Terri asked, on the floor with one eye open.

'Once I thought I wanted to be an actress.' Mary smiled. 'I studied for a while. Then I thought I was going to get married. I didn't think I'd end up teaching class singing in a school. But you see, Terri, if you don't reach for the stars, you won't hit the trees. Always reach for the stars. Promise me?'

'Of course,' said Terri. 'I wouldn't do anything else.'

With Mary's coaching and the exercises she practised every day at home, Terri slowly felt her throat opening, lengthening and widening and the voice starting to form lower and lower in her body. It grew stronger and clearer, rounder and more beautiful. Her throat didn't hurt any longer after she'd been singing. And when she and Joe had sex, she felt the primal call that Mary had talked about rising in her again, while he pushed himself in towards the central force that could give life to her voice — and could have given life to children had she let it.

Singing began to seem sexual. After a while, Terri wondered how it could ever have been anything else. The physical process of the voice, she told the puzzled Joe in Edinburgh, connected all the vital organs, and more, if you were doing it right. 'It's a force that travels all the way from the centre of the earth through your feet and into you, then upwards through its expression to reach out to the whole world!' she enthused, lounging on their bed with a can of lager.

'Cut the bullshit, babe,' Joe shrugged. 'You sing nice so you make money. We're doing well. We got fifteen quid today.' He tapped her throat. 'That,' he said, 'is our rent.'

'Ah, well.' Terri gave up trying to share her image of a pantheistic universe united by the power of sound. 'At least you've got some common sense.'

But in Edinburgh, Terri missed Mary from the middle of her central force. She'd try to phone her from a call box, but Mary was rarely home when Terri was free to ring; and she couldn't let Joe know that there was someone she loved more than him. He must have sensed it, because he was becoming possessive and jealous.

Spending the summer in Edinburgh had seemed like a good idea at the time, but he didn't want to go home. It wouldn't be long before the festival finished; autumn would arrive and the weather would turn chilly. Then nobody would want to listen to a wee girl from the Gorbals busking inexpertly imitated opera arias, and they'd have to find other work, preferably indoors.

She thought of Joe as a friend and companion, a bloke to hang out with, share the rent and enjoy sex (better now that she was finally on the Pill). Yet he seemed to think she was his property, like a dog or an ice-cream. He'd be furious if other lads tried to talk to her when she was out singing; he'd never let anyone else dance with her if they went to a disco together, even if she wanted to — 'It's only a *dance*,' she protested after he pulled a fellow smaller than himself away from her by the lapels, punched him and got them all kicked out. It was a little like football: she couldn't understand why anyone would take something so meaningless so seriously. On good days, she missed Mary and Robbie. On bad days, she missed Finn too.

Eventually Joe hit her, not once but several times, and she began to think that football was not such a good comparison. Meandering out of the casualty department with a patch over her eye, she knew something had to change. She was nineteen; she had to escape before it was too late. It would have been so easy to give in to the lassitude, the helplessness — the knowledge that escaping was not so simple, that if she left Joe and struck out alone, worse things by far might be waiting for her. There was one open window, though, and she'd tasted its fresh air. Never was she so free, so happy or so much herself as when she sang. Her voice wasn't her choice, but it was her greatest, perhaps her only, asset; and as she walked home, aware of surreptious glances at her damaged face — curiosity or shock — its presence gleamed like a Belisha beacon, showing her where to cross to the other side.

★   ★   ★

Guidance, prays Terri, inside the church in Bruges. She screws her eyes shut, and waits, and waits. Nothing happens. Peace, perhaps, is an end in itself in the Begijnhof.

Above her, the bells sing out the hour: it's four o'clock. She floats back into the present. Time for tea, maybe a little more chocolate — then preparation for the reception. The temperature is dropping. When she pauses on the step outside the church, she detects, with a Scot's infallible instinct for bad weather, the scent of snow on the breeze.

16

A slash of crimson through grey: the red carpet
is ready to welcome the dignitaries, bridging the
pavement to the hotel's ballroom entrance. When
Terri and Teo arrive arm in arm, their warmest
coats wrapped against the icy night, the cameras
swoop at them. Terri shields her eyes from the
flashes with one arm. Several reporters stand
nearby, filming pieces-to-camera; others scribble
shorthand or thrust microphones towards the
arriving VIPs. The foyer's chandeliers catch the
brilliance and magnify it.

'Terri Ivory! Is it true that you'll never sing
again?' shouts one of the journalists.

Terri halts unintentionally, wobbling on her
high heels and wondering whether to punch him.

'Ignore it, darling,' Teo whispers, arm around
her shoulders.

She shrugs him away — protectiveness is not
her style. Catching the journalist's eye, she grips
him in the stare equivalent of the stocks. 'If
anybody should say that, I, *personally*, shall put
his nose in a sling,' she declares, before gliding
on through the doorway.

Teo slides her coat away, his eyes full of pride.
Terri's hair is wound into a smooth French knot
and she's wearing one of her best strapless ivory
gowns, tight though it is, her bare throat showing
off her largest rhinestone necklace. Teo is in
dinner jacket and black tie. 'Imagine this,' he

says, handing in the coats at the cloakroom. 'Who'd have thought it, twelve years ago? Or twenty? Can you believe we're really here?'

'I'm pinching myself too.' It's true: Terri Ivory from the banks of the Clyde, accompanying her lover to a swanky ceremony second only to the Nobel Prize itself? Robbie would have had the whole neighbourhood laughing at her. Get a grip, hen, Finn would have grumbled; the Gorbals is good enough for me so it's good enough for you. Yet this is no time to go soppy — and when Teo smiles at her with all the tenderness of an adoring hound, her innards choose this moment to rebel. Bad evening for that, she reminds herself. Tonight she has to stay on-message. 'Well, then. Let's have some champagne.'

Around them, a marsh of voices ripples under the high ceiling. Snatched breaths of different perfumes tickle Terri's nose as she navigates through the party towards the grandscale windows, which overlook the Minnewasser. Her tight gown cuts into her underarms and the top of her breasts. Her reflection stares back from the glass, superimposed on the floodlit night, as silver and black as an old film. Outside, a few flakes of snow have begun to fall.

The crowds part and let Teo through to join her, a champagne flute in each hand. A cabinet minister from London turns to greet him, then one from France, and an associate of Mandela himself from South Africa. Terri watches him approach. How he's changed; his self-respect has finally returned, outwardly at least. He's shaved within a millimetre of skinning his chin; his hair has been cut — actually *cut* — and his shoulders look broader while his stomach looks narrower. Still, she notices his fingers moving, itching for their tobacco.

'You must be so proud of him,' the wife of the prize committee's chairman enthuses, shaking her hand. 'It's a work of genius. I'm convinced he'll win. Of course,' she adds, laughing, self-conscious, 'nobody tells *me* anything. I'm just *the wife*.'

'I know that feeling,' Terri tells her. 'I had a husband once. Before Teo and I met.'

'And do you have children?'

'A daughter, Juliette. She's just started university.' Terri turns to smile at Teo, who bows slightly to her companion.

'I didn't realise,' the chairman's wife says. 'Somehow I hadn't expected you to do anything except sing.'

'It's never easy to get the right balance,' Terri remarks. 'It's a rare treat to be the accessory tonight. I can just enjoy the party and feel proud of my man!'

'And is it true that you're planning to retire from the stage?'

'Please excuse me a minute.' Terri's smile atrophies. 'I must powder my nose before dinner.'

A gong sounds in the hallway and a master of ceremonies declares: '*Mesdames et messieurs, le dîner est servi dans la salle des fêtes.*'

Teo and Terri, hands touching, pause at an easel to find their places on the list and see who

329

else is on their table.

'You've won,' Terri hisses.

'You think?'

'Otherwise we wouldn't be on Table One with the Chairman and Nelson Mandela.' The nominees have been spread around the other tables, one on each of the top four. 'They wouldn't put you all together or you might start fighting.'

'You are clearly more familiar with such occasions than I am. Come then, my darling, let's go and get our prize.'

'*Your* prize.' She takes his arm. 'What do you think it'll be?'

'Sweets. We'll share them on the bus.'

'I hope it's lemon sherbets.'

Sailing into the hall, Teo and Terri greet acquaintances, smiling and waving as they pass. Their names are printed on tiny white place cards; the table, close to the platform and its microphones, bears a centrepiece of blood-coloured flowers. White-gloved waiters pour wine, while everyone shakes hands with their companions for the evening. Admiring remarks are exchanged on the beauty of the hall — wood-panelled, generous-windowed, lit discreetly but for the TV lights; the cameras are preparing to relay the ceremony live after dinner.

Terri, transfixed by the saintly smile of Nelson Mandela, turns her charm towards him and persuades him to talk about how he sees the political situation developing in South Africa. Under the table Teo presses her knee. Small talk, scallops and palate-cleansing sorbet go by; then roast lamb with flageolet beans. 'Beans: a deliberate attempt to embarrass whoever must make a speech later!' Teo remarks. The whole table of twelve people laughs, hard.

Terri knows this type of laughter. Responses to Teo these days are no longer suspicious or fascinated, as they were when she first knew him, but sycophantic. Perhaps the former — fameless but genuine — had been preferable. She wonders how many people in this hall have actually read his work; how many have the faintest idea what he had gone through before he produced it. They think he's grown from shattered man to artist, and from artist to celebrity. Underneath, he's the same shattered man.

She thinks of everything that Nelson Mandela has experienced. All those decades in prison; and now here he is at a luxurious ceremony to present a prize in his name. It's unimaginable. Yet he, unlike Teo, seems comfortable in his skin. There's a lightness to the air around him that brightens everyone else when he appears. What is his secret? She makes a mental note to read his autobiography as soon as she gets back to London.

'She makes everything possible,' Teo is telling the entire table, arm around Terri.

'Ah, she's your muse?' Nelson Mandela, seeing Teo's besottedness, grins from ear to ear.

'It's not just the singing,' Teo confides. 'Terri bakes the best cakes in London. One slice of her cherry and almond gateau and I can write for a whole day without stopping.'

'You're a lady of many talents, then.' The chairman turns to Terri. 'I never thought I would find myself asking a great diva such a question, but — you are fond of baking?'

'The two aren't incompatible,' Terri says, laughing. 'I adore cooking. Though of course I'm never able to do it much when I'm on the road. When I was a wee girl and didn't know I could sing, I used to think I'd be a dinner lady in a school someday.'

'I think,' says the chairman's wife, 'as someone who can't sing to save my life, that singing is the most amazing gift anybody can have. There's no sound more miraculous than a great voice.'

'Like yours, Terri,' the chairman adds. 'You've given us all so much joy.'

A lump rises to Terri's throat as she smiles and thanks them, trying to convince herself that the chairman's statement was not deliberately made in the past tense.

Nobody mentions the prize. Terri begins to tell a story about the time her costume caught on a protruding piece of metal when she was trying to make a stage entrance from the top of a ladder. Behind the chatter and clinking crockery, her mind drifts from Teo towards Alistair, by way of the beans. She can no longer see a bean without thinking of his rations. One moment he'd been a strapping youth with everything to play for. Now, is he, too, a shattered man like Teo? Has Teo changed as much as Alistair has?

'What is it?' Teo asks. 'Where are you?'

'I was wondering what you were like before I

332

met you.' She keeps her voice down. 'Before the war.'

'What do you think I was like?'

'I don't know. But . . .'

'But what?'

'But Alistair. He's like a different lad — you haven't seen him. You'd be shocked.'

'No, I wouldn't,' says Teo. 'Just sad.'

A wave of tiredness is breaking over Terri; it feels like a long time since she locked her front door that morning. Uncharacteristically, she leaves half her apple pie.

★ ★ ★

Before the coffee arrives, the lights dim; a young jazz musician is welcomed onto the stage and sings two numbers at a piano and microphone a few feet away from their table. Terri protects her right ear with one hand. The chairman excuses himself to prepare for the big moment. Mandela gives Terri a wink. Teo quietly pulls from his pocket a sheet of paper covered in his close-set handwriting — an acceptance speech which he's written in Bosnian. 'In case I lost the paper,' he tells Terri. 'Anyone who found it might have thought I expected to win, or something evil like that, so I made sure they couldn't read it . . .'

The chairman, who's slicked back what's left of his hair, strides to the microphone and taps for attention; behind him the ten members of the jury are filing into place.

'I won a prize at school once,' Teo whispers to Terri. 'For needlework.'

'*Votre attention, s'il vous plaît!*'

Terri detaches herself, listening to the chairman's speech in French, which she understands little more than when she first met Teo. Her eyelids feel weighted with exhaustion and her dress is constricting her lungs like a killer snake. In her throat, a sandy, scratchy sensation lurks between sips of wine. Has she talked too much? Or is she imagining it? She can't tell what's real. Alistair haunts her, with Teo's past. What are they doing, eating this lavish meal and drinking vintage Bordeaux, when Teo would not be here at all had he not been through years of starvation, bereavement and state-sanctioned murder? Tonight is a mark of recovery, but how deep does it go?

'And now we come to the highlight of this evening,' declares the chairman. 'The presentation of the Mandela Award.'

The speech drags on. Outside, the snow is settling; the glimmer from the windows turns paler and bluer. Tomorrow morning, there will be ice. The juxtaposition of winter night and lavish wood keeps drawing Terri's eyes away from the chairman and off towards unknown territories.

Two words jolt her back into her body.

'Teo Popović!'

There's a roar of approval, a surge of applause and a prerecorded fanfare. Teo stays perfectly still for a second, his face showing nothing whatsoever. Then he turns and embraces Terri. 'Darling! You did it!' she cries, throwing her arms round him, and as she does so something gives

334

way in her dress with a tearing sound that only she can detect amid the racket.

Teo gives her a long kiss. Then he whispers, 'See you later,' checks his pocket for his script, and makes his way up the stairs towards the microphone. Terri smiles fixedly, one hand negotiating with her dress, hunting for the damage. Cameras whirl forward, the flashes shiver through the room; all the guests are on their feet, applauding. Even the other nominees are cheering. Teo is suddenly to be one of the most famous authors on the planet. Surely now he'll never again sleep out on the métro? On the platform, Nelson Mandela clasps Teo's hand before handing him a heavy glass sculpture, which Teo pretends he's about to drop. They pose for photos together.

Terri, moved beyond words, wipes a stubbornly forming tear from her eye with her free hand. Around her torso, the silk is beginning to slide. The rip is on the right, starting from the waist and extending upwards and downwards along the seam. Squinting towards it, she can see tiny white threads popping out of their holes — more, she's sure, with every breath. She wears no bra with this dress and its boned bodice. If only she can stop it from falling off in the middle of the biggest evening of her lover's career.

'*Merci beaucoup.*' Teo speaks into the microphone. Silence falls. 'I am sure you will forgive me,' he continues, 'if I make this speech in English — my reasons will be apparent very soon. I'll be brief, because you know the book, you know what happened and there are just two important words to say: thank you.'

Applause blares out; Teo takes a long breath.

'Thank you, Mr Mandela, Mr Chairman and all the committee for their kindness in choosing my poor old novel to honour with this prize. Thank you to my agent, my several publishers and the generosity of everyone who has made it possible for me to complete what was, as you can imagine, a slightly difficult process in which I relived the events of the early 1990s. And I would like to add that if anybody had told me then that tonight I would be standing here, accepting this generous award from some of the finest people in the world, I wouldn't have believed it. To me, this proves that life and time can heal the unhealable, at least a little. The past cannot return, but the future can bring us to some very surprising places.'

Teo pauses and looks straight at Terri. She blows a tiny kiss towards him. 'And now,' he says, 'I want to thank the one person who has done more than anyone else to help me bring this book into being: the lady in my life, Teresa Ivory.'

'No!' Terri mouths, hoping he'll see. What if someone insists she sing? That would be unthinkable. Perhaps the tear in her seam would give her an escape route. She can't stand up in front of the cameras if her dress is falling off, even if her voice works.

'Teresa has been my inspiration, my muse and my tower of strength for many years.' Teo won't take his eyes off her. 'I don't know what I'd do without her. We've led necessarily separate existences . . . '

Terri bites her lip. Why does the entire world need to know this?

' . . . but I am hoping that we may make some changes to our lifestyle. I'd like to take this opportunity not only to thank her for all she has done to help me, consciously or not, but — I would like to say the following in front of everybody.'

As Terri watches, transfixed with horror and powerless to stop him, a frisson goes round the hall. Teo sinks on to one knee. 'Teresa Ivory,' he declares, 'I love you with all my heart and soul. Please would you do me the honour of agreeing to be my wife?'

Terri's face, neck and shoulders turn as hot and pink as beetroot soup. The cameras swing towards her; one hand clutching her split seam, the other at her face, checking her temperature, she's in need of a third hand to find her evening bag and a handkerchief within it. She grabs a napkin instead to mop her forehead — less than dignified. She can't seem to get her breath. How could Teo do this to her? In public, in front of Nelson Mandela, live on television? She could shake him. She could *kill* him. And she's terrified to let go of her dress.

'Terri,' says Teo.

Terri understands that she has no choice. She begins to get up from the table, but in her confusion she takes one awkward step and her heel catches in her hem. With a sickening jolt, the damaged seam gives way all along the bodice. The dress may have been way too tight, but now it really is going to fall off and there's nothing she can do about it.

'Excuse me,' she stammers. And instead of going up the platform stairs to join him, she pivots left towards the nearest exit and sails out to solitude and safety.

17

'Ivory,' says Terri, 'comes from elephants. Like me.' Wrapped in her hotel dressing-gown, she lifts the dress off the bed where she'd dumped it. 'Look at it. It's split right down the side.'

'I don't care.' Teo strides across the room for the twentieth time since his return. In the winter night, a stray church bell is striking three.

'What did you want me to do? A striptease for peace?'

Teo puffs on his pipe, silent.

'I didn't mean to humiliate you,' Terri protests. 'I thought, on balance, that it would be a lot more embarrassing for both of us if my dress fell off in front of TV cameras from thirty countries.'

'You know what they thought. You know what everyone thought.'

'Since when do you care what people think?'

'All I wanted was for you to say yes. You didn't need to get up at all. You could have sat at that table, said yes and smiled sweetly.'

Terri grits her teeth. He's right, of course, but she hadn't thought of it at the time and now it's too late. She attacks instead of defending. 'I wasn't the one making an assumption that someone *would* agree to marry me in front of thirty TV cameras.'

'Bitch,' Teo mutters, head in hands.

'Don't call me names.'

'You deserve worse.'

339

'I'm going home,' says Terri.

'Fine. Go. Get out. You think I ever want to see you again?'

Terri hesitates, balancing on a single cell; to one side lie the words: 'Come on, darling, we can work this out.' On the other side lies her suitcase.

She's said the words many times before. She chooses the suitcase.

★　★　★

Terri packed her rucksack in 1976 and left Joe in Edinburgh; she walked to the coach station without a backward glance and boarded the next bus to Glasgow. It was winter and the wind was ferocious, laden with ice from the outer Hebrides. Terri had twenty pounds, Katharina's address in London, and one handkerchief from a set Mary had given her for her birthday. In the rucksack she'd stuffed together her clothes and her volumes of songs. On the side of her face, a darkened patch of skin showed why she was leaving. She'd tried to conceal the storm-coloured bruise with make-up; you don't want the whole world to know about a thing like that. Let alone Finn.

Hauling herself and her luggage off the bus at last, Terri stared at the grey street, the brown office blocks and the gloomy sky settling towards dusk. Never before had she been so glad to see Glasgow. After strapping on her backpack she set off at a brisk pace, up the hill towards the street where Mary lived. She desperately needed Mary's magic teas and ointments, her healing hands, her sensible words. Or maybe she just needed to see her.

She stood outside the block, ringing the bell. No response. Terri pushed the small yellowed button again and again until her finger smarted. This felt familiar — she'd done it before. Mary might be inside, ill, sleeping, lonely. She tried to peer through the front window, but the light was bad, the interior wasn't illuminated and she could see nothing. Nor was there any sign of Mary's cat.

'Please,' said Terri aloud, pressing.

Above her, a window opened and she saw a neighbour she recognised peering out, her hair in curlers for the night. 'Hello, hen,' said the woman. 'Are you looking for Miss Hoolihan?'

'Aye,' Terri called back. 'How are you, Mrs Cook?'

'Och, I'm no bad. But have you no heard, Mary's gone?'

'*Gone?*' Terri's mind spun: what did 'gone' mean? Away out, or moved away? Dead? 'Will she be back soon?' she ventured, hoping Mrs Cook couldn't see her face.

'She's moved away.'

'But where? Do you know how I can find her?'

'Your guess is as good as mine, hen. I'd have thought she'd tell you more than she told me.'

'I've been living in Edinburgh,' Terri explains. 'I haven't seen her for ages. I didn't know.'

'May be that she got another job, somewhere a bit less rough. Why would a nice young woman like her stay in a place like this if she didn't have to? Perhaps she finally found herself a man.'

341

Terri tried to protest. Mary had loved her work here; she was drawn to troubled places and people because she had the gift to heal; she wouldn't ever have moved away without at least leaving a note. The words wouldn't come out in the right order.

'If you hear where she is, would you let me know, please?' she asked instead, scrabbling for some paper in her rucksack to write down her mother's address.

Mrs Cook, peering over her windowsill, hesitated. 'You're the lass that sings, aren't you?'

Terri nodded. Somehow, that had become the way everyone described her.

'You'd better come up.' The buzzer sounded, and the grateful Terri took the steps two at a time.

Inside, Mrs Cook sat Terri down in a big armchair, provided tea and began to explain.

'Our Mary's never been in a shred of trouble, far as I know,' she said. 'You can tell a good person when you meet one, don't you think so? But it began with those herbs. You know she taught school singing and the church choir too. Well, there was a wee boy in the church choir practice who had a fever, and she took him home with her and made him a drink with a herb.'

'It didn't make him sick, did it?'

'Heavens, no. The fever went almost at once.'

'Then — ?'

'Then his mother wondered why. She didn't like it.'

'Why not? Was she mad?'

'She didn't like it that Mary had taken a child

342

back to her home, even if he was sick and needed to be looked after, and even though she, the mother, wasn't at home to take care of him herself.'

'I'm sure Mary just wanted to help.'

'Well, this was the church choir, not any old sing-song, and this halfwit mother went to the priest objecting to the choirmistress taking a young lad to her home, and he wrote to the bishop, who wrote to the cardinal. Next thing we know, Miss Hoolihan was removed from her choir. And then the children at school heard the story and started dressing it up and passing it around and turning it into something it wasn't, if you know what I mean. They started to throw things at her. And not just the children. Much of what was thrown was words, though nobody could prove anything bad had happened. It was all made up and malicious. But one day very quietly she upped and left. I can't say I blame the poor lass.'

'Oh my God.' Terri covered her face with her hands. She didn't know what to say.

'If you find her, hen,' said Mrs Cook, 'tell her we know she's all right? We know she didn't do anything wrong. That lass doesn't have a bone in her body that's not blessed with goodness.'

The tea dried up in Terri's mouth. Mary had been sacked by the same church the practices of which had left Terri pregnant because birth control was evil, which in turn forced her into what it deemed the murder of two babies, which otherwise would have had Joe for a father and given the lot of them a life of abject misery? And

343

healing was suspect if it was herbal, and a woman a potential criminal if she tried to help a sick child?

'Thank you for telling me the truth.' She gave Mrs Cook a kiss.

Her backpack straps cutting into her shoulders through her old coat, Terri plodded away downhill. Waiting for the bus south to her mother's, she knew that on arrival she'd face a barrage of 'I told you so,' at best and, at worst, 'What's he done to your face? No more than you deserve, I'll warrant . . . ' She gave up on the bus and began to walk.

The Usher Hall and her job in the pub had been a welcome refuge, and more than that when it led her to Katharina — but she always had to face Joe when she went home to their bedsit after work. Finding another job had to be easier than staying with him. Terri remembers the cinema car park. He wasn't worth her tears, but she still wondered what had gone wrong so much so that their world of just four years ago felt like another lifetime. The trouble was that he knew where to find her. Obviously she'd go to her mum. She'd hoped that Mary would let her stay; now it seemed that she might never see Mary again.

Terri turned a corner and the wind flung itself into her face. She screwed up her eyes against it; her ears ached with cold. Home couldn't be a solution for long. The one other person she could call was Katharina herself. The strangeness got stranger by the moment. Terri, thinking as she walked, made a decision that, while apparently random, was still a decision. If her mother said that she had deserved what Joe had done to her, she'd phone Katharina. And whatever the result was of that conversation, she would leave the Gorbals for ever.

Terri climbed the stairs and walked along the damp-infested corridor to her mother's door. It was no different from before, yet somehow, even though the house of bedsits in Edinburgh hadn't been exactly a National Trust showpiece, Terri noticed things that had escaped her for years: brown circles of fungus on the ceiling; a smell in the entrance that was urine and always had been; rust on the window edges that wouldn't lock as a result. Not that anyone here had much that was worth stealing.

'I told you so,' said Finn, looking her up and down. 'You can't say I didn't. Well, hen, you'd best come in.'

'How's Robbie?' Terri asked. Her mother seemed to have aged in the past six months. Terri gazed at her, willing her to go dancing to mouth music at the pub. She knew Finn would never do that again.

'Your brother's out gallivanting. I suppose you'll be wanting some tea. What's happened to your job?' Finn filled the kettle with a long-suffering sigh. Her shoulders in her old blue housecoat had acquired a defeated aspect, an incipient stoop with pronounced angles, the twists of which mirrored the bitterness underneath.

'I left,' Terri said.

'You gave them more notice than you give me, I hope?'

'No, I just left. I had to.'

Her mother swung round and assessed her face and its bruise with a sharp glance. 'What's he done to you?' she snapped. Then she added, without waiting for Terri's answer, 'Well, it'll go in time. I'll warrant it was nothing more than you deserved.'

Terri stood up. 'I need to find a phone box,' she said.

Twelve hours later she was on another coach, bowling south down the M1 towards London and the address that Katharina had given her. It was as if Mary, vanishing, had managed to send Katharina into her life to rescue her instead.

★ ★ ★

Moving on is occasionally the best thing you can do.

'It's not that I don't want to marry you,' Terri ventures, before she opens the suitcase. 'It's just that I'm not a hundred per cent certain, not enough to stand up and say yes in public.'

'Go on, make it worse,' Teo growls.

'It felt like you were trying to trap me. You just decided I'd say yes, or that I wouldn't dare say no. And that upsets me.'

'I know, it's Teo's fault. It's always Teo's fault. Let me touch something, and it'll fall apart. Let me love someone, and they vaporise.'

'What do you want? You'd rather I'd been dishonest? You'd rather I'd jumped up and hugged you and said 'oh darling, I'm yours for ever' on international television, dress or no dress, and then we'd have come back here and I'd have said: 'actually, *no*'?'

'What I want is for you to say yes and mean it.'

'I can't, and you know it.'

'So, what are we doing here?' Teo's gaze pierces Terri; she feels she's raw meat over a fire.

'You tell me. Popping the question that way was your idea.'

'I can't go on like this.'

'Neither can I.'

She feels Teo about to speak; but he stops. There's no need.

⋆   ⋆   ⋆

Julie is in the Junior Common Room, her knuckles knotted as she stares at the screen. The image of Teo is dead centre, on one knee on a platform, uttering a proposal of marriage, extending a hand forwards — and as Julie watches, her mother, clutching weirdly at the side of her dress, rises and steams towards the door like a luxury yacht setting out to sea.

Julie pulls herself off the sofa, feeling woolly, all limbs, feet and confusion; eventually she forces herself to run back to her room to find her phone, trying not to howl aloud. What's *wrong* with her mother? How can she do a thing like that to Teo, after all these years? She gets through only to the voice mail; naturally, Terri had switched off her handset for the dinner.

Julie can't remember the first time she met

347

Teo. She retains a distant imprint, but couldn't have put a date on it: just a whiff of tobacco, a hangdog face with dark circles under darker eyes, a tender hand on her hair, and a French children's book — she couldn't understand a word, but she'd liked the pictures. He'd drifted between the background and foreground of their lives; she's not sure at what point she'd understood he was more than a friend to Terri, sleeping where her father used to sleep. If it had bothered her, she doesn't remember that either. Perhaps it is not only her that Terri regards as a millstone. Perhaps it applies equally to him.

Resolved, she packs a bag and looks up the timetable for trains to London the next afternoon.

In the morning she attends a lecture which she scarcely hears, then delivers a slapdash essay to a supervisor's pigeonhole at a neighbouring college. She allows a suitable number of hours for Terri to travel back from Bruges — over the years she's learned to calculate to within fifteen minutes the time it will take her mother to come home from a variety of international locations. Finally she cycles off to the station, leaving a note for Irina.

★ ★ ★

Terri has been back for eighteen minutes and is leafing through the Yellow Pages for a clothing repairer when she hears the key in the latch. For half a second her heart overturns, expecting Teo. Instead, Julie's light step sounds in the hall. Terri dives out of the kitchen.

'Darling, what are you doing home? Are you OK?'

'I saw the awards on telly.' Julie hasn't even put down her bag. Her eyes are full of anger. 'Mum, how *could* you?'

Terri darkens. 'Is that why you're here? To yell at me about last night? I need that like a hole in the head.'

'So do I, Mum. I can't believe you did that to Teo! What did he do to deserve it?'

'Come upstairs and I'll show you exactly what happened.'

Terri takes her daughter's arm and marches her to where the split evening dress lies splayed on the bed. 'As you can see, it's strapless, and it's split. The whole world would have seen your mum in the buff. That would have been fun, wouldn't it?'

'Better than what you did.'

'Oh, you think so, do you?'

Terri tries not to show that she's quailing inwardly with her first suspicion that perhaps Julie's right and she's wrong. She ushers Julie into the bedroom armchair, crouches next to her and explains the full story as simply as she can.

'But why don't you want to marry him?' Julie protests at the end.

'Because I don't. One day you'll understand.'

'You want to be free, don't you?'

Terri feels Julie's gaze hardening, accusing her. 'I value my independence, but there's nothing I'd like better than to have a loving partner to come home to. It's just that he isn't that partner.'

349

'But what about him? What about *me*?'

'Darling,' Terri tries to soothe, 'it's not your problem.'

'Of course it is.'

'And why?'

'You make it my problem. You'd always rather I had no father than give up your freedom, and even when you'd grown up without a dad too! You never hide anything, you go off with your Hollywood stars or your conductors or just blokes you pick up — you don't give a damn what anybody thinks. But I love Teo like he *is* my dad. Don't you ever think about him? He loves you!'

'Don't shout at me.' Terri controls her tone. 'You've got a dad, remember? And you don't seem to like him any more than I do.'

Julie flinches; Terri can see the pain coursing through her and hates herself for causing it. It's not Julie's fault if her father is too absorbed in his new family to spend much time with his old one. She's about to try to take Julie in her arms when the girl pulls away. 'You want your flings more than you want a proper relationship,' she says. 'It's disgusting!'

'Oh, and that's all right for your generation but not for me because, shock, horror, I'm past fifty and I'm supposed to be a dignified matron? It's disgusting, is it? It's your generation that's promiscuous, your generation that'll go to clubs, swallow pills that fry your brain and sleep with anything that moves.'

'I've never slept with anybody except Alistair!' Julie lets out a sob.

Terri is starting to feel too angry to comfort her. 'So tell me, if you're being the wise adult here, why do you think Teo is the perfect man for me to live with, for ever and ever till death us do part? He's damaged, Julie, he's complicated and self-destructive, and if I let him he'll destroy himself and me too.'

'You could rescue him.'

'For Christ's sake! Julie, you've got to learn this now: you can't change a man. You must never, ever get together with somebody with the idea that you can change him, heal him or save him, because you can't, and nobody can. I'm not a lifeguard, I'm not a St Bernard dog bounding through the snow with a barrel of brandy and I'm not the angel at the top of the bloody Christmas tree. I'm a *woman*, an ordinary human being, I've been in this world for half a century and I know what life suits me.'

'There's nothing remotely ordinary about you.' Julie blows her nose.

'Past the crap, I'm as ordinary as you can get, and you know it.'

'But you never think of what's best for Teo . . . or for me.'

'Of course I do! You don't seriously believe that Teo would be a good substitute father for you?'

'He loves me and I love him.'

'You marry him, then.'

'Oh, Mum!' Julie howls, 'why can't we just be a normal family?'

Terri reaches for her daughter's hands. She's glad when Julie lets her hold them. 'How many 'normal families' do you know?' she asks. 'There's no such thing, not any more.'

'I'm so confused.'

Julie tips forward; she puts her arms round her mother and holds on. Terri strokes her back and notices that her heart is pounding and there's sweat on her neck. She shouldn't have to feel this way, not at nineteen. Is this her, Terri's, fault? She wants to cry in sympathy, but that wouldn't help.

'Everything's topsy-turvy,' Julie sobs into her shoulder. 'Everything feels inside-out and back-to-front and I don't know which way to look.'

'Darling, hush. I promise you, those precious 'nuclear' families don't solve a damn thing. You get beneath the surface of every so-called family and you'd be shocked to see what's really going on under the keeping up of appearances. You think Bernard, Jane and Ellen are a normal family? Your half-sister's going to be a headcase in her teens because her mother never gives her a moment to be herself without being shouted at.'

'Don't be horrible about Ellen.'

'I'm not, I'm being horrible about Jane. I'm sure she's a good doctor, but that doesn't make them a happy family. Don't you remember, you ran away from them?'

Julie lowers her eyes. 'It's not a reason not to try.'

'I'm sorry.' Terri tries a different technique. 'I know it's upset you. But can't you see? You have to be honest, you have to be true to yourself. If you're not, if you just do what other people expect of you, you end up making everyone miserable, especially yourself.'

'But sometimes,' Julie points out, 'they're miserable anyway.'

'Well, try being happy first. Find your own path. You're supposed to be grown-up now, you needn't depend on me to make you happy. What does make you happy?'

'I miss the way Alistair and I used to be.'

'Oh, darling.' There's nothing Terri can do about this, inevitable though it is. She stands up and pulls Julie after her. 'Come on, I'll make us some tea. And there's cake. I'm trying not to eat it.'

Julie trails out of the room and disappears downstairs. Terri, feeling as if a cylinder inside her chest has emptied itself out, heads back to the kitchen.

Just as she's wondering where Julie has gone, she hears, from the basement, the sound of the piano and a slender voice rising quietly over the top. Julie is playing chords and doing some warm-up exercises.

Terri stands motionless, listening. Could *that*, after all, be what makes Julie happy?

18

Julie and Alistair take a taxi from the bus station to the college, as Alistair is still on crutches for his knee. Julie watches him, anxious, as he surveys the grey turrets above the gates, the strolling tourists with their cameras, the fleets of bicycles and the tree-protected river. He says little.

'I thought we could go to formal hall,' she ventures. 'They do it three times a week and I don't usually go, but it's a good value, three-course meal.'

'Formal what?'

'It's sit-down dinner in the main hall. We have to wear gowns, or I do — '

'Dressing-gowns?'

'No, these black college robe things — they make us look like vampires — it's quite funny, really . . . ' She stumbles over her words, too many of them. 'I thought it might be fun for you to try it.'

'Don't try to make me have fun, Jul. It's good enough just to get out of the sodding flat.' Alistair tries to grin.

'I'm glad you're back.'

He gives a snort. 'I'm not.'

'What do you mean? Why not?'

'I'm going back, soon as I can.'

'*What*?' Julie is horrified. 'But how *can* you go back?'

'How can I stay here?' he retorts. 'My mates are there and I'm damned if I'm going to sit around skiving in Falcon fucking Park.'

'But . . . '

'Don't, Julie. You don't understand.'

'Too right I don't.' She bites back the words.

She's booked a camp bed from the porter's lodge to bring to her room — she doesn't want to risk rolling over onto one of Alistair's injuries on her own narrow mattress. Irina, having spotted her wheeling the contraption through the courtyard, with Alistair hopping on his crutches alongside, comes running down.

'*Ochin priatna!*' She beams at Alistair, shaking his hand hard. 'So wonderful to meet you at last.'

'So you're Irina,' he says, assessing her figure in her cashmere jersey. Irina's expression grows faintly glassy. Alistair either sees straight through her or sees nothing at all; it's hard to tell which. Julie, watching his face, feels a knot tautening inside her. In the taxi, she hadn't wanted to admit it was there.

'You are staying how long?' Irina smiles as hard as she can.

'Just tonight, I think.'

'So you come to hall and meet our friends,' she encourages. 'Charlie and Raff are looking forward to this.'

'Right. See you later.' Alistair turns away towards the staircase. Julie gives Irina a nervous glance, then hurries after him.

In Julie's room, Alistair says little while he unfolds the bed and dumps his sleeping bag on top of it. Her books and manuscript paper sit on the desk, gathering dust; she's done no work for days, mainly because she hasn't been there. She went down three days ago for Darren Hanley's memorial service, where she cried for four hours even though she'd met him only twice, for two minutes apiece, in Catterick. She was unsettled on two counts: first, because that bomb could so easily have killed Alistair instead; yet also she felt like a spare part while he greeted the other lads who'd been with him in the Snatch and were also recovering, and a commanding officer who was back on badly needed leave. Cambridge might be a world that wasn't hers; but in that company, she had no place at all.

A sheaf of communications had been waiting for her in the porter's lodge: a note from her tutor telling her to make an appointment to see him, phone messages from several supervisors demanding to know where she and her essays were, and a card from Chris the organ scholar saying that she's much missed at choir and he hoped everything was all right. She was almost relieved to be back.

'How do you like Rini?' she asks Alistair brightly.

'She's nuts, isn't she?'

'Do you think so?'

'Completely fucking nuts.'

'Maybe she is, a bit — she's sort of dramatic — but she's very sweet. Very caring.' Julie thinks of Irina hugging Knut the toy polar bear.

'This 'formal hall' . . . Can't we just go out for a curry?'

'But everyone's dying to meet you! They've all

been hearing about you for so long, they really want you to be there . . . '

'Who's 'they'? Your posh boyfriends?'

'I don't have posh boyfriends.'

'Charlie? Raff? Who the fuck — ?'

'Charlie fancies Rini, and we think Raff's gay but he won't admit it. We're just friends.'

Alistair watches Julie rummaging through her papers. 'These people don't know they're born.'

'They have different lives, that's all.' Julie opens packets of soup and puts sliced bread into the toaster.

'It's not 'all'. You don't know how it feels, Jul.'

'Mainly because you won't tell me.'

Alistair has consistently refused to describe his life over the past months. He accepts a mug of soup, his gaze hard and resentful. There's an odd look to him which is easier to see now that he's out of the flat: his focus is missing. At least half his mind is permanently somewhere else. Though Julie knows it's not his fault or hers, she wishes frantically that she could bring it back.

'Have a rest,' she suggests. 'I've got to write to all these people.'

Alistair mutters 'Whatever,' through toast and peanut butter. When it's finished, he pulls off his shoes, stretches out on Julie's bed and is soon out cold.

Julie, at her desk, begins to scribble replies and excuses. Alistair snores behind her. Her grovels are necessary, but she has little conscience. Harmony and counterpoint exercises have never felt more pointless; essays on Italian baroque opera bore her to tears, especially after the sight of Darren Hanley's mother sobbing her heart out on Sue's shoulder. Her only sincere apology is to the conductor of the chamber choir.

'*Dear Dr North,*' she writes, '*I am so sorry to have missed the last two practices. Some very difficult things have been happening and I had to go home. Please may I come and see you, because it is very hard to —* '

There's a snort from Alistair. She glances round. He's on his back, one arm shielding his face. His limbs are twitching while he mutters something unintelligible. Dreaming; reliving something, curling into the foetal position, letting out some weird, stomach-sourced noises that sound like sobs.

'Al?' she whispers, going to him. When she puts a hand softly against his shoulder he moans quietly, then lets out a flooding muddle of words — she can't make out all of them; some are expletives, others are names. She identifies 'Han'; something about high heels. There's a tuneless kind of tune, vaguely like a Christmas carol. Then a howl.

That curdles her into action; she bends to kiss him. 'Al, wake up — you're having a bad dream.'

There's an abrupt movement, a flip and flash of a limb, and something strikes the side of Julie's head. The world twists and she sees the floor leaping up towards her. She's too shocked to wonder what happened. A second later, Alistair is crouching beside her, calling her name, his face terrified.

'God, I'm sorry,' he gasps. 'I didn't mean it. I didn't. Julie, speak to me, are you all right?'

Julie, forcing back tears of fright, sits up and tries to nod.

'Are you sure? I didn't hurt you?'

'Unless I've got a black eye, no.' Julie tries to calm her breath.

'No, you haven't. Jul, I was dreaming, I was back there and . . . '

'It's OK. I know.'

'How do you know?'

'You were talking in your sleep. It sounded so . . . so . . . I just wanted to wake you up.'

'Over there, if someone wakes you up like that, they could have a gun against your head. God, Julie, I'm sorry . . . '

'You're not there, you're here with me. You're safe now.'

'I'm with you. I don't know about safe.'

Julie picks herself up and forces her feet towards the basin. The hot water on her face is a comfort; she hadn't realised she'd turned so cold. Shivering, she feels faint and nauseous; it must be the shock. 'Al,' she begins, 'what do you do, out there, if someone *does* wake you up and they *do* have a gun?'

'They haven't, yet.'

'But what — I mean, would you shoot them? Would you get to your gun in time?'

'Course. You're never parted from your weapon.'

'Never?'

'Never. They lie around in the tent and you always have it beside you when you sleep.'

'But do you ever use it?'

'Do I — ?'

There's a moment of blankness, a gulf like a mountain ravine between their understandings.

'Do you ever have to fire it? Have you ever had to — like — shoot someone? Kill them?'

Alistair turns away. 'Christ, Jul,' he says. 'What do you think we do all day?'

★   ★   ★

As dusk descends, Julie manoeuvres Alistair into the showers and persuades him to wear a tie. She borrows a gown from the porters' lodge and is putting on mascara when Irina taps on the door and invites them to pop in for sherry before going up to hall.

Alistair stands politely beside Julie in Irina's room, adding few words while Charlie and Raff hold forth about essays, golf and the bridge club, which Julie admits, reluctantly, to joining from time to time. He's assessing the cushions, the iMac, Knut the bear; she catches his eye over a sherry glass and he winks. It's the best moment of the day — a flicker of hope left from their old world.

'I hadn't thought,' he says, following the others through the courts to the hall. 'You always say you don't fit in and you don't belong here, but it looks to me like you fit like a glove.'

'Oh, Al,' she protests.

'You've got all these dead posh friends, they like you and you like them. What's the problem?'

'I'm not like them, though.'

'Sure you are. Diva mum, lecturer dad, posh as it gets.'

'I'm only here because my dad insisted. And *you* insisted too. Don't you remember?' Distressed, Julie catches Irina's attention and conveys that the others should go in ahead and save them places.

'So if you don't like it, don't stay.'

'What do you *want* me to do?' Julie pulls him aside from the stream of students in black gowns, flapping towards dinner like a flock of crows.

'Jeez, Jul, do what you fucking like.'

'Just come inside and have some food. You haven't eaten anything since our toast. No wonder you're in a bad mood.'

'I'm not in a fucking bad mood.'

He looks like a creature cornered by hostile dogs. She's never seen such an expression on his face before, or anyone else's — except possibly Teo's, once when she walked in while he was having a row with Terri.

'Will you try, at least? You might actually enjoy it.'

'Oh, I *actually* might, might I?'

Julie stands still, at a loss. She simply doesn't know what to do. Whatever she chooses will probably be wrong.

Irina bounds out and solves the problem by clutching Alistair's arm and saying, 'Darlings, please come in now, we are waiting for you and they are about to say grace.' The tension slackens; a moment later they're crossing flagstones to the hall door and the vaulted interior.

The dons are arrayed at the high tables, placed

horizontally at the far end. The students cluster on benches at long trestles perpendicular to their superiors. Overhead, wooden beams line the peaked roof like whalebones. Julie, Alistair and Irina are the last in; a gabble of chattering spirals around them from the students in their gowns. 'Load of bloody vultures,' Alistair mutters.

'Give them a chance,' Julie begs, relief sweeping her at the sight of Charlie and Raff waving and gesturing; they've kept places towards the end of a table. She'd never have thought she'd take their part; but she doesn't see why Alistair has to dismiss an entire roomful of two hundred people at one go. True, the ex-Elthingbourne crowd on the other end of their table aren't her favourite people, but Charlie and Raff have become her friends. They're fine, once you get used to them.

They're just in time for grace. Everyone stands, gowns drooping from their shoulders, while a classics student intones in Latin. Afterwards, they sit down and continue talking as if nothing had happened.

Charlie turns to Alistair. 'It's great to meet you at last. Julie never stops talking about you.'

'Thanks, mate.' Alistair stares with some distaste at the wine that Raff's preparing to pour him. 'Any chance of a lager?'

'I'll organise it.' Charlie bounds off to speak to a waiter. Julie notices the Elthingbourne girls, Tansy and Natasha, looking Alistair up and down over their wineglasses.

'You're students and you have people waiting on you?' Alistair says to Charlie when he returns.

362

'Only in hall. It's the same as it was hundreds of years ago, they say. Oh, and our rooms get cleaned. Poles, mainly. Dead gorgeous, some of 'em.' Charlie folds his arms behind his head and glances at Irina, presumably to see if she's jealous. 'All these Polish women coming over here — I can't understand why our girls aren't more worried about it. I mean, they're all slim, they're all beautiful . . . '

'And they're taking all the jobs,' Alistair points out.

'That's not the case,' Raff argues. 'They do jobs that nobody else wants to do. The ones our lot think are beneath them, cos they just want to go out and get pissed.'

Julie stares into her plate, wishing that the entire hall would dematerialise and take her with it. Fortunately Alistair doesn't volunteer any information about his mother — though in some ways, his maximum-density silence is worse. Her heart twisting, she pictures Sue setting off for work from Scargill Tower after dark.

'You're in the army?' Natasha asks him from the other end of the table. 'D'you know Prince Harry?'

'Never met him.' Alistair makes an effort to smile.

'Do you have a gun of your own?'

'Sure. SA80 A2 LSW.'

'What's that when it's at home?' Tansy giggles.

'It's a kind of machine gun. LSW means light support weapon.'

'Alistair's a hero,' Charlie encourages. 'He

tried to save his friend when their truck was attacked.'

'Ooh,' says Tansy, 'will they give you a medal?'

'Don't care,' Alistair says. 'I couldn't save anyone. Nothing'll bring him back. Not a subject for polite company.'

'It's OK, Al,' Julie whispers. A waiter places a starter in front of her — salad with grapefruit and avocado. She pushes a yellow segment around the plate. Thinking about the memorial service, she can't swallow it.

'I wouldn't want to spoil this refined atmosphere with tales from the big bad real world,' Alistair is remarking.

'Al, everyone knows what happened. They're on your side.' She presses his knee, but he pushes her away so hard that she jolts Charlie's arm and there's a clatter as his plate tumbles on to the floor.

'Sorry!' Julie dives under the bench to retrieve it. 'Oh, Charlie — all your salad. Have mine, I don't want it.'

'It's OK,' Charlie assures her, but he looks unsettled. Julie notices Irina's cat-eyes flick sideways to the door, outside which Vaslav often lurks with a cigarette while he waits for them to finish dinner. 'I'll get you another lager,' Charlie says to Alistair.

'Thanks, mate. Answer to all our problems, lager. That's what makes the world go round.' Alistair thumps his glass on the table. 'And bring back conscription, that's what I say. Compulsory military service — that'd sort out the knives and guns on the streets. Teach kids some discipline, show 'em what toughness really means.'

Several students glance round and stare. Raff looks aghast. 'You're saying you'd force every kid to risk his life, with no choice?' he protests.

'Like I said, it'd sort a lot of the crap round my way in south-east London.'

'Sorry, mate, I know you're a hero and all that, but I can't possibly agree with you.' Raff is as perturbed as Julie has ever seen him — he'd never cope with an environment like Alistair's camp, that's for sure. 'Some people just aren't cut out for that life. It's a basic human right, not to be forced to go to war.'

'Tell that to the fucking fanatics we're up against,' Alistair remarks. 'They don't know the meaning of the words 'human rights', even in Pashtun.'

'I think he's right,' Natasha remarks. 'Turn all the yob gangs into cannon fodder! That'd solve everything.'

'I don't feel great.' Julie mumbles. 'Shall we go, Al?'

'Why? You said this was fun.'

The main course arrives — slabs of beef in pinkish gravy with metal dishes of potatoes, broccoli and Brussels sprouts to hand round. Julie, staring at the meat soaking in the remnants of its own blood, loses anything that was left of her appetite. Across the hall, a group from the drinking society are chucking bread pellets at each other. There's a tinkle of breaking glass.

'They are such babies,' Irina protests.

'Pass the spuds?' says Natasha. Julie passes them.

'Pass the sprouts,' says Alistair. His south-east London voice pronounces it as 'spraaeouts'.

'Pass the *spraaeouts*!' Two of the Elthingbourne boys with Natasha and Tansy pounce on their opportunity. 'Pass the bleedin' *spraaeouts*!'

'A line from Shakespeare's famous play 'Chav and Juliet'!' Tansy declares.

'Shut up,' Julie advises the girl quietly; Alistair's whole body is tensing.

'Shu'up! Shu'up! Shu'up yer face!' The public-school kids, a safe majority, fall over each other, hooting with laughter.

'Here you go, mate, here's yer spraaaaeouts!' yells the boy next to Natasha, picking three green balls out of the dish and batting them through the air. One of them strikes Alistair just above the eye.

'Al, everyone teases everyone about their accents all the time,' Julie tries to warn him, but it's too late. She ducks towards the wooden panels as the commotion bounces off the walls and windows. Plates leap from the table as if in shock therapy, gravy splays across the girls, who must be glad of their gowns' protection; Alistair is on his feet, shoving table and bench away from him, and reaching for his crutches. The students at the far end transform in a flash from bullies to scared, sheepish children.

He limps towards the sprout-thrower, who's still clutching the vegetable dish, and hoiks him to his feet by his striped collar. 'Out,' he barks.

Julie had expected tactless questions, challenging opinions, disagreements, but she'd never imagined a schoolyard brawl about Alistair's accent, let alone over Brussels sprouts.

'Hang on, mate, I really don't think that . . . I mean, all it was . . . ' The boy, smaller than Alistair, is quaking visibly.

'Al, your leg!' Julie protests.

'Outside.' Alistair, ignoring her, jerks his head towards the door with the assurance of one who's become used to scaring individuals from another culture into obeying him. More dismayed by the moment, Julie suddenly understands that Alistair has acquired authority. Whatever he was taught in Catterick, whatever he learns day by day out in that remote camp, something's emerged from him that she'd never known was there. It's not only that he's grown up; rather, he's found himself, or, as Teo might say, found his own voice. And she's not sure she likes it.

'What *is* the meaning of this?' The college master himself is in front of them, arms folded. 'Young men, this will never do. I must insist that you leave this hall, *now.*'

'We were just going, sir,' Alistair declares. Goading the unfortunate student with nothing more than willpower and one gesture of a crutch, regardless of his own painful ribs and knee, he manoeuvres him through the doorway. Julie dashes after them to the courtyard, where Vaslav is enjoying a peaceful cigarette.

Seeing the open space inviting battle, and the hulk of the Lithuanian bodyguard slouching nearby, the unfortunate student does all he can do: he yells for help. Two porters surge out from the lodge; each grabs one of Alistair's arms.

'Get off me!' he protests. 'It's not your problem.'

Julie runs to them. 'He's just back from the war, please don't hurt him!'

'He's your guest, Julie?' The elderly porter, who'd handed the camp bed over to Julie, is fond of her; she spots sorrow in his face.

'Please let him go, Mr Simmons,' she begs. 'He's not well. His ribs aren't right yet. Nor's his leg. Please let me look after him.'

A curl of cigarette smoke reaches them from Vaslav, who's watching everything with apparent amusement.

'I don't need bloody looking after.' Alistair shakes the porters away. 'Leave me alone. I'll get the next bus home.'

'Al — '

'Keep out of it, Jul. I'll get my stuff.'

'Normally I'd call the police if someone attacked one of our students,' Mr Simmons growls. 'But you're Julie's friend, so just this once I won't. But I shall wait to escort you off the college premises myself.'

'It's the bullies you ought to kick out.' Julie rounds on him while Alistair turns his back and heads for her staircase. 'Those idiots making fun of him. Not someone who's just been injured in a war.'

'I know that, love,' says Mr Simmons. 'But I'm not the one who makes the rules.'

★ ★ ★

368

Julie sprints after Alistair. In her room, he chucks his T-shirt and toothbrush into his backpack.

'No sex, then,' he says.

Julie stares at the floor.

'It's no good, Jul. You're one of them now.'

'Al, you've got to stop this them-and-us thing, it's not right.'

'What was all that, then? I didn't fucking start it.'

'You didn't have to get violent. Like I said, everyone's fair game here, it's normal.'

Alistair turns, his face scarlet. 'If you've been in a war, and some guy throws things at your head and your eyes, what do you do? What do you *think*, Madam Opera Singer's Nice Little Girl? Where I've been is no place for you, or your stuckup friends. I'd like to see them lot last two seconds in Catterick, never mind the full Monty. Don't cry — it won't help you or me or anyone. Now do you see why I want to get the fuck out of this stupid country?'

'I'll come home with you.'

'No! I'm sick of you mummying me all over the place. Leave me alone.'

And with that he grabs his coat from the chair and his pack from the floor, then his crutches; he pushes past her and is gone. Julie stands as still as if her feet had been pinned down by icicles.

Half an hour passes before Irina peers in to find Julie on her bed, sobbing into the pillow. She vanishes, then reappears carrying Knut.

'Oh, Rini.' Julie takes the bear in her arms.

'How is he?' Irina sits beside her and strokes her hair.

'Knut?'

'No, silly. Alistair.'

'It wasn't his fault, you know.'

'Of course not — he's not well. Something's shaken him up.'

'*Something?* Seeing his friend die and only just avoiding it himself.' Julie sits up and blows her nose.

'Do you think he killed anyone?'

During this very long evening, Julie has learned that the niceties of whether or not Alistair has had to kill someone couldn't be less relevant. 'Sometimes they were under fire all day every day, days on end,' she reports. 'They do what they have to, to stay alive.'

She senses the information sinking in, and Irina's understanding shifting and breaking, just as her own had earlier.

'Oh Julie, this war . . . we all thought it was so far away.' There's a crack in Irina's voice. 'The news cleans it up and keeps it distant, but it's here, ruining lives of people we love.'

'He wasn't like this before.' Julie sits up and blows her nose. 'He's changed. You do believe me, don't you? He's turned into — I don't know what he's turned into. A sort of machine.'

'A soldier.'

'Yes. Maybe he kills, and maybe he saves people's lives too — he doesn't even think about it any more. Or he didn't until he came home. He doesn't know where to put himself now, Rini, he only wants to go back.' Knut's synthetic fur is velvety against her face; she hugs the bear, fighting tears — not of misery

370

as much as bewilderment.

'Darling, I know. I can see he will have changed. What are you going to do? Change with him?'

'I have to call Mum, I want her to know what's going on.'

'Shall I stay?'

'Yes. Please.'

★　★　★

Terri feels battered by silence. She's not used to it. The cacophony of airports with flight numbers calling in many languages; the melange of noises backstage in an opera house — singers vocalising, phones ringing, lifts pinging, announcements on the tannoy; phone calls from Martini, sometimes daily; silly questions from interviewers; traffic and ambient pop during shopping trips, children's shrieks in the playground when she mothered Julie. That's her soundworld. Not silence.

She's been ploughing through some of Pauline Viardot's songs at the piano, picking out the tunes with one hand. They're beautiful, she thinks, direct but imaginative, tuneful and with plenty of opportunity to show off. She hums: a simple, sweet song of longing for a missing lover, dedicated of course to Turgenev. '*Hai luli, hai luli, Ah, qu'il fait triste sans mon ami.*' How sad it is without my love.

The accompaniment isn't complicated, so she strums some of the harmonies and mouths the words — she doesn't dare to sing out. It's a bit like the 'Eriskay Love Lilt': '*sad am I without thee* . . . ' The pairs of broken lovers meet and merge in the notes, as fresh now as they were when Pauline set them down over a hundred years ago.

Terri hasn't spoken to Teo since Bruges.

★　★　★

The telephone jolts her back to earth. 'Mum?' In a great rush, Julie pours out the full story of Alistair's ignominious departure. 'I don't know what happened,' she finishes. 'I didn't know people could be so changed in a few months.'

'Thomas Hardy once said: experience is not as to duration, but as to intensity,' Terri remembers; it's one of Teo's favourite quotes. 'Darling, he's not going to get back to normal overnight.'

'He won't get 'back to normal' *ever*.'

Terri knows she's right, but dares not say so. 'Go to bed, sweetheart, try and sleep,' she encourages instead. 'I'll call Sue first thing tomorrow and see what's going on. Will you be OK?'

'I think so. Irina lent me Knut. Thanks, Mum, night night.'

Terri ought to rest too, but she has no Teo to soothe her, nor an outsized teddy bear by way of substitute. She goes over for the hundredth time the events that led to her and Teo leaving Bruges barely on speaking terms. Her mind trawls every stage like a deep-sea fishing vessel. The net traps snowflakes as large as petals, the split seam gaping over the too-too-solid flesh beneath, Teo bemused at the microphone, the door looming ahead. Each time she explores the debris, she finds the same notions flapping around out of their element. Even if she hadn't fled, even if she'd played the game for the cameras, the result would have been the same: she'd have had to tell Teo afterwards that she didn't want to marry him. She wanted everything between them to stay as it was. That would have upset him even more than being rejected on TV. How could he pull such a stunt in the first place? How could Teo, of all people, be so crass?

Terri drums her heels on the mattress. She'd thought Teo valued, as she does, honesty to self and others, genuine feeling and humane action. But she's never won anything of the stature of the Mandela Peace Award. A Gramophone Award for her recording of *Der Rosenkavalier*, a Grammy for *Tristan und Isolde*, a South Bank Show opera prize and an honorary doctorate from the redbrick university that happened to employ her ex-husband, though nice, weren't quite the same. Maybe Teo is less resilient than she'd thought. Maybe he, too, won't go back to his old self any time soon.

One thing is certain. She can't return to the stage yet; she can try to salvage her relationship with Teo, but may not succeed; Julie, at college, is shedding a skin and has to be left in supportive peace; so she, Terri, is alone and, but for the shadowy companionship of Viardot and Turgenev, underoccupied. She must be able to do something positive.

She'd never quite worked out what Mary, in

Glasgow, did when she wasn't teaching, but she suspected she spent her spare time on good works: helping people with those healing hands, the herbs she brewed, the strength she could impart merely though being there. Mary had spent much time helping her. She could help someone. She could help Alistair.

19

On the seventh floor of Scargill Tower, Terri knocks on Sue's door, carrying a plastic bag distended by a cake tin, a bunch of daffodils and a CD. 'Half a mo,' calls Sue's voice. Waiting, Terri sniffs the air. A pong of drains, or worse, emanates from the bowels of this building — rather an appropriate metaphor for that type of smell.

'It's got worse,' she remarks when the door opens.

'You'd never believe it.' Sue ushers her in. 'We've been on to the council, but they don't want to help. Keep on saying they'll take a look, but they never do. It'd cost them, see?'

'That's a pretty bad smell. Someone should find out what it is.'

'We did. It's a blocked sewer. It's overflowed. A group of us went down to find where it was coming from and it's the most disgusting thing you ever saw. Believe me, you don't want to know, no more than the council does.'

'They've got to sort it.' Terri pushes the cake tin into Sue's arms. 'It's their job. You can't live with that.'

'Way I see it is, those of us who work for ourselves do our jobs. Those who work for someone else don't.'

Terri has worked for herself all her life. 'I couldn't agree more,' she says. 'Yes to tea, by the

375

way. Where's Alistair?'

'In his room. You heard about the other night?'

'Julie's version.'

'Probably not much different from his. He's worn out, though. I keep telling him he's got to look after those bones, but he just wants to magic himself better.'

'Of course he does. He's young. It's the state of mind I'm more worried about. Do you remember him and Julie ever arguing before, in all this time?'

'Oh, Lord, it always looked so perfect — love's young dream, and that. I couldn't imagine them two falling out.'

'And after me and Teo . . . Sue, when did you last have a nice man in your life?'

'A man, couple of years. A *nice* man, couple of decades.'

'We should try speed-dating,' Terri smiles. 'They say it works a treat. Can I go and see Alistair?'

'Help yourself. He should be so lucky, the ungrateful sod.'

Terri strokes the tabby cat, which is mewing hopefully at the sight of food, even if it is cake. Then she taps on Alistair's door. A grunt comes back.

She finds him in bed, playing loud pop music through inadequate headphones. He barely looks at her.

'Al.'

He opens one eye.

'Turn that off, please, and talk to me.'

'What?'

Terri leans down and pulls the headphones off him.

'I was listening to that.'

'That is not worth listening to.'

'I don't want lectures.'

'I want to know what happened in Cambridge.'

'That's just what you *don't* want to know.'

'Julie's upset.'

'*She's* upset? Fucking hell, I'm the one who got picked on and kicked out.'

Terri sits on the bed. She can't help surveying Alistair's shoulders and the hairs that investigate the air above his T-shirt. For several years she's been trying hard not to imagine her daughter in bed with this boy. She loathes the idea of Julie's delicate limbs being crushed under the weight of a sweaty male body, pumping at her as if she's a slab of meat, but now he's lying there like a slab of meat himself, unwashed, unkempt. She imagines him in the desert disaster — his friend dead while he lived, glimpsing the tiny fibre of fortune across which one could have been exchanged for the other. The look in his eyes doesn't amount to bitterness; just blankness. The sort of emptiness she remembers from Teo's face when she first knew him.

'Please don't blame Julie,' she says.

'I don't. But I don't want to go there again.'

'Fine, that's your choice. Now, why not get up, have a shower and come and eat something?'

Alistair turns his head to the wall. 'I've got a headache.'

'I bet you have, playing that racket. You'll be deaf by the time you're forty.'

'I'm nearly deaf already. Guns and stuff. It's bloody loud, Terri. Music's nothing.'

'I'll bring you some tea.'

'Terri, for Christ's sake, just leave me alone!'

'OK,' says Terri, smarting, 'be like that.' She sails out of the dark room with head aloft.

★　★　★

A phone book lies open on the kitchen table beside the teapot. 'Dunno who to ring first.' Sue pushes a milkless mug towards Terri. 'Council or the MoD. I usually can't get through to neither of 'em.'

'Why don't you both come over later?' Terri sips. 'I'll cook supper.'

'That's kind, love, but I'm working tonight. How's Julie? Did you talk to her?'

'She's upset by how much he's changed.'

'Thing is, he *hasn't*.' Sue stirs sugar into her tea. 'He's the same as he ever was. It's just he's the same person who's been through something terrible. I guess he's grown up.'

Walking home a little later, Terri reflects on this. It makes sense; so it was with Teo. Your essence doesn't change, but what happens to it in such extremity? Growth — in which direction? She remembers Mary and her fireplace in winter, which she'd used to show her the properties of strange substances. One Christmas Mary gave her a chemistry set, full of fascinating powders and crystals. She refused to take it

378

home in case Robbie managed to blow up the block with it, but in Mary's flat she watched her beloved teacher throw salt into her log fire and turn the flames lavender. Some blue crumbly stuff — copper sulphate, said the label — turned them sea-green.

'Magic,' breathed Terri.

'Not magic — but all the more miraculous because it's not,' said Mary.

Teo used to insist that he hadn't been changed by his experiences, only 'repointed'. Painful to place him in the past tense, like Finn, Robbie, Mary, Joe, the two babies she hadn't had. Oh, and Bernard. She'd forgotten about him.

No sooner has the name 'Bernard' crossed Terri's mind than her mobile rings, signalling the man himself.

'That's odd,' she remarks. 'I was just thinking about you.'

'I wouldn't make a habit of that.' Bernard is at his driest.

'You could make more of a habit of calling your daughter. She's having a hard time.'

'Terri, don't *start*, please. I'm calling because Jane and I are bringing Ellen to London for a half-term treat next week and we thought of coming to visit you.'

'Oh.'

'We thought it might be nice for Ellen to see Julie.'

'I'm sure it would. As you know, Julie's at college.'

'How's Teo? Recovered from his award yet?'

'Don't ask.'

'How are *you*?'

'Definitely don't ask.' Then Terri's mind makes an unexpected connection. 'But why not come and have lunch?' she adds. 'I wouldn't mind asking Jane's advice about something.'

She's rarely heard Bernard's voice sound as startled as it does in response to this.

★　★　★

Seeing Bernard back in the house, Terri feels as if a column of equations disguised as soldier ants is parading over her skin. Watching him — she's sure his ears have grown more pronounced — and Jane, who towers over her in high-heeled boots, she wonders how they could have had a child as sweet as Ellen, who bounces straight up to hug her.

'You should get that crack seen to, Terri.' Bernard hangs up his coat as if he's never been away. 'It's not going to get better on its own. And the roof needs attention.'

'The roof needed attention when we moved in, and the crack's been there since the war. The house is still standing. I can't think about that kind of expense at the moment.' Terri smooths back her ex-husband's daughter's hair and kisses her on the forehead.

'Aren't you going back to work?' Jane demands.

Terri smarts — does Jane think she's being self-indulgent by staying offstage to recover? 'Of course,' she retorts, 'but not until *my laryngologist* says I'm ready.' She enjoys outstaring Jane, but wishes she wasn't the shorter of the two — and that her money worries could be less real than they are.

'Where's Julie? Isn't she here to see her father and sister?' Jane asks.

'She's got supervisions and a concert with her choir. The college terms are very short and intense, you know. Oh, no, you wouldn't — you didn't go there, did you? Coffee?'

'Tea, please, no sugar.' Jane sits down, casting about for her child. 'Ellen, what are you doing? Come here!' The little girl has wandered through the drawing room to stand with her nose to the window, gazing in longing at the plastic-shielded swimming pool.

Terri serves spaghetti with a sauce she pretends she's made herself, plus a salad, and cake to follow. Ellen chatters, when she's allowed to, about school and ponies; Jane watches to make sure she doesn't kick the table leg, spill her food or speak out of turn. Terri notices a glazed look gelling on Ellen's face after she's been scolded for an unintentional transgression several times too often.

'So.' Jane dabs tomato sauce from the corner of her lips, 'I understand you wanted to ask some advice, Terri. Is it about your voice trouble?'

'Not at all.' Terri is already wondering whether her idea is sensible. But, faced with the fall-out between Alistair and Julie, and Sue's despair over finding trustworthy outside help, she feels as much out of her depth as they do.

'It's Alistair.' She explains: the blast, the physical recuperation, the mental effects.

'Headaches? Blackouts?' says Jane. 'Does he have flashbacks to what happened?'

'He certainly has nightmares, and his mood swings around. Some days he's fine, just cross and frustrated, but Sue says he has panic attacks. She thinks it's almost like a kind of culture shock. I think in the First World War they'd have called it shell shock.'

'No, definitely,' says Jane. 'It sounds like a classic post-traumatic stress disorder. He should probably see a psychiatrist. It's important to get treatment. Apparently the prisons are full of ex-servicemen who've been disturbed by their experiences, haven't had any help, and turned to drugs or alcohol. Sometimes they react to everyday situations too violently, which means they end up being prosecuted when what they need is actually medical or psychiatric support.'

Terri's innards lurch horribly. She thinks of what Julie had told her: the porter threatening to call the police. 'Do you know if there's any medication that could help him?'

'No, he'd have to ask his own doctor about that. It wouldn't be right for me to suggest anything, especially without seeing him.'

Terri doesn't like to explain that Alistair has been resisting attempts to get him to an army counsellor. 'Their place is on the way to the station. I thought maybe we could drop in. They feel so isolated, so forgotten ... '

'Hmm,' says Jane. 'I don't want to interfere, but if it'll make him feel better short-term ... '

'That block is no place for Ellen,' Bernard interrupts.

'Why?' Ellen asks.

'Because it's not. Supposing you ladies go together, and we'll wait here or meet you at the station afterwards.'

'Whatever.' Terri glares. She knows that Bernard's real issue is that Scargill Tower is no place for *him*.

★ ★ ★

The smell of sewage dominates the front hall and the lift isn't working. Jane gamely takes the stairs; Terri does her best to keep up. She's conscious that Jane isn't only taller than her but also younger and fitter.

'Disgusting,' Jane remarks, her nose scrunching. 'That's a public health hazard. Is anything being done?'

'They keep calling the council.' Terri feels something light brush across her face — an insect? She thinks she can hear a soft buzzing from the depths of the stairwell. The flies are congregating to investigate the smell, beating the council to it.

A minute later, Sue and Jane are facing one another in the Rosses' doorway.

'Come in, Dr Mason, nice to meet you,' Sue says. She gives Terri a kiss, then shakes Jane's hand gingerly, as if afraid of breaking something brittle. 'Sorry about the mess.'

'No, I'm more concerned about your drains.' Jane swings off her coat. 'So, I understand you're having some trouble?'

'That's one word for it.' Sue pours tea. Terri

383

keeps quiet, stewing silently over the notion that Jane and Julie have the same surname.

Jane explains her reservations about examining anyone else's patient. 'He ought to be under local professionals.'

'It's not like we haven't tried.' Sue has spent the past week trying to coax Alistair out of his room, away from the bed and the computer. Without the safety valve of Julie, his mood hasn't so much swung as plunged, and kept plunging until she wished it would swing again.

'But there must be systems in place to assist soldiers returning from conflict zones,' Jane says.

'Oh, there are, there are. But *he* doesn't want to do anything.' Sue's tone is acid. 'He calls the counsellors 'trick cyclists'. It's like he thinks it'd be a black mark against him when he goes back, or something.'

Jane draws in her breath. 'I'm sure he's wrong. I'd certainly hope so. Shall I have a look at him, if he feels like it?'

Terri twists her hands in her lap while Sue tries to tempt Alistair into the kitchen. Voices, first quiet, then slightly raised; at last Sue returns. 'He says go in, but sorry about the mess.'

'Right you are, then.' Jane gets up, as brisk as if she's about to go into battle herself. Terri and Sue exchange glances; they settle down to wait.

The ebb and flow of voices in the bedroom gives them little idea of what's passing between reluctant doctor and even more reluctant patient. Terri can hear Jane's accent, but not her words; Alistair's monosyllabic responses; then a more extended explanation or argument, she can't tell which. There's some rustling. Then the sound of the computer printer. Sue and Terri exchange bemused glances. Voices — and silence. As if someone has been stunned speechless.

The door opens and Jane appears, several folded pages of printout in her hand. 'I think that was productive,' she says.

Terri and Sue chorus questions.

'Mostly he wanted to tell me about how his friend was killed,' she explains. 'He's carrying quite a burden of guilt, though of course it's not his fault. But no, it'll take a while for him to process that.'

'Do you think it really is whatever they call it — post-traumatic whatsit?' Sue asks.

'No, there's no doubt at all. That's bound to be it.'

'What do we do?'

'Well, of course this isn't my exact area of expertise, but what I think is this,' Jane begins. 'First he should see a psychiatrist who can give him a proper diagnosis. That will provide him with an out, in all likelihood — they could organise a medical discharge if they feel it's appropriate, and then he can enter a programme of psychiatric care, maybe with medication to see him over the hump. Antidepressants have a lot of bad press, but I find them extremely useful, I prescribe them rather frequently and I've seen people derive considerable benefits from them. As for money, there should be a good package for him if he's medically discharged and after that he should be entitled to a range of state benefits. Then gradually, it ought to be possible for him to think about finding work. Maybe the supermarket will have him back, or they could put him into a job that's less intensely physical if his leg isn't up to the stacking. Of course he should go to a therapist, two or three times a week if not five, so that a professional eye can be kept on his state of mind. And he should definitely stay at home where you can care for him.'

As Jane speaks, Terri watches Sue's face transform slowly from hope to incomprehension.

'And for goodness' sake,' Jane finishes, 'ring the council and do something about those drains before the flies eat everyone alive. You know, there's a mosquito in his room. Right, Susan, thanks very much for the tea, I'd better be off. My husband and daughter will be waiting.'

'Say bye-bye to them from me,' Terri grunts. 'I'll stay here a while.'

'Terri, I still don't know what all of this is to *you*, but never mind that,' Jane returns. 'See you again.'

Sue, stone-faced, sees Jane out. From Alistair's room, the silence expands fold upon fold, keeping the two women in its thrall while they listen for Jane's footsteps tapping down the stairs. Terri almost finds it in her to wish that Jane would meet the gang on her way out.

'I'm sorry,' she manages to say. 'I'm so sorry. You don't have to believe her if you don't want to.'

'She meant it,' Sue responds. 'Oh God, Terri, I

might never get out of here again. And he mightn't, and that's worse. Terri, he's not yet twenty! And she's talking like he'll be damaged and labelled for years, maybe the rest of his life. What are we going to do?'

There's such anguish in her face that Terri can hardly bear to look at her. 'Sue, it's just one person's view. It's not her area of expertise, she said so herself, and she doesn't have to be right. Heck, I wonder what she told him . . . Let me go and see him — I feel responsible.'

Terri finds Alistair where Jane must have: in front of the computer, typing an email to Gerry with two fingers and Spellcheck.

Terri puts a hand on his shoulder. 'What did she say?'

He shrugs her off without looking up from the screen. 'Stupid stuff. I don't care. Doesn't make any fucking difference.'

'After what you've been through,' Terri says, her mouth dry, 'I think you're entitled to have a little flip if you want to.'

To her surprise, he grins. 'Like I said, doesn't make no difference. Not now. It's . . . ' He trails off, hunting for words. Terri sits on the bed and waits.

'You see,' he begins, 'it's hard trying to tell people what it's like. Everyone wants to know, but nobody who's not been in it can ever really get it. So, you're in this fucking rough environment, and then your best mate dies in front of you and you can't save him: he's dead, you're alive, and you have to live with that. All the training says you have to expect difficult

387

times, you have to get back to the job, you have to — like Prince Harry's hat, you know? I saw it on TV, it said 'We Do Bad Things To Bad People' on it. You know you have to do these things, and you have to carry on, because if you don't, you and all your other mates will die too. And it's tough, Terri, it's bloody tough, the bad people really *are* bad, they'll kill us anytime, and there's no other way, d'you see?'

'Yes, I see. Go on.'

'Then you get back here and suddenly everyone's like, oh my God, he's got post-traumatic stress disorder, let's give it a medical label when you can't save your best mate and he dies coughing up blood in your face. I can still taste it, Terri. I can smell and taste it the whole time. And they make out there's something more wrong with me if I don't want to go soft, and if I don't want to tell everybody every last detail. I know I'm telling you now, but you're different — I know you, I just don't want to tell some fucking sanctimonious doctor, not her, not nobody.'

'It's OK, Alistair. Go on.'

'So there I am, one minute we're larking around like we do, then there's this bang, a few seconds later my best mate dies in my arms, I pass out — and I wake up in bloody Birmingham. And I don't know where I am or what I'm doing there — and the lads are thousands of miles away, they're still going through it and all I want is to be with them and help them. And here everyone says, oh dearie me, you've been to war — let it all hang out,

388

don't bottle it up, have a good cry and you'll feel better. See a psychiatrist, have a label stamped on you for the *rest of your fucking life*, get yourself medically discharged then go and sponge off benefits because you've had a nasty experience, poor little boy, there there. I mean, it's shit. It's just shit. Thing is, *you* know that there are things you can't ever know. But that silly cow, she thinks she knows it all. Fact is, she hasn't got a clue.'

'Another of my bright ideas. I only wanted to help, and I'm sure she wanted to as well.'

'Julie's step-mum, right?'

'I thought she might be a good doctor. I just have a problem with her because she married my ex-husband.' Terri doesn't often admit this.

'It's OK,' says Alistair. 'It's not your fault, Tez. I feel sorry for her. Because if anything goes wrong for her, she won't bend, she'll break. You see?'

'Perfectly.' She could hug Alistair for disliking Jane.

He sits, silent. His eyes seem to bore through his computer screen and out the other side, past the walls, the tower and London, out to the space where the way he's been taught to think doesn't make sense any more, where the rules have fallen to pieces and new ones, learned specially, won't knit up; and where the fragments of his world lose their gravity and spiral away through air that's not pure enough to hold them together.

'What did you call me?' Terri asks.

'Tez. New name. D'you like it?'

She smiles. 'Come and have tea tomorrow.'

'Thanks, Tez. Cool.'

'I'll see you then,' she says, and pats his wrist. Sweat, heat, pulse, warmth. Has anybody called her 'Tez' before? And why wouldn't he talk to her before, but now that Jane has had a go at him, he suddenly opens up?

She sets off through the fetid air of the tower block and back to a place that, in the sixty-odd years since the bomb hit Livingston Road, has forgotten what it's like not to be safe and steady and doesn't want to remember.

20

'The thing is,' says the TV producer, 'we're about living artists. Modern culture. You know, what culture means. How culture's anything you want it to be. It can be graffiti and the Arctic Monkeys, not just some fat old lady warbling in an elitist theatre nobody can afford.'

'I'm not dead yet,' Terri points out. 'And I'm trying to lose some weight.'

'Of course, Miss Ivory, I wasn't suggesting that was you, but your pitch is about this Pauline Viardot lady, not about yourself. But we hear there are reports that you might be forced to retire. We might be interested in covering that story.'

'Thanks for that,' says Terri at her most sardonic. 'And by the way, you're talking bollocks. Culture is *culture*. The development of the human being beyond the animal, to its greatest creative and communicative potential. Your crap isn't culture, it's a pathetic, politically correct cop-out. Good luck to you.' Hanging up, she crosses the producer's name off her list.

She hasn't felt right since Jane's visit to Alistair three weeks earlier. Something as noxious as the tower block's sewers seems to have crawled under her skin and stayed there. Taking it out on a twenty-something TV producer who's either half-witted or half-stoned doesn't help as much as she'd like. By late afternoon, she feels worse.

391

Never mind the government's anti-ageism regulations: responses from three or four different TV companies have left her in no doubt, despite roundabout language, that they're only interested in presenters under thirty, preferably with a regional accent, either from an ethnic minority or loudly blonde. Terri explained in her best Glaswegian that she *is* blonde, if resprayed, and could be as loud as anyone required. 'I could give you the phone number of a producer on Radio 2,' suggested a youth who'd drawn a blank at Terri's name and the information that she was a singer, aged fifty.

'Pauline *who?*' said the head of culture, whom she called next. 'Ivan *what?*'

After three more producers have offered nothing but answering machines, two of which are full, Terri stops, for the moment. She goes to the basement and begins the gentlest of warm-up exercises. Never give up. Terri Ivory was not born to give up. Outside, the weather is positively Scottish: the March north wind is whistling down the chimney and tossing handfuls of raindrops against the window.

Between chords, Terri becomes aware of another sound: a tapping on the front door. Probably someone wanting to read the meter, or persuade her to change her electricity provider. She stumps upstairs to investigate.

Alistair is outside, hair bedraggled and jeans soaked through.

'Jesu Maria!' Terri ushers him inside.

'Sorry,' Alistair mumbles. The plaster is off and he can move without crutches, but he still has a limp — Sue insists that it will go, with time and physiotherapy. He places the greater part of his weight on his right leg; the left foot drags slightly, scuffing one side of his shoe. Terri remembers him jogging uphill, racing Julie after the exams, getting himself 'army fit'.

'Tez, sorry to land on you.' He stands off balance in the hall, dripping. 'You'll think I'm thick.'

'Try me. What's going on?'

'It's just . . . would you come down the supermarket with me? I promised I'd do the shopping for my mum tonight, but . . . '

Alistair's silence is louder than his words. Terri knows, from conversations with Sue, that it's the everyday annoyances that they take for granted, like supermarkets, traffic jams and junk mail, that can faze Alistair the most, bringing on the panic attacks that he doesn't like to acknowledge. Terri pulls on her coat and grabs her largest umbrella.

'You should make a list,' she suggests while they walk down the hill, pressing the umbrella against the wind. 'Lists help.'

'Yeah, the therapist told me to do that. That's one reason I don't.' Alistair grins, more to the ground than to her. He's visited the army counsellor twice, and doesn't think much of him.

'Have you talked to Julie?'

'Nah.' He doesn't elaborate.

She changes the subject; she's put foot in mouth too often recently. 'So, what do you need?'

'Usual. Loo roll, pizzas, bread, biscuits, peanut

butter, orange juice and that. Mum's into orange juice all of a sudden. Says it's good for us.'

The supermarket sprawls under a Victorian terrace on the hilly high street. The buildings must once have been beautiful, Terri thinks, but the layers of grime and the general air of neglect have left the place feeling sorry for itself, and its occupants likewise. She counts items on her fingers.

'What are you doing?' Alistair asks. She's pleased to see, in the supermarket's bright lights, that his face looks reasonably engaged.

'Making your list. You can remember each thing you need by giving it an image. Number one, loo roll. Image: self-explanatory. Number two: you could visualise a two made of bread. Then the orange juice: imagine, say, a carton of it bent into the shape of a three.'

'Clever.'

'My teacher, Mary Hoolihan, showed me that.'

'Your singing teacher?'

'Not exactly. She was a sort of mentor.' Terri has never found a satisfactory way to describe Mary. 'She taught class music and singing at my school and rehearsed the church choir, and she land of took me under her wing. She was the one who got me started.'

'Sound like a good person.'

'She was. So good that someone felt threatened and kicked her out.' Terri gives a brisk smile. 'All right, number one. Where's the loo roll?'

Alistair knows the supermarket backwards. He steers the trolley as if it were a tank, greeting some of his old workmates on the way, introducing Terri as a neighbour and friend of his mum's. Halfway up an aisle, he stops and loads in the cheapest large pack of loo roll.

Terri is finding this trip more fun than she'd expected. 'Number two: bread.' They laugh together at the implanted image of the edible two. She's starting to wonder why he'd bothered asking her to go with him.

It's only when they're facing the chiller cabinet of fruit juice that the trouble kicks in.

'Which one does Sue like?' Terri surveys row upon row of cartons and bottles. Alistair, beside her, is standing stock still. 'Al?'

Cartons of orange juice with 'bits' or 'smooth, no bits'; organic; organic Fairtrade; made from concentrate; freshly squeezed large; freshly squeezed small; 'family size' made from concentrate; mixed with cranberry, blueberry, grapefruit, carrot, ginger and/or yogurt; blood orange; oranges from Florida; oranges from Spain; chilled, to consume within two days; long-life, unchilled, to consume within two years . . .

'All I'm trying to buy,' Alistair says through clenched teeth, 'is a carton of orange juice. What am I meant to do?'

'Take the cheapest.'

'But look.' He points at the numbers. They're irregularly measured: price per litre, price per half-litre, price per carton; a special offer, three for the price of two — is that better value than buying a cheaper carton in the first place?

Sweat gleams on Alistair's forehead. 'Why do I

have to stand here working it all out for hours, when *all I want is some fucking orange juice?*'

'Steady on.' Terri places a hand on his elbow. He pushes her away.

She remembers Kipling's poem about keeping your head when all around you are losing theirs. 'Like I said, just take the cheapest,' she says, then places some cartons in the trolley and pushes it away from the offending shelf. Alistair drifts beside her — gone. She notices passers-by, young women, mothers with whingeing toddlers, elderly men in anoraks, glancing at him — is it her imagination or do they disapprove? A strapping lad like him, wandering along, dazed, limping, sweating? If only she could tell them where he'd been . . .

'Let's get out of here,' she suggests. 'Come home with me and I'll give you some dinner.'

Alistair, his panic subsiding, can only nod and thank her.

* * *

'Does it happen a lot?' Terri asks her guest, eating fish, oven chips and salad in her kitchen.

'Sometimes.' He's concentrating on his plate, his energy returning as the food kicks in. 'Usually when I don't expect it.'

'What does happen?' He's shovelling super-sized forkfuls of fish into his mouth; she'd forgotten how much young men eat. There hasn't been one in the house for a while.

'Something sets it off . . . I dunno what. It's like, the light. Or the shelves. Or people

. . . yesterday, I was in Woolworths, and this kid on a scooter comes zooming round a corner without looking where he's going and his mum's busy hitting his brother somewhere else, so he slams straight into me. And I . . . '

Terri puts down her cutlery, aghast.

Alistair shakes his head. 'I could have fucking *killed* him. It's just that if someone hits me, I don't always remember that I'm not supposed to hit back, I nearly didn't remember that it's just a stupid kid who shouldn't be riding a scooter in a shop but doesn't know better cos no one never told him. I got a fright, that's all — but there's this moment when in your head you don't see a dumb kid, you see a bloke with a beard and a Kalashnikov, and there's nothing you can do about it. Gerry told me he had this mate who came back, and some guy bumped into him by mistake in the pub — and he went nuts, he beat him up and he's in bloody Wormwood Scrubs now. At his trial all he said was 'too much sand'.'

Terri watches him, his head bowed and turned slightly away; there's a faint tremor in his wrist that she hadn't seen before. Next month they should all have been celebrating his twentieth birthday together.

'And you see these rows of orange juice and that,' he goes on. 'It's like, choice is supposed to matter. You can choose between all these different brands and prices, and you have to choose, you can't just take a carton of juice and get the hell out. You have to stand and think

397

through this crap for ages. And there are lads out there being killed, when there's no choice at all — '

'Al, it's OK. We're home now.'

'I don't know what to do.' Alistair looks away from her. 'I know it's happening, but I can't stop it, and I can't just snap out of it, see? I would if I could, honest. It's not fair on my mum, she's got enough problems, and all I want is to get back there, but there's my bloody leg and as for the ribs, I don't know how long it's going to take . . . '

'Al, hush.'

'Sorry, Tez. It's not your problem. I shouldn't be here, I'll go now.'

'Sit down, Al, *please*. Just come over whenever you like. Promise?' Terri leans across the table and reaches towards his hands. She doesn't touch him; instead, she invites him to touch her. She waits, palms upward. The defensive, angry eyes return her gaze — back from another world. With the slowest of motions, he takes her offered hands, grasps them, squeezes.

Neither of them moves as the air closes in. Terri suspects she may panic too — her heart is racing, maybe another hot flush, and her tongue feels like paper. If she tries to stand, her knees will shake and she may fall. She doesn't try. She pretends it's not true.

'All right?' she ventures.

'All right. Thanks.'

The grip relaxes; breath flows as the spell breaks. 'How about some more fish?' says Terri.

★ ★ ★

'You're well out of it,' Stefan says, pouring slivovicz. Sonja passes Teo a dish of Turkish baklava chopped into bite-sized pieces. He chews one, laden with syrup and pistachio; its flakes stick to his teeth. Outside, the night is deep indigo over the Bosnian hills.

The stupid thing is that he understands. If his dress had been about to fall off, he'd probably have done the same. That doesn't stop it hurting. The sharp point, piercing to the heart, is that Terri won't commit.

'Fine,' says Stefan. 'I wouldn't marry you either if I was her.'

'The great thing about family is you can always rely on them for support and encouragement.' Teo fills his pipe.

'You should have ditched her long ago,' says Sonja. 'You should be with someone who can give you children.'

'I'm too old to be up half the night changing nappies. Also — Terri does love me. But she has a particular life and it happens to suit her more than it suits me.'

'We'll find a wife for you,' Sonja declares. 'A Bosnian girl, someone who knows where you're coming from.'

'Even *I* don't know where I'm coming from any more. I don't belong here now, but I've never belonged in Paris either. Let alone London.'

'Come on, folks. It's past one and Sonja's cutting hair in seven hours' time.' Stefan stretches his arms and smiles at his wife.

Beyond the window the dusky slopes are dotted with lights. Even now, Teo half expects to hear gunfire, but there's only the distant buzz of cars changing gear and some tinny pop music from over the road.

He lies in his cousins' spare bedroom, listening to the night. Even if Sarajevo is full of ghosts, they're from a time gone by, a time when he didn't know that Terri existed. The biggest comfort, in a plane of existence without her, is to find his way back to another, which he'd inhabited before he met her.

Stefan has to go to Mostar to visit a new business partner. Tourism there is developing at quite a rate and they're thinking of redeveloping a restaurant together in the old town, close to the bridge. 'Want to come along?' he asks Teo over breakfast and *razgalica*.

Teo stays silent.

'You've got to do it sometime,' Stefan encourages. 'You've taken the first step. Now maybe it's time for the next one.'

'Going home . . . '

'Going back, anyway.'

'It's home. It always was. Perhaps I shouldn't have left.'

'So come with me today.'

Teo stops thinking. If he thinks, he won't be able to move. He has only to walk to Stefan's ancient Trabbie and get in. He watches his feet shunt across the damp road towards it, watches his hand rise towards the handle. The inside stinks of petrol and stale biscuits. Teo fastens the seatbelt. Stefan starts the engine and the car begins to move. He toots as they pass Sonja's salon.

Teo watches in detachment. They snake up and down the hills, out of Sarajevo and into the valley, as beautiful to him as Shangri-La, which meets the Neretva and follows it to Mostar. He knows every bend in the route; he thought he'd known all the eateries that pepper the roadside, but now there are many more. The water that dances through the riverbed is still the colour of idealised malachite.

'The house . . . '

'You don't have to do that if you don't want to.'

Teo looks at Stefan's prematurely aged yet contented face: plump cheeks, designer specs, neatly trimmed blond-grey moustache. He'd spent half the previous evening talking about the pros and cons of different cars; he wants to ditch the Trabbie. Under his smartest shirt, he's developing a paunch. During the siege, Teo remembers folds of skin where now there are rolls of fat. He doesn't begrudge his cousin's Swedish husband his success. He could have got out, gone back to safe, civilised Scandinavia, but he'd chosen to stay. If Teo bears anyone a grudge it's himself, for leaving, for not being strong enough, for not wanting to see where the house had stood.

'There's no reason anyone should be strong enough for that,' Stefan points out. 'We're only people, you know. Trying to get on with things. Just because some goons blasted us to hell and gone, that doesn't mean we're superhuman if we make it — we're bloody lucky, that's all. You deal with it as best you can — and you've done better than most people, with that book.'

'The fucking book is a fucking excuse. It's a way of not facing the reality.'

'I'd think the opposite.'

'So does everyone. That's how I get away with it.'

'Jesus, mate, stop beating yourself up! It's *not your fault.*'

Tunnels, twists and bumps in the road; a lorry in front slows to a frustrating inch-a-minute uphill; across the valley, the unearthly whiteness on the mountaintops that looks like year-round snow is an illusion caused by sunlight on limestone. The angles at which the rays refract are as familiar to Teo as the rhythms of nursery rhymes. Last time he saw those hills, they were full of snipers.

'All right?' asks Stefan.

'For God's sake, stop saying that!' Teo snaps. 'I'm fine.'

If he were to tell Stefan everything that was churning about in his head, his cousin would turn the car round and drive straight back to Sarajevo. A signpost goes by: 'MOSTAR: 6 km'. By the roadside, between the farmhouses, in little fenced-in areas, indeed wherever there is room, he spots makeshift graveyards bearing thickets of white headstones, obelisks and crosses packed densely together.

★ ★ ★

The car judders along the road towards the old city. 'We may as well go see your bridge,' Stefan says. 'Get it over and done with.'

He turns up a hill to park, and Teo jolts from side to side as the Trabbie grumbles about the gradient. When they climb out, Teo notices that the air smells different. Fresher. He catches the scent of coffee and cigarettes from a chrome-decored café on the first corner they reach, the whiff of pine from the hills, garlic from a restaurant where Stefan automatically pauses to assess the competition. No gunpowder. No decay. Across the road, a building he remembers as a grand nineteenth-century marble block housing a bank and some of the smartest apartments in East Mostar stands in ruins, like the Roman Forum but destroyed only fifteen years ago. Inside it, trees, strong and young, shove bare branches through what used to be bedroom windows.

'Not rebuilt, then,' he remarks.

'Nobody seems to know who should rebuild that. It's a Habsburg block so they think the Habsburgs should do it. Austria, anyway.'

'I can imagine what Austria would say about that.'

While they walk, Teo's eyes stray towards a busy café, its walls simple and bare, the wooden tables and chairs hosting groups of men in late middle age, most of them smoking and sipping coffee from small cups; some are playing chess or backgammon. Teo notices a crutch beside one of them; his left leg has been amputated at the knee.

The impression of a town comes not from what you see there, but rather from the feelings those sights inspire. You grasp its essence in the faces of the children; their brothers and sisters who had never been born; the depth of the wrinkles on their grandparents' foreheads; a generation that should have been in its forties now, but is missing; the limps, the laughter, the desultory stone plaque beside the road that says: 'DON'T FORGET.' He watches two young backpackers photographing the sign. War, or its aftermath, has become a tourist attraction.

Walking down the hill towards the Neretva, the old town and the Stari Most, Teo halts in his tracks outside a souvenir shop that sells metal coffee pots, ceramic jewellery and pictures of the bridge; there's a wicker basket containing what appear to be . . .

'Those are *bullet cases*.'

Stefan blows cigarette smoke. 'There were a lot of them lying around. Some clever sod decided to make them into pens and sell them to tourists.'

'I don't believe it.' Teo picks one up. The brass glints in his hand, dully golden. The ink of the ball-point that's been fitted inside it leaves a blue stain on his index finger. 'This thing could have killed someone.'

'They're helping people to earn a living now,' Stefan points out. 'Look, Teo. Here we are.'

Teo looks. Staring at the pen had been an evasion tactic, because he knew that there, in front of him, in another second, he would see the

404

image that graces the front cover of his book, symbol of the tragedy of Mostar: the bridge, the Stari Most. Or its replacement.

He'd known about it; Sonja had told him. Style, not substance. Like everything now. They walk to it in silence and climb the ridged limestone that peaks over the centre of the Neretva. The stone is slippery underfoot and Teo concentrates on staying upright.

'If people thought about the content, not just the look,' he remarks, 'we mightn't have the problem of fake drugs.'

'I'm not with you.'

'You see,' says Teo, hanging on to the bridge's railing, 'there are places in the world where organised crime rings are manufacturing pills that look like real prescription drugs: the packaging is perfect. But there's nothing medicinal inside the pills. So people pay a fortune for them, swallow them, then die. If people weren't so easily fooled by outward appearance, that wouldn't be possible.'

'Are you saying you think this bridge is a fake drug?' Stefan indicates some Japanese tourists, taking photographs and exclaiming on the beauty of the view. An old mosque with humped dome and minaret stands near the river, in the shadow of the hill. The mountains rear up, free of fighters. Teo stares at the Hum, the mound-like mountain he used to love for its magnetic energy, which he'd imagined fed the town with life and warmth. It's not dead; only twisted. At the summit there poses an outsize concrete cross.

'The church says that's a symbol of reconciliation,' Stefan remarks. 'Bloody likely. It's a provocation to everyone else. Another land grab.'

'Don't get me started,' Teo growls. He pauses at the side of the bridge, one foot higher than the other, and stares into the furious current. A muscular young man in swimming trunks poses on the parapet at the summit; the Japanese tourists stand by with their cameras.

'He won't jump unless they pay him.' Teo divines. 'A fine-looking boy. He should meet our Julie.'

'You have to stop thinking of her as your daughter.' Stefan tells him. 'You have to move on.'

Teo stands at the summit of the bridge, gazing about. 'I just wish that in the middle, there was something real. Something with soul.'

'In Terri?'

'No, here. Terri's got a soul, even if sometimes she sells it.'

'Let's go and have lunch at the place I'm checking out,' Stefan suggests. 'That's real. Especially the fish.'

'Stefan, you're heartless.'

'What else is new? Come on, we'll meet Zoran and try the grilled snapper.'

Zoran's restaurant is a short walk from the Stari Most. Stefan assesses the location: an old stone house with a sizeable riverside terrace and perfect views. As a tourist magnet, it couldn't be better. Most people lunching there have come up on day trips from Dubrovnik, clustering through the narrow stone streets, buying those odious pens. Teo leaves half his snapper but accepts extra wine, which Zoran, keen to impress Stefan, insists is on the house. Across the restaurant, Teo spots a copy of his book lying under someone's camera and a cotton hat.

'I got it all wrong.' Teo picks at his tobacco.

'What?'

'The fucking book. It's turning this place into Theme Park Bosnia. Mostar City, Hollywood.'

'*Jaha*,' says Stefan in his best Swedish. 'Sold the film rights, have we?'

'Shut up. People read the book, then they want to come and gawp. 'Oooh look. Here's where all those people died. Oooh, look, a bombed-out building. Let's go find a landmine! That wasn't the idea. That's not why I bloody wrote it.'

'I'm sorry I brought you,' Stefan declares, 'and I can see why Terri chucked you. For heaven's sake, Teo, it's awful, but it's over. We're going forward. We've got to move on.'

'No,' says Teo. 'It's not over and it won't be until there's some absolution for the suffering. You're only seeing the business potential. I'm looking at people who live here, who've lost limbs and families ... The place is stuck. Absolutely stuck. Can't you feel it?'

'Jesus, Teo, we went through it like you did, we lost friends, we lost most of Sonja's family. I don't want to be ruled by that loss any more. Tourism is good for us, can't you see? It brings in money, it creates jobs, so we can build and hope and be creative. If you're proactive everything becomes possible.'

'I wonder how many charities there are here. Mental health, orphans, prosthetic limbs . . . '

'Go on, give all your money away. I won't stop you. I know you're crazy.'

'No, I'm thinking . . . '

'What?'

'When we've finished the wine,' says Teo, 'let's take a walk past the theatre.'

★ ★ ★

The National Theatre stands on a small paved piazza in the centre of East Mostar: a concrete cube from the forties, its façade splattered with bullet holes. Across the square, Teo glimpses another graveyard, fenced off, its tombstones closely crammed. Children play around the fountains, chasing each other and squealing in the early spring sunshine; their mothers lounge at white plastic tables outside the theatre, drinking coffee and keeping a quarter of an eye on their offspring. A huge advertising hoarding on the wall beside the damaged theatre shows a young couple staring, mouths and eyes stretched with delight, at a piece of paper offering them a whole four per cent interest on their savings. The theatre is presenting, less glitzily, a cut-down version of *Tosca* with piano accompaniment.

'I'd like to bring Terri here,' Teo says.

'Teo, get over it. Put her behind you. She can't even sing any more. Everyone's saying she'll never get back now — not with all these babes around like Varya Petrovna with big boobs and dyed hair.'

'Terri's boobs are fantastic, take it from me. And she's been dyeing her hair for decades.'

'That,' says Stefan, 'is precisely my point.'

'She's a pro. If I ask her to sing here, she'll agree.'

'Forget it, Teo. Now, listen.' He puts both hands on Teo's shoulders. 'Do you want me to come with you to your house?'

'I'm not going.'

'Are you sure?'

Teo gazes towards the graveyard, screwing up his eyes against the sun. 'I know what it looked like. Next time, perhaps.'

'There'll be a next time, then?'

'Yes,' Teo declares. 'I'll be back.'

21

'Ready?' Anita's hands are poised over the piano keyboard.

Terri fills her lungs and lifts her soft palate. 'Ready.'

Anita plays a chord. Terri lets the note emerge in a hum, rises up the arpeggio, then lets the sound open gently.

'Beautiful!' says Anita. 'Well done.'

Terri knows she's been here before. 'It's all right? Really?'

'Of course. Next one.'

Half-watching a red bus pulling up a few metres from the front window, Terri continues. Her laryngologist usually knew what he was doing. His advice was normally right. He'd said she could start again. She hopes this occasion won't be the exception that proved the rule.

'Good,' says Anita. 'Good girl.'

Terri hears Mary's voice for a second: 'Good girl . . . ' with the Irish twirl of the consonants. Drinking herbal tea in her front room on a Glasgow winter night, and feeling relaxed, calm, at one. Just thinking of it makes her want to sing, to get the emotion out so that it doesn't clog up her body.

'It's good, Terri.' They've finished the exercise. Terri gazes at Anita as hopefully as she'd have assessed Mary's expression when she was sixteen. 'How do you feel?' Anita asks.

410

'Fine. No problems. A little nervous. I need to do my relaxation exercises more often. Now that I'm not on the phone to Teo for an hour a day, it should be easier.'

'You must miss him.'

Terri feels a stabbing sensation, like being punctured by a knitting needle. 'Not really,' she says.

'Well.' Anita, ever tactful, changes the subject. 'It's time to think about how to ease yourself back in.'

Terri has been thinking of little else. In discussions with Martini, Beethoven's *Fidelio* has been mooted; so has Strauss's *Capriccio*; and *Rosenkavalier*, of course, but that's rather close to the bone at present. He's evasive about the film pitch. And nobody has said a word about Wagner.

The session over, Terri pulls on her coat and hugs Anita, hard.

'*Brava*, darling,' Anita says, hugging back. 'Good girl.'

At home, she rings Martini. 'I've decided to have a party.'

'Oh, God.' He isn't amused. 'Please, no Russian billionaires, I beg of you.'

'Don't worry, it'll be very Bohemian. Terri's salon, just like the old days.'

'Good girl,' says Martini.

Why is everyone saying 'good girl' to her, as if she's a dog? Hoping that it's just affection, Terri prepares to make some calls.

★ ★ ★

411

In Scargill Tower, affection is not top of the agenda: Sue and Alistair, cooped up together in the flat over what's become a stinking open sewer, are at loggerheads. Alistair derides his therapist and is frustrated, underoccupied and angry; Sue is drinking too much beer; and whenever Terri visits them, she feels there's one more sideswipe than last time, one extra snide remark. Now the atmosphere makes her itch to get out.

'It was more peaceful out there with the suicide bombers,' Alistair grumbles, when Terri arrives in the middle of a screaming match.

'Maybe you can make him shut the hell up.' Sue, flushed with fury and frustration, pulls out two bottles of beer and plonks one in front of Terri.

'Not for me, thanks,' says Terri. It's eleven o'clock and Sue, whose shifts finish in the wee hours, has only just surfaced from sleep.

'Suit yerself.' Sue virtually throws the bottle back into the fridge.

'What's going on?' Terri demands.

'Nothing.' Alistair storms back to his room.

Sue, head on arms, begins to sob. 'I can't cope. What am I meant to do? All day, every day, it's just us, and the gang — and those stupid cats . . . '

'Sue, *shhh*,' Terri pleads. In his room, Alistair is tapping on the computer keyboard so hard that each letter seems to shake the walls.

'I mean, all I'm trying to do is survive and look after him.' Sue dissolves into a fresh flood.

'But I can't stand it any more. I don't know what to do.'

'Tell you what,' says Terri, 'why not let him come and stay at my place for a few days? Tonight, if you want. It'd give you both a break. I'm all alone, it'd be nice to have someone in the house. And I'm having a little do tomorrow night — I could use an extra pair of hands.'

'Well, if you're sure,' Sue ventures. 'If you don't mind him being your daughter's ex and that? It's kind of you, Terri. Really kind.'

'Not at all,' Terri assures her. 'It'd do all of us good. Will you join us for the party?'

'Thanks, love,' Sue says wryly, 'but if I've got a night off to myself, I'm damn well going to put my feet up for once!'

★　★　★

It does feel odd to invite Julie's former boyfriend to be her house-guest for a long weekend. But as she admits, walking up the road with him and his overnight bag, she has an ulterior motive.

'I'm throwing a party,' she tells him. 'I was hoping maybe you could help me with things.'

'What things?'

'Preparing the food, handing it round, pouring the drinks, clearing up — as long as your leg's up to it. I won't drag you to the supermarket, I've ordered everything online and it'll be delivered tonight.'

'Cool,' Alistair mumbles. He can't quite meet her gaze. His stubble looks sharp and slightly golden under the lamp-posts. Terri reaches up and rubs his cheek.

'You'll need to shave, of course.' She smiles, wondering how he'll react. To her relief, he smiles too.

'Why're you having a party? Is it your birthday?'

'I'm having a party because it *isn't* my birthday. I want to try something.'

'Like what?'

'Singing. Just something gentle, to see if I can.'

'So who's coming to this party?'

She tells him. Martini, naturally; Roger, her favourite accompanist; the new chief conductor from a big national opera company, with whom she's never worked; Dora, her American haute-couture friend; a fashion journalist she's known for two decades; some neighbours who used to feed her cat when she had one, when Julie was tiny, and many more. 'Lots of different people,' she says. 'The typical Ivory Trail Mix.'

'What'll they make of me?'

'They'll adore you, darling. Everyone adores you. And they'll respect you, too, for what you've been doing.'

'Bollocks. I don't even respect myself.'

'Well, you should.'

'Don't tell me what I should or shouldn't do. You're not my CO or my mum.' He's starting to slouch and mutter — and by now Terri knows these signs.

'Too right I'm not!' She rounds on him, stopping in their tracks. 'Now, *listen*. You're not going to take that sulky tone in my house, my lad. You're not going to sit about feeling sorry for yourself and yelling at whatever happens to be nearest. You will get back your once-perfect manners — and yes, Alistair, they used to be very good — and you will make the effort to behave like a decent human being. Then maybe you'll wake up one fine day and find you are one. Otherwise, you can go back home right now, because I won't have it otherwise.'

Alistair, faced with this outburst from the strongest diva in south London, can do nothing but knuckle under. 'Sorry, Tez. I didn't mean it.'

'I know you didn't. Come along, now, and we'll have some tea.' Terri hooks her arm through his and marches on up the hill.

* * *

Of course, she'd bargained without Julie wanting to come home — a message on the answering machine reveals that she does. College is freezing, she hates the course and she needs to sleep for a week. 'Christ,' Terri exclaims, more to herself than Alistair, 'don't youngsters do anything but grumble these days?'

'I don't really want to have to see her,' Alistair says. Terri has made up a spare bedroom for him — he shouldn't be in Julie's room with all its associations. He's a guest in his own right. 'I can just go home again,' he suggests.

'Certainly not! Don't even think about it.'

Terri phones Julie and explains. There's a long, long silence.

'I thought you'd be busy,' says Terri.

'I thought I lived there,' says Julie.

415

'It's just bad timing, sweetheart.'

'Yeah. Right.' Julie hangs up without saying goodbye.

Alistair is lingering nearby, waiting for her, a steaming mug in his hands. He raises it towards her. It's so long since anyone brought her a cup of tea in her own house when she wasn't ill that Terri begins to smile and can't stop.

★ ★ ★

Julie, burning with pain, goes for a long walk around town; this time it doesn't help. The fury is still alive and intense. When Irina looks in, she finds Julie has scattered the contents of her cupboard and chest of drawers all over the room and is shoving items into a case, several at a time.

'What are you doing?'

'Going to Paris, for good.' Julie doesn't stop to look at her friend. Her hands are shaking with anger.

'What? To Teo? Julie, wait!'

'Why? I should have done this months ago.'

'Don't be so hasty. You can't decide a thing like this on the spur of the moment. What happened?'

Julie shakes her head. 'I just have to go.'

'Have you phoned Teo yet?' Irina demands.

'No.'

'For goodness' sake, phone him. He might be away. Don't you remember . . . ?'

'He's just back from Bosnia.'

'How do you know?'

'I saw him on TV. There was this story about how he'd been back to Mostar for the first time.'

'Are you sure you want to go and stay with him? He sounds nuts,' Irina points out. 'Especially since he's broken up with your mother.'

'It's not so much that I want to stay with him, more that I want to work for him.'

'Doing what?'

'Admin. Secretarial stuff. I *know* he needs help. I saw his desk.'

'What about your course?' Irina's eyes fill; this time, Julie means it when she says she's going for good.

'I can't hack it. I'm getting nowhere, I'm only here for my dad, it was never what I wanted to do.'

'Don't say you're going altogether. Ask them to defer your place. You could start again next October.'

'Maybe, but maybe not. I'll get to Paris first. Then I'll call them.'

'What's done it, really? Is it us?'

'No, Rini, of course not! But . . . ' Julie wonders how to tell Irina how shaken she is by the revelation that her mother has conscripted Alistair to stay and help with her party, which means Julie can't possibly go home. She's never thought before that just because she hasn't spoken to Alistair for a month, that means they'll have broken up for good — yet now it's clear that they can't be in the same house at the same time. She needs to escape. And if Alistair can go to her mother, then she can go to Teo.

Alistair is good at skulking in corners. 'Come on, Incredible Hulk,' Terri summons him. 'Stop loitering and give me a hand. You can slice the baguettes.'

She feels lighter both on her feet and in her mind now that he's there, even if he talks little while they set to work. Once Terri would have hired caterers. Today she's decided to save several hundred pounds by doing the job herself, with her new assistant.

'What shall I do with these?' Alistair asks. He's cut each baguette into neat rounds and arranged them on Terri's baking trays as she'd shown him.

'They're going to be Italian bruschetta. Now, pop them in the oven under the grill setting and toast them on each side. Make sure they don't burn. Then please brush them with olive oil. Meanwhile, I'm chopping tomatoes, garlic and olives and we'll pile that on top of about half of them. And for the others, a selection of aubergine, chargrilled artichoke hearts, sundried tomatoes and mozzarella . . . '

'You must pick up ideas for this stuff all over the world,' Alistair remarks, eyeing Terri's international selection.

'Mostly Italian, darling, and what isn't Italian is usually French. Except for the salmon and salads, of course.'

'Why don't you just get crisps?' Alistair asks. 'Tortilla chips with dips. Dead easy.'

'Well . . . ' Terri is embarrassed to find she's embarrassed. 'I want it to be special.'

'It's about seeing your mates, though, isn't it? And it'd be less aggro for you to organise.'

'Yes, but some of these 'mates' I haven't seen in ages and I want to make them feel good.'

'And then? When they do?'

'When they do,' says Terri, grating a carrot, 'I intend to sing to them.'

'So *you* should be the one feeling good.'

'If I manage to pull this off, then yes, I will feel very, very good.'

'Right, I get it. I'll look after it all for you, Tez. I'll be head of the Mess.'

'Not too much mess, please, darling. I could always pretend you're my son.'

'Or not,' remarks Alistair. 'You'll be wanting the living room hoovered, won't you?'

'Darling, you're *wonderful*. Thank you.' Terri tosses sultanas into the grated carrot with a little orange juice as dressing, humming to herself. What a comfort to have a young man in the house; what a relief to see that the same Alistair she's known all this time is still there, somewhere underneath. The change of scene is doing him a power of good; since her lecture on the way home, he's been perfection itself. For her, he makes an effort. Poor Sue. Terri takes a giant salmon out of the oven, unwraps the foil and pokes at it to see if it's cooked. It, too, is perfect. So are the bruschettas. Today, she is certain, everything will be perfect.

The sound of the vacuum cleaner reaches her ears, as comforting as tiger balm. Her own cakes weren't elegant enough, she'd decided — besides, there was too much else to do — so she's ordered several outsize French fruit tarts from her favourite patisserie. Lifting them carefully from their boxes, while her stomach grinds with longing, she arranges them on her widest plates where they sprawl, golden, green and crimson, exuding butter and syrup; next, she sets out a cheeseboard with five carefully contrasted French cheeses and some Portuguese membrillo, a garnishing of grapes and a few marigolds. It's spring again, at last, and it's bringing life, hope and healing.

Just as these thoughts are warming her through, the phone rings. There's a familiar greeting.

'Teo?' Terri sits down, fast.

'I thought you should know,' says Teo, 'that Julie is here.'

'What? What do you mean? What's going on?'

'She wants me to tell you that she has decided not to go back to Cambridge.' He sounds formal and distant. 'I've tried to persuade her to change her mind, and I hope she'll try to defer her place rather than leave outright. But in the end it's her decision.'

'But — '

'She is planning to stay here and work for me, until she has a better idea of what she wants to do, and how, and where.'

'But Teo — heavens! Put her on, *please?*'

'She says she'd rather not speak to you yet, she knows you're busy throwing your party. To which neither she nor I appear to be invited.'

'You're both supposed to be busy in other cities,' Terri points out.

'Terri, listen, I want to ask you something.'

'The answer's no.'

'You don't know what the question is.'

'Teo, it's over.'

'I want you to come to Bosnia.'

'For God's sake. I just told you, it's over.'

'Teresa, I am relaying a professional invitation direct from the culture minister for you to come to Mostar to sing, if you can and will. We're organising a charity concert.'

'Mostar isn't on my scheduled flight path right now. Teo, I have to go, I've got guests turning up soon.'

'Well, then. Enjoy yourself. Call me if you change your mind.' Teo rings off.

So much for her day of perfection. Terri drums her feet, hard, then slices an artichoke heart and munches it with an illicit bruschetta. Alistair can't hear or see her; he's still upstairs, cleaning the bathroom. What kind of girl runs away from a fine university and elects instead to work as dogsbody for her mother's ex-manfriend? A girl, Terri suspects, who is very, very angry.

Alistair, his tasks accomplished, asks if he can use the computer. Leaving the salmon and the salads shrouded in clingfilm in the fridge, the bruschettas and tarts on the sideboard and the cheese under a glass dome, Terri installs him at her desk with a cup of tea, then goes down to the studio to make certain that her voice will behave. She won't press it. Just a few exercises. The afternoon is quiet; in the garden, daffodils droop in the pale sunshine.

When she's finished, there's still no sign of Alistair, so she goes up to see what he's doing. He is hunched at the desk, glaring at the screen, the tea cold and untouched beside him. The screen displays a picture of a desert camp.

'Is this what you do all day?' Terri asks, without a hint of sarcasm.

He nods.

'Looking for anything that will help your mates?'

'Anything that will tell me what's really going on. Rather than what the news says.'

Terri shakes her head. What a tragic waste, she thinks. All those strong young lives, snuffed out or irredeemably twisted, and for what?

'Alistair, is stewing going to help?'

'No.'

'So why do it?'

'I don't know. I just feel like — in my head, see, I'm not here. I'm still there. And it takes me so effing long to type the messages, I hate that.'

'Have you tried going for one day without logging on?' Terri sits on the desk and swings her legs.

'Once or twice, but . . . '

'Come on, darling,' Terri encourages. 'Come downstairs. Just for today, try to pretend you're living here, in the present, with me. I'd love it if you'd give me a hand with the salmon. I need lots of cucumber sliced very finely to decorate it.'

Alistair abandons the computer and follows her.

★   ★   ★

Five hours later, the drawing room is a mass of guests, standing, sitting and reclining. Candlelight glistens on skin and jewellery and bounces off the sides of wineglasses; laughter pierces the space like birdsong. Empty bottles litter the kitchen surfaces and used plates are piling up in strange formations. The salmon and its cucumber scales are nearly gone, the carrot salad has been plundered down to the last dotted sultanas and only three bruschettas are left. Now the guests are swarming by turns over the cheeseboard and the dessert.

'My word,' says Martini, munching apricot tart, 'what a wonderful evening. It's just like old times.'

Terri kisses him on the cheek. She's wearing ivory as usual, this time a new trouser suit that fits and doesn't show too much flesh. Flitting from group to group, fired up by adrenalin, she refills glasses, laughs, flirts, introduces people to one another, whether familiar old-timers or glamorous newcomers. Several friends are looking about for Teo — or maybe she's imagining it. How odd to have a party without him. Thank heavens for Alistair; a helpful pair of male hands minus emotional thumbscrews.

'Your helper's a nice lad,' remarks the conductor's boyfriend. 'Is he Polish? Where did you find him? Was it through an agency?'

'I'd like the phone number of your caterer,' says the fashion journalist. 'My daughter's getting married next spring.'

'Where's Julie?' asks Roger, Terri's accompanist. 'How's she enjoying Cambridge? My nephew went up last year, he's having a whale of a time. He's captain of the college rowing team.'

Terri replies to all of them with hugs, kisses, a radiant smile or a refill of wine. Alistair's clearing abandoned plates and keeping the dishwasher busy. Terri finds him unpacking the latest clean load.

'Come and have a drink,' she pleads. 'I didn't mean you to spend the whole time working.'

'It's OK.' He keeps lifting out the plates. 'I don't know what to say to all these people anyway. Someone asked what I was doing before, and I told them and everything went quiet, so I thought I'd do something useful instead.'

Most of her long-acquainted guests, Terri thinks, should recognise Alistair from the photos of him and Julie that used to sit around in the kitchen and the drawing room — she'd removed them before he came to stay. Some might remember him as a young boy; they may not know him now that he's a man, and a complex one. Slightly tired, sore-footed and relieved to have a moment's peace, Terri absent-mindedly watches his back and shoulders bending, lifting, turning. Sweat patches darken his T-shirt.

'All right, Tez?' he asks, glancing round.

'Yes thanks, darling. I'm going to take the plunge now. I'm going to sing. Come and listen?'

'Should I?'

'Of course. I want you there.'

Terri has some quiet words with Roger, who opens the piano. They will do Bach's 'Bist du bei mir' and Schubert's 'An die Musik'.

424

'What's that?' Alistair looks over her shoulder at the music.

'A wonderful song called 'Be thou with me'.'

'About God?' Since returning, Alistair hasn't had much time for God, if indeed he ever had.

'No, about love. It's one of my favourites.' She turns to Roger. 'Ready, darling?'

'Terri Ivory, if you're ready to sing,' Roger replies, 'then I'm ready for anything.'

★ ★ ★

Alistair sits cross-legged on the rug — not too far from the door, so that he can bolt if necessary. A reverential atmosphere infuses the room while people settle to listen. He thinks of Han, singing in drag a few days before he died.

What would the lads say if they could see him now? He doesn't particularly care. He's seen his mate killed, he's fallen out with Julie, and there's nobody here who knows the reality of life in battle; if going through it was tough, it often feels worse to be stuck at home, able to do nothing, among people who still think that the comparative price of crisps is important. A pity Teo isn't around — he's the one person who would understand, though he also has most reason to hate a soldier. Teo had sat in that same kitchen less than a year ago, telling him that armies exist for one reason: to wage war.

Yet faintly, while the guests around him clap a welcome and Terri beams her most charismatic smile at her adoring friends, Alistair feels a nudge of memory — Teo again, years ago,

425

talking about how he first met Terri. He'd been on the point of suicide, he said; then he went into a theatre and heard a voice. Alistair, not knowing why another person's voice should make anybody change their mind about living or dying, had taken it with the proverbial pinch of salt.

He remembers the Mozart that Julie brought him. She walked into his room and put a silver circle into a machine and a moment later he was in heaven. And Julie was in those sounds, part of an aural landscape more beautiful than anything he'd ever seen. Environments of sound, he'd realised, can move. You can't take a forest, a lake or a beach with you to the other side of the world, but music can go anywhere and keep its atmosphere, its message and its impact. He hadn't thought about it then; he was just glad it was there with him in his room.

And now Julie's mother, as beautiful as a twenty-year-old with her ivory suit and perfect performer's poise, is making her announcement. 'I'd like to sing for you 'Bist du bei mir', by Bach. In case you don't know it' — she looks straight at Alistair — 'the words mean: 'if you are with me, then I go happily towards death and my peace'.'

Alistair has never heard Terri sing before.

Julie had wanted to drag him to the Royal Opera House. 'Me? For fuck's sake!' said Alistair. She cajoled — Terri would give them complimentary tickets — but Alistair refused. 'Pile of snobs,' he said, 'why would I want to go there? Don't like it anyway.' 'Twit,' said Julie.

'How can you know if you never try?' Still, he hadn't gone. Terri once offered to take them both to Milan — Alistair was only seventeen and refused (he cringes to remember) because he couldn't speak Italian and he'd thought all Italian men were gay.

Roger plays a sparkly pattern of chords and Terri takes a breath.

Alistair had found Julie's choir beautiful, with its twenty or thirty voices. But the music emerging from Terri's throat — if it is indeed from the throat — seems to set off a resonance within his body that is like nothing he has ever experienced. He's heard opera singers by accident, warbling away on Classic FM, in shops or at underground stations, but that was ambient background noise, Muzak like any other. If that was what Julie's mum did, fine, as long as he didn't have to listen. But *this*?

This is the woman who'd marched him up the hill and told him not to sit in her house sulking? The same person who'd patiently steered him through the orange juice ordeal? The Terri who sat in their kitchen cuddling the cats and refusing milk in her tea, joking with Sue and making her laugh?

The sound flowers from the pit of her stomach, he thinks, not her throat. It emerges from her very centre, from the spark in the depths of her being that makes her alive. He couldn't have been more astounded if he'd found a bar of gold on the stairs at Scargill Tower. If an angel streamed out of a cloud and revealed the nativity star, if a rainbow let him climb its curve, if Darren Hanley came back to life, none of that could be more astonishing than the transformation, in front of his eyes and ears, of capable, Scottish, cake-baking Terri Ivory into . . . *this*.

Alistair doesn't believe in God, but if there is a God, or anything that's greater than we are and has some clue about what's going on, that is surely what's entered Terri and is speaking through her song to everybody in the room, all as dumbstruck as he is. Now he knows what happened to Teo in Paris twelve years ago. It's a form of surrender. A giving-up of everything you thought you believed, felt, wanted or hoped, because nothing could be more true, or more real, or more important than this. And having heard it, having felt it once, how can you live without it?

Once, in the tent before Christmas, they'd been telling stories, most smutty, some supernatural and ghosty because it was so dark, but one bloke — he thinks it was Ben — had talked about seeing a vision. He'd been driving a lorry somewhere in Poland; there was a point of pilgrimage, a vision of the Madonna, and he'd experienced it himself. He'd seen the Virgin Mary with his own eyes, he said.

There's nothing virginal about Terri, but she's all the more miraculous for that. What a woman, what a glory. She was more than a woman: she was perfect and fulfilled, not a nervous little girl who happened to be pretty. It was Terri, not Julie, who stirred his soul to its depths, Terri, not Julie, who revealed all that a woman could be,

428

Terri, not Julie, who could show him marvels to restore his spirit, as if one soul could pour itself into another, quenching its thirst, until it overflows.

When the second song, the Schubert, finishes — he'd loved it even more than the Bach — Alistair sits frozen to the floor. Everyone else is applauding, laughing, hugging her. She seems overwhelmed — flushed in the face, trembly in the hands. Of course, Alistair remembers, as if from a great distance, she hadn't sung publicly for months. She chose those songs because they were relatively easy. This has been about making sure she can do it at all.

He pulls himself, with some difficulty, to his feet. It's as if he's been through a watermill and come out drenched and very clean, with all the nonsense washed away. Feeling shaky, he sidles across to her.

'Well, Alistair,' she says, laughing, 'so, you heard me sing, finally! What do you think?'

'I don't know what to think,' he admits. 'It's the most incredible thing I ever heard in my life.'

'Come off it, darling. But thanks, I'm glad you listened.' She reaches up and kisses his cheek.

Alistair wants to scream. She'd linked her arm through his yesterday, going up the hill. It felt cosy, female and so on, but he hadn't thought twice about it. She'd slept in a bedroom across the landing from his, and he'd never thought of her in there with everything about her blue, white and gold; he'd not agonised that he couldn't hear her breathing or see her face, or ever thought there'd be a reason he'd want to.

He's been calling her Tez because he felt that comfortable with her.

'Al,' she's saying, 'why don't you give everyone a refill? I think they need one after that.'

'I need one myself, Tez.'

'Tez?' the gay agent echoes. 'He calls you *Tez?* What is this, *Footballers' Wives?*'

'Tez of the d'Urbervilles!' Terri returns.

'Darling, you were wonderful,' cries Dora, the American woman from haute-couture. Sounds of triumph and American exaggeration. What can he say to Terri later, when everyone's left? In his spell at war, he'd known what he was doing, as far as anyone did; there were patterns of reaction, routines that you learned to follow, turning good sense into good reflexes. But nothing had prepared him for this. This is impossible. For Christ's sake, *she's Julie's mum.* That reminder is good sense; but there's no reflex to complement it. Feeling that he's experienced another, more personal explosive device, Alistair drifts to the kitchen and uncorks bottles of red and white wine.

'Thanks, sweetheart,' says Terri, smiling into his eyes as he fills her glass. Then she carries on talking to Dora, as if the world hasn't changed at all. Probably, for her, it hasn't.

★ ★ ★

Terri closes the door behind the last guest at 2 a.m., with a sigh of contented exhaustion. 'Well,' she says, 'that was an evening to remember.'

430

'You could say that,' Alistair remarks.

Relieved, she kicks off her shoes; at once she's three inches shorter. Gazing up at Alistair, it occurs to her that he could pick her up with one arm if he chose to. Or he could have, if she were still her old weight instead of her new one.

'I can't thank you enough,' she says. 'You don't know what this evening meant to me.'

'Nor me.' She can't read the expression that crosses his eyes. Something she's never seen before on that face. A question? A plea? Or is he simply even more knackered than she is?

'How about a good Scotch whisky?' She pours them in the kitchen, hands him a glass, then leads the way back to the deserted drawing room where the embers of the fire glow with red heat, black coalite and white ash, and the candles warm the air, slightly smoky and scented with amber. She remembers an evening like this with Teo — the first of her parties that he'd been to. She'd sung some favourite arias, then some duets with Felicity Lott while Graham Johnson accompanied them, and after everyone had gone she and Teo made love in front of the fire for an hour and a half, ending up under the piano. So, magic is still possible without Teo. When she glances at the space beneath the Steinway, her scalp prickles very slightly.

Alistair perches, awkward, on the sofa across the room, cradling his tumbler. Terri slobs into her favourite chair, legs across its arm. 'Cripes, my feet! Those blasted heels. I could do with a good massage.'

Alistair says nothing and doesn't move.

'So, who did you talk to? What was your highlight?' Terri loves having post-mortems about parties. Who'd hit on whom? Which married man was pretending he wasn't, for the benefit of which woman? Was the food all right? 'Do you think,' she says, 'that the carrot salad went well with the salmon?'

'I wouldn't know,' Alistair says quietly, 'but it beat the hell out of army rat packs.' He doesn't seem able to meet her gaze.

'You all right, Alistair?'

'Terri . . .'

'I thought I was Tez.'

'Tez. I mean, Tez. I can't believe I never came to hear you sing before.'

'You enjoyed it?'

'I never heard anything like it.' Alistair, looking at his feet, has hardly touched the whisky. Terri takes a long sip of hers. Wonderful. Tastes of home.

'I'm very glad,' she says. 'That means such a lot to me.'

'Does it?'

'Of course. It means a hundred times more that you should enjoy it than that someone like Dora or Martini should. They've heard the songs a hundred times, you see.' Terri yawns, stretching out her legs. 'But if you expect not to like them, then find you do — now, that's special.'

'I just felt — I don't know how to put it.'

'Try.' He looks so shy, awkward and stunned that her heart melts for him.

'That second song — what was it called?'

' "An die Musik".'

'Everyone knew it but me. What does it mean? The words? Was that the 'be with me and I'm happy to die' song?'

'No, that was the Bach. 'An die Musik' is by Schubert. It's an ode to music. It says: 'Oh blessed art, how many times you have eased my troubled soul; I thank you.' It says it at greater length, of course, but . . . '

Alistair's whole body has begun to shake. He curls downward over his knees, sobbing long and hard.

Terri's world tips over as she jumps out of her chair to hold him and soothe him, and next thing she knows she's on her back on the sofa, his mouth kissing her larynx and the threads of grey in her hair that escaped the highlighter, and the extra plumpness around her shoulders and breasts that had split her dress open in Bruges, and she knows it's the Mary syndrome, she's just done for him what Mary had once done for her, but crucially, she isn't a teacher and Alistair is a grown man of twenty and a passionate one brimming with much-frustrated hormones, and since they are utterly alone with the candles burning low, the fire so very warm, the curtains closed and the piano silent and the guests gone and the clearing up can be done tomorrow, there is absolutely no reason why they shouldn't do what they seem to be doing in any case, not out of choice, not even thinking about it.

'Slowly,' she whispers.

He listens, obeys. Moves in, as deep as he can. It's perfect. When she thinks he can't go further, he does, and she gasps out, her skin alight, balancing on the brink.

'Terri.' He's half-conscious, alive completely in his body.

'Hush.'

He pulls off his shirt and burrows at hers so that their skin is in contact. Something rips. She tugs off her bra and he presses his face into her breasts. Has she ever wanted anyone or anything this much? If so, she's forgotten. She flings a cushion away so she can lie flatter, wriggling off the last of her clothes; freed of them, she wraps herself round him and lets him move as hard as he wants to. His head goes back, he lets out that deep shout from the source of all sound and as she feels him bursting like a river from its banks, she gives herself up and falls with him through the whirling, living space into the darkness.

22

At first light Terri opens her eyes. Alistair is asleep on top of her, his breathing slow. There's stickiness all over her belly, her thighs, her sofa and what remains beside and under her of her trouser suit. She's certainly been sweating, as it is a hot situation to be in, a candlelit, fire-heated room with a heavy young man acting as your duvet for the night.

She extricates herself; he turns over, mumbles, but doesn't wake. Upstairs in the twilight, the bathroom is a relief. A shower staunches the stickiness, the hot water soothing her still painful feet and comforting her as she hurtles towards the crash that must follow the crazy high induced by the stupidest thing she has ever done in her life.

In her unused bedroom, she crawls under the covers. The sheets are chilly, but she's glad to be there. Amazingly, she has no headache, even though she must have been drunk, as must he. There's no other explanation.

She turns platitudes over and over, searching for one that helps. Two consenting adults. We enjoyed it. He's not with Julie any longer, I'm not with Teo, we're both free. As long as nobody knows and it never happens again, nobody will get hurt. Worst of all: it's only sex.

The door creaks; she half sits up. She can see

him hesitating outside, his bright eyes sleep-clouded. A rush of guilt and tenderness takes hold of her; she slides across the bed and pats the space next to her. A second later he's there, bulky and warm, with cold toes, and her body zaps into awareness. He reaches out for her; she can't not respond.

'I'm sorry,' she says. These are the first words that have passed between them for six hours.

'I'm not.'

'We shouldn't do this.'

'Fine time to say that!'

'But . . . why . . . ?'

'Because I want to.'

'I'm thirty years older than you. I've known you since you were fifteen. And you are my daughter's former boyfriend.'

'So what?'

'So plenty . . . I'm sorry, it's my fault, I wanted . . . I don't know . . . '

'You wanted a very good fuck. And you got one.'

'I wanted to — to comfort you or something.'

'I wanted *you*. And I wanted you to want me, not 'want to comfort' me. And don't say you didn't, cos I know you did.'

She pulls away and feels about for her slippers. 'I'll make some tea.'

'I'll come with you.'

His eyes trail her as she takes her dressing gown from the peg. Excess plumpness, cellulite, wrinkles setting in — what would a boy of twenty want with this?

Amid the anarchy of plates and glasses left

436

from the party, Terri sits cradling her tea opposite Alistair at the round kitchen table where they've sat so many times with Teo and Julie. He waits for her to speak. As the senior partner in this mess, she must take the lead; she's responsible; she should have been *in loco* mother-in-law, not lover.

'Last night was wonderful, but we can't carry on,' she begins. 'You know that, don't you?'

'Why not?'

'You know why not.'

'Julie and I are finished. It's you who's like me, not her. I think I'm in love with you, Terri. We're two of a kind. We've both got nothing except ourselves.'

'Everyone,' Terri suggests, 'has nothing except themselves in the end.'

She pulls breakfast things out of the fridge: bread, butter, jam, Alistair's favourite peanut butter. She leaves the orange juice where it is.

'You know, I grew up much the way you did,' she remarks, 'only without satellite TV, mobile phones and hot water. I didn't know my dad either. Though I had a brother once.'

'What happened to him?'

'He died.'

'I'm sorry.'

'I seemed to spend a lot of time looking after people.'

'I thought, with the singing, that you only looked after yourself.'

'Thought, past tense?'

'Until yesterday I thought that. Then I heard

you sing. I got it all wrong before.'

'Is that what changed?'

He stirs his tea, eyes lowered: lashes long, capable hands with their lamb chop palms, the neck strong and solid. Looking at him turns her inside out. 'You'd better go home,' she says.

'I don't want to.'

'You have to. This mustn't happen again and nobody must know about it. *Ever*.'

'Terri, I don't *want* to stop. Please let me come back tonight.'

'Julie's — still — my — daughter,' says Terri.

★ ★ ★

Her panic only begins to subside when Alistair and his overnight bag are out of the house. He's left behind an imprint, as if he'd forgotten to put his aura back on. It lingers like a cloak of static. The crumbs of toast and peanut butter on his plate. The hollow of his head on the spare pillow. His mug holding leftover tea, a muddy footprint on the hall floor, dark stubble from his razor sprinkled into the basin, the disarrayed sofa, the stains. She grabs the cushions and pulls off the loose covers. It's a good excuse to have them cleaned. Her white suit lies on the floor, crumpled, as if she should be inside it, crumpling too.

Terri picks it up and feels the crash descending.

★ ★ ★

Julie surveys what should be Teo's desk, wondering where to start.

'Please don't throw anything away.' Teo is pulling on his coat, about to take the opportunity to visit an estate agent. 'I have to be able to find things.'

'You will,' his new assistant promises, wondering how he imagines he can find anything in the desk's current condition. 'And if the phone rings, I'll answer it in French, OK?'

'Let the machine get it. That's why it's there. I'll see you in an hour or two.'

'*Au revoir*,' Julie says, beaming.

Teo, halfway out, turns back. 'And don't forget to ring your mother.'

Julie hasn't touched a telephone — his or hers — since she arrived. He's letting her sleep on the sofa until she can find herself a room elsewhere. She's so happy to be here, away from college, England, and both her mother and father's psychological reach, that she sings while she breaks down Teo's 'piles' into manageable sections. She can sing anywhere. It's not what you've got, she decides, it's what you do with it.

Teo has a great many pieces of paper, though, and he's let them accumulate like snowdrifts, without rhyme, reason or filing system. The Parisian view she'd hankered for — the awning of the corner café, the narrow street opening on to the boulevard Saint-Michel where it borders the Luxembourg Gardens, the students sauntering by, the deliveries, the shouts, the sheer Frenchness of it — all that fades as Julie tussles with organising the unorganisable.

'It won't be all *grand crème* and karaoke,' Teo warned her when she arrived in a heap of fluster and relief from the train.

'I don't expect it to be.' It was good enough that he'd recognised he needed an assistant and that it might as well be her. But now, facing the reality, Julie experiences her first doubts. How *do* you organise someone like Teo? Even her indomitable and millstone-sensitive mother hadn't managed that. She creates piles of letters alphabetically by sender, then rearranges them by topic, then yet again by date. They all work, but which will work best for him?

Soon the afternoon has gone and her head is bursting with frustration and uncertainty. P for publisher, X for Xenia his agent, March 2006 — yes, *really* — for the date of a letter, T for translation, R for Russian translation? No wonder the place is a mess: Teo has no more clue about it than she does. Which, coming full circle, is why he's agreed to have her there in the first place.

With a clonk of closing door, he's back; on her knees among the piles, Julie glances up, guilty. He's assessing her, half annoyed and half pitying. 'I'm getting there,' she insists. 'I am.'

'Did you phone your mother?'

'Well . . . '

Teo takes the telephone handset off its stand and drops it into Julie's lap. He scoops up a heap of papers and puts it back on the desk where it had started. Then he grabs a second armful and dumps it straight into the waste paper basket.

'Phone her,' he says. 'You can't put it off for ever. You can't keep running away.'

'You're not my dad.' Julie, sulky, stares in dismay at the brimming bin.

'This was your idea. You've been accepted, not invited. So kindly get on and do it.'

Julie takes a breath and dials.

★ ★ ★

Terri is in bed, alone, with the curtains closed. She's answered no other calls all day. The machine is clogging up. She's only answered this time because her alert read TEO. And it wasn't Teo at all, but Julie.

'I want to leave uni and defer my place to next year,' says Julie. 'Do you think they'll let me?'

'What makes you think you can do that?'

'I didn't have a gap year — and I can learn more by working for Teo here in Paris than . . . '

'Oh Jeeee-zus,' sighs Terri. 'Jul, please put Teo on.'

Teo takes the phone.

'She's staying with you?' Terri snaps.

'Until we can find her a place to share with some girls her own age, she can stay on the sofa.'

'I don't want her there.'

'Hang on, Terri, what's such a big deal?'

'I don't think it's appropriate for a young girl suddenly to foist herself on a middle-aged man and insist on being your house guest. Who knows how it'll end up?'

There's a shocked silence. Then Teo protests,

'Terri, what are you suggesting? What do you take me for?'

'Just send her back. I'll give you the train fare.' Terri, tired and upset, feels her self-control flying out of the window.

'Terri, this is ridiculous. I'm hanging up.'

'I want her *home*!'

With a click, the phone goes dead.

★   ★   ★

In Paris, Teo turns to Julie. 'That does it,' he says. 'You can definitely stay.'

★   ★   ★

The next day at lunchtime, Julie wanders out onto the boulevard Saint-Michel, trying to remember which way to look first when crossing the road. She's on a hunt for accommodation agencies, and, heading towards the university, cafés and bookshops that carry adverts for flatshares. Browsing, she spots cards offering hostels, apartments, rooms in student houses. In a café uphill from the place de la Sorbonne she stops to refuel with espresso. Leaning on the bar to drink it, she notices the animated features of some students clustering at the tables and half hears, half imagines their discussion; she wishes she could join in, but they're talking too fast for her to follow. Her French has a long way to go.

Teo has drafted a letter of agreement setting out her salary and working hours, and they've both signed it. Now she can spend her wages as she likes: she can find her own room, sign up for a language course, or look for a singing teacher. The boulevards gape after Cambridge's narrow lanes; the Luxembourg Gardens look straitjacketed compared to the blowsy greenery along the Backs. But Julie is determined: she will become a *parisienne*. Sipping her coffee, she notices the students watching her with curiosity and, she hopes, approval — a pale boy sporting a froth of dark curls, a girl with delicate features behind fashionably strong-rimmed glasses. Doors swing in her mind, revealing new panoramas; there's a world here, and she's in it. She can choose.

Of course, she couldn't choose what had happened to Alistair and their relationship. And yet . . .

She could have tried to talk him out of joining up, but she hadn't. She knew the dangers, anybody would, but she'd decided not to interfere. If she'd attempted to stop him, he'd only have dug his heels in harder, accused her of holding him back. But at least she would have known she'd tried. Some drip of doubt might have got through. She could have told him, as Teo had, that armies exist to wage war; that there's no glory in taking another life or in dying for a misguided cause. Yet he'd thought, somehow, that he wouldn't have to — how could he? All that talk about humanitarian aid . . .

Or was he just saying that to make her feel better? He'd known. Of course he'd known. She'd been naïve. And maybe, while knowing, he hadn't cared.

Julie feels tears brewing up, threatening to drip

into her coffee. She's dimly aware that the students are still glancing her way, the curly haired youth in particular. Perhaps one of them will approach her. She could make friends, if she chose. But right now she's too upset. She pays for her coffee and turns to leave.

Back in Teo's flat, there's no room for self-absorption; she spends her time answering his phone ('*Bonjour, c'est le bureau de Monsieur Popović*'), typing his correspondence — at least she can decipher his handwriting — and occasionally taking him a refill of very sweet Bosnian-style coffee, which he's taught her to make. He's ensconced at a table in the bedroom with his laptop, tapping away to his heart's content and puffing on his pipe.

'Wasn't it a good idea of mine to employ you?' he announces.

'*Kava*,' says Julie — her first word of Bosnian. She presents him with a cup.

'It's *šutkuša*. Say it?'

She tries. 'Zhootkoozha?'

'Late-afternoon coffee. It's meant to relax us. See you later, my dear.'

Relaxing it isn't, not at that strength. Julie drinks it anyway. She's learning to trust her instincts. She knows she's done the right thing: now that she's here she must work hard, make friends, learn the language, try to get over Alistair if she has to. She can't stop change, but she can choose how to manage it. She can't pick her parents, but she can decide to reinstall Teo into her life where her father should have been. She'll persuade college to keep her place open for next year, just in case. And if her mother wants her, she knows where she is. The fact is, she decides, her mother has become almost as much a millstone to her as she, Julie, had once been to Terri.

The telephone rings in her right ear. '*Bonjour, c'est le bureau de Monsieur Popović,*' says Julie.

'It's me.' Her mother's voice. 'How are you?'

'Fine. I've got a job, I'm looking for a room and I'm learning French.'

'Ah.' Terri sounds, briefly, floored — perhaps because the confidence in Julie's tone isn't wholly fake. 'So you really are Teo's secretary?'

'His PA,' Julie corrects her. 'Mum, you sound knackered.'

'I am. Very. Now, is Monsieur Popović available in his *bureau* to talk to me?'

'He's writing and asks not to be disturbed,' Julie informs her.

'Oh, for God's sake, go and get him. He will want to talk to me, he's already left me three messages today.'

Julie slinks to Teo's door and peers round. 'It's Mum,' she mouths, and watches myriad shadows cross him as he takes the phone.

She tries not to eavesdrop, but it's difficult. The words seem fierce, with feelings to match. She tries to concentrate on typing. '*Chère Madame Farinet, je suis très heureuse de vous confirmer . . .*' This is definitely the best way to learn French.

'Julie?' Teo calls. 'Come here a minute, I need to ask you a question.' Intrigued, she goes to his doorway.

'Your mother,' Teo continues, 'has agreed to sing in a charity concert I'm trying to arrange in Mostar in three months' time. It will be her first public gig, as it were, after her break. It's a little place with big emotions. I'd like you to sing with her. Will you?'

'What?'

'My two favourite girls together, mother and daughter, one coming back, the other setting out. What do you say?'

'What would we sing?'

'I don't care. Your mother will think of something.'

'But me *with* Mum?'

'Please, Julie. I'll need your help as my administrator to set this up, but what I want is for *you* to *sing*. It is a charity fund for the music therapy centre, to help the victims of the war and their families. It's not only the money, though, it's the attention of the world that's needed, and if your mother sings, there will be attention. You see?'

'But why me too?'

'Because I would like you to,' says Teo.

Julie's mind throws her a ticker-tape parade of images: her mother taking curtain calls at Covent Garden, La Scala, Vienna, Paris, flowers raining down as she stood shining in the spotlight. 'I can't possibly sing together with her, I'm just studying and she's — she's *Mum*.'

'I believe you can,' he says, pressing her hand. 'And perhaps more importantly, so does she. Julie, we want to give you something special.'

'What, like a heart attack?'

'Darling, what can I say to persuade you?'

'You can't.'

'There must be something we can do. A deal. Think of a condition, something you really want.'

'How about . . . ' Julie stalls. 'Perhaps — if you make Mum let me stay here and stop bugging me about uni?'

'Done. Shake on it?' Teo holds out a hand. Julie, looking into his hangdog eyes, takes it. She's scared by the idea of singing with Terri, but she'll do it for Teo, because she is loyal to him and he has faith in her; and because it's Mostar; and for Alistair, who happened to be English but could have suffered in exactly the same way if he'd been born Bosnian, Iraqi or Afghan.

* * *

Terri — who is indeed knackered, but not for the reasons Julie had assumed — wonders what Mary would have advised.

It's some time since she last tried to track down Mary. She'd tried the Public Records Office, but although it could have helped her to trace any Hoolihan ancestors — had she known where and when Mary was born — it wasn't much use for finding someone who is, presumably, still alive.

She types MARY HOOLIHAN into Google. She finds historical Marys from Newfoundland, Salford and Ireland, but few present-day ones, except some Americans who, on further

447

investigation, sound unlikely — she can't imagine Mary living in Florida. She scans genealogy forums by the dozen. She discovers a short story by W. B. Yeats about 'the daughter of Hoolihan'. Google asks if she really meant Mary *Houlihan*, which she didn't; she can still picture the 'oo' by Mary's unanswered bell. She calls up the Glasgow phone book, only to discover, after several minutes, that she's searching through the residents of Glasgow, Kentucky.

It's a long time since she was last in Glasgow, Scotland; after Robbie died and Finn moved south, there'd been no reason to go, except for work — and Scottish Opera hasn't booked her in years. Today the place holds little for her except dodgy memories. Not that the ones here are shaping up much better. She hasn't attended mass since she was a teenager, but just as she'd taken to the Begijnhof in Bruges, hunting for guidance, now she feels a longing for good, old-fashioned absolution. It has struck her with horrible force that she has to cut Alistair out of her life.

She's coaxed him to her, made him depend on her, turned herself into a rock of support — now she'll have to undo all that good by pulling herself away, like a rug from under his feet. And how will that affect him? He's already shaken, confused and vulnerable. She longs to get her guilt off her chest — yet she knows that she can never feel better about it, no matter how many Hail Marys she says; telling a priest would be useless; but she certainly can't tell anyone else.

If singing a charity concert in Bosnia will earn her Brownie points with the Almighty, then she needs them. Badly.

23

'I don't understand.' Sue stands on the Livingston Road doorstep, arms folded, her gaze behind her glasses one part puzzlement to two parts fury.

'Come in,' says Terri.

'No, thanks. I don't get it. You come round the whole time, you make out you're our best friend and suddenly — slam.'

'Please come in.'

'You're a snob like all the rest,' Sue accuses. 'Patronising us as long as it suits *you*.'

'Sue, *please* come in and let me talk to you.'

'Sod that. It's been two weeks.'

'I know. How's Alistair?'

'How do you think?'

'Listen, I'm packing, I'm going away for a while. I've got to go to America, to see people and plan things, have some coaching with a . . . '

'I don't care what you're doing in bleedin' America. All I can say is, if that's what your 'friendship' means, the Americans are welcome to it, cos we don't bloody want it.'

'But if you won't even — '

But Sue has gone, marching away down the hill without a backward glance. Terri, numb with misery, turns back to her suitcase.

She's resolved on total removal. Dora has invited her to stay on the Upper East Side; Katharina is in New York, and Terri hasn't seen her for years; also, she can consult any one of the several top-notch vocal coaches she knows in the city. The trip is a measure of last resort.

He started to ring at 9 a.m. the next morning and continues, once every fifteen minutes on bad days, every half an hour on good ones. She doesn't answer. Her telephone displays the number that's calling, to make certain she won't miss Martini with a shout from La Scala, but there's little need for it. Remembering the supposed proclivity for violence among war veterans, she'd been terrified for a while, but now she's sure he's not stalking her physically — whenever she goes out, she glances over her shoulder, but he is never there. Yet that's almost worse, because it means he's cooped up in the flat fighting with Sue; and she can no longer help. It's a nightmare and it's all her fault.

At night, alone, Terri remembers him. Many times she's had flings, delicious one-night stands when you give a little and take a little, everyone's happy and physically calmed, and so what? It's natural to crave physical closeness. When you're riding the waves of the moment like that, why should you stop to think? But one phrase returns and returns, like a mantra: how could she have been so stupid?

★ ★ ★

In Paris, Julie is trying to learn not only French, but also some rudimentary Serbo-Croat. 'Bosnian,' Teo corrects her. 'There's no such thing as Serbo-Croat any more. They've done their best

451

to separate Serbian from Croatian and Bosnian from both.'

'But how?'

'A bunch of nationalists started making up words to change them into separate languages. It's like striking down the Tower of Babel, splitting people up instead of bringing them together. Welcome to the Balkans.'

She can hardly believe the amount of work it takes to organise a single concert in another country. Unintelligible contracts arrive, and would have been equally unintelligible in English. To check them she has to locate a Parisian lawyer who understands Bosnian. The theatre revises its estimate of the cost, upwards. Then Teo decides that the event needs international PR, and delegates the appointing of a press consultant to Julie; she has to visit several high-powered women, all of them in jackets and jewels, to decide which to choose. Teo gives her extra cash and tells her to buy herself some decent clothes rather than wearing her jeans and blue cardigan every day.

After a week on the sofa, she's found a room in a shared flat, not far from the Gare du Nord; the area is cheaper than Teo's *arrondissement* and comparatively run down, populated by shadier characters, while the cafés lack the polished décor and the banners of handwriting from Rimbaud or Rostand that feature at the eateries near Teo's. It's more like Falcon Park, and Julie feels less self-conscious here. The flat is on the top floor of an apartment block built around a small courtyard; her room offers a view of rooftops and sky ('Ah, a Parisian garret,' Terri says approvingly). It's a narrow space with a single bed and one rickety cupboard, but that's all she needs.

Her new flatmates, Monique and Anne-Marie, are fun, friendly and not much older than she is; best of all, their English is limited so she's obliged to speak French with them. Monique works as a PA for an accountancy firm and wears tight skirts; Anne-Marie is Monique's school-friend and though she has a dogsbody job in the archives at the Musée d'Orsay, a fabric hairband around her forest of curls makes her look incongruously like a tennis champion. They're both fascinated when Julie tells them about Teo, her mother and her singing; even better, they like hearing her when she vocalises in her room.

At first Julie worried that she'd be gooseberry as the third girl; but on her first day, after she'd unpacked and arranged her room, they'd knocked and insisted they should all go out for a coffee; later, they cooked her dinner and wouldn't let her help. She felt overwhelmed with welcome and warmth. While they cooked, she put away two glasses of wine at the speed she would have with Irina, Charlie and Raff, but soon she realised that she was way ahead of them. This is France. You pour small glasses, not big ones; you sip them with your food. Leglessness is frowned on. Besides, it's good to wake up on Saturday morning with no headache, feeling fresh and eager for a run in the Luxembourg Gardens en route to Teo's for a briefing on the state of the concert.

Saturday afternoon is free. She wanders through the Left Bank, window-shopping, people-watching — they watch her back — taking in the bright pale air, the sunshine, the spring in her own step. After crossing a bridge to the Right Bank, she finds herself passing a row of pet shops, where puppies, kittens and rabbits play in large glass tanks, waiting for good homes. At first Julie's aghast, but then she spots a family with two small daughters inside one shop, transfixed by a pair of Golden Retriever puppies. The proprietor, in a white coat, lifts out one of the little dogs as tenderly as if it were a baby. The children cuddle it while it licks their noses. Soon money is exchanged and the puppy is carried away, wagging its tail, to its new family.

Julie wanders inside to take a closer look at the remaining puppy snuffling around in its space, suddenly deprived of its brother. She has never had a dog of her own, much as she would have loved one; a dog is a lot of work, and needs a routine that the family couldn't have, Terri explained when Julie was tiny and hankering for a four-legged friend. Naturally, this mightn't be the time for such a commitment, not unless she's staying here for ever. She could, of course, do worse than stay . . .

The proprietor, no doubt seeing her anguished expression, lifts the other puppy out of its pen and lets her hold it. Its big paws and damp nose are so soft and eager that she can hardly bear to put it down again. 'I think I'm in love,' she tells the proprietor, much to his amusement — probably because her French is incorrect. But she has to be realistic; their little flat is in no way suitable for an animal that, however cute, will soon be almost larger than their kitchen. 'Don't worry,' he assures her. 'He won't be here long. We French love dogs — puppies like this one are usually adopted extremely fast.'

'I'm glad.' Julie gives the animal a regretful kiss on his right ear, and hands him back. Leaving the shop, dogless, she pauses and takes a last gaze at the little Retriever, who's already being fussed over by his next set of admirers.

'*Vous voudriez adopter ce petit chiot?*' someone asks her.

'*Oui, je l'adore!*' Julie responds at once, before looking round.

The question has come from a curly haired youth about her own age, carrying a violin case. She wonders why so many people here have curly hair — it doesn't seem such a fashion sin as it does in England. Then she notices he looks familiar.

'We haven't met,' he answers her unspoken question, 'but I've seen you before. You were in the Rostand, at the bar, crying into your coffee. I wanted to ask you why, but you left before I could find the courage.'

'I'm sorry, my French is very bad,' says Julie, though it's already incrementally better than it was that first day.

'Not at all, it sounds excellent,' he assures her.

She's not sure she should be talking to a stranger — but she definitely, unquestionably, likes the look of this boy, his friendly eyes and the reassuring sight of the musical instrument.

'I study at the Conservatoire,' he explains, seeing her looking at the violin. 'Hard work, but I love it. Do you like music?'

'I sing,' Julie tells him. 'Actually, I was studying music at university, but I dropped out a couple of weeks ago and came here instead.'

'But that's amazing! My mysterious, weeping stranger is a musician too? Are you in a hurry? Would you like a coffee?' The lad indicates a café round the corner. And Julie, who would never, ever have done such a thing in London, or anywhere else until now, falls into step with him.

'*Je m'appelle Frédéric,*' he says, holding out his hand. 'Everyone calls me Freddy.'

'Julie,' she replies, with her happiest smile.

They pick their way through to a corner of the café, past tables and chairs laced with newspapers, umbrellas, coffee cups, the remnants of omelettes and glasses of wine or *citron pressé*. Julie's innards give a little lift; it's as if she has found her way into a world that she's been standing outside, desperate to enter yet lacking a pass. She wonders if her French will be up to sustaining a conversation with Freddy, but he slows his speech for her; if she goes wrong, he corrects her, not bossily but in order to help. 'This is the best way to learn,' he declares. 'May I be your new French teacher?'

She hadn't realised that she could explain herself in French, but he makes it easier for her. He listens, chin on his clasped hands, violin case tucked out of the way between his chair and the window, while Julie describes Teo, her mother, her decision to drop out of university. She wonders whether she should be telling a strange boy so much, so quickly, but there's something about the way he listens that makes her open up; every time she tries to hold something back, he encourages her with the slightest of prods to continue. He looks interested — genuinely so. That helps. There's lightness in her mind. 'I feel free,' she confides in him. 'I've never felt this free before.'

'It's good?'

'It's great!'

'I'm very glad.'

'And you? Tell me about you and your violin.'

'It's not so exciting. No famous parents or step-parents. I live with my family near the Bastille, I study. Lots of practising! But I love music more than life, so it's not so bad.'

'Exactly.' Julie smiles.

'I'm doing a little concert soon at the Conservatoire — we have a lunchtime series where we show off. Would you come?'

'I'd love to, if Teo doesn't need me.'

'Bring him too. I'd be honoured to meet him.'

'I'll ask.' Julie watches him write down his phone number and the date of the concert on a napkin, then gives him her own number without a moment's hesitation. He programmes it straight into his mobile phone.

'So Teo is like a substitute papa for you?' he asks.

'Kind of. It's weird, but I don't know one person at home — in London, anyway — who has a normal family.'

'Don't worry, there aren't many here either,'

he reassures her. 'Mine is OK, but I think we are an exception. I look at my friends and I think it's a miracle. What's 'normal', anyway? A lot of us, me and my friends, we feel that we've created a family among ourselves. We choose each other and we look after each other.'

'But it's never quite as strong,' Julie suggests. 'I'd definitely choose Teo if I could choose a dad — but my mum would have to as well.'

'*Ouais.*' Freddy sips coffee. 'I guess it's true that you can't really choose your family until you choose to make your own.'

'For the moment, I think I'll stick to cuddling the puppies in the pet shop!'

'For the moment.'

He smiles into her eyes, and Julie suddenly realises that she hadn't heard what he'd said; she was too busy looking at him.

'I hope you can come to the concert.' Passing her the napkin, he pats the back of her wrist.

'Thanks. I'll be there.'

'And by then your French will be even better!'

'I like speaking French. I know I'm not good at it, but I enjoy it. It's almost like you can become a different person if you're speaking a different language.'

'*Chapeau!* I take my hat off to you — you will soon be perfect.' He pauses. 'And in a way, if you will permit me — you already are.'

'*Tu es trop charmant!*' Julie declares, giggling.

When they say goodbye, he kisses her on both cheeks; watching him walk off, glancing back and waving over one shoulder, Julie has the odd sensation that she's known him for years. With him, she'd felt confident, funny, comfortable: herself at her best. She'd felt happy. She can't remember when she last felt so happy talking to anybody. She certainly can't remember the last time she'd felt so at ease with Alistair — though that, of course, was surely not his fault.

She wanders home along the Seine hardly sensing her feet on the paving stones. By the time she's back at the apartment, though, she's falling off her high, Alistair's image thrumming behind her eyes. After all this time, after everything he's been through, how can she just accept his reluctance to see her and contemplate waltzing off with someone else? He must surely want to have her back soon — and what will she say to him if she starts seeing Freddy? She dials Scargill Tower; no reply. Then she tries her mother, but the answering machine informs her that Terri is on a plane to New York.

'Don't worry,' Anne-Marie tells her, showing her how to arrange an elasticated fabric hairband to best effect. 'We'll go dancing and have fun. You'll see, everything will be fine.'

'But how?' wails Julie, staring at her sophisticated new look in the mirror.

'I don't know,' Anne-Marie admits, 'but it usually is. Stop worrying so much, Julie! You know what I think? Every time you start enjoying something, you feel you have to stop yourself because it's wrong. But it's not! Mostly, you know, we do get through our bad patches. You might find your heart's stronger than you think.'

'Really?' Julie is inclined to believe Anne-Marie, whose mother had died when she was ten. If anyone knows about bad patches, it's her.

'You'll see. The only thing that really heals is time. *Alors*, Julie, you look cool. Ready to go? Dancing shoes?'

Julie stands up. 'Dancing shoes!'

★   ★   ★

Terri, in New York, spends three happy days with Dora, letting off steam. They eat together, drink together and laugh so loudly that heads turn in the restaurants. Then she goes to Dora's shop and buys two suits and a concert dress at wholesale prices.

'Green? Are you sure?' Dora says.

Terri swishes round in forest-coloured net and silk. 'It's time for a change,' she declares. The dress goes with her eyes, which hover between green and blue but are more interesting when the green is emphasised. After Bruges, Terri thinks she may have had it with ivory.

'It didn't split because it was ivory,' Dora points out. 'It split because you, darling, got porky. We'll sort you out. You and I are going to the gym every day as long as you're in town.'

'Definitely a reason for me to find my own place!' Terri decides. But when she does find a short, inexpensive let — a one-bed flat not far from Dora's that belongs to a friend of hers who's away for a month — it turns out that there's a gym in the basement. There'll be no escape.

Nor is there any escape from herself. When she turns out the lamp and watches the shifting

460

patterns of headlights from the street below, it's as if she can still hear the telephone ringing in Livingston Road, still feel Alistair's lips on her neck, still see Sue's face, accusatory and hurt. Had Alistair confessed? Has she ruined his recovery? If Sue knows, would she tell anybody, and if so, would it reach the tabloids or, worse, Julie? Terri buys some over-the-counter herbal sleeping pills which help to stave off the thoughts that flap around her like ravens.

But if one thing is worse than running away from Alistair, it's speculating about what would have happened if she hadn't. There'd be an affair, and people would learn about it; there'd be gossip and, no doubt, disgust; sooner or later it would end, and finally she'd find herself out in the cold, with nothing to look forward to except, possibly, more short, meaningless flings with tall, disastrous men. And her daughter, the one person in the world to whom she truly belongs, would never speak to her again. If she had to choose between Julie and Alistair, there would be no choice; nor could there ever be. As things are, if Julie should learn the truth, Terri could lose the entire infrastructure of her life.

She fights the temptation to run down to the deli for the biggest bagel or muffin she can find. Pounding the treadmill instead, with Dora on the next machine egging her on, she decides that exercise is the answer, at least in the short-term. It will not only rescue her figure, but it stops her thinking, buoys up her mood and helps her sleep. She's so out of shape that Dora's intensive fitness programme leaves her exhausted; but it

461

brings relatively rapid results. 'Except that I eat like a fucking horse,' she confesses.

'Darling, you were eating like a fucking horse in any case,' Dora points out. Dora's doctor recommends a laryngologist in an Upper East Side hospital and Terri takes herself there for a discreet check-up. After peering at her throat with a variety of contraptions, and asking her to sing some simple exercises, he tells her she's making excellent progress. 'Take it slowly and build up your technique carefully, just as you are and I reckon you can be back onstage comfortably in a month or two.'

Thank heavens she's doing something right.

Mostar will be a boon: a chance to ease into performing without the pressure of Covent Garden or the Met. Julie tells her, by email, that Teo is engaging an international PR manager, but that the theatre is tiny. She hums through arias and duets. She's perturbed by Teo's insistence that Julie should sing. Is it a PR stunt: 'Mother and daughter share the stage for the first time'? That would be unfair to them both. Still, Julie deserves a chance to air her beautiful voice — and, perhaps, to see whether this is the path she really wants to follow.

Terri experiments. There aren't many suitable duets for two sopranos. But there's the letter *canzonetta* duet from *The Marriage of Figaro*; and a duet by Pauline Viardot, 'Havanaise', which is extremely difficult. Could Julie manage it? If she could . . . It occurs to her that if Teo is effectively using her and Julie to stimulate publicity for his good causes in Bosnia, then she can use Teo's publicity to raise interest in her film. If she wheels out the best songs of Pauline Viardot, and Teo and Julie wheel in some journalistic bigwigs and a TV crew, it can't hurt.

She asks Dora to scan the Viardot duet, which is full of Spanish virtuoso glitter, and emails it to Julie in Paris with a note: 'Can you do the upper line?' This could also be the chance she's longed for to sing her favourite Viardot song, 'Les étoiles', for voice and piano with a solo violin thrown in for good measure. The voice should be a mezzo, but Terri won't let that be a problem — her range should cope, and if not then she'll transpose it herself. She emails Teo: 'Can we have a violinist?'

She spends her days planning, hunting, practising, visiting art galleries, browsing the shops — though she prefers to support Dora's business rather than the big department stores. She tries valiantly to resist bagels in favour of salads with fat-free dressings, then pumps away in the gym alongside a range of New Yorkers who are either grotesquely fat or terrifyingly thin. After a couple of weeks her clothes begin to feel a little more comfortable.

Then, abruptly, one day she succumbs to a fermented mix of guilt and anxiety and tries to phone Alistair. After his persistent calls to her, he won't answer. Suddenly it's her phoning him — if not every half an hour, then certainly several times a day — to no avail. 'This is surreal,' she tells Dora, who knows that there's been an infatuation, but not that it was acted upon. 'First he won't leave me alone. Now he won't answer my calls.'

'That's logical,' says Dora.

★ ★ ★

Katharina invites Terri to tea in her apartment on Riverside Drive. Terri automatically feels a whisper of trepidation as she goes up the Gothic mansion's front steps and explains herself to a sepulchral doorman. She's never stopped being in awe of her former heroine. Whenever she sees her, she pictures that face as she'd first seen it, on an LP sleeve in the firelight of Mary Hoolihan's front room, and the voice as she'd first heard it, as powerful as an Amazon out of a Greek myth. And then the day Katharina walked into the pub. Part of her, faced with Katharina Strashilova, is still the little girl from the Gorbals.

'Terri, *dearest*.' Katharina, exotic as a peacock in a purple kaftan and a great deal of eye make-up, greets her with three kisses. 'Come inside and tell me everything. It's been *such* a long time.'

Terri had always wanted to tell Katharina everything, but never managed to. She'd revered her since the first day Mary played her her recordings; she wanted to love her as much as she loved Mary. But it was difficult, and it's no easier now. Katharina's walls are plastered with posters from her performances and those of her friends', including some of the biggest conductors, tenors and pianists of the twentieth century. Terri browses the signed photos that adorn the

464

entrance hall from floor to ceiling, while Katharina instructs her housekeeper to make coffee. Katharina, unlike Terri, had married money and she has never wanted for luxury since she stopped singing. She's good at spoiling Terri, too, at least outwardly, and has ordered cakes from the most expensive patisserie on Fifth Avenue. But Terri's telling of 'everything' always ends up much truncated.

'My darling,' Katharina interrupts, while Terri is explaining how Julie has a lovely voice but is vacillating over developing it, 'did I ever tell you about the time I sang *Roméo et Juliette* with Giuseppe di Stefano?'

She has, of course, many times; indeed, Terri had named her daughter after that role, one she'd never sung herself, expressly in Katharina's honour. Now, as usual, she smiles and pretends that it's news. Tea with Katharina has always meant listening, not talking. In Terri's current mood, that's fine.

★　★　★

Back in the apartment, Terri lies on the floor, knees up, head supported by a book, doing her exercises. Rooting the voice in the earth. The voice of Persephone, she thinks, a call from the core of the planet. She breathes steadily, closes her eyes, visualises. Her voice expresses her central force, her life force. A manifestation of the earth's energy, the divine energy, as Mary would have called it. That energy is everything we are. It drove the great creators, the writers, composers, performers, scientists, philosophers, prophets. It filled Jesus and Abraham, Muhammad and Krishna ('Don't tell them at church that I said that,' Mary remarked). It's the energy that brings us love, that makes us merge with a lover to create a child. It binds us together in one great chain of humanity. The only difference is how we channel it. Terri channels it through her naturally beautiful voice.

'You have to stop thinking,' said Mary. 'To feel the energy you must ignore those noises in your brain, stop worrying about who you are, why you're who you are, how you're going to get home or what you're going to eat for dinner. You live only in the flow, as the energy manifests in the circuit of breath. From there, you can radiate that energy out so that others will benefit from it.'

Yet it can all go horribly wrong. Singing and sex may have the same root in Mary's famous energy, but that's no excuse; if she's damaged the already devastated Alistair by confusing them, she has only herself to blame. If only she knew how he is; perhaps she's worrying needlessly. Meanwhile, she'll have to live with this guilt and anxiety, probably for a long time.

She lies still and breathes. What of the future? To reformat yourself after so many years requires the courage of a trapeze artist flying from hold to hold, without a safety net. Terri is by no means sure that she can do anything of the kind. Her only certainty is that if the alternative is losing Julie, she must find that courage, no matter what it takes.

★ ★ ★

Julie and Teo cross Paris together by métro to listen to Freddy playing his violin in the concert hall of the Conservatoire, which is based in a concretey complex called the Cité de la Musique.

'You like him?' Teo asks Julie at the end. She's been sitting motionless for the whole hour, eyes and ears fastened like pins to Freddy's every note. The last piece, in particular, had transfixed her: the 'Poème' by Ernest Chausson. She seemed to hear in it myriad images: an exotic garden, unfulfilled passion, an overwhelming sense of mystery — it seemed to trace a story without possessing a narrative. Perhaps she was imagining it.

'He's wonderful,' she says, watching Freddy take his bow.

'Been seeing him?'

'No, no — but we've had coffee a couple of times. And lunch once.'

'So, shall we take him to Mostar with us?'

'Mostar?'

'Your mother wants a violinist to play a Viardot song with her. He plays nicely and I think you might like him to be there . . . no? We kill two birds with one dropped penny!'

'Oh Teo . . . ' Julie flushes amethyst. Just as she's reaching her purplest, there's a cry of 'Julie!' and Freddy, case slung over one shoulder, is beside them, beaming, reaching out a hand to greet Teo, whose face breaks into its most charming smile. Freddy, thinks the bedazzled

Julie, is the sort of person who will make everyone smile simply by being there.

'I enjoyed your playing very much.' Teo pumps the offered hand. 'Bravo.'

'It's a joy to meet you, Monsieur Popović. I was so moved by your book.'

'Julie, *what* a nice young man. My dear Freddy, have you time for a coffee with us? There is something my assistant here and I would like to discuss with you.'

'That would be wonderful! And please tell me, as we go — how was the last piece, did you think? The Chausson 'Poème'? Because it's the first time I've performed it. It's very difficult and I was worrying about how it would come across.'

'It's superb,' Teo affirms, 'and what I'm about to suggest might give you a chance to play it again.'

'I'd love that. It needs a lot of playing in, because there's so much in it. You know, it is quite literary — it was modelled on a story by Turgenev called 'The Song of Triumphant Love'.'

Julie and Teo stop in their tracks with astonishment, then exchange glances, wondering whether to explain why to the bemused Freddy. Julie's head begins to spin: perhaps this is all meant to be? The sense is so strong that it's positively frightening. It's almost as if the whole thing has been settled in advance by providence, which had failed to consult them.

Teo takes charge, sensing her confusion. 'This is a delicious irony, my dear fellow,' he tells Freddy. 'I have been trying for years to write my own version of that story, because I am a writer who, like Turgenev, loves, or loved, a singer. Terri, my singer, wishes to sing songs by Turgenev's singer, Pauline Viardot, at our concert in Mostar. So, were you to come with us and perform with her in a song by Viardot, there would be nothing more appropriate for you to play as your solo than this beautiful work.'

'Mostar?' Freddy's smile shines around the café like the sun itself — or Julie thinks it does. 'How amazing — of course I will! It would be a privilege. I'll play the Chausson and anything that Madame Ivory would like. It is genius to find music by Viardot. And maybe we should include also some Fauré?'

'The 'Pie Jesu' is my party piece.' Julie sits up. 'Why?'

'Perfect!' Freddy claps his hands together. 'Because Pauline Viardot's daughter Marianne nearly married Fauré. They were engaged, but she broke it off — she was a little scared of him . . . '

'Don't tell me,' said Teo. 'She could sing?'

'She could! I was reading all about this when I learned the piece. Turgenev always hoped she would sing professionally, but she didn't want to . . . '

Julie is barely listening; her imagination is in overdrive. Freddy in Bosnia! She's wading into a swamp of confusion — because giving up on Alistair would be altogether wrong. It's not that she doesn't still love Alistair; she does. Yet when, under the table, Freddy's foot brushes her ankle, briefly but deliberately, her heart gives such a vault of joy that she wants to turn a cartwheel.

'You're in love,' Teo says, sarcastic, ushering her back to her desk in the flat. 'That, my dear, is *all* we need now.'

Julie's fingers fly faster and faster over the computer keyboard while she drafts the newly devised programme for the concert.

'Be careful, Julie.'

'Do you think I need to be? He's so lovely.'

'I mean, be careful *with your spelling*. I need you to concentrate!' He pats her shoulder. 'I'll make some coffee to tempt you back to earth.'

★   ★   ★

Terri has been in New York for nearly a month when Martini phones. Her neighbour from Livingston Road has contacted him, after a spot of detective work, to ask where she is. High winds have knocked some tiles off the roof of her house and there are ominous signs that damp may be getting in through the crack at the front.

'Fuck,' says Terri.

She hadn't left keys with anyone else before she set off for the States; Alistair has them, as he has for some years. She'd been too preoccupied to remember to ask for them back. In America she's paid her way on her carefully saved emergency fund — if this wasn't an emergency, she doesn't know what would have been; but there is no way it will stretch to the cost of a new roof and major repointing.

'A stitch in time saves nine,' her agent reminds her.

'Very dry, Martini. I guess I'll have to go home.'

* ★ ★ ★

Two days later she's standing outside her house, looking up. The damaged tiles lie where they'd fallen, fractured grey lumps close to the front steps. The wind is still intense, tugging at her hair and ears on the exposed hill; branches have crashed into the road, torn cruelly from their trees. The plane had dipped and plunged its way east for seven hours and she's barely stopped feeling queasy. Trepidatious, she unlocks the front door and goes in.

The smell of damp, which she knows too well, hits her at once. Without shedding her coat, she runs upstairs and from the landing opens the hatch into the loft, standing on a chair to reach inside for the pull-down ladder.

The roof has leaked badly. Patches of dark on the exposed floorboards show her where the water has come in; a box of ancient junk belonging to Robbie — old schoolbooks and a football scarf that she couldn't bear to throw out — has been drenched and ruined. If something isn't done fast, the boards will rot and might fall in. Noxious circles have already appeared on her bedroom ceiling. At the front of the house, the wall beside the crack feels dank.

Terri busies herself with the Yellow Pages. 'Yes,' she says to the bored receptionist at one

471

firm, 'it *is* an emergency.'

The high winds — presumably induced by global warming — have brought a sudden boom to the building business. 'Everyone is having problems,' a sympathetic Pole tells her, explaining why his firm is over-subscribed. Terri drums her heels, then pulls on hat and gloves to go down to the high street and seek face-to-face contact with any building firms she can find, or at least some recommendations from local shopkeepers.

The first office she tries brings her no joy — nobody is remotely interested in her roof. Insurance claims are two a penny at the moment. The newsagent next door displays cards for local companies in its window. Terri jots down numbers in a notebook, her mind whirring through calculations — scaffolding, materials, two or three men to work for — how long? A week, two weeks, longer? How long does it take to repair a roof, let alone replace it? What about the cost of fixing the crack? Supposing the whole thing is due to subsidence and she has to have the house underpinned?

She becomes aware that someone is watching her. Turning, she finds herself face to face with Sue.

'You're back.' Sue doesn't look as if she wants to be hugged.

Terri hesitates. 'Sort of.' She tries to smile. 'There are some problems with my house. How've you been?'

'Well as can be expected, thanks very much.'

There's a long pause.

'How is Alistair?'

'He's gone north. Staying with his mate Gerry. It's all easier up there, the family lives in a house that doesn't have a load of stairs and Gerry can drive them both to appointments and the leisure centre and that.'

'Is it helping?'

'He needs more help than I can give him,' Sue says, expressionless, 'but it sounds like he's doing OK. They go swimming, they have physio, there's a decent army therapist, and best of all he's with his mate who's got the same problems. He needs his own kind, Terri. It's like after what happened, he belongs to them now, not to me.'

'Are you coping OK?'

'I cope. But I miss him. I miss my little boy.'

'Oh, Sue.' Terri holds out her arms, expecting rejection, but instead, Sue surges forward and returns her embrace. And hugging her eases Terri's spirit better than all the health food and gym-going in all her time in New York.

'Terri,' says Sue, 'I should tell you — I know what happened.'

'You do?' Alarmed, she backs away.

'Like he didn't have it written all over him?' Sue's smile twists; the sinking sun glints off her glasses. 'I knew something was weird, so I grilled him until he owned up.'

'You're his mother, you would see it.' Terri wants to sink through the paving stones to the centre of the earth.

'I know my own boy, or I used to.'

Terri, numb, waits for Sue to go on.

'You know what I thought?' Sue says. 'That

you wanted to treat him like your son, because you didn't have one. And then it went wrong.'

Apologies have never been Terri's greatest strength; in the opera world, she feels, they can be an indication of dangerous weakness. Fortunately, Falcon Park High Street is no theatre. 'I don't know what to say except that I'm sorry,' she says, improvising frantically. 'I know it shouldn't have happened, but it did and I can't undo that. Can you ever forgive me?'

'I won't pretend it's easy.' Sue pauses. 'I was bleedin' livid. But it takes two, don't it? It's not just you, Terri. He should've known better. And so should I, I should've seen it coming and warned him off.'

'I didn't see it coming myself,' Terri admits. 'Won't you come back to the house and we can talk properly?'

After a moment's thought, Sue nods; turning up the hill, they fall into step together. It's such a relief that she is there, as she used to be, that Terri wants to sing for joy.

'I've missed you,' she says.

'Me too, I missed you,' Sue admits. 'To be honest, that's what hurt most of all.'

At the house, Terri thinks better of tea and pours celebratory wine for both of them, although it's only half past five. Then she gives Sue a guided tour of the leaks.

'My brother John'll find you a good builder,' Sue says, gazing around; she hasn't been to the top of the house before. 'Get you sorted in no time.' She takes in the number of bedrooms

— mainly disused — and the paper-filled lair that is Terri's study.

'I'm very worried,' Terri admits, back downstairs. 'I don't know how much damage I've done to Alistair, and if I'm why he's had to go away I don't know how I can live with myself.'

'Stop panicking, love. There's only one reason he's gone: it's cos he was nearly killed in a sodding war and he has to be where he can get better. Not everything is *your* fault, you know. You're not so important. You don't rule everyone's lives.'

Suitably humbled, Terri turns away to hunt for some crisps in the cupboard. 'Should I go and see him?'

'No way,' says Sue. 'You've done your best to heal him.'

'Jesu Maria. I should learn to mind my own business.'

'In a way, it was your business.' Sue drains her wineglass. 'Terri, can I ask you a question?'

'Go on?'

'Why do you keep those bedrooms empty upstairs? Two of them, isn't it?'

'One was my mother's when she was alive. The other was meant for my brother, Robbie, who died. Our au pairs used it.'

'Why d'you stay in this house, love?' Sue sits forward. 'I was watching this TV programme, right? It was all about decluttering your home. What these people were doing with their houses was hanging on to things that they couldn't let go. Stuff they couldn't make themselves chuck out. When they did, they felt great.'

'I haven't got too much clutter, just too much space. Anyway, the house may be falling to bits, but I like it. I like sitting in this kitchen. I like my studio, and having parties, and the pool is great in summer. I couldn't have that anywhere else, could I?'

'Sure you could, if you wanted. But when I was really angry with you, I started thinking that what you really wanted was more family. Other children to look after.'

Terri says nothing. She's thinking of the empty bedrooms, adjacent to Julie's. Rooms for her mother and brother? Or rooms, perhaps, for the two children she hadn't had?

★ ★ ★

The reassuring voice of the nurse: 'Teresa? You're going to be just fine. The doctor's removed the foetus.'

Herself, stupid kid, asking: 'Was it a boy or a girl?'

The words coming back: 'It was a boy.'

The next time, she hadn't asked.

★ ★ ★

'I thought maybe I could help Alistair,' she tells Sue eventually, one hand on her own throat. 'The music. He loved it so much — it really got to him — it released something in him, or I thought it did. Sometimes I feel medicine can't cure much at all, that healing has to go deeper than popping pills. I hoped music could do that.

476

But maybe there are some things that even music can't reach.' She's slowly recognising that a hitherto unsuspected reason might underpin her grudge against doctors.

'What they all say is that it's time.' Sue evidently can tell what a raw nerve she's hit. 'Some things medicine can't cure, some things music can't cure — and some things, even love isn't good enough. Then you have to leave it to time.'

'You're right,' says Terri. 'I know you're right.'

On the doorstep, the two women embrace.

'You're not planning on telling Julie any of this, are you?' Terri pleads at last.

'Hell, no. Poor kid, she's been through enough. Like my mum used to say, least said, soonest mended.'

'Thanks so much . . . and if there's anything I can do . . . ?' says the still-mortified Terri.

'There's not. But thanks. I'm glad we're friends again. 'Bye, love.'

'Oh, Sue.' Struck by an idea, Terri runs after her. 'Hang on. Did your stink trouble in the tower get fixed?'

Sue stops short, then laughs, sardonic. 'You kidding? We've all complained again and again, and nothing happens. I don't know what we're supposed to do. We're living over an open sewer! The insects are having a field day, we're all getting bitten.'

'Right then,' says Terri. 'In that case, maybe there will be something I can do. I'm going to make some calls. All right?'

'Whatever you like, love,' says Sue, mystified.

Back inside, a quick Internet hunt reveals the number Terri needs: BBC London News. She leaves a message on its answering machine: 'Hello, this is Terri Ivory, the opera singer. I have a story that may interest you, please call me back.'

★ ★ ★

A few days later Julie, in Paris, is practising her songs for the Bosnian trip while Freddy sits with Monique and Anne-Marie in the kitchen, drinking coffee and channel surfing on the TV. Through the vibrations of the Viardot duet, she thinks she hears Freddy shout: 'Julie! *Viens ici, c'est ta mère!*'

She scoots into the kitchen. Her friends have stumbled upon the early evening news on BBC World: there, striding through the darkest depths of Scargill Tower's basement, is her mother in an ivory trouser suit, covering her nose with a handkerchief and talking to a reporter named Sunil about the months of public health hazard and the dire condition of the block. Nothing had been done despite repeated calls from residents, Sunil reports.

'The council small print contains plenty of information about how to make a complaint, and then about what to do if you're not happy with the way your complaint has been handled,' he says into the camera. 'But it seems there's another stage too: have a local celebrity ring the BBC. I'm glad to say that the builders arrive tomorrow morning to begin clearing this up.'

'Thank you, Terri.' Sue shakes her hand on behalf of the residents.

'My pleasure,' Terri says gracefully. 'It's the least I can do. I grew up in the Gorbals and watched my mother's health being shot to pieces by living in appalling conditions that were never fixed. In those days I could do nothing about it. Now I can.'

'And we understand that soon you're off to Bosnia to give a charity concert, raising money for families still blighted by the effects of war?' Sunil asks.

'That's right. Maybe we can talk about that another time.' Terri smiles. 'It deserves a slot to itself.'

'Maybe we can.' Sunil looks delighted. 'And so, from a very smelly place, it's good evening from BBC News . . .'

Julie feels the admiring eyes of her three friends turn towards her. She flushes. 'That's my mum,' she says.

24

Sarajevo Airport had reopened to international flights relatively recently, Terri remembers. If Teo had wanted to go back sooner, it would have been a complicated journey involving planes to neighbouring countries followed by extended rides on dubious buses. Now you can fly direct on a budget airline in two hours. As the plane touches down, she peers out at the hills and feels a shock at the strangeness of it: this is the homeland of the man who had spent longest in her life.

She hasn't seen Teo since Bruges. She hasn't seen Julie since she upped sticks and headed for France. A mysterious boy called Freddy has appeared in Julie's emails, Teo has invited him to Mostar to play his violin with them and she knows nothing more than that. Julie, who seems to have discovered her 'event manager within', has hired the best arts PR in Paris; the international press will come to Mostar in force. And Terri is still far from sure what will happen when she starts to sing.

She walks through customs into the airport to find them all waiting for her, propping up some high tables at a coffee bar: a gaggle of figures, some familiar, others less so. Her gaze lands at once on Teo, who is looking relaxed in a leather jacket that must be new; perhaps he's rejected patched corduroy at last. At his side is a lithe and

480

beautiful young woman — for a second, she scarcely recognises her own daughter. Julie's hair has been cut into a sleek bob and she's wearing something in which Terri has never seen her before: a suit. The perfect image of a young professional manager, she's wielding a clipboard and is managing to keep an eye on its information, furnish her arriving guests with coffee and flirt with a terrifically handsome boy with a violin case by his feet, all at the same time. A camera crew, black-clad, spike-haired, is checking its equipment behind them. Teo spots Terri first; she takes a breath, then goes to him, hands outstretched.

He kisses her on both cheeks, which wasn't quite what his gaze had led her to expect. 'Terri, you're here.'

'Yes. At last. Hello, Julie.'

'Mum!' Julie hugs her. She's wearing perfume and makeup.

'You look wonderful, darling. So elegant! I haven't seen you for *ages*.'

'You look good too, Mum. We're nearly ready, but we're still waiting for Roger, and Isabelle from the *Independent*. Sergei and Irina are coming later, but they'll make their own way.'

'You asked them?' Terri growls.

'Sergei Ivanovich has pledged a huge amount of money to the charity,' Teo explains. 'I suppose that if I'd managed to drown his guests, he might have had other ideas.'

'Mum, this is Freddy.' Julie pulls forward her violinist friend. 'He's going to play 'Les étoiles' with you, and some other pieces.'

'*Enchanté*.' Freddy kisses Terri's hand.

Terri thinks of Alistair, heading north to be with his friend rather than his mother. Julie, she can see, has eyes for nobody but this young man, and no wonder. That's how fast love can hit you. Five years of Alistair, endless assurances of undying devotion, then all it takes is one bolt from the blue. It occurs to her that maybe Alistair hadn't been so much Julie's boyfriend as her security blanket.

Roger and the journalist, Isabelle, arrive together on the next plane, one tall, lanky and bespectacled, the other short and cheerful, with a perceptive gaze. More introductions, greetings and kisses. Terri downs her coffee, disoriented more by the people she knows, or had thought she knew, than the people and places she doesn't.

Julie claps her hands and takes charge. 'Good, we're all here now. Everyone ready to go?'

She shepherds the party and all its gear out to the car park and a minibus that Stefan, Teo's cousin's bizarrely Swedish husband, has elected to drive for them.

'We meet at last.' Stefan shakes Terri's hand — not altogether approvingly, she senses. 'I am doing the catering and driving, and if you like, my wife, Sonja, will be very happy to look after your hair.'

Terri is so surprised that she laughs aloud, which, fortunately, makes him laugh too.

Isabelle touches her arm. 'I saw you on the London news sorting out that tower block,' she tells her. 'I thought you were *brilliant*.'

'Thanks,' Terri says. 'I've got to be good for something, I guess.'

'Ah, I'm a big fan. You must talk into my tape recorder while we're here.'

'Tape recorder?' echoes Terri. 'I haven't seen one of those for a while.'

'Antiquated, but I trust it. At least the cat can't tread on it and delete my interviews!'

'Sometimes old stuff is the best. Like me,' Teo says. 'Terri, why don't you sit in the front with Stefan?'

Soon Terri is watching Sarajevo spread out around her. She'd seen it often on the news, being shelled and sniped — she was still with Bernard then and she can almost hear his voice making clever, sardonic comments while the screen depicted buildings collapsing and children with horrific injuries. Stefan points out the Holiday Inn, where the foreign reporters had been based during the war. It looks smaller than she'd expected, but distinctly familiar. Now the reality of everything she'd seen on the television finally begins to sink in.

'It's good of you to come all this way,' Julie says to Isabelle, who's on her right, taking in the passing views.

'It's good of you to put on the concert, and it's a wonderful excuse to come here at last,' she replies. 'I've always wanted to see Bosnia.'

'Why's that?' Teo asks.

'I have this theory that damaged and recovering places attract damaged and recovering people,' Isabelle suggests. 'I identify with Bosnia. I lost my parents and my sister within a few years of each other and I have some silly notion that I might have more in common with people here than with a lot of my friends in London.'

'You're right,' says Teo. 'I've become aware of this since I came back. I've found that you have to be very careful who you're dealing with and why they are here. I'm told it's become a haven for organised crime. And beyond that, there are so many ghosts. Perhaps I'm one myself.'

'In that case, I think you're a very benign one,' Isabelle laughs.

Terri lets the others talk as she watches the road curving round the hills. It's getting dark. Once they reach Mostar, Stefan will take them all to Zoran's restaurant, which they've done up and expanded in partnership. Across the valley the mountains' lower slopes are carpeted with trees; at the top, odd exposed limestone under the rising moon gives the false impression of snow.

Teo looks happier and more confident than Terri has ever seen him. Something about this makes her feel hurt, even mortified. She tries to break the ice.

'Did you go back to your house?' she asks.

'There's no house to go back to.'

'The site of it.'

'No.' He says nothing more; awkward, puzzled, she pulls back. Her eyelids are twitching with exhaustion and her empty stomach is making some embarrassing grinding noises. Teo won't talk and she can't eat, so she retreats into a nap.

At some point she becomes aware of Stefan pointing at a dark ribbon at the bottom of the valley. 'The Neretva,' he says. 'We'll be there soon.' Terri nods and dozes off again. When she awakens, she is in Teo's town.

Stefan turns sharp corners on the potholed road. 'So,' he announces, 'first we go eat, then we go sleep. Yes? We are having the best spring lamb for dinner.'

Terri is surprised to find how easy it is just to agree. Nobody is treating her like a diva, for once, and it's refreshing not to be pandered to, not to be treated any differently from anybody else just because she can sing. At one time she might have insisted on a limo to transport her in comfort to Mostar; muddling in on the minibus, though, is more fun. Besides, it had never occurred to her to do anything else.

Stefan pulls up in a makeshift car port outside the restaurant. A powerful whiff of garlic and olive oil turns Terri nearly faint with hunger. She'd been on the point of asking to go straight to her hotel to get some sleep. But a few minutes later, ensconced at a long table with the entire party on a candlelit terrace by the river, she finds she's tucking into some of the tenderest meat she's ever tasted and the local wine, as Teo had always said, is rather good.

She gazes around at her companions. Isabelle has engaged Teo in a detailed conversation about the shortage of musical instruments in Mostar; Freddy and Julie, side by side, are hardly talking, which means there must be a powerful attraction between them; the camera crew drink beer and joke together; Roger, on her left, holds forth about the recitals he's been giving recently with Varya Petrovna.

'Do you rehearse at home with her?' Terri asks. 'Have you ever seen her bathroom?'

Teo, at the other end of the table, is evidently enjoying his chat with the young woman journalist. Something's wrong; the more Terri tussles with what it is, the more she knows it's her fault. What's done can't be undone; but how can she ever begin to put it right, now that she has travelled so far down the track in a different direction? What, in any case, is 'right'?

'Are you tired?' Roger asks her.

'Knackered,' Terri admits. 'But I'll sleep well and be fresh as a daisy tomorrow I'm looking forward to having Sonja do my hair.' Sonja, on Roger's other side, beams at her.

'You will feel tired here,' Teo remarks. Perhaps his radar is still attuned to her voice. 'It's one of the first things I noticed when I came back. Exhaustion gets to you very fast in Bosnia.'

'I can feel that,' Isabelle comments. 'Is it the altitude?'

'No, we're not that high up. It's more that a little energy doesn't go far. It's hard work, being here. There's so much hurt around that you can't help but be affected.'

'I'm tired because I've been travelling all day.' But even as Terri speaks, she wonders whether this is the reason. She's barely seen anything yet; only this restaurant and a few bumpy, hilly streets. Can atmospheres get into your bloodstream that quickly?

'You'll sleep very well. And I'll give you a guided tour tomorrow.' Teo promises, over the last of the wine.

Teo and Julie have booked their team into an Ottoman-style guest house in East Mostar, close to the National Theatre; it's set in a protective courtyard, enclosed by a stone wall covered in luscious creepers. Terri and Julie, who once would have shared a room, are instead at different corners of the landing; Isabelle's room is opposite Terri's and Roger's is downstairs at the back. Freddy occupies an annexe over the breakfast room; Terri wonders whether he'll stay there. Teo, Stefan and Sonja are lodging at Zoran's apartment further out of town.

Terri takes in the tranquil enclave, the scent of some early roses and jasmine, the warm welcome from the proprietor, Hasan Ibrahimović, who immediately brings out one of her CDs for her to sign, then shakes Teo's hand, congratulating him on his award. They leave their shoes in a row on the front step, Turkish style; inside, lovingly carved golden wood seems to calm the atmosphere, lining the ceiling, the staircase and the window casements.

'You see, we should have been enemies,' Teo explains, patting Hasan on the shoulder. 'I'm a Bosnian Serb Orthodox Christian, theoretically, and he's supposed to be a Muslim. We're not meant to get along. We do. Some people think that's a problem.'

'We both want the same thing, Teresa,' says Hasan. 'To support this beautiful event that has brought you to Bosnia to sing for us.'

487

Terri beams. Such words often greet her on the Diva Drag — but this, she knows, is different; something unique and genuine. She doesn't know what the concert will be like, but she senses that it will resemble nothing she's experienced before.

'I'll show you to your room.' Teo picks up her case. Terri lets him, hoping that maybe he wants to talk after all.

★ ★ ★

Teo, who knows his way around the house, unlocks a door to the right of the landing; Terri finds herself in another ornately carved interior, with a divan bed along one wall and, opposite, an antique wardrobe in dark wood, intricately inlaid with mother-of-pearl. 'Thank you, Teo,' she says, smiling, trying to hide how tired and anxious she is.

'My pleasure.' He gives a short, formal bow; he seems about to leave.

'I wanted to show you something,' she adds quickly. She can feel him watching her while she opens her suitcase and takes out her new concert dress.

'Green?'

'Do you like it?' Terri holds it up against her.

'It's nice. Not how we're used to seeing you. What's happened to ivory?'

'I'm getting too old for that. Even brides look silly in white and ivory past a certain age.' Not that this is any time to talk about weddings. She could kick herself.

Low voices reach them from the courtyard garden; Freddy and Julie are sitting on a bench under a trellis of vines, talking. Teo and Terri gaze out at them.

'I hope they can make a better go of things than our generation has,' Terri remarks. 'They've got their whole lives ahead of them. Maybe they'll know better than to screw things up.'

'On that merry note,' Teo grunts, 'I shall let you sleep. I'll meet you tomorrow at ten at the café outside the Hotel Bristol and I'll show you Mostar. You'll be rehearsing in the theatre in the afternoon, and then Stefan will set up some space at the restaurant for you to give your interviews. Will that be all right?'

'Fine, thanks.' Terri's solar plexus stings at the coolness, even indifference, in Teo's voice as he says goodnight. She hears his shoeless steps padding down the wooden stairs — she's relieved that he doesn't stop to say goodnight to Isabelle. Hanging up the green dress, she reflects that she should be pleased for him: he's come home as a national hero. Maybe he could only reach this self-assurance without her? However much he used to think she helped him, perhaps she'd only held him back?

And her? Heading for a come-back? Or alone and all washed up? The concert will be her moment of truth. Trying to forget about the lot, Terri sinks gratefully to sleep.

25

Terri and Julie stand together at the top of the Stari Most, watching a youth clad only in swimming trunks pose on the parapet as if there's no such thing as gravity. His skin is tanned a rich gold; his muscles look as if he spends half of each day in the gym and the other half in the river. Far beneath the peaked bridge, the Neretva flows like torrential liquid jade under the morning sun; coppery light brushes the pine trees on the mountains and glances off white limestone on the Hum.

Terri steps forward and places some change in the swimmers' box, which another boy holds out hopefully towards passers-by. The young man on the wall nods an acknowledgement, then extends his arms towards the sky. He springs — and in the fractured moment it takes for him to curve down and plunge into the water, Terri takes in the bronzed body glinting against the green and gold background and imagines, for a second, a falling angel.

'I'm enchanted with this place,' she thinks aloud. 'I feel as if I've stepped inside Teo's head.'

'I'm not sure that's such a great place to be,' Julie says, grinning.

'You like working for him?'

'Oh, he's basically impossible. But he's like family, so it doesn't matter. He expects me to make order out of chaos, but when I do, he grumbles that he can't find anything. I'm getting used to it.'

The swimmer has surged against the powerful current to the riverbank and is drying himself down; soon he'll be back to repeat the performance. Terri and Julie wave — he doesn't wave back — then turn towards the centre of town where they've arranged to meet Teo. They wander past what used to be Mostar's grandest hotel, but is now a bombed-out shell in terracotta stone. Perhaps, Terri reflects, the town is much like Teo himself: a mingling of past tragedies with a certain confusion over the future. She notices a buzz of reconstruction, cranes and cement mixers, targeted in spots calculated for maximum tourist appeal; but elsewhere the once-grand architecture lies wrecked, some of the ruins bearing Warning notices, others plastered with billboards displaying giant images of the latest sports car, a new variety of chocolate biscuit or skinny girls pouting over purple lace underwear. Not far from the bridge, a beautiful young Roma woman in a colourful robe, carrying a baby, approaches them pleading in broken English for money. The child, about a year old, is so cute that Terri reaches into her purse and donates. It's not much; it may help.

'I guess that's all any of us can do,' she remarks to her daughter as they wander on.

'What?' Julie, lost in a daydream, isn't listening.

'Help a little. When you're faced with destruction on this scale, it's hard to think of anything to do that can really help. What we can do is sing. And draw some attention to it. Now, you know that bit in the Mozart . . . '

★ ★ ★

They're sitting over coffee in the open air when they smell Teo's tobacco. Terri battens down the hatches as he approaches; the rush of emotion is stronger than she expected. She has never encountered Teo before in a place where he thinks he belongs. To London, Paris, Bruges, he was a stranger, however celebrated; the more people assured him he was part of the cosmopolitan life of a city, and was respected there and loved, the more alien he'd seemed to feel.

Watching his badger-haired head and his dark eyes surveying what remains of his town, a gentle understanding curls, blanket-like, around Terri. Here he's part of the place, just one more person — yet his traumas symbolise everyone's. She reaches out a hand to him. He takes it briefly and squeezes; he won't look at her. The old current is still there. With a stab of anxiety, she wonders whether he feels it too, or if he's become immune.

'Let's walk,' he suggests.

Soon they're strolling down a busy street away from the old town; on its other side, the city looks wholly different. 'West Mostar,' says Teo. 'The Catholic side, the Croatian area. They've done a lot more rebuilding there.'

'And this road? I get the feeling that crossing

492

this road is not something you want to do,' Terri remarks.

'Welcome to the Bulevar Revolucije. It was the front line in the war. My mother-in-law ran across it one time. A bullet singed the back of her hand.'

Terri takes in the paving stones, the trees bending under the wind off the river, the cars trundling over the tarmac. She tries to imagine the gunfire. Signs of destruction linger all around.

'Look.' Julie pauses to stare at a ruin of carved flesh-coloured stone, set back from the road beyond a patch of long grass and dandelions. 'That must have been the most astonishing building.'

'It was,' says Teo. 'Julie, no.' He holds her arm. 'Don't go on the grass, it could be mined. It'll be decades, maybe centuries, before this place is safe again.'

'And yet people think Bosnia is 'all right',' Terri says. 'It isn't, is it?'

'Of course not. That's why you're here. Isabelle's been talking about that very hard already. That will be the centre of her article: that people have short memories. A place is bombed to bits, then they move on to bomb another and leave everyone trying to pick up the pieces, although they're too shattered to think straight. And the tragedy is that if it's forgotten, if it is not put back together, the whole thing could happen here all over again.'

'So how *do* you put it back together?' Julie asks.

'Piece by piece. Brick by brick, one at a time. You can't do it overnight. God may have been able to create a world in seven days, but given the ineptitude of human beings who were fashioned in His image, it's more likely that it took him several million years.'

Julie's mobile rings and Terri sees her face illuminate as she reads its screen. '*Salut,* Freddy!' She drops behind to talk.

'And Alistair?' Teo asks Terri, glancing backwards.

Terri says nothing. The ghost of her night with Alistair hangs like a sword of Damocles over her head; luckily, nobody else can see it.

'He's practising, he'll meet us at lunch.' Julie rings off.

'So, are you and Freddy . . . ?' asks Terri.

'We're just good friends.'

'Stuff and nonsense!' Teo adopts his best P.G. Wodehouse English. 'You spend every spare moment with that boy.'

Julie turns pink. 'We're fond of each other. I mean, he's lovely. But I worry about Alistair and what he's going to say . . . '

Terri closes her eyes for a moment. Her daughter is in palpable denial. 'When did you last see him?'

'When he came to college.'

'Julie, that's months ago.'

'But I can't just abandon him!'

'Do you talk often?' Teo asks.

'No. He doesn't seem to want to talk to me. I email him. Sometimes he writes back.'

'And what does he say?' asks Terri.

'Not much.'
Terri and Teo exchange glances.

★ ★ ★

On the stage of the theatre, Terri faces her daughter amid surroundings of concrete, wood and brown brick. Roger is at the piano, a reassuring figure smiling at them through his glasses. 'Mozart first?' he suggests.

But for their run-through after breakfast, this is the first time that the two of them have sung together outside their home. In the duet from *Figaro*, Terri, as the Countess, is dictating a love-letter to her maid, Susanna; Julie, with her higher, lighter voice, echoes her phrases, reading back the *canzonetta* as she writes it down. The acoustic flatters them; the theatre is a pleasant surprise, neither too large nor too 'dry'. Julie's voice sounds purer and finer than Terri had anticipated; singing at college has clearly done her good. There's a core to it now, a silvery quality that responds naturally and gracefully to the music's nuances — Julie is turning from a girl who can sing into a woman with a talent. At the end, Terri realises she's been so busy assessing Julie's voice that she'd completely forgotten to worry about her own.

'You sound fantastic, darling.' She embraces Julie.

'So do you!' Julie hugs her back, glowing. Her face is alight, full of music and hope. 'Mum, this feels good. I was so scared, I didn't think it would, but it does.'

The Viardot 'Havanaise' is less simple, though — full of rapidly twirling lines that they have to sing together, it soon has them practising slowly, bar by bar, until their initial exhilaration has virtually evaporated. They can't afford to relax just yet.

Freddy is in the stalls, listening, violin case beside him. Terri sees the theatre lights catching and silvering his lavish curls. He's someone in whom all the dots join up. While the rest of them, to one degree or another, are missing connections and prone to blind spots, Freddy's synapses are simply where they should be; he has consistency and direction, and he lacks self-conscious insecurity. How on earth, faced with this adorable, intelligent and clearly devoted boy, can Julie think she must hang on to Alistair, guilt or none?

If Julie knew that Alistair had declared himself in love with another woman, she'd be upset; but also she'd be free to start the relationship with Freddy that she obviously longs for. But if she knew that that woman was her mother . . .

'Terri?' Freddy waves from the stalls. 'You want to try 'Les étoiles'?'

Terri has been eyeing this song for years. It's one of Viardot's best, the voice and the violin mirroring each other while the words, by the Russian poet Afanasi Fet, carry them up through the transformative effect of the heavens at night. Freddy plays the introduction with Roger; and Terri hears the melody she loves ringing live at last out of his violin. It's always been present in her mind; in his hands, it becomes real for the first time.

That's why Julie could be happy with this boy. And the fact that he's pitched up with a violin piece based on Turgenev's 'The Song of Triumphant Love' is too much of a coincidence to be a coincidence. Terri senses symbols and pointers — but frustratingly, Julie has to see them too. If she could bring Julie and Freddy together, would that offset her guilt over Alistair? Or would she just be a meddling mum who'd only make things worse?

'It's so beautiful!' Freddy enthuses. 'Let's start again.'

Terri peers past the stage lights into the auditorium; Teo is lurking near the door at the back of the stalls. She can only see his outline, the curve of his shoulders, the faint slouch that creeps into his stance when he's not in public-figure mode, and the gleam of a black iris in the shadow. Then her mouth turns dry and she reaches for her chair and the bottle of water beside it.

Another awareness has begun to crawl across her as a flood might fill a room, rising inexorably inch by inch. She can climb on to the furniture to escape it, but it will overcome her eventually: for now, of all times, she understands with certainty that she loves Teo, loves him entirely and without doubt, and she's lost him.

Here, in his home, it's as if she's seeing him for the first time. Is it because the balance has changed? Because his dependence on her has passed? Because she'd taken him for granted? Or because Alistair has turned her upside down and shaken her enough to reset all her perspectives? She'd thought he might have broken her feelings for Teo; instead, the sickening chill of nerve endings expanding and contracting beneath her skin tells her that they're stronger than ever.

How can one night, one unintended, unthinking encounter that lasted only a few hours, come so close to wrecking so much?

She forces herself to concentrate; her voice is working so well that it seems insignificant compared to the chaos inside her head. Teo has freed himself. Maybe he's met someone else. And if he ever finds out about Alistair, he'll despise her every bit as much as Julie would. She seems to do nothing except make mistake after mistake. The stronger the love, the more vulnerable you become, she reflects. Perhaps this is how you discover which knot will hold best under strain. But, God, the pain when they give way.

Drifting from rehearsal to lunch and back again, Terri tries to shield her mind from the assault of excess feeling. The rest of the afternoon must be devoted to hard work. A runthrough for the lighting crew, a few passages to tidy up with Roger, another few with Freddy. Two interviews with local press, two with international, from Paris and Milan — Isabelle's will wait until the next day. These prove a welcome distraction. Terri, facing the journalists, drinks so much coffee that her hands shake. She tries to say the right thing. She talks about war and recovery, healing and music, love and hope, and the interviewers lap it up.

When she finally leaves her corner at the restaurant, stretching limbs stiff from sitting for too long, she spots Julie waiting for her at another table, looking as intensely worried as Terri is herself.

'I just spoke to Sue,' Julie begins. 'She says Alistair's coming home tomorrow.'

Terri stalls. Her caffeine-laden innards are still threatening palpitations. 'Yes . . . ' she ventures.

'She says he doesn't want to see me.'

'You haven't seen him in a long time,' Terri points out softly.

'But I don't understand. I think I should go back and try to sort it out. You see, if I get a plane first thing in the morning . . . '

'What?' This is worse than Terri had expected. 'Julie, *no*.'

Julie is so startled that she doesn't reply.

'You can't do that.'

Julie has become very good at leaving a place in the hope of finding something better in another — even if she occasionally does the opposite with people. It's time to tell her some home truths about both.

'This weekend, my angel,' Terri begins, 'you aren't just a student or a PA: you are a professional singer. That means that you've been engaged to do a job, and you must do it. People are depending on you.'

'But Alistair depends on me more than anyone else!'

'No, Julie, he doesn't — you just want him to.

499

You're not hearing the reality. He's said he doesn't want to see you. That sounds fairly definite to me.'

'I don't believe it. It can't be true!' Julie's cheekbones are carmine.

'Julie, listen. You're not leaving this town until we've done the concert. Is that clear?'

'You could do it without me.'

'I can't and I won't. Alistair will be in exactly the same place when we go back on Monday. For Mostar and us, this is a big weekend. For him, it's just two more days. Look, you can't keep running away. You have to wake up, face up and move on. And that means singing tomorrow, with me, onstage. End of story.'

'I feel so lost. I don't know why I can't help him.'

'Sweetheart.' Terri takes her hand. 'I've felt like that about Teo for over twelve years. I know it's hard, but the choice isn't only yours: it's his as well. You're asking for trouble if you try to hang on to a man who doesn't want you to — even if he *is* injured and traumatised. You're not twenty yet. You could be missing out.'

'You mean . . . ?'

'Your lovely violinist.'

'He's not mine.'

'He'd like to be.'

Julie hesitates. 'Do you think Sue's telling me the truth?'

'Sue always tells the truth — that's why I like her. I've met a lot of people in the music business who don't. Darling, seriously: you have to let go when something has run its natural course.' Terri loathes the platitudinous sound of her own voice, so self-consciously soothing, so deliberately wise — when underneath she's wondering how to hang on to any shred of Teo that's left for her.

Zoran brings over a clay carafe of white wine and pours them two glasses. Terri pounces gratefully on hers, while Julie stares across to the mountains, biting her lip. Nearby, another restaurant pipes out folk music, a motor-scooter putters up a hill, a few drunk tourists caterwaul, and underlying everything the whirling whisper of the river continues.

'Can I ask you something, Mum?' says Julie.

'Of course. Anything.'

'Am I a millstone dragging around your throat?'

The sentence thumps into Terri like a rugby ball. '*What?*'

'Because I wondered if it seemed, like, when I was little, that . . . '

'Julie, why did you use that word? Millstone?'

'Mum, when you were in hospital . . . I found your diary.' Julie stares down into her wineglass. She can't look Terri in the eye.

Terri scrolls frantically through what she recalls — which is not much — of the diary she'd kept when Julie was six years old, just after she and Teo had got together. 'Oh, Jesu Maria.'

'I know I shouldn't have read it.'

'But you did. And?'

'I started thinking you weren't the person I thought you were.'

'Do you know how long ago I wrote that diary?'

'I sort of worked it out roughly, but . . . '

Terri jumps to her feet and begins to pace around. 'Julie, nothing is easy. Nobody said it was meant to be. It's bloody tough to combine a career and being a mum and it gets to all of us from time to time. But that doesn't mean I don't love you! Can't you see that?'

'It still felt horrible.'

Terri wonders how to put into words the difference between the state of being a child, when things are true or false and last for ever, and the state beyond, where nothing exists except endlessly mutable shades of silver, 'I know it hurts the first time you understand that your parents are fallible,' she suggests. 'But don't you *know* that I could never not love you?'

'Did you really feel that way, though? Back then?' Julie is a little girl again as she speaks; she may be nearly twenty, stylish and self-assured on the outside — but now she seems so childlike that Terri's heart crumbles.

'Yes,' she says quietly. 'I did, on that one particular day. But that was then. It was one moment in our lives, and only one. I wrote it down to get it off my chest. Don't tell me you've been stewing over this ever since my operation?'

Julie's silence tells her all she needs to know.

Terri leans towards her. At one time, she might have let rip about how ridiculous this was — that to take as gospel one sentence written in haste and exasperation thirteen years ago makes no sense. But Terri does nothing of the kind. What's at stake is her closeness to her daughter, and she's recently come to appreciate its full extent. That's what matters. Besides, she has learned a new skill: how to apologise.

'Julie, it wasn't meant for your eyes,' she begins. 'I'm sorry you saw it. One day, when you too are stressed out with juggling a young family and a career, maybe you'll understand. But for now, you've got to know that it's not the half of my feelings for you. I'll love you until the day I die, and beyond. You're the most precious thing in my life and you always have been. Please will you forgive me?'

Julie throws her arms around Terri and bursts into tears. Terri kisses her cheek and strokes her hair. This girl is not her best friend; she's her daughter. However much she's tried to pretend that it need be no different, it is, and it always will be. She has to lock away that night with Alistair; only its concealment can let her be close to Julie again. She will have to trust Sue, and Alistair himself, to keep the secret for her.

There's a quiet cough beside them; inter-locked, they glance up. Freddy is standing there, smiling as he usually does and looking vaguely embarrassed.

'Freddy, darling, come and join us.' Terri switches on her smile, forming a silent prayer that Julie can follow this relationship through; then maybe she'll have done some good.

Freddy begins to talk about his explorations, post-rehearsal, in the old town. 'I bought you a present,' he says to Julie, bringing out a small tissue-paper package. Julie's face lights up: inside there's a pair of beaten copper earrings that suit her to perfection. Under the vines, the evening is turning muggy; humidity seeps out of the Neretva as if the air itself is thirsty. Terri's head thumps. Perhaps it's just the effect of the wine on what — incredibly, after Zoran's lunch — must have been an empty stomach. She wanders away to leave the youngsters alone together. Sometime this evening, she must speak to Teo in private.

But when he arrives for dinner with the rest of the party — which now includes Irina, Sergei, Vaslav, a crew from *Newsnight* and a representative of the *Corriere della Sera* from Milan — it's clear there'll be no chance to talk to him for some time, if at all.

The dinner passes in a stupor of promises, gratitude and an apparently limitless parade of food. Isabelle is ensconced with Teo at the wrong end of the table, interviewing him over her whirring old tape recorder. Terri, stuck beside Sergei, spends most of the main course insisting to him that her voice really will be fine this time, honest to goodness. Exhaustion washes over her in a torrent like the Neretva.

She watches Teo talking to Isabelle. The journalist is wearing a wedding ring, but that's no guarantee that she wouldn't fancy seducing the occasional willing interviewee. She's an intelligent girl, dark, slim and intuitive; Teo clearly responds to that, as well as to her sensible questions. She wants to see the music therapy centre and meet the directors of the charity — something that Terri realises, with shame, hadn't occurred to her, so busy has she been preparing for her performance. It's nearly eleven thirty and she must sleep; the big day begins in just half an hour. She tries to resign herself to the inevitable: what's the point of being Queen Canute, trying to command the tides? She'd had her chance. She is where she is as the sum total of her own decisions, made over years and decades; if she doesn't like it, she has nobody to blame but herself.

She's about to make her excuses and leave when a group of young people crowd out on the terrace in an explosion of colour and noise; they're about to gather around the next table when one of them spots Teo. There's a surge of delighted greetings. One boy is carrying a guitar case.

Teo catches Terri's eye and beckons her over: 'I want you to meet some friends.' These youngsters, he explains, are all local musicians — three of them play in the town's small orchestra, and several others are students and budding professionals who love to sing folk music. All of them will be at the concert tomorrow. She sees joy in their faces as they recognise her. She calls Julie and Freddy to meet them.

'What is it like, the folk music here?' Freddy asks, with his most charming French accent. 'I have not been lucky enough to hear it.'

'What's it like?' The boy with the guitar at once flips his case open. 'We show you!' The others need no further bidding. The guitarist ready, the group lean towards one another over the table and a second later the whole terrace is bright and rich with their singing. Terri half expects Zoran to shut them up. Instead, he and Stefan stroll out of the kitchen to join in.

A minute later Terri, too, is lost. This is some of the most haunting music she's ever heard. The melody aches, the rhythms are intricate and irregular yet hypnotic, the harmonies as scrunchy as anything ever penned by Puccini. The young musicians sing together almost as a choir, in harmony rather than unison — they know this song as well as a gathering in Liverpool would know the Beatles. The music's atmosphere penetrates the spirit of every listener, as humid as the Mostar air and as full of troubling wonder.

Freddy dives into a corner with his violin case and tunes up the instrument; Julie stands beside him while he tries to play along in the third chorus, by which time the melody is growing familiar. 'It's in *seven?*' he asks the guitarist, who nods without missing a beat. Terri hears Julie's voice blending with the others, the violin and guitar — wordless, of course, but all that matters is her willingness to be part of it.

There's a cheer when the song is over; Freddy and Julie are hugged and kissed, and the young Bosnians pull over chairs for them, Irina and Vaslav. Terri wonders whether a new security crisis has demanded the Lithuanian's limpetlike presence at Irina's side — but as she watches, Vaslav manhandles Irina towards him, wraps her in a sacklike embrace and plants a long kiss full on her lips. Julie begins to laugh and can't stop. Terri looks on, puzzled, while Julie mouths 'Well?' — at her friend, and Irina, grinning from the depths of the body-guard's arms, holds up a thumb to the sky.

It's clear nobody intends to stop singing anytime soon. The *Newsnight* crew confers, then dashes off to fetch its equipment. Isabelle, fascinated by the music, wanders across to join the singers, so Terri slips over the terrace to take her chair beside Teo.

'*Sevdah*,' says Teo, by way of explanation. 'I wrote about it in the book.'

'I haven't got that far yet,' Terri admits. 'It hurts too much.'

'Never mind.' Teo shrugs. 'The music speaks more than the words. This is the folk music of what used to be Yugoslavia — it's the one thing that unites the Balkans. We have *sevdah* all the way from next to Italy almost down to Turkey, and you can hear the influences — the Gypsy style from Hungary, Sephardi music from Spain, the rhythms of Turkey, the flowing melody of Italy and Austria. And those wailing effects are middle-eastern, like the Muslim call to prayer and Arabic music from north Africa.'

'What are the words about?'

'The usual. Love. Loss. Life.'

'Songs of triumphant love?' Terri suggests.

Teo closes his eyes while the singing pulses through the night. 'When I hear these sounds,' he says, 'I know I'm home.'

'And your songs?' The guitarist, beaming at Julie and Freddy, invites them to contribute. 'This is *sevdah*, our music, but now let's sing something from Britain or France.'

Julie and Freddy exchange looks, hesitating. Terri understands: the pair of them scarcely know any folksongs at all. Tunes, perhaps, but not words. She jumps to her feet.

'I can sing you a Celtic song from Scotland if you like,' she declares, picking her way around the table edges towards them.

'Mum!' Julie cries. 'Sing to us!'

Silence falls as suddenly as the sounds had begun. Terri sees Teo following her every move, her daughter glowing with pride just as she used to before this mangle of a year had tried to grind up their relationship, and the eager, expectant faces of the young Bosnian musicians gathering close around her. She closes her eyes and, very softly, begins to sing the 'Eriskay Love Lilt' that she had sung to Mary, all those years ago.

> *Vair me oro van o*
> *Vair me oro van ee*
> *Vair me oru o ho*
> *Sad am I without thee.*

At the end of the stanza she casts a gaze in Teo's direction, under half-opened eyelids. This song is for him. And the Bosnian guitarist, listening to the melody and the mood, lets his fingers brush over his strings until he finds the harmonies; gently, he begins to pluck out an accompaniment.

> *. . . By love's light my foot finds*
> *The old pathway to thee.*

At the end there's silence while the magic hangs in the air, savoured by the whole gathering; as it dispels, the young people begin to clamour for more. Terri smiles and shakes her head. 'Not now,' she laughs. 'It's your turn. More *sevdah!*' And she leans over her new friend's shoulder and twangs his guitar strings before making her way back to Teo, whose handkerchief has changed position since she began the song and whose eyes look more moist than before in the candlelight.

The guitarist whispers instructions to Freddy, who experiments, plucks, bows something then nods, ready; and soon the musicians are back in their element, blending together through the shared, compulsive rhythms and melodies. Terri, slumping into her chair, takes a long swig of wine. Teo lifts her hand and kisses the back of it. 'A beautiful song,' he says. 'Old for you, but new to me.'

She nods, silent. Here, where she feels she's wiping clean the palette of her life in the green Neretva, it would only take one gesture to change everything for herself and Teo. She could say 'I must go and sleep; it's the concert tomorrow.' Any sensible singer would do that. Yet instead, she could let him know how she feels, with one touch, one instant, across the scant six inches between their hands. It would be so easy — if she dared. A tiny gesture carrying an outsized admission; the abandonment of all remaining pride. Accepting her love for Teo, and admitting it aloud, should be no big deal compared to her throat operation — yet it feels far more daunting, with much more waiting to be won or lost, healed or destroyed. Minute after minute passes, but Terri and Teo sit motionless amid the music, side by side, listening without speaking.

The *Newsnight* team come back, clattering about inside the restaurant as they organise cameras and microphones. In a moment they'll flood the candlelit terrace and the golden light over the river with fierce TV illumination; the mood will break and it will be too late. Perhaps it already is. She's worn out, she might say the wrong thing. If that happens, with the concert tomorrow, it could mean calamity. She should go to bed. There might be another chance in the morning.

On the other hand, there might not.

'Teo,' says Terri.

She puts one palm flat against his sleeve and strokes it slowly, feeling the smallest ridges in the cloth through her fingertips. She stares at some breadcrumbs that dot the tablecloth, the chewed olive stones in their terracotta dish, a platter of abandoned fish bones. Scarcely able to look up, she knows he's turning towards her; after a protracted moment in which nothing is focused except the guitar and the song, she begins to sense, via his wrist alone, something coursing through him that might be gentleness, might be wonderment.

A flood of *sevdah* echoes in her ears; the once familiar warmth of Teo's arm encircling her sends sine waves of joy through her body. She lets her head lean on his shoulder, as she rarely has before, and feels the touch of his lips on her hairline.

'Are you sure, Terri?'

'Yes.'

'Kiss me, then.'

Terri turns herself upwards, and does. 'Welcome home,' she whispers.

'You have to mean it this time. There'll be no going back, not again.'

'I love you, Teo.'

'I've waited a long time to hear you say that. Say it once more and maybe I'll believe you.'

She fights a moment of humiliation and lets it melt into humility — same root, different effect. 'Yes. I love you.'

'I love you too. Stay with me.'

'Yes. Yes, please.'

A moment later the camera lights are on, dazzling everyone, and the *Newsnight* team is filming the singers, the floodlit river and the bridge behind them. 'Come along,' Teo mutters through the jubilant volume. 'Let's get out of here.'

* * *

It rains in the night, long and hard. Terri stirs herself sometime in the small hours to close the window. The air is clearing when she glances out at the courtyard, scented with jasmine under the scudding clouds. Teo is fast asleep behind her; she moves softly so as not to wake him. She doesn't want to break the spell. Perhaps when they go home — or when she does, since Teo *is* home — they'll fall into their old rut; but perhaps they won't, if they've both grown enough to move beyond it. She doesn't know. It's a risk she'll have to take. So, too, is Alistair; all she can do is recognise that one day the story may come out, try not to let it, but hope that if it does, it will be long ago enough not to matter so much any more.

Terri pauses. In the courtyard below, at the table under the canopy of vines, two figures are ensconced on the bench. A slanting ray from a lamp in the downstairs window illuminates the curve of Julie's cheekbone and the dark half-moon of her eyelashes. The vine leaves shelter them from the dissipating rain. As Terri watches, Freddy reaches towards Julie's hand and picks it up gently. He kisses her fingertips one by one. Terri wonders how long they've been there. The *sevdah* had sounded as if it would go on for hours, as Teo told her it would while they sloped away. She has no idea whether it's closer to midnight or to morning; tonight, they're all in a dimension beyond that.

Softly, Freddy tips Julie's face towards him and kisses her. And Terri wonders whether there's such a difference between the shock of wonder that she's witnessing in them, discovering it and each other for the first time, and what's just passed between her and Teo after thirteen years together, on and off. Terri has always believed that there's an infinite number of ways to feel and give love. But real love, pure love, when you're lucky enough to find it, is usually the same.

When they go home, she'll burn the diary. She'll burn every other diary she has ever kept, too — most of them are hidden under the bed that had once been her mother's. If her voice comes back to its former strength, she will be grateful for ever; if not, she will cope as best she can, and better, because she will no longer be alone. As for her Viardot and Turgenev project, if she finds someone to 'action' the film and launch her into a new career as TV presenter, she will be grateful too; if not, she might consider spending some time here in Bosnia, teaching people how to sing, helping them to find their voices. On balance, she might do that anyway. To the east, the first streaks of dawn are brightening in the sky.

26

Terri and Teo go down to breakfast together, to the considerable amusement of Hasan, who stacks extra bread, cheese and jam in front of them with two large pots of *razgalica* and a knowing remark about coffee being good for energy levels. There's no sign of the other guests. 'Either they have already gone out,' Hasan explains, 'or they don't want to get up! Isabelle took her camera for a walk, and your daughter and her friend only came home at four, so we may not see them for a while.'

'We're all very silly,' Terri beams. 'It's our concert tonight. We should have been resting, not partying.'

'We met some of the music students,' Teo explains, 'and they started to sing . . . '

Hasan nods; he's seen it all before. 'More coffee?'

'Yes, please!' Terri and Teo chorus.

'OK, I make coffee, then I must prepare the last room for the other lady who is arriving today. I think she comes for your concert. She is maybe another journalist. Your press attachée has done a very fine job.' He points at the day's newspapers, which are plastered with photographs of Terri.

Terri hasn't stopped smiling since she woke up. She and Teo clink their coffee cups together and sit quietly for a while, relishing the morning scents and the rapidly intensifying sunshine.

'Darling,' Teo begins, filling his pipe, 'there's something I'd like to do this morning. It won't take long, but it's not going to be fun. Will you come with me?'

'Anywhere,' says Terri.

★ ★ ★

They have one hour before the final rehearsal. Terri bangs on Julie's door to wake her; when there's no reply, she bangs on Freddy's in the annexe instead. Two sleepy voices reply that yes, they will be there on time.

Teo and Terri, hand in hand, wander out of the courtyard into the busy market street of East Mostar, where Teo stops to buy flowers from a stall: an armful of white blossom, clinging to its branches, cherry and white lilac. He knows the florist and engages her in a long chat. Her features are deeply wrinkled under her headscarf and she walks with a slight limp.

'We used to buy flowers from her in the old days,' Teo tells Terri. 'She's only my age.'

Terri understands. This woman will have lost her loved ones — a husband, maybe children; goodness knows what she, a Bosniak Muslim, experienced here in the 1990s. After everything, she is back at her stall, selling flowers. 'What else could she do?' Teo remarks. 'She's wonderful. A very wise person.' He smiles. 'She was saying how lovely you are.'

'Let's walk,' Terri says. 'Is it far?'

'No, but it's uphill. Are your shoes comfortable?'

'Fine.' Terri takes the blossoms and follows him.

Away from the main roads, the mountain track grows steeper as they climb, stony and slippery after the night's rain; the air is laden with the aromas of damp earth and grass.

'I used to run up here when I was a kid,' Teo remarks. Terri fills in the missing information: Teo's children used to run up here too.

They round several hairpin bends; looking back, Terri sees Mostar in the valley, the river an enchanted serpent with the rebuilt bridge a golden triangular scale on its back.

'Don't go off the road,' Teo reminds her, glancing over his shoulder. Terri, trailing behind, is ashamed to be out of puff.

The last two minutes pass in silence. Then she sees something, half hidden by the rampant greenery that's claimed back this territory: the burned-out shell of a house. Teo slows down, then stops.

Nothing remains of the windows; only fragments of the walls, grey stone, streaked with carbon where the flame fingers had left their prints. Plants — ivy, bindweed, sycamore and a crab apple tree — have encroached on every corner of what used to be Teo and Mila's kitchen, where they fed the children and relaxed on winter evenings after work. And where Teo had done likewise as a child, with his parents and siblings; and his father before him.

Teo stands lost in thought, his face betraying little.

'Is there as much here as you expected?' Terri asks, tentative.

'I didn't expect anything. But that's it. My house. Except, it isn't. The spirit's gone. Houses have spirits, Terri, and sometimes they die too.'

'Where shall we put these?' Terri's arms are full of Teo's flowers.

'Wherever you like. I don't know where their graves are.'

There's another long moment of silence. Terri can hear a cuckoo calling, deep in the woods. She goes forward to the spot that had once held a garden gate and places the branches of blossom on the grass.

'Tell me?' she ventures.

He points up the hill. 'They used to roll burning tyres down here to attack the town. But sometimes there were people with guns behind the tyres. You know what they were trying to do, don't you? It was absolute ethnic cleansing, the invention of it. They were chasing people out of the land they wanted to take. Here, it was the Bosnian Croats trying to get rid of the Bosnian Serbs and shift the Muslims they couldn't kill from West Mostar to East. Everyone has a story. Take my florist friend; she came from a village where the men were all massacred. Take Hasan; he lost three-quarters of his family, he was put in the concentration camp they made on the heliodrome, and he's lucky to be alive. And . . . .' Teo trails off, staring towards the top of the Hum, where the giant cross looms against the sky, claiming the ground in full knowledge of its own cruelty.

'Were you here?' Terri presses.

'I came home.'

'And found this.'

'I can see it all as if it were yesterday. But it's very strange: time passes, things move on whether you like it or not. There's nothing here. This is only soulless stuff. I thought I'd be devastated, coming back. But it is simply — not the same.'

Terri finds a rock at the roadside and sits on it. 'I never told you this,' she begins, 'but I also lost two children. Actually, I didn't lose them. I aborted them.'

'How old were you?'

'Sixteen. Then eighteen. I was too young and I had a frightful boyfriend. I left him after he beat me up. I never told you about that either, did I?'

'No, you didn't. In thirteen years. But I don't blame you, either for keeping quiet or for doing what you did under those circumstances.'

'I'm glad I have Julie.'

'She's a gem. Treasure her.' Teo puts an arm around Terri. 'Marry me, and we'll pretend she's my daughter too. I'll adopt her.'

'We can pretend just as we are,' Terri suggests.

'No, this time we get married. I'm not letting you go again.'

'We're standing here, in front of your house, and you can still say that . . . ' Terri, hand against her throat, gazes at the wreckage of Teo's home.

'If they'd come an hour later, I'd have been in there,' he confirms. 'And for fourteen of the last fifteen years, I regretted that I wasn't.'

'Your burns . . . '

'The burns,' says Teo, 'are the least of it.'

Terri feels a twang of anxiety as Teo turns his black eyes towards her and fixes her gaze. 'There's something else?' she divines.

'There is. Something I've never told you, or anyone else. I want to tell you now. It's not in the book. It makes nonsense of my book, my prize, everything. And if you still want to marry me after that — well, we'll see.'

'Teo, I don't mind if you don't tell me,' Terri says, shivering despite herself. 'There are some things that should never be told.'

'You don't want to know?'

'I do. But it's up to you.'

'Then listen.'

★ ★ ★

'I said in the book,' Teo begins, 'that I came home from teaching school to find the house burning. It's true that I came home and found this. But it wasn't from school. It was summer 1993, Mostar was under siege and I was in the fighting, like everyone else. I was a healthy man in my late thirties, so of course I was conscripted and put on the front line. There was no choice — these thugs would come round and grab you if you hadn't joined up, and force you to. So I'd fight twenty-four hours, go home and sleep, then go back. That's just how it was, that's what we did. And every time I came back I was dreading it.

'One time I found Mila's mother sitting in our kitchen, with a plaster on one hand. She wasn't a

Catholic, Terri, she was a Muslim. Mila's family were Bosniaks, but her mother happened to live on the west side. They evicted her from her apartment and sent her to the east. They forced the Muslim citizens of West Mostar to run to East Mostar across the front line — that road I showed you — with bullets flying all around, and those who made it must have had some blessed charm about them. She'd run, Mila's mother, she'd gone in her long skirts carrying nothing, she just picked them up and ran and ran. Mila put a plaster on her hand because she had one graze from where a bullet had crossed her skin. It was a kind of miracle. A single sticking plaster.

'I was out there with my gun, Terri, I had a gun just like Alistair has one. I was fighting to save my family and my friends and my city. And some people thought I was on the wrong side because I'm a Serb, while others thought I was on the wrong side because I married a Muslim. And still more thought my Muslim wife and her family were on the wrong side because she married a Serb. You see how fucking stupid it all is?'

Terri takes his hand and waits, feeling his pulse thumping in his veins.

He stares at the ruins of his garden wall, his eyes unfathomable. 'When you're shooting,' he goes on, 'you don't always know where the bullets go. People fall, you don't know if you shot them or someone else did. They travel a long way, these bullets. The ones that came down from the hills and hit the buildings may have flown a mile, maybe more. You pull the trigger and it goes and you don't know what's happened. It's not chaos, Terri; it's worse. And then I came back, and I saw the house beginning to burn, and the soldiers wandering out, laughing, buttoning up . . . '

'No,' says Terri.

'I knew that inside I would find my wife, my mother-in-law and my daughter, dead. Raped, shot, then burned, how else can I put it? And my son with them.'

Terri puts her arms around his waist and holds on to him — as if it would make any difference.

'Terri, I had my gun and a few bullets left. I went crazy. I killed them, face to face, and watched them die, and relished it. And, Terri, they were people too. They had families, I'm sure. I don't know why they did what they did. They became machines in war, not able to think or feel. They behaved like machines, so I treated them accordingly. But, my dear, I'm still a murderer. Because of me, there are children somewhere in Croatia who grew up without their fathers.

'There are lots of us in the Balkans. There are commanders, people who ordered the building of concentration camps, people who blew up homes, bridges and airports, walking around here free as air. Some of them are still running the damn place. I'm not the worst; I did what I did for love. But if you marry me, you're taking on a killer.'

Terri feels peculiarly calm, as if she'd known it all along. 'What did you do afterwards?'

'I went in to see if there was any hope . . . The

521

smoke got to me pretty fast.' He points to one side of the garden, where apple trees are in bloom; it used to be an orchard. 'I managed to stumble out as far as there, then I lost consciousness. I might have died, but one of my neighbours found me on his way home. He could see what had happened, but he spotted that I wasn't dead and he just picked me up, God knows how — he slung me over his shoulders and carried me to his place. He saved my life. When I woke up, I could have killed him for it.'

Terri gazes into the undergrowth at the scattered stones that had fallen from the walls. 'And now?'

He shrugs. 'It's so strange. In my mind, it was all still alive, burning, until today. I'm almost glad to find it is dead. It's finished. It's entirely finished. I can see that now.'

'And when you take the métro . . . ' Terri, who never cries, is in tears.

'Everything's a whitewash, Terri. The book is pretence. A way of denying what I did, not confirming it, do you see? I'm a sham, and however much I try to move on, this is me, this is who I am, where I come from and what I did. Do you still love me, now?'

Terri takes both his hands, her mind seething with questions, but not ones that she wants to ask him. Questions about whether you can ever know another person thoroughly; how far you can trust yourself, someone else and the love between you; how the revelation of one misguided night spent with the wrong person might destroy more trust than the confession of a wartime murder can; how much of it is a gamble.

Maybe it's all a leap of faith. If you never leap, you never reach the next level. Terri thinks of the young man on the Stari Most, plunging into the Neretva. When has she ever shirked a challenge? She is Terri Ivory, and if there is an extra mile to go, Terri Ivory sets off at once, flying the flags. This may be the longest extra mile of her life.

'I don't know what our future could hold,' she says. 'I don't know whether it's the right thing for either of us, but I do know that I've been an idiot, that I love you and that I will accept you as you are, no matter what happens next. Will you forgive me?'

'Forgive you? What for?'

In the ruins of his garden, Teo kisses Terri for a long time through her tears. Then, with one last glance at the blossom in the grass, they turn away down the hill, towards the living and waiting town.

★ ★ ★

The concert starts late — concerts usually do here, Teo tells his musicians. If you put eight o'clock on the ticket, that's not when the curtain goes up, but the time people begin to arrive. Later, when everyone's there, more or less, someone might think about ushering them inside.

Backstage, flowers fill Terri's little dressing room — the largest bouquet is from Sergei. All she can see in her mind's eye is the white lilac that Teo had left on the mountain in memory of his family. She warms up as usual, and test-drives a few of the duet passages with Julie.

'Break a leg, Mum.' Julie smiles, exquisite in her grey silk, shining with the unmistakeable glow of newly found love. They join hands, then set off into the light together, to a crash of applause. Terri feels Julie's hand, chilly with nerves, slip away from her palm; her own quickened heartbeat threatens to swamp her larynx. Yet in the spotlights, the fear drains: the innumerable moments she has stood in front of her audience in the past surround her like a magic circle of protection; and her daughter, who has learned to switch on her charisma just as Terri can, is ready to meet this challenge, and depending on her to make it possible. Roger's accompaniment begins to unfurl at the keyboard. Terri has no more time to pray before she begins the dictation of the Countess's letter.

And there it is: her voice, back again, flowing as if it's new, lifting her up after itself; and Julie, her sternum opening out, lets her ray of sound echo her mother's, matching her like the shadow of Terri's own youth reborn.

After the Mozart, their 'Havanaise' duet fizzes through the theatre: despite, or perhaps because of, her concentration and the increased connection between her and Julie, Terri half imagines another figure standing alongside them: perhaps the ghost of Pauline herself merging with the spirits of Finn, Mary, Katharina and Anita, into one dark, generous and blessed figure: her good genius, her guardian angel. The presence is so intense that, if she'd had space to think between the notes, she might easily have wondered whether it was real. They sing; and while the song lives, it is the summit of all their reality, the past, the present and the future, whatever it may bring.

In the wings Terri and Julie embrace; listening to Freddy and Roger spin the dusky magic of their Chausson, they stand together, entwined and silent, riding on the current of music and time.

Terri kisses Julie, then makes her way back onstage for her solo Viardot songs. Soon she is singing 'Les étoiles', aided and abetted by her daughter's new lover — one who will remain firmly where he belongs, on the other side of the piano. The violin's sweetness warms her through, the surprised audience listens, agog, and Terri lifts her voice into Pauline's enraptured phrases, arching in alternation with Freddy on his violin and Roger doing his best to control the bumpy piano in the background.

Afanasi Fet wrote, and Terri sings, in French: '*I stand and stare motionless, my gaze upon the stars; and between myself and the stars there weaves a secret bond. I imagine . . . I know not what I imagine. A far-off sound like a holy choir, the stars, golden, tremble sweetly. Now do I love them more than before, the stars, the heavenly choir.*' Simple, beautiful and perfect.

Freddy hugs her at the end; Julie, whose solo will finish the programme, is battling tears. 'This Pauline,' Freddy enthuses, 'she's a genius!'

'I know that and you know that,' Terri declares. 'Now maybe everyone else will know it too. Thank you for playing it with me.'

'Ready, Julie?' says Roger.

'Whenever you are.' Julie straightens her shoulders, lifts her head and strides out to take the stage in her mother's footsteps.

'Go, angel, go,' whispers Terri, watching her from the wings, while the spotlight casts chiffon-delicate shadows through the Grecian grey dress. Roger plays one chord and Julie's clear voice, pure as a diamond, utters the first dreamlike note of the Fauré 'Pie Jesu'. 'Lord, grant them rest.'

Terri stands transfixed. This glorious young artist — for artist she is — is her little girl?

'She must go for it,' whispers Freddy, watching beside her. 'She must sing. She's too wonderful not to.'

'Maybe now she will,' Terri nods. 'She's been fighting it. But you can't fight a voice. You don't have it; it has you.'

'Just like love.' Freddy's face seems garlanded in joy as the applause crashes out and he drinks in the sight of Julie, bathed in pearly stage light, raising her arms and thanking her audience.

Julie is back with them a second later. 'Was it really OK?' she asks, like an eager child. But it's Freddy to whom she goes first, Freddy who embraces her and tells her how marvellous she is. Terri looks on, smiling to herself: Julie has climbed the next rung at last.

Finally, Teo walks on to the stage. He reads

out a passage of his book; after that, he announces that the concert has attracted international donations of a hundred thousand Euros towards the continuing efforts of the town's music therapy centre, which had pioneered the clinical use of music in the treatment of children traumatised by war, and is now turning its attention to a second generation — one in which children have been affected by the traumas that their parents experienced.

'War is not something that happens and goes away,' he declares. 'It stays with you. It passes its effects down through the generations. There is no way to stop that until all wars are stopped. I doubt whether we shall live to see that day, in the world that surrounds us now. But here, inside this shell-scarred building in a town that knows too much about war, I swear on my family's memory that I will never stop hoping and believing in that possibility.'

Ahead of them, the audience, its silhouettes as black and silver as ghosts, rises to its feet and cheers.

★ ★ ★

The crowd begins to disperse through the dark square, past the fountains; lingering groups of friends cluster at the plastic tables, enjoying a last chat over drinks. Backstage, Terri and her team embrace each other, exhausted and elated all at once. Terri rubs off her stage make-up and changes out of her concert dress. Tomorrow will carry her back to earth and reality. She seems to have lived today in a dream; the trick will be to take its atmosphere home with her.

Stefan and Zoran are catering a celebratory meal on the restaurant terrace. The journalists have to leave early in the morning, so decide to head back to their hotel to pack. Terri hugs and thanks them. Isabelle promises to send her a copy of her article. The correspondent from *Newsnight* promises to let her know when the report will be broadcast, and adds that she'll recommend to her boss that they should look at Terri's Pauline Viardot project. 'I thought the Viardot songs were a *knockout*,' she adds.

Terri waits for her to leave before she packs up. She needs a moment alone in her dressing room to absorb the return to silence through the humidity, the intensity and the relief. Just to stand and breathe for a few seconds, to make sure she is still in one piece. At last, she zips her green concert dress into its carrier and bundles it, her other paraphernalia and as many bouquets as she can manage out of the theatre. Across the square, the close-packed obelisks of the grave-yard shine pallid under a full moon.

She could have sworn that she was alone on the piazza, when out of nowhere she feels a touch on her arm.

'Terri Ivory?'

The voice is almost familiar. A whisper from a long-ago past.

'Hello?' says Terri, turning, looking into an elderly pair of brown eyes split horizontally by bifocals.

'I don't know whether you'll remember me.

It's rather a long time since we last met, so it is.'

'I know your voice. But . . . ' The accent — the mixture of Irish and Scottish . . .

'My name is Mary. Mary Hoolihan.'

'Really?' demands Terri, disbelieving.

'Yes,' says the puzzled woman. 'That's my name. Probably you've forgotten me, but when you were just a girl you used to . . . '

Terri drops her bouquets. She drops her concert dress in its carrier, her shoe bag and her handbag onto the stone paving and her shriek sets dogs barking through three streets around them. She hugs Mary so hard that she nearly lifts her clean off the ground — for Mary is no longer the statuesque, witchly beauty she remembers, but a bird-like woman who must only be in her sixties but seems to have shrunk nevertheless. Or maybe it's just that Terri has grown.

'I tried to find you. I looked everywhere! *Where have you been?*'

'Ah, well,' Mary says, her smile sending a thrill of recognition through Terri. 'You're such a star. At first I worried after you disappeared to Edinburgh, but then I thought, well, you're a lively girl, you had your young man — you won't want to know me any longer, and fair enough. Next time I heard of you, you were doing so well that I didn't want to bother you. Then you did better and better. I have all your records. And I play them to my youngsters now, my pupils who want to sing or act or learn to use their voices. I always play them your records, just as I played Katharina's to you.'

'If you knew how I've missed you — I've been

kicking myself for losing you for thirty years!'

'I didn't want to be found,' Mary declares. 'But now I do. You'll have heard that nice Mr Ibrahimović talking about the English lady who is taking his very last room? That's me.'

'And after three decades, you came all the way to *Mostar* to hear me?'

'I heard on the grapevine, around Christmas, that you'd been having a problem and I started to be very worried about you. There is that niggle on the neck, you know, when you sense something is wrong with someone you care for. Later I found this concert on the Internet — it was the first chance to come and see how you were. It sounds as if the problem has cleared up.'

Terri's eyes fill. 'Did it sound all right? Did you really think so?'

'Of course. If anything, dear, you've improved. The voice may not be young any more, but you have the benefit that getting older brings if we're lucky: a little wisdom.'

Terri stands grinning stupidly. After all these years, and at the end of what must be the strangest day of her life, she simply doesn't know what to say.

'So, we're here. Both of us.' Mary gives a satisfied smile, her chin lifted. 'I'm so pleased to see what a superb woman that scrappy little girl has grown into. You had the courage to leap across borders, *a chroí*. You needed to cross all those boundaries to get to where you are today. But you had some confusion, I felt, about where our natural boundaries lie.'

'You thought I was making land grabs?' Terri smiles.

'You were justified and you won. In our hearts the boundaries can sometimes feel like the borders here in the Balkans.'

'You mean, we mess them up all the time?'

'We do,' Mary agrees, 'because we're only human, especially if there is nobody in our childhoods who can draw the lines for us in the right place. But then you see that what counts in the end is the ability to transcend this, with love, and forgiveness, and our capacity for both.'

'Come to dinner.' Terri links her arm through Mary's. 'You must meet my daughter and my partner, Teo, and all the others. And we'll eat. And sing.'

'What do they sing here?' asks Mary.

'Sad songs,' says Terri. '*Sevdah*. Some call it soul, others call it love. But for me, they are songs of triumphant love.'

★ ★ ★

Alistair lifts T-shirts and a fleece out of his cupboard and piles them on to the bed. His rucksack hangs upside down, drying out after a good wash, ready to hold his luggage; his plastic 'comfy box' is already half full. The air in Scargill Tower is fresh and clean.

'I won't forget you, you know,' he says to the woman who leans against the doorframe, watching him.

'We'll be friends, won't we?' Julie says.

'Yeah. Hope so. I guess we went through too

531

much together not to be.'

Silence falls; Julie can barely begin all that she wants to say. 'What time is the train?' she asks instead.

'Four.' Alistair is heading for Brize Norton.

'Nervous?'

'What for?'

They look at each other across Alistair's comfy box; he's taking a lighter duvet, as the lads have told him it's hot as hell now. Julie imagines him back in uniform, back in action with his replaced knee, sleeping in the breeze-block and canvas tent in the desert night. Then she thinks of Freddy and Teo in Paris, and her imminent audition for the Paris Conservatoire, to which Freddy has goaded her into applying.

'I still don't understand why you want to go back,' she says, feeling lame.

'I don't expect you to. Look, it's not because I believe in some cause or because some plonker of a prime minister says I have to, or any of that shit. I'm going back, Julie, to help my mates. We're doing it for each other. Things we never imagined we could do. You can only do those things for people you're close to.'

Julie watches him fold up the duvet as small as it will go; it takes up most of the box. The penny is falling once again.

'And me?'

'You're going back to Paris to learn to make the most of that voice,' he instructs. 'Anyone can go to war if they have to. Not everyone can sing like you. You don't know yet what you can do for people if you sing.'

'How do you mean?' Julie can tell, from the shadows that cross his eyes, that this has more significance than she knows.

'Just believe me. That's all. Will you tell your mum something from me?'

'Yes?'

Julie had tried to persuade Terri to come to Scargill Tower, but she was busy. First she had to organise the builders and the scaffolding; then she had a meeting with Martini, the conductor of Covent Garden and the director of a new production of *Der Rosenkavalier*, then a trip to the town hall which had something to do with Teo's residential status after they get married; finally, tea at Fortnum and Mason with a very old friend with an Irish name, celebrating something that Julie couldn't quite understand from her mother's hasty yet ecstatic explanation.

'Tell her,' says Alistair, 'that she mustn't worry. Tell her that it was the best thing that could have happened.'

'What was?'

'She knows. When she sang, she hit something in me that was new, or had gone out, or some shit like that. She helped me to see that people can become so much more than people — so good things can happen, things can get better.'

'What things, Al?'

'It doesn't matter. There was a problem. A misunderstanding. And I want her to know that it's OK now. Do you promise?'

'Yes,' says the puzzled Julie. 'I promise.'

'Good. Thanks.'

'She sent you something.' Julie pushes a plastic carrier bag towards him; it contains a cake tin, emitting a strong whiff of chocolate, brandy and fruit.

'Alistair?' Sue looks in. 'Your uncle John's here with the car. We'd best get going if you want to catch that train.'

Alistair and Julie don't meet each other's eyes for a minute.

'Well. I'll see you when you're on leave,' Julie says.

'I'll call you.'

'Take care of yourself. I'll miss you.'

'No, you won't. But it'll be good to see you next time, and to hear what you're doing with that voice of yours. 'Bye, Julie.'

★ ★ ★

In front of Scargill Tower, Julie stands on a concrete step and watches Alistair load his stuff into John's boot. She waves while the car trundles away towards the high street and, beyond it, the station; beyond that, the return. When it's vanished, she turns away to walk home. A new song is waiting there for her to learn to sing it.

Acknowledgments

My profound thanks to everyone whose generosity and expertise has enriched this book.

For insights into the weird and wonderful world of opera I am hugely indebted to Marie McLaughlin, whose advice has ranged from the essential to the magical. I would like to thank Nina Stemme and Katerina Karneus for their insights into the challenges of singing Wagner's *Tristan und Isolde*; the vocal teacher and coach Gerald Martin Moore; the consultant otorhinolaryngologist John Rubin; the voice coach Tessa Wood; and several people who kindly talked to me about their experiences, but asked to remain anonymous.

I could not have tackled the military issues without some vital conversations with John and Patrick Sanders, to whom I am deeply grateful.

My visit to Mostar in 2007 to attend the world premiere of the opera *Differences in Demolitions* by composer Nigel Osborne and poet Goran Simic was one of the most moving experiences of my life. Vast thanks to Ian Ritchie, Tina Ellen Lee and Opera Circus for this, as well as to Nigel and Goran for the inspiration of their beautiful work. Special thanks too to my brother-in-law Ben Mandelson for his advice about *sevdah*.

The words of Pauline Viardot's song 'Les étoiles' are by Afanasi Fet and the translation (from the French version) is my own. The

'Eriskay Love Lilt' is a traditional Scottish folksong. Turgenev's story *The Song of Triumphant Love* is available in a volume of his short fiction, *First Love and Other Stories*, published by Oxford World Classics. An excellent biography of Pauline Viardot, *The Price of Genius* by April Fitzlyon, was published by John Calder, but is currently out of print.

Numerous books about Bosnia have played an important part in my research, notably *Bosnia: A Short History* by Noel Malcolm (Pan Books) and *Unfinest Hour: Britain and the Destruction of Bosnia* by Brendan Simms (Penguin). For further reading about music in post-war Bosnia I recommend *When Swan Lake Comes to Sarajevo* by the distinguished violinist and conductor Ruth Waterman.

Last but never least, I would like to thank my agent, Sara Menguc, for her sharp eye, sensible advice and tireless support; my editors Carolyn Mays and Kate Howard, and everyone at Hodder; the violinist Philippe Graffin, for commissioning the concert script without which I might not have begun this book; and, of course, Tom, who as ever deserves the fictional 'Mandela Peace Prize' for his supportiveness and understanding.

Jessica Duchen, London 2009

www.jessicaduchen.co.uk

We do hope that you have enjoyed reading this large print book.

Did you know that all of our titles are available for purchase?

We publish a wide range of high quality large print books including:
Romances, Mysteries, Classics
General Fiction
Non Fiction and Westerns

Special interest titles available in large print are:
The Little Oxford Dictionary
Music Book
Song Book
Hymn Book
Service Book

Also available from us courtesy of Oxford University Press:
Young Readers' Dictionary
(large print edition)
Young Readers' Thesaurus
(large print edition)

For further information or a free brochure, please contact us at:
Ulverscroft Large Print Books Ltd.,
The Green, Bradgate Road, Anstey,
Leicester, LE7 7FU, England.
Tel: (00 44) 0116 236 4325
Fax: (00 44) 0116 234 0205

Other titles published by
The House of Ulverscroft:

HUNGARIAN DANCES

Jessica Duchen

Karina's life was once mapped out for her — she was meant to follow in the footsteps of her Hungarian grandmother, a world-famous violinist. Instead, she's a teacher, a mum and wife to Julian, a very English husband who's not always in step with her. But when disaster befalls her best friend, Karina feels forced to question the very foundations of her existence. Encouraged by a chance encounter with a like-minded musician, she begins to delve into her grandmother's Gypsy past, and to discover the secrets of her Hungarian family history. Life will never be the same again. Like most people, Karina isn't sure the life she chose was the right one. But she is willing to take drastic steps to change it.

WHEN I FOUND YOU

Catherine Ryan Hyde

When Nathan McCann discovers a newborn baby boy half-buried in the woods, he assumes he's found a tiny dead body. But then the baby moves and, in one remarkable moment, Nathan's life is changed forever. The baby is sent to grow up with his grandmother, but Nathan is compelled to pay her a visit. He asks for one simple promise — that one day she will introduce the boy to Nathan and tell him, 'This is the man who found you in the woods.' Years pass and Nathan assumes that the old lady has not kept her promise, until one day an angry, troubled boy arrives on his doorstep with a suitcase . . .

LOVE AND SUMMER

William Trevor

It's summer in Rathmoye and when a stranger appears photographing the mourners at Mrs Connulty's funeral it doesn't go unnoticed. Florian Kilderry couldn't know that the Connultys are said to own half the town: he has come to Rathmoye to photograph the remains of its burnt-out cinema. But Mrs Connulty's daughter resolves to keep an eye on Florian Kilderry, and witnesses the events that follow . . . Out in the country, Dillahan, a farmer and a decent man, was accidentally responsible for the deaths of his wife and baby and had later married Ellie. But Ellie falls in love with Florian, although he's planning to leave Ireland and begin anew after what he considers to be his failed life . . . and a dangerously reckless attachment develops between them.

THE MORE YOU IGNORE ME . . .

Jo Brand

Alice is five, old beyond her years and convinced she needs five personalities to cope. Her family, in a cottage in Herefordshire, are a bit weird. When her mother climbs naked onto the roof with Alice's pet guinea pig in her arms, she's whisked off to the local psychiatric hospital. Keith, Alice's father, is severely tested by his in-laws, whose disturbed behaviour terrifies the community. Alice's one hope, which gives meaning to her life, is Morrissey of The Smiths. Desperate to see him sing live, and just as Morrissey seems within her grasp, her mother contrives to reappear on the scene, dragging behind her a new man . . . Can mother and daughter be reconciled? Or is the stage set for more heartbreak than Alice can imagine?

THE SOLITUDE OF PRIME NUMBERS

Paolo Giordano

A prime number is a lonely thing: it can be divided only by itself, or by one; it never truly fits with another ... Alice and Mattia are alone. Alice bears the scars of a skiing accident that nearly killed her, and Mattia lives with a guilty secret that lies at the heart of his disabled twin sister's disappearance. They each recognize in the other a kindred, damaged spirit — their destinies seem irrevocably intertwined. But when Mattia accepts a mathematics posting that takes him thousands of miles away, it seems that love might just be a game of numbers after all; until a chance sighting by Alice of a woman who could be Mattia's sister forces a lifetime of hidden emotion to the surface.